MW00719444

This is a work of fiction. Similarities to real people, places, or events are entirely coincidental.

FIRE LANDS

First edition. July 7, 2019.

ISBN: 978-1393060840

Written by Christopher Metcalf.

Table of Contents

I would like to dedicate this book to the love of my life, Dolores. Without your support, nothing is possible.

A special thanks to Bishop O'Connell, author of the American Faerie Tale Series, who gave me the nudge I needed to bring this book to light.

And a special thanks to Barry B, Tony Morris, K'wan Foye, and my father Brad Metcalf who all inspire me in one-way shape or form.

A novel by: Christopher Metcalf

Chapter 1

The people in the world of Delos needed a hero. An explosive light resonating in the grim darkness, a gift from the gods sent to fight tyranny and oppression.

Evorix wasn't their hero, never would be.

With a deep sigh, he yanked the head of his axe out of the skull in front of him and wiped the blood and brain matter across his leather breeches.

Battle exhausts everyone, even the most battle hardened. And for those who survive, it's a curse. A curse that can only be cured by dying in the next battle. But Evorix was never that lucky.

He was a mercenary in Batopia, a lawless land in the north of Delos that was a cesspool of the worst kind. He had been hiding in the north for almost a year, longing for a way to get back to his old life.

I hate Wolfryan raiding parties, he thought.

A silky black raven squawked behind him, cracking the still air. He turned his neck slightly, and watched the bird fly over his shoulder, its white droppings splattering against his leather pauldrons as it climbed higher into the sky.

Damn Delosian ravens, worthless animals, he thought, smearing the white droppings off his armor. *Gods, I hate this damn place.*

He spit a stream of tobacco juice from between his pursed lips, the majority of it hitting the dead body in front of him. The sun overhead beamed down on his bald black head as the beads of sweat slowly dripped off the stubble on his chin.

Glancing at the bodies around him, Evorix snorted and then took a long pull off of his canteen. The field lay littered with the dead and those who would be joining them shortly.

He slammed his axe head into the wet ground and leveraged himself up with a loud sigh. The sound of his joints popping and creaking an unwelcome sound. He walked toward the woods on the far side of the blood drenched clearing and took to the grim task of dispatching the unlucky mercenaries still alive.

He drowned out their moans and gasps they made after the knife slid across their throat. After he was finished, he walked over the threshold of the woods with his axe swung over his shoulder.

Glancing into the sky for any birds large enough to swoop down on him, he misstepped and stumbled over a tree root. He struggled to his feet and swiped the palm of his hand over his sweat drenched face and then turned around.

Damn, I really hate this place.

With a quick glance over his shoulder, he grabbed his pack and walked out onto the road leading to the village of Pistoryum. The dust swirled around his ankles as he walked, the smell of blood heavy on his leather armor as he approached the gate.

He stayed in the shadows as he meandered his way to the closest bar in the village.The few coins he managed to take off the dead jingled in the pouch hanging from his belt. He slipped into the bar, the patrons barely noticed his hulking frame.

He wasn't handsome by Wolfryan standards, but he would do as a bed warmer in Batopia. His most noticeable feature were his eyes, one dark green, the other a smoky hazel.

He sat down at a table and ordered a mug of ale with a mutton pie to eat. He ate quietly and after he finished, he pounded his battle scarred fist on the table and looked around.

Where's that barmaid? He took another pull on the brittle wooden lip of his mug. *Haven't got all day. I need another...*

He stared at the man next to him in disgust as he watched him shovel more gruel into his mouth. Shaking his head, Evorix glanced at the faces around him.

Never can be to careful.

Among the sporadic wooden tables, men and women played different card games. Evorix glanced up in time to see a man fall out of his chair, a knife buried to the hilt in his throat. The ace of spades tumbled from the cuff of the gamblers sleeve.

Stupid, really stupid. Never keep an ace up your sleeve, to obvious.

The guards dragged the dead man through the bar, his blood leaking onto the boards underneath him. They pushed the patrons walking in front of them out of the way as they worked their way to the rickety door. They launched the body out into the street for the feral dogs to finish what the gamblers had started.

Evorix glanced up as another brawl erupted over a prostitute behind him. He glanced over his shoulder and watched the man taking the worst of the beating yank a knife from his belt.

Evorix stared at the knife. *Oh, that's not sm—*.

A guard standing nearby swung his sword down and cut the attackers hand off, the knife clattering harmlessly on the floor. The guard ripped the man's head back from behind and ran his blade through his back. The bloody tip of the blade exploded through the man's sternum, splattering blood over Evorix's boots .

"Down boss," the guard said, pointing to the other man as he sheathed his sword.

The local watering hole was called The Blade, the local mercenary hang out. But it was more of a shanty than an actual functional tavern. The rotting wood on the exterior of the building allowed the cold wind to blow through the cracks, chilling its patrons to the bone.

The prostitutes above him leaned over the railing and talked amongst themselves. For a good time with them it was only a few coins and Evorix snickered as he heard the loud moans from behind the slim wooden doors on his left.

He pulled his hood closer to his face, flexing his arthritic fingers as he spun a coin on the table. Although he didn't stick out in the tavern among the other patrons, he was still an imposing figure, his shoulders tight around his dirty stained blue tunic. He continued drinking and before he knew it, he looked at his empty mug with one eye closed and took a quick look around.

Empty and down to my last few coins. Damnit.

His eyes scanned the bar, trying to spot an ale someone left unattended. Two men argued beside him about the Wolfryan emperor and his iron grip on the throne.

He hiccupped and thought. *Oh, if they only knew.*

One of the patrons shoved the other, escalating the argument. Evorix used the distraction to pull both mugs over to him. He drained them, burped and then pushed them back.

He pushed himself off the bar stool, stumbled over to a vacant table and sat down. He squinted at a young boy as he ambled over with a pitiful look, grimy hand out. Evorix stared at him, then pushed him to the ground with his large palm. With a drunk chuckle, he snatched a mug of ale as it passed by.

The server turned around and said, "That's fa' somebody else!"

Like I care.

After a long swig, he burped again and then flipped a gold coin onto her serving plate. He pushed her and said, "More...now."

He glanced at his feet and scooped the ragged boy off the ground. He tossed him onto the opposite bench with a flick of his wrist. Using his thick index finger, he slid the mug of ale across the table to see what the boy would do. Looking at it, the boy licked his lips and reached for it like quicksilver.

Evorix yanked the mug back. "Tsk,tsk,tsk."

He pulled one of his last silver coins from his breast pocket. "Spirits will take your pain away for a moment boy, but silver..." Effortlessly, he rolled the coin over his knuckles and stared into the boys soft brown eyes. "This will haunt your nightmares no matter how much of it you have. It consumes my soul. Now begone," he said, flipping the boy the coin. The corner of his lip upturned in a half smile.

The boy gave him a toothless grin and vanished.

Damn shame he won't live through the winter. Actually, none of these poor bastards are going to make it. He looked around at the smiling faces. *Never enough food to go around, only flesh.*

A prostitute caught his stare and walked over to his table. She picked up the coin he had been spinning and pocketed it.

"Fancy a ride? I'm better than most in here," she said, standing over him as she ran her calloused fingers through his hair.

"Not interested. Now leave me to my drink," he replied, staring straight ahead.

She leaned in closer and placed his hand on her breast. "Now what do you think?"

He smiled and stood up, his legs wobbling. She took his hand and led him to a room. Walking through the doorway, she slipped out of her dress and laid down in the flea ridden bed. She waved him over with her dirty index finger. He walked over to her, towering above her as she unbuttoned his pants. He pulled his tunic over his head and laid beside her.

Her fingers and mouth found every ache on his chiseled body. She heard him groan as she slowly started to ride him. She leaned back and hooked her arm around his neck. Evorix put his hands on her waist and when he finished, he wiped the sweat from his brow. With a deep sigh, he rolled over and fell asleep for a few hours. When he woke up, he pulled his pants back on at the edge of the bed.

"You're right. That was better than most," he said, pulling his filthy tunic back on.

He walked to the door and left one gold coin on the dresser. He exited the room and sat back down at his table, peering at the tables in the smoky room. Seeing nothing, he drank several more mugs of ale over the course of the next few hours until the purse swinging from his side was empty.

Brooding about his misfortunes, he cracked his knuckles thinking of when he would get his revenge on the emperor. He was not normally a drinker, it left you out of control and to lose control meant a quick death.

Finally, his head dropped onto the table and he passed out. A lone figure sat tucked away in the shadows of the tavern wearing a forest green cloak with a fur-lined hood. He had been watching Evorix drink and had patiently waited for his opportunity. Evorix should have been paying closer attention, he had too many enemies.

The silent figure sipped his mug of ale every few minutes and glanced around trying to blend in with the shadows. As he scanned the faces, he noticed that no one seemed to see him sitting by himself as he tapped his long thin fingers on the rickety table. Silently, he approached Evorix from behind carrying a large bucket.

The cold water he dropped on Evorix's head had the desired effect he wanted. Like lightning, Evorix rose from the bench and drew his sword from its worn scabbard. His legs wobbled for a moment and then he bent over and vomited.

Ach, yellow bile. Should have eaten something other than the mutton pie. I never drink, I should have known better. What the hell happened, and why am I all wet?

He wiped the back his sleeve across his mouth to clear the bile off his face and then spit the remainder out of his mouth. He patted himself down and looked around, his body swaying with every hiccup. After his last hiccup, he felt his wet pants and squinted through the smoky atmosphere. He blinked the smoke out of his eyes and sat back down. He returned his sword to its sheath and stared at the man in front of him with mild amusement.

"Who are you supposed to be then?" he asked.

The cloaked man sat down across from him and said, "I am the breeze rolling through the grass, the salt in the ocean, and the key to unlocking your miserable existence." He looked around to make sure they weren't overheard and said, "Unless you like living like a pig in this cesspool."

With a snort, Evorix picked up his empty mug and raised it in his direction. "And I thought I was drunk because you definitely ain't rolling through my grass, body parts ain't right. And I hate salt, oh how I hate the taste of salt. Now you called my tavern a cesspool." He slammed his knife into the gnarled table. "Be careful with your words *friend*, you may offend me."

After a moment of silence, Evorix lit his pipe, pressing two fingers over the embers.

The stranger continued. "I am—-"

Evorix muttered as he puffed, "Pissing me off. Now, I didn't tell you to sit, or ask you to. So, piss off and leave me to my drinking."

"I am—-"

Evorix glanced up again, his eyes leveling with the strangers. He couldn't get a good look at the strangers features because his hood was pulled as tight as his own. A wisp of smoke came from under Evorix hood. "Perhaps you didn't hear me the first-time. Piss off!"

The other patrons quieted down to see if the yelling would escalate into a brawl. Disappointed, they went back to their drinks. The stranger made eye contact with Evorix again and dropped a leather purse onto the table.

"I'm looking for an old friend. Perhaps you have seen him?" he asked.

"Nah, don't think I have," Evorix said, cleaning the brown tobacco stains in his pipe.

"His name is Evorix Vispanius, former prefect to Emperor Tiberius. Have I found him?" the stranger asked.

Only for a moment, Evorix's eyes betrayed him from under his hood. He drew a sharp breath and his body stiffened.

How does he know? I need to remain calm and not kill him. Be tough to explain it.

His eyes darted around the room, searching for a trap, or any other men intent on killing him.

Evorix's hand crept to the bone handled knife on his left side, but at the last moment he pulled it away. While Evorix stared around the room, the stranger dropped a large coin purse in front of him. Evorix eyed the purse in front of him and licked his lips, his greed taking over. He picked the pouch up and opened the strings.

"If I'm the prefect Evorix Vispanius you're looking for will depend on how many coins are in here. And who the hell you are, besides an annoying prick," Evorix said.

The man ignored his insult. "There's five hundred coins in the there," the man said.

The stranger pulled his hood back and smiled wide.

Evorix's eyes bulged wide before he snatched his knife from its sheath. "Gius Flavius. You got a lotta nerve coming here after what you did,"

Evorix slammed the knife into the table and then slowly pulled his other knives out and placed them on the table, a cold dead look in his eyes. "Give me one good reason why I shouldn't kill you right now."

"I just gave you five hundred reason why. You're a greedy son of a bitch Evorix, so listen to what I have to say or kill me."

Evorix took a deep breath, looked at the purse and felt his own. "Alright, I'm listening," Evorix said, pushing his back against the booth he was sitting in.

Gius nodded at the purse and Evorix looked at it, his lips tight. Evorix picked it up and glanced inside and then dropped it in disgust. Rubbing his fingertips with a frown, he stared at Gius.

"I thought you knew better than to give me Wolfryan gold. I wouldn't spend this if it was the last currency to buy ale with," Evorix said, throwing the purse back in front of Gius and readied himself to leave the table.

"Don't be an idiot. There's plenty more where that came from. It all spends the same," Gius said, spinning a coin on the table. "Besides, I'm paying you to listen."

Evorix paused, sat back down and lit his pipe again. "Alright, I'll play along. What do you want, Gius?"

Gius took a long sip of his ale and then said, "I want you to kill Octavius."

Evorix coughed as the smoke left his lungs. He leaned forward and laughed until he had trouble drawing his breath.

"You always were a dreamer, Gius. Even if you could get to him, Asinius would make sure whoever assassinated him would suffer greatly before he gave them the gift of death," he said.

"Octavius isn't untouchable, Evorix. We got his father and now the Rebellium needs your help. You were at one point one of the best warriors in Delos before you became prefect. Hell, you killed more men than Jonas the headman." Gius cleared his throat and leaned in to deliver the last of his message. "And the reason I came out of hiding was to ask you personally."

"Been rehearsing that speech haven't you? Octavius ain't a threat, he's just another emperor. Besides, I hear that disgusting fat bastard is sitting in luxury being fed grapes by naked boys," Evorix said.

Gius sighed. "What do we need to give you for your help then?" he asked.

"The world," Evorix mumbled, picking dirt from under his nails.

Gius shook his head and tapped his chin. Without a word, he grabbed Evorix by the back of the head and with a quick pull slammed his head onto the table. Knocked unconscious, he fell off the bench.

Gius picked up the coin purse from the table, stooped down and slung Evorix over his shoulder. Their server came up holding a fresh mug of ale as he walked away from the table.

"He won't be needing it my dear, but I do," Gius said, taking the mug.

"Hey, who's gonna pay fa' that?" she asked in her northern accent.

He slipped two gold coins into her calloused hand and closed it. "I will. And you never saw us, right?"

"Alright ya lardship as you wish," she said, moving on.

The other patrons didn't notice nor care as Gius carried another drunk into the blistering cold. The wind, hail and freezing rain hit him in the face as he pushed the tavern door open. Trudging through ankle-deep snow, he carried Evorix to the room he was renting at the Sleeping Aardvark, an inn on the edge of town by the icy waters.

The Sleeping Aardvark wasn't glamorous, in fact, it was nasty. The sign hanging over the door had a black aardvark with red eyes painted on it, but the sign had seen better days. In its current state, it looked more like a fat rat than an aardvark.

The old black-and-white bordered Batopian flag flying over the door of the inn was torn and stained with blood from battles long forgotten. The bones of the dead soldiers who fought in them long since pulverized into dust.

The walls of the inn smelled like rotten fish and the patrons didn't smell much better as they lounged around void of emotion, most of them in a drunken or drugged stupor. Green algae oozed from the well in the courtyard giving anyone who drank it terrible dysentery.

Gius had paid a month's rent with one silver coin and gave the innkeeper another one to keep his mouth shut. The innkeeper didn't bat an eye as he handed Gius his room key. There were plenty of criminals who came to the Sleeping Aardvark to disappear, it was nothing new.

The innkeeper looked over the rim of his round metallic glasses as they entered. He was scribbling something in his ledger as Gius walked by.

Gius heard the innkeeper mutter to a patron, "I serve anyone, even Wolfr—-"

Without looking at him, Gius cut him off and said, "Mind your business old man or I'll cut your tongue out."

Gius steadied himself as he walked up the stairs, straining with each step. Each stair creaked under their combined weight as he neared the top. Stepping onto the top board, it splintered into three pieces. He lost his balance and threw Evorix onto the landing with a strained grunt. As his ankle twisted, he heard his big toe snap. Soft curses escaped his lips as he bent down and grabbed his ankle.

He put as much weight as he could on his ankle as he stumbled down the hallway. He fell into the wall several times, but managed to drag Evorix by the arm to his room. As they cleared the door, Evorix rolled face first onto the floor.

Letting out a heavy sigh, Gius sat down on the lumpy bed and pulled his boots off, favoring his sprained ankle. He knew he had no right to ask for Evorix's help. The physical and mental pain they both suffered was enough for any man to endure.

All the politicians, army commanders and merchants in Wolfrya who associated with Octavius wanted him dead for the part they believe he played in Tiberius' death. Few if any of the politicians left opposed the newly minted emperor. Evorix had failed in his duty to protect Tiberius, something his son would never forget.

Tiberius, Octavius' father was more prone to exterminating other races than his son was. The peasants called him Clockwork, because his penchant for violence was as reliable as the continuous tick of a clock. Evorix's failure carried an automatic sentence of death and Octavius wanted the debt paid in full.

A plan had been hatched by the Rebellium council for Gius to recruit Evorix and have him assassinate the emperor in Iceport. It was a suicide mission no doubt, but only a few men in Delos could pull it off and maybe survive. Gius didn't know how he was going to get Evorix on board, but he had no other choice. Octavius had to die.

Either Evorix joined the Rebellium, or Gius would kill him and protect the plan. It's always about the plan. But the one absolute Gius knew in the equation was Evorix would kill anyone if the price was right.

He knew that killing people never really bothered Evorix. If people were innocent, he still killed them, only faster. A target was a target, it didn't matter the age, gender or occupation, nor did he care. Princes to paupers, he had killed them all.

A man who felt wronged like he did, was doomed to die alone like he was, needed to serve a purpose, a valiant purpose. Gius wanted to make sure if Evorix did die it would be for a greater purpose, The Rebellium.

Chapter 2

Iceport, the capital city of the Kingdom of Wolfrya was on the east coast of Delos where the crossroads of the kingdom met. It was the largest city in the world, mightier than all the southern tribal tent cities, the only free people left who opposed the Wolfryan aristocracy.

Emperor Octavius Victorus stared at his slave as he poured Tramonian wine into his empty lead goblet. The emperor's taste for other wines had diminished over the years because of his constant consumption. He always wanted to appear more refined than he was, but even if he was refined, it wouldn't have showed in his daily life.

The emperor's wine was imported from the Kingdom of Tramonia far to the west on the opposite coast. The wine was only produced in Sorra, the capital city rivaling Iceport in size and commerce. The king of Tramonia could only sell his potent exported commodity to Emperor Octavius by royal decree.

As the most expensive wine in Delos, only the emperor could afford to drink it anyway. The wine fetched a huge price on the black market and most of the bandits and highwaymen who went after the merchants carrying it were Warlord Three Toe's men, ruthless mercenaries who thrived on hijacking goods.

The king of Tramonia, Aksutamoon disappeared recently along with his latest shipment he was hand delivering after the latest shipment had been hijacked. It was rumored he disappeared in Drathia, a no-man's land south of Batopia.

Octavius' slaves clammy palm slipped on the wine handle as he poured the wine in front of him. The wine splashed across the emperor's forearm and stained his white sash inlaid with gold and silver thread. With no hesitation, the emperor's prefect, Asinius Pelagius slid his sword from its sheath and bent the shaking slave over the oak table. He chopped the slaves head off, but it took two sword strokes to finish the job. The blood dripped onto the floor as the body spasmed across the food on the table.

Asinius was a shell of what he once was. The years had not been kind to him and his old war wounds plagued him on the coldest and rainiest days. The physicians told him he needed more exercise, but the last time he ran or rode a horse was during the campaign to crush the Ba warriors, warlike creatures who lived in the Fire Lands.

Few if any legionnaires like him survived the Battle of the Fire Lands, the Delosian losses were catastrophic. Tiberius lost three quarters of his men and men like Asinius did not have fond memories of the battle, only the carnage.

He had the look of an old grizzled veteran. His tan eye patch covering his right eye was tight against his gaunt face. He tried to keep his salt and pepper beard trimmed daily, but his hands usually shook in the morning. He wasn't sure, but he was forgetting random things throughout the day as well. His beard was a style from days past when prefect's were worth something, but their respect had died amongst the peasants and the aristocracy when Tiberius was murdered.

Asinius took a haggard breath and thought of the battle that changed world history.

"*Front rank, kneel,*" *Asinius shouted.*

The soldiers took the command in stride, many of the legionnaires familiar with the sound of his voice. The Ba warriors crashed into the front line, slaughtering most of his men. Asinius heard their screams and the roar of the warriors as he battled for his life.

As the Ba drew back for another charge, Asinius' men tried to reform. Tiberius rode forward to Asinius' position to see the battle up close, his retainers floating in front of him, shields held high for any stray arrows.

"*End this, now,*" *Tiberius shouted, sitting in the saddle next to him.*

Asinius swung his blade in front of his face and then raised his sword above his head. "*On me you bastards,*" *he commanded.*

His men stood up and marched forward. Out of the corner of his eye, he could see several Ba warriors galloping into their flank, buying time for their shield brothers to regroup.

Asinius watched as the riders bore down on Tiberius. He pointed his sword at the emperor behind him.

"*To the Emperor!*"

Asinius slammed his heels into his horses flanks and rode back to the emperor. He dismounted in front of Tiberius' horse, pulled a pike against the inside of his boot just as the riders slammed into them, their lances aimed low.

Asinius heard the roars a few feet away. Before he could blink, the warriors crashed into him and his men. Asinius thrust his pike up and gored the lead rider in the chest. Another rider on his right with a red rope tied around the tip of his lance aimed it at him.

The lance penetrated Asinius' armor and slammed into his hip. Asinius ground his teeth and groaned. He freed his sword and slashed at the warrior as he fell to the ground and passed out.

He woke up several hours later in a medical tent with Tiberius standing over him.

"You're still alive?" Tiberius asked.

Asinius nodded and stared at his shattered hip.

"I am promoting you to prefect for your sacrifice. You saved my life and for that I am grateful. Heal up and report to the castle for your new assignment," Tiberius said.

Asinius could only nod, the pain to great for him to speak. The emperor withdrew with his entourage and left Asinius to revel in his glory.

Asinius snapped back to reality and glared at the slaves cowering in the corner. He touched his hip and winced even though the pain was long gone. He motioned for the others to pull the headless body from the table as he picked up the slaves head and threw it to the dogs below. Octavius roared with laughter as he watched the hounds tear the head to pieces.

"Asinius, you always know my wishes before they reach my mind," he said, picking up a handful of ripe purple grapes from the table.

He shoved them in his mouth with a grunt and then grabbed a leg of mutton. With a satisfying groan and an eyeroll he was in bliss. Food was one of the boy kings greatest pleasures, other than his sexual debauchery.

The throne he sat on was made from the bones of Rebellium commanders neatly stacked on top of one another. They sat on top of a base made of solid gold, surrounded by skulls that had been dipped in liquid silver.

Wolfryan's believed to sit on your dead enemies was a sign of good luck to come. His father's throne had been made of stone, but blood now stained it. It was a constant reminder for those who failed to protect him. Octavius had it broken into smaller pieces and placed around the dias below him as a reminder of what happened when his father let his guard down. He firmly believed compassion for the masses killed his father and he wouldn't make the same mistake.

He shouted for more wine and another slave came to the table. The slave stood in a pool of blood, hands trembling. The man tried to concentrate on not dropping the lead lined carafe as his pulse quickened. Octavius stared at the slave as he bent over to retrieve the dirty lead bowls. The man marshalled the goblets and silverware onto a tray for the other slaves to clean while Octavius stared at his rear end.

Octavius licked his lips as the man's toga slipped up to his mid thigh. When he finished, he motioned for him to lean forward. "Come to my room later with a few of the others and I will show you the meaning of lust," he said.

He ran his stubby pinky finger with a long yellow fingernail along the slaves ear cooing sweet nothings into it. The slave blushed, bowed his head and then left. Octavius licked his lips again and stared at him as he walked away.

Asinius shook his head in disgust as he watched the emperor fart and then burp as he reached for more food.

Ovtavius' favorite food was mutton and pork, but he recently started having headaches at the back of his head and neck, so he tried to cut back. A feat to difficult to master.

"Asinius, why have we not found that traitor Evorix?"

"Evorix will continue to escape us if we keep sending mercenaries after him, Imperator," Asinius said.

"Then who shall we send?" Octavius asked.

Asinius shrugged. "We may need help from the southern tribes or we will continue to have body parts sent back to us. I don't know who can kill him," Asinius said.

"What about you?" Octavius asked, raising an eyebrow.

"Imperator, I'm an old legionnaire who wouldn't stand a chance against him. We fought together and I saw him kill more men than I could count, if I go, I'm a dead man," Asinius said.

Octavius stopped eating and wiped the back of his hand over his lips. A quizzical look crossed his features as he smacked his lips together. "What good are you as my prefect then, Asinius?" He held his hand to his temple and rubbed it. "My head is pounding again. Fetch me some of my belladonna flowers."

Octavius was not in good health, his stature far from impressive. He was short, barely taller than a boy of twelve. And when he drank, he usually tortured and maimed people with a wave of his hand. He was indifferent when it came to torture, especially women and children. They meant nothing to him.

After his father was assassinated, Octavius became indifferent to death. A piece of him died with his father and then he withdrew with his belladonna leaves and became distant to everyone, even his closest advisors.

Asinius believed that's where the change had occurred like most others in the court. Octavius was always a mysterious child, prone to pranks and bouts of laughter, but where a child was, a drugged tyrannical half wit stood in his place.

The belladonna leaves helped influence his decision to kill the empress of Wolfrya and then cut her into a thousand pieces. He had her ground up and fed to the poor because she didn't tickle his fancy any longer.

Deep in thought, he moved his index finger under his nostrils as droplets of blood fell onto his toga. He glanced around, saw no one was watching and then spilled wine over the center of his toga to cover the stains.

"I need a new toga," he roared.

His slaves rushed from the room and brought a freshly pressed replacement. They helped him undress, his bloated figure in clear view of Asinius who turned his head in disgust.

Usually, Octavius' nose bled daily, but he had been able to cover it up for the most part. It seemed the more he drank and chewed belladonna leaves, the worse it became.

A sharp knock sounded behind the four inch thick oak doors at the front of the throne room. They swung open and a group of men walked in. The palace guards snapped to attention as the group walked by, their boots clicking on the black marble.

Asinius raised his hand in the air with a closed fist, signalling his men to stand at the ready. Three guards broke formation and stood in front of the dias steps with their spears crossed.

The guards confiscated the men's weapons as they approached. Octavius was leery of anyone who approached him and if he did meet with someone, they would be unarmed. The men who marched in were covered in mud and filth from the road. They knelt before the stairs as they approached, their red cloaks shred at the bottom.

The scale segmentata armor under their torn white tabards was bloodied from whatever fighting had recently taken place. The men placed their hands over their hearts.

"We are but dust in the wind, Imperator," they said in unison.

The recent skirmish they were in was at the edge of the Batopian wilderness in search of Evorix. No Wolfryan's were welcome over the border and if they did cross over, their tabards were returned torched from the fire where they were burned at the stake.

Not saying anything in response, Octavius nodded and held his hand out. A large ruby in a platinum setting hung from his left pinky. The leader of the small band approached the steps with his standard bearer and attempted to ascended them. As they neared Asinius, the standard bearer slammed his lance onto the marble.

"Imperator, Lord Marus has returned."

The Wolfryan flag that hung by the standard bearer was white with a bust of Octavius's face, this one was splashed with blood. Before taking his first step, Asinius held a vine branch across the man's chest.

"Watch yourself, Marus."

"Touch me again and I'll gut you, now move," Marus said, pushing past him.

Asinius smiled and stepped aside. Marus reached the top step quickly and approached the throne. He put his hand under Octavius', held it and took a knee. "We have returned, Imperator."

"Lord Marus Atticus, commander of Legion I. What news of your mission?" Octavius asked, looking for his belladonna leaves.

Asinius walked over and handed them to him. Not turning his head, Octavius shoved the leaves in his mouth and stuck them in his bottom gum line.

"Imperator, we were ambushed and I lost most of my men. I believe Evorix is in the fishing village of Pistoryum on the northern coast. But we couldn't get there," Marus said.

"I don't care where he is and I care not that you were ambushed! I want him dead, stuffed and in my hall by the summer. Do you understand me?" he asked.

"I need only hear to obey, Imperator," Marus replied, bowing lower.

"I don't need your poetry, Marus. I need your skill in tracking my prey. Hell it should be easy. Haven't I killed everything he ever loved?"

"You have Imperator, right down to his dogs," Marus said.

"Then bring me his head," Octavius said.

Marus nodded and bowed again before standing up.

"You may stand next to Asinius," Octavius said with a wave of his hand.

Marus walked over and stood near Asinius, trying his best not to hiss an insult at his bitter rival. Marus' heart was cold, twisted, sinister even. His jet black hair recently began to thin and streaks of silver had started to run through it. He carried the title of Legatus, a title he was proud to carry.

Wolfryan legatus' were Octavius' mouth pieces, his private police force sent to find any disloyal politicians and legionnaires.

He was a wolf in sheep's clothing and tried to keep the emperor's ear at all times. He knew if he lost it, it would mean a loss of favor and the unlimited power that came with it.

Octavius processed what he was being told and then pushed himself off the throne and stumbled toward Marus, hallucinating. He slapped Marus across the face with the back of his hand, the spit from the corner of his mouth peppered Marus' armor. More annoyed than hurt, Marus instinctively reached for the knife at his side.

The guards could hear Marus groan as he remembered it had been confiscated. Before he could move his hand from his waist, a knife was at his throat from behind. Asinius pressed it against his jugular, then yanked his head back. Marus swallowed the lump in his throat, his palms sweaty.

"Your orders, Imperator?" Asinius asked, tightening his grip on Marus' hair.

"Orders, yes, kill...wait...where...where am I? Asinius, why do *you* have a knife to my loyal commander Marus' throat? Marus, what the hell are you doing here. Where ...where the hell is that traitor Evorix?" Octavius asked, rubbing his temples in confusion before he collapsed back onto the throne.

"Shit, here we go again. Guard, pick the emperor up and bring him to his chambers. You know the drill, two men at each window, four to the door. Move out," Asinius said.

One of the men picked the emperor up and cradled him in his arms as he threw up. The guard dropped him on his face and held his hands up in disgust with vomit smeared across his breastplate. The others put their hands over their mouths and tried to refrain from laughing.

Asinius looked down at the emperor and motioned his men to pick him up again. The guards carried him away to sleep it off, and Asinius secretly hoped he wouldn't wake up.

"I'll kill you for that, Asinius," Marus hissed before he descended the stairs to rejoin his men.

"Get in line," Asinius said before he walked out onto the balcony.

Chapter 3

Evorix

1 year earlier

E vorix walked through the garden, his hand brushing against the thorn bushes that prickled his palm. He smiled, a sad smile. He knew the war with the Ba pridesman would end soon and it would most likely be his death.

He snapped a violet flower off its stem and turned to his wife Alecta. Brushing the hair off her ear, he slid the flower behind it. She smiled and brushed her hand against his.

"I love you," she said

"As do I," he replied, staring into her eyes.

Their courtship had been arranged by his father and it combined the two most powerful houses among the lesser lords of Wolfrya.

"I have to go to the palace and tend to Emperor Tiberius," he said as they approached the villa.

Their villa was a gift from the emperor. Evorix was still shocked by the gift, a rare glimpse of goodness from an otherwise deranged man. He marvelled at the bleached white speckled stucco glistening in the early morning mist and the trees he had planted with Alecta that adorned the front yard.

"I love the oak trees we planted," he said, gazing up at the leafy limbs.

"Me too," she said.

He sighed and winked at her. "Gotta be going. I'll see you later in the throne room," he said, pecking her on the cheek.

He watched her walk into the villa and then mounted his horse. He cantered out of the courtyard and passed the peasants leading their carts to the trade district.

What a beautiful day, he thought as he rode under the portcullis. He saluted the guards in the watchtower and continued down the road.

His horse trotted to the stable where he dismounted. A stable boy ran up and took the reins from him.

Evorix smiled and flipped him a gold coin. "Don't spend it all in one place," he said.

He walked the short distance to the palace, saluted the guards and walked into the throne room. Tiberius sat on the throne listening to Evorix's father, Rotix, and his brother, Palix. They were talking about something, but he couldn't hear from where he was standing.

Tiberius waved him toward the steps. Evorix bowed and held his blue stoll from falling onto the ground.

"Imperator," he said.

"Evorix, prepare the throne room for the poor to collect their stipends," Tiberius said.

Evorix bowed again and made eye contact with his father and brother. They only made eye contact for a moment and then went back to talking to the emperor. As they talked, the poor were led in by the Imperial guard.

Evorix's father and brother stood behind Tiberius, their eyes searching the crowd for any perceived threat.

A herald stood atop the stairs and shouted, "Our exalted emperor Tiberius will now give out your monthly stipends."

The guards shoved the peasants into line as they fought each other to be first in line. Evorix glanced at his father and brother who stood side by side behind the emperor whispering to one another. Their eyes darted around the room looking for any threats.

It all happened so fast. The distraction at the side door beside the throne drew everyone's attention from the emperor. Several men broke through the mass of people, hacking and slashing at the guards lined up with their backs to the door.

Evorix drew his sword and shouted, "Protect the emperor."

A woman standing next to Evorix screamed as a man knocked him to the ground. Evorix looked up and saw the blood running down the steps. Several of the Imperial guardsmen lay with their throats cut, their swords still in their scabbards.

A quizzical look crossed Evorix's face as he watched his father and brother pull their knives from Tiberius' back and hurtle him down the steps. Evorix didn't have time to think, the man who knocked him down swung his sword at him.

Evorix knocked the blade to the side, cut the man's shins with his own blade and then kicked him away. He regained his feet, shoved his sword through the man attacking him and then sprinted for the throne. His brother and father pulled their swords and crossed them in front of their faces.

"Move aside son, this was bound to happen," his father said.

Evorix pulled his dagger and threw it at his brother and hit him in the throat. Palix fell to his knees, eyes wide. As his body rolled down the stone steps toward the emperor, Evorix engaged his father.

The two battled for several moments trying to find weaknesses. His father took a step back and slipped on some blood. Evorix seized the moment and ran him through. His father's warm blood flooded over his bare hands.

Rotix smiled, blood dripping from his lips. "For the——."

Evorix thrust his wrist dagger under Rotix's chin, cutting his sentence short. He kicked his father off the blade and down the steps. He exhaled loudly and then rushed to the emperor and knelt by his side. Gripping his trembling hand, Evorix pulled his head into his lap.

"I failed you, Imperator," Evorix whispered.

Tiberius' lips twitched and his eyes went blank as a low sigh escaped his lips.

Asinius rushed in with his guardsman holding Evorix's wife and best friend, Gius Lupinius. Asinius stared at the body of the emperor and shouted, "Arrest the assassin."

Evorix stood up and said, "I killed the men responsible," he said, pointing to the bodies.

Asinius gave him a cold stare and pushed his wife to the ground. "You're the assassin. Now arrest this traitor."

Octavius stormed into the room, spittle dripping from his lips. He saw his father at the foot of the steps and ran to him. Sobs wracked his body as he cradled his head.

Evorix heard him muttering, "No, no it can't be. Someone help him!"

Asinius walked over to Octavius and put his hand on his shoulder. He whispered into his ear and then stood beside him.

A guardsmen slammed Evorix over the mahogany table from behind and tied his hands behind his back. He stood him up as Octavius walked over, tears falling from his eyes. He slapped Evorix across the face, stood nose to nose to him and hissed, "You'll pay for this." He stormed past Asinius and walked out of the throne room with his guards in toe.

A guardsman shoved Evorix toward the door. "Move!"

Evorix reached out to his wife and as he did Asinius slapped his hands with the flat of his blade. Evorix recoiled from the blow and looked at Gius as he walked by.

"Sorry about this. Never expected you to survive," Gius said.

Evorix paled and then slammed his forehead against Gius' nose. Gius collapsed to the floor. The guards marched him to a holding cell deep within the bowels of the castle. They unbound his wrists and shoved him in, then slammed the door shut.

Evorix's eyes searched the cold bare room. There were no windows, only a bucket to shit in. The hay had been recently removed and he had a suspicion they wouldn't be bringing it back.

He sat down on the ice cold ground, his back against the slimy wall. He stared at his hands, the blood drying on his fingertips. The smell made him vomit. He spit into his palms trying to rub the blood off with his blue stole, but to no avail. He looked at his coveted stole in disgust and threw it to the other side of the room. His whole life had changed in the blink of an eye.

I killed my father and brother. God's forgive me.

For the first time in his adult life he cried, not because of what he did, but because he knew they would sentence Alecta to death because of his failure. He dried his eyes and looked around making sure no one saw him. The guard posted outside of his cell yawned and went back to sleep.

He tried to look out the window but couldn't. He picked up a pebble near his foot and threw it against the opposite wall. It made a clinking sound and then rolled away.

The guard turned his head to look. He slapped his spear butt against the iron bars. "Quiet traitor," he mumbled before dozing back off.

Evorix stood up and paced the cell. He soon found what he was searching for. He found a sharp piece of stone stuck out from the wall by his foot. He coughed loudly and broke it off with a quick stomp.

He heard a voice down the hall yell, "Brutus, prepare the traitor. We will come and get him in an hour."

Evorix knew precisely what that meant. Getting information was what he did best. He was one of the best tortures with hot iron pliers in the castle. People would say anything to make him stop. He picked up the rock and felt along the edges. Jagged and formidable, it was a simple brutish killing machine. He looked around the room and knew what to do. He slammed his palms against the wall and gasped for breath. As he clutched his chest, he fell to one knee. "Please help," he mumbled, pulling on his tunic.

The guard glanced over his shoulder with a sigh and flung the door open. "What's the matter?" he asked.

As the guard lowered his head to check on him, Evorix slammed his makeshift knife under his chin. The blow didn't kill him instantly, he lingered for a few moments clutching at Evorix's tunic.

Without much effort, he pushed the rock up further and finished him. He lowered the man to the floor, then stripped him. The pants were too tight and the shirt made him look like he had one too many dinners. But the shoes, the shoes fit well.

He pulled the guards hauberk on and adjusted his helmet. The spear lay by the cell door and he quickly picked it up. He broke the shaft over his knee as another guard walked down the steps. Evorix sat where the guard had been sitting and lowered his head onto his chest. The other guard walked up and nudged Evorix with his boot.

"Bill, I'm not covering for you if you're drunk again. Get up," he hissed, jabbing his spear into Evorix's ribs.

Evorix glanced up. "Surprise," he said, jamming the broken spear head into the man's groin.

The guard flopped to the ground, blood dripping from the corner of his mouth. Evorix got to his feet, dragged the guard inside the cell and then ran for the stairwell.

He navigated his way through the dungeon, stopping only to drink from the pools of stagnant water puddling in the crevices of the wall.

Finally, after what seemed like a hallway that would never end, he reached the main floor of the castle. As he exited, he saw Alecta's corpse, her tongue protruding from between her lips.

The other members of the Rebellium swung next to her from thick strands of rope. He took a step toward her body, but a group of legionnaires ran past him. He ducked back into the shadows of the buildings.

I'm sorry, Alecta.

A single tear fell from the corner of his eye. He looked around and saw a horse tethered to a rail near him. He untied it, slipped into the saddle and rode off toward the Batopia wilderness.

Chapter 4

Where the hell am I? Evorix asked himself, looking around the room.

He searched for anything that may cause him harm and with a pained grunt, he pushed himself up to his knees. He noticed Gius asleep in a chair, his chin resting on his chest.

Gius was a few years older than Evorix, his crooked teeth stained brown from the tobacco he chewed. His black curly hair had one silver streak running through it making him look like a skunk.

With his eyes closed, Gius said, "Morning."

Evorix attempted to shake the cobwebs from his hungover brain.

How did he find me? he thought.

Evorix rose to his feet and coughed. Gius lowered the legs of the chair he was sleeping in back to the floor and stood up.

He took a step forward. "Are you open to hearing my plan yet?" Gius asked.

"What plan?"

"Killing the emperor," Gius said.

Evorix nodded and then ran his hand over his skull. "I'm listening."

A slick smile crossed Gius' lips.

Nonchalantly, Evorix asked, "What do you need me for, Gius? I'm not your answer." He briefly looked down and said, "I kill without remorse. Some find this valuable and others find it disturbing. Is that the skill you seek?" he asked, feeling his tunic.

Gius pointed to a tunic hanging by the hearth. "That's precisely what I need."

Evorix nodded his thanks and pulled his tunic over his head. He flung it over his shoulder and then grabbed the one drying nearby.

Gius went to his satchel near the door and pulled out a stained and bloody piece of parchment. After unrolling it, he read it to Evorix.

I, Octavius Victorus hereby authorize the extermination of any and all members of the Rebellium. Men and women found guilty in absentia for the murder of my father Emperor Tiberius Victorus. These citizens must be brought to justice and punished for their disloyalty. The person at the top of this list must be crucified for his crime and burned at the stake. Bring me Evorix Vispanius. Find him, torture him and kill his family and friends. But his heart and head belong to me.

Emperor Octavius of Wolfrya

Gius rolled it up and looked at him. "Found this on a man I killed a few months ago. You do know you still have a price on your head?" Gius asked.

"I know," he said, a slight smile at the corner of his lips.

Evorix wanted to be left alone and it looked like that idea was slowly being snuffed out. Pausing, he sighed and put his fingers on his chin.

Well, looks like all I am is a killer. Once a killer, always a killer.

Interrupting his thoughts, Gius said, "I know you want revenge, but you can't do it from here. They will just keep coming for you and staying here puts all these peasants in danger. Ride with me and we can rid the world of tyrants."

Ignoring Gius, Evorix walked over to the water basin and washed his face free of the vomit and debris. After a few moments of silence, Evorix chuckled and dried his face on a nearby linen cloth.

"Tell me why should I give a damn if these peasants die, they ain't my people." Their eyes met. "I've lost the person who mattered the most. You should remember that. So, no I won't help you. I'll get my revenge on my terms, not on yours."

Gius shook his head and sighed, "I must have the wrong man. The Evorix I knew was no coward. Good day to you," he said curtly, opening the door, his hand slowly moving toward the blade stuffed in the back of his breeches.

"That's more like it. Now back to the tavern I go. Good luck in your quest to save Delos, Gius. I'll be right at home with the whores and fatherless children waiting for my moment." He spit at Gius' feet and glanced up. "I ain't the man you came to find. I'm just a washed up prefect," he whispered, patting Gius on the shoulder.

Gius sighed and pulled his hand from the knife handle. He would kill Evorix when he was asleep just to put him out of his misery. No use draining his life force out as he looked into his pathetic eyes. He watched his former best friend amble toward the stairs. Evorix's feet crossed mid step and he tumbled down the rest of them like a tumbleweed.

"Poor bastard," Gius muttered, closing the door.

The patrons didn't even glance at the bleeding lump of flesh at the foot of the stairs. With only his pride damaged,

Evorix crawled to the banister and pulled himself up. Once he regained his legs, he brushed himself off and walked to the tavern door, head held high. As he reached it, the door swung inward and knocked him to the floor.

Three rugged mercenaries strolled in and glanced at the patrons faces. They wore white tabards that were freshly pressed with a black axe and a red spear crossed on the front, the sign of Wolfryan bounty hunters. Evorix took one look at the men and knew who they were.

Can't these bastards leave me be?

The leader of the group walked to the desk and asked the innkeeper if he had seen a man that looked like Evorix. For a brief moment, the innkeeper paused not sure what to say. He shook his head no.

The leader of the group grabbed the innkeepers shoulder and stabbed him in the neck. The patrons stared at the blood dripping from the mahogany ledge as the man's body collapsed.

The leader turned around and said, "Now that I have everyone's attention. Who knows the whereabouts of the former prefect, Evorix Vispanius?"

No one spoke, nor did they move. They were there to get drunk and forget their past. Not to memorize who came and went in their seedy inn. "Oh, did no one hear me?" he asked, looking around.

A wicked smile crossed his featuress when he noticed Evorix on the ground. He did the best he could to hide, but even with his body in a half hearted dead pose, they knew. Mercs always knew what they hunted.

"Looky who we have here boys," the man said, glancing at his companions. "On your feet you worthless piece of shit. Been hunting you for awhile. It's about time I found you."

A crossbow bolt grazed the leaders ear and sunk into one of the attacker's chests behind him. The man glanced at the bolt and then fell to his knees. The mercenaries sword dropped from his hand and clattered on the floor near Evorix.

Someone jerked Evorix up and held him in a choke hold as a human shield. He squirmed trying to free himself as another bolt hit the second attacker who was charging the stairwell.

The man bounded up five steps and then came rolling back down. A bolt stuck out of his forehead and as he hit the floor the shaft broke off. Blood flowed out in front of the stairs as Gius descended from above with a limp. The souls of his boots soaked with blood as he reached the bottom floor.

"I would let him go if I were you," Gius said, reloading his crossbow, his voice like steel. He crossed into the light and pointed his hand-held crossbow at his target.

"Gius Lupinius, I thought you might be floating round here. I always knew you were alive. Guess I should have checked under your hood when you were brought to the gallows. A mistake I won't make twice," the man said, trying to hide behind Evorix.

"Last warning, Viscus," Gius said, circling him.

Evorix growled. "Viscus..."

Gius circled Viscus and stopped. "Last chance."

"You wouldn't da——"

Gius pulled the knife from his waistband and threw it at Viscus before he could react. The weapon went end over end and embedded in his skull. Blood smeared across Evorix's cheek as the body fell backward.

"Been waiting a long time for that moment," Gius muttered, pulling his blade free. "He was partly responsible for killing my kids," he said as he turned around, his face flushed.

Evorix felt compassion for his old friend for a moment and then chuckled as he knelt next to Viscus. He bit into a gold coin he found in Viscus' pocket.

"This is real gold. And I bet he has more." He ripped Viscus's tabard open and cut a coin pouch hanging around his neck with a laugh. "Yup, I was right."

He shook the pouch near his ear and heard the clinking coins inside. "Oh, a private stash. These coins are what I'm looking for," he said, flipping one in Gius' direction. "Go find a whore."

Gius rested his blade over Evorix's shoulder and lifted his head up with the flat of the blade. "I disapprove of your looting habits. The dead are not to be picked clean. It angers the Gods," Gius hissed.

Evorix pushed the blade away, muttered under his breath and continued his looting. "He has gold teeth, what an idiot," Evorix said.

"Have you no decency?" Gius demanded.

Evorix yanked the teeth from Vicus' mouth, stood up and then urinated on his corpse. With a sinister smile he said, "Decency... nope, fresh out. He's lucky you killed him. I wish I could bring him back to life and kill him again."

"Ugh."

"We best be going," Evorix said.

"So, you're in?" Gius asked, regaining his composure.

Evorix felt the blood on his neck. "Ain't got a choice now. Can't hide here anymore."

He zipped his pants up with a grunt and then sprinted outside. Gius followed behind him and jumped on his horse. He pointed at the mule tethered next to Evorix.

Looking down at him with a smug smile, Gius said, "It's the only animal I could find for sale in this shithole. And I paid a fortune for it. Worthless thing cost me a thousand Wolfryan coins. So, hurry up and get on!"

The mule swung its tail and hit Evorix in the face with a loud whine. Evorix slapped the mule and said, "Gius, I ain't riding this thing. I'd rather walk."

"Suit yourself, I'm riding out," Gius said, holding his hand over his brow. "Look, over the horizon," Gius said, pointing his finger at the dust cloud beyond the ridge.

Evorix watched the dust for a moment. "You know on second thought." He glanced at Gius and then the dust cloud as it moved closer. "I'm going to ride with you," he said.

"There's probably too many to fight, we'll have to hide. We'll lose them in the forest," Gius said.

Awkwardly, Evorix got on the mule painted like a zebra.

Who would paint a mule?

Shouting over his shoulder, Gius said, "Keep up, or die. Same rules apply like they did in our old unit."

After riding through the night and taking multiple shortcuts through Whispering Woods, they managed to lose the bounty hunters.

The Whispering Woods were where the Batopian wilderness began. It was said to be haunted by the souls of fallen legionnaires who deserted and were killed by their own men.

Evorix and Gius took a break halfway through the forest to let the animals rest near a secluded pond. Gius went on foot in search of food and Evorix started a small fire. An hour later, Gius came back with several rabbits hanging from a tree branch. Neither man talked while Gius prepared dinner. Evorix puffed on his pipe and blew smoke rings into the air as he leaned his sore back against a tree.

He finally broke the silence and said, "They say this woodland has demons, killer trees and other creatures just as terrible in the vast darkness." He glanced around after he said it, staring at every tree to make sure they didn't move.

Gius laughed and pointed to a tree with a wind chime hanging from it. "There are your ghosts. A tribe of wild men who don't live far from here use it as a scare tactic. They have helped the Rebellium from time to time," he said, turning the rabbit over he had on the skewer.

"Can they help us reach your fort?" Evorix asked.

"Doubtful, they only protect themselves. There are only a handful of warriors with no wives. They worship the god Eltel," he replied.

"The god of death?" Evorix asked, pausing between puffs.

"Yes, the very same. The men who wander in here in search of treasure usually become their sacrifices. The Rebellium brings the tribesmen food for free passage through their land, the others..." He snapped his fingers. "Shouldn't tread here." Gius laughed and continued, "The surprise is there is no treasure."

Evorix pushed himself to his feet with a smile, walked over to where Gius was sitting and said, "Must have gone pretty bad for you to come out of hiding, old man. Pistoryum is a dangerous place for someone like you."

"Someone like me?"

"Yea, you know. A timid—-"

Before he could finish his statement, Gius elbowed him in the balls. He fell to his knees and held his crotch, gasping for air.

"You dirty rott—-" Evorix muttered through clenched teeth.

Gius grabbed Evorix's tunic, closed his fist and then punched him across the jaw. Knocked unconscious, Evorix crumpled at his feet.

"Timid." Gius snorted. I'll give you timid."

He picked Evorix's pipe up, rubbed the stem on his tunic and then lit it. Gius dragged him under a tree by his feet, smiling every time he heard his head bounce over a rock in the road. After securing him to the tree, Gius returned to the fire and continued preparing his meal.

Chapter 5

Octavius' snores woke up the male slave in his bed. One slave slipped out from under his flabby arm and woke him up. Octavius yawned and looked around the room as the sunrise illuminated it.

He struggled for a few minutes to get out of bed. Finally, a slave helped him up, then laid down beside the bed. The slave wore a soft brown bear skin so the emperor's naked feet never felt the cold marble. The man grimaced in pain as Octavius stood on his back and stretched.

Every morning, the emperor stepped on a slave to remind them who was in charge. The bed chamber was lavish, his bathtub was made of gelded gold and his goblets and silverware were made by the best silver and lead smiths in Delos.

All of his togas were made from the finest imported silk, courtesy of the southern tribes. His balcony overlooked the city of Iceport in its entirety. The locals called the city Iceport because of the large blue and red icebergs floating in the bay's semi frozen ocean.

His slaves threw rose petals out in front of him as he walked over to a bubbling hot tub. He dipped his toe in to test the water and moaned. "Ahhhh."

He lowered his naked body into the water and sighed. The slaves washed him above the water and below as he laid his head onto the tubs edge.

He made eye contact with a younger slave and nodded at his crotch. The slave removed his toga and washed Octavius' penis under the water.

One of the slaves handed Octavius a cup of wine. After taking a few gulps, the slave took the goblet back and wiped his mouth. Octavius licked his lips and stared at the man. The man shaved Octavius' face and massage his shoulders. He did his best to ignore the emperor's gaze, but he felt his eyes undressing him.

A polite knock sounded from outside the bedchamber. One of the guards looked at the emperor who waved his hand dismissively. The guard opened the door and two guards crossed their spears in front of the emperor. The men who entered stood and waited for the spearmen to move.

"Let them pass," Octavius said, glancing around one of the guards. The spears lifted and Asinius approached the tub.

"Imperator, what are your wishes?" Asinius asked.

Octavius closed his eyes and leaned back again, letting his naked slave work his hand below the water. He groaned in pleasure as he lifted his head up.

"Asinius, why are you disturbing my morning rituals?" Octavius managed to gasp.

"Imperator, Marus came to report his findings this morning," Asinius said.

"And?" Octavius asked.

"He's outside. I haven't heard his report because you slapped him across the face for his failure to find Evorix and then he attacked you last night. Do you not remember, Imperator?" Asinius asked.

"It's a little hazy for me at the moment," he replied, raising his head off the ledge of the tub. "Did you say he attacked me, prefect?"

"Ye—-"

Octavius waved his hand to stop him from answering and said, "I must have started it. Marus is more loyal than you could ever hope to be, Asinius. I don't know why I bother keeping you around. You're just a lazy worthless crippled old goat. Now that you've ruined my morning ritual, I'll start my day."

Asinius' face reddened. He bristled at the insult, but remained level headed. He clenched his right fist repeatedly until his knuckles turned white. After regaining his composure, he looked at Octavius' favored guards standing in front of him with arrogant smiles on their faces.

Octavius rose from his bath water bloated. Asinius gagged and turned his head as a slave hurried to put a robe on him. After putting on the robe, Octavius walked to his balcony and spit over the side and hit a woman pulling a cart below him. He shrugged and spit again as she continued to struggle down the road. Asinius walked up from behind and stood next to him.

"Prefect, bring Marus to my chambers. I would like to talk to him about a mission I want carried out," Octavius said without looking at him.

"As you wish, Imperator."

An hour later Asinius and Marus walked into Octavius' chambers. The emperor was sitting at a table eating a roasted turkey leg.

"More wine!" he shouted, ringing a bell by his side.

Bowing at the waist as he got closer to the table, Marus said, "Imperator."

"Ah Marus, my most trusted and loyal scout, come closer."

Marus gave a sly smile and a wink to Asinius, then stepped in front of him. Asinius clasped his hands behind his back, trying to refrain from striking him. A low growl escaped his lips as he watched Marus walk over to Octavius.

Octavius flicked his wrist as if he were an annoying fruit fly and said, "You are dismissed worthless ape, I mean Asinius."

The emperor's bootlick guards chuckled at his misfortune. Asinius paused and tried to control his temper. He took a step forward as he reached for a knife in a sheath attached to his forearm, then caught himself. Instead, he bowed low and touched his forehead. After the emperor was no longer looking at him, he left the room.

"Marus, I have an assignment for you," Octavius said oblivious to the previous day's events.

"As you wish Imperator. What do ask of me?"

Looking around, he waved Marus closer to him and whispered in his ear, his voice an octave higher.

"Your first order of business is to execute Asinius. You're my new prefect. He's trying to take my crown." Octavius' eyes flicked widely in their sockets. "He cannot be trusted," he hissed, spit leaking from the corner of his mouth. "He's an ape, a traitor to the crown."

Marus pulled his head back, noticing the dribble of spit from the corner of Octavius's mouth and said, "Are you sure that's what you want, Imperator?"

Marus asked him quietly so he had an option to turn back. The emperor killed on a whim. He had an air of indifference about crucifixions and beheadings. It was the best way to keep the populace loyal.

"Yes, why would I say it if I didn't want it done?" Octavius asked, the white spit continuing to drip from the corner of his mouth.

"He has men who are loyal to him in the castle and other places in Iceport, Imperator. What—"

"Kill them too. I want them all dead!" he screeched at the top of his lungs.

Marus put his fist over his heart and bowed his head.

"On me!" he shouted to his men as he stormed out of the chamber.

• • • •

ASINIUS LOOKED AROUND his sparsely decorated room as his slaves packed his belongings. He was in the process of donning his armor when one of his loyal slaves Herius told him of the conversation between Marus and the emperor.

Not wasting time, he ordered his men to form in a square formation in the courtyard of his villa. He limped down the steps and when he reached the bottom, his breathing became labored. He felt a pain radiating over his shoulder, down his arm and pulsating above his heart.

"M'lord, we have assembled the men and have readied your escape route," said one of his commanders.

He grunted at the man and looked around at what would no longer be his home by nightfall. Ofcourse, he had seen the writing on the wall when he left the palace, Hersius' warning was just a confirmation. He knew they could only hold the emperor's troops off for so long. He planned to fight a leap frog defense and escape into the marsh with as many of his men as possible.

Herius handed Asinius his helmet made of a copper and zinc compound, painted with white pigment. Attached to the helmet was a palladium mask with a large teardrop under one of the eyes.

It was the helmet of Wolfryan prefect's and they were handed down from father to son as the succession went on through time.

To be a prefect, a man had to be of pure blood, pure Delosian blood. The bloodline would have had to extend back to the beginning of the Delosian empire, hundreds of years before.

"The enemy approaches," one of his sentries positioned in the guard tower above him shouted.

"How far away?" Asinius shouted back.

The guard turned back around and shouted in pain. He grabbed his stomach, fell backward and smashed into the square. His body made a sickening crunch as it landed among Asinius' other troops.

"I guess they're within arrow range," Asinius muttered to no one in particular.

"Your orders, m'lord?" one of his commanders asked.

Asinius grunted and walked to the center of the courtyard. He shouted at his men to close the square, backs to one another. His men stood far enough apart to fight effectively, but not so far apart that they couldn't protect one another.

Asinius' riveted segmentata armor glistened as the sun beat down on them. His hoisted his tabard above his head, displaying the Wolfryan coat of arms.

"No prisoners, no mercy!" He bellowed as he threw the tabard onto the ground in front of him and spit on it. For good measure, he rubbed his heel over it, smearing it with dirt. His men cheered and formed a tighter defensive stance.

Sweat poured down Asinius' leathery face and over his eye patch. The first ranks of the enemy, ill equipped from the haste of Marus' marching order appeared over the hill.

"Ready your bows!" shouted one of his commanders.

Asinius spit again and raised his arm up high, then brought it down. The first flight of arrows thumped from his men's bow strings and over the wall of his villa. His soldiers cheered as the enemy screamed out in pain. But their cheers were short lived as the retaliatory arrows landed among his men.

"Give 'em another," shouted a commander, standing beside him.

"They don't stand a chance, Lord Asinius," the man said before yelling for another round.

Asinius smiled. He knew it would only be a matter of time before the legion broke through the courtyard's wooden gate.

"Archers to the top wall," Asinius shouted, slamming his mask over his face.

The archers ran to the wall and fired another three volleys. Before they could recover, another volley answered theirs, knocking a handful of men into the courtyard ten feet below.

Asinius looked for his archery commander after they blocked the next flight of arrows. The commander was sprawled out beside him, an arrow standing straight up in one of his eye sockets.

"Damn the Wolfryan aristocracy," Asinius mumbled, picking a wounded man up off the ground.

He sent him back to his villa where a healer was treating the wounded. Another volley came in as Asinius' back was turned. One of his men shielded him as the arrows rained down. He pushed himself up, but the man's weight on his back was too much for him to move.

"Get off me soldier," Asinius shouted, his helmet a few yards away.

The weight on his back eased and Herius pulled him to his feet. "He's dead, m'lord."

Asinius could only nod as he watched his men hide behind their shields, the arrows shattering against them. Screams of pain resounded in his ears as his men fell one by one.

Joining his men in the center, he stood shoulder to shoulder with them as volley after volley kept them pinned down.

"We need to retreat," one of his officers said as an arrow pinged off his shield.

Asinius nodded and at the top of his lungs, he shouted for a withdrawal and his men retreated with him. They reached the door separating his villa from the courtyard. A handful of arrows landed at their heels as they stumbled through.

More of his men collapsed as the multitude of arrows pinned them to the ground. The sound of battle blew through his ears like a freight train. He limped over to the cemetery beside his villa and scooped up a handful of black soil. He let out a deep sigh as he watched the dark granules fall between his fingers.

He muttered, "The hours of our lives are measured in grains of sand." He paused for a moment, said a prayer and then prepared for his last stand.

"Make your last stand here," he said, drawing his sword across the sand.

There was a loud bang at the gate and he watched it break into several pieces. The legionaries dropped the battering ram at their feet and broke through. Sandaled feet stomped through the villa and into the inner courtyard. Marus' men marched four abreast, dust floating up around their ankles.

The white tabards of Wolfrya fluttered as a light breeze blew through the yard. The legionnaires shields butted up against one another as they marched in perfect unison. They split into two columns and surrounded Asinius and his men. Marus rode into the courtyard, his red cloak swaying in the breeze. He looked around from his perched position, a smug look on his face.

"It looks like your time finally ran out. Pity too, I thought for sure you would eventually outsmart me. But it looks like you were all show, Asinius. No action as my mother used to say," Marus said.

"Brave words from a man sitting on a horse in a sea of the best warriors *I* trained in Delos. Besides your mother only said that when my dick wasn't in her mouth, " Asinius said, banging his sword over the rim of his worn round shield.

Marus roared, his fingers clenching his horses reigns. "Asinius, I would love nothing more than to cut your impudent throat. But we all have orders and mine are to extinguish your life force with torture. So, lay down your arms with your men, come quietly and I will allow them to live," he replied, glancing at his pristine fingernails.

"My men will never surrender and you know that. But I will surrender to you when Iceport no longer has icebergs, or perhaps when you take your tongue out of the boy's ass!" Asinius hissed.

Asinius' men catcalled and jeered at their opponents as Octavius rode up from the rear of the column, his short round frame bouncing in the saddle.

"Kill them for God's sake," Octavius said as he reigned in beside Marus.

Asinius swallowed his spit. "Ah, the worthless emperor of Wolfrya has arrived." Asinius made a crude gesture and shouted, "Death to the aristocracy."

Asinius' men looked at him over their shoulders and banged their swords with a responding war cry. The end had come and even his slave Herius was armored and ready for battle. A hole in the circle opened and Asinius walked out, Herius close on his heels.

One of the emperor's guards lifted a crossbow up to Marus. He aimed and fired a bolt at Asinius' chest, but

Herius leapt in front of him at the last moment taking the blow of the quill.

Asinius' men rhythmically thumped their shields and pulled him behind them. A horn blew a long note from their defensive position and his men charged out, breaking formation. The two similarly armed groups clashed throughout the courtyard.

Asinius' men were outnumbered three to one. Limbs and heads were hewn from the owners bodies as the fight raged, both sides inflicting heavy casualties.

As the battle raged, Marus watched Asinius limp into his villa, his men covering his retreat. Marus dismounted and sprinted to the door. After reaching it, a large man with a long white beard shoved Marus to the ground from behind.

Spitting sand from his mouth, Marus stood up, pulled his shield to his face and extended his sword over the edge. He squared off in front of the door with his old friend Peltrasius, a legendary legionnaire in Iceport.

"Peltrasius, stand aside. My quarrel is not with you. Lay down your arms and I will do my best to help you join my ranks. You're a good legionnaire."

Peltrasius spit on Marus' tunic, a slight smile crossing his lips. "Death first."

The two men faced off and engaged. Peltrasius lunged forward and knocked Marus to the ground again. Marus rolled over backward and stabbed up with his sword. The blow penetrated Peltrasius' armor, disemboweling him. Falling forward, Peltrasius' weight pushed Marus to the ground. They landed on the blood-soaked sand and with great effort, Marus rolled the dead man off of him.

He pulled his sword from Peltrasius' stomach in time to see the last of Asinius' men put up a futile resistance. The wounded from the villa joined the last of their unit and fanned out in front of the door. Most were badly wounded and clung to their weapons, some barely holding on in a final act of defiance.

Marus heard their shields clink together as they formed a formation similar to that of a turtle's body.

"Forever loyal to Asinius!" shouted one of the men as they marched into the legionnaires. Shortly after the two groups engaged, Asinius' men were put to the sword.

Marus grabbed one of his men from behind and yelled, "Bring Asinius back to me, now."

He sighed and wiped his brow, checking himself for wounds. He glanced down and saw he was standing on a severed arm. He picked it up and stopped one of the men walking past him.

"Does this belong to you?" Marus asked.

The legionnaire looked at him and then shook his head no.

"Ah, well doesn't really matter. Find the owner," he said, shoving the severed arm into the man's chest.

The other legionaries with the man laughed at him as he attempted to wipe the blood off of his blue stole. Going back into the blood drenched courtyard, Marus saw Octavius pulling the blue stoles off of some his dead legionnaires.

Marus walked up to him and placed his hand over his heart and bowed. "Asinius escaped," he said, barely above a whisper.

Octavius' face turned blue, his lip quivering. He turned around and stormed back to his horse. Before mounting, he turned back to Marus. "That's one prefect, don't fail me again."

He yanked his horses reigns, turned it around and cantered off followed by his household guard. One of Marus' men, his red cape cut in half from the battle sprinted to where he stood scanning the villa.

"M'lord, the men are chasing Asinius down in the swamps. Will you be riding with us?" asked the man, mounting his war horse.

"No, I will oversee the cleanup and find any treasures he may have hidden. Bring me back his head," he replied.

"And the body?" asked the man, pulling a spear stored on his saddle bag.

"Leave it for the buzzards. Just remember what I told you earlier," he said, walking back into the villa.

The legionnaire nodded and rode off followed by the others. Marus scanned the villa and checked the walls first, the most obvious place to hide treasures. He tapped his knuckles against the wall, probing for a hollow place. The walls yielded nothing. He tossed the furniture around the room trying to find any trap doors in the floor boards.

In frustration, he stormed back into the courtyard and back to his horse. As he was mounting, he looked at the cemetery and a newly erected cross. He stared at it for a moment and then dismounted. He pointed at one of his commanders.

"Get a shovel," he shouted.

He directed the man on what he wanted shoveled and then backed away. The dirt flew over the man's shoulder until he hit something metal after a few feet.

Marus' men pulled a chest out of the ground and broke the lock off of it. Marus flipped the lid open and picked up a silver goblet. There were all sorts of treasures. Coins, goblets, plates, rings, pendants, Ba warrior jewelry from the last war, a treasure trove from years of collecting.

"This must be his retirement." Marus said to his men with a chuckle. "Close it up."

"Shall we deliver it to the emperor?" asked one of his men.

"Why? He didn't find it. Return it to my quarters," he said before galloping off.

Chapter 6

G *od damnit that hurt. If I get my hands on him, I'll tear him limb from limb*, Evorix thought, rubbing his jaw.

Gius looked over his shoulder, pointed at the crackling fire and said, "If you want dinner, it's over here on the spit."

Evorix pushed himself up from the tree he was laying against and mumbled, "That's the second time you knocked me out. It won't happen again. The way you hit still proves you're timid."

Gius walked over to Evorix and chuckled. He kneeled and cut his bindings off and gently touched Evorix on the shoulder.

"If you want to live forever, you can leave now. I won't judge you. *Or*, you can join us and we can dispose of Emperor Octavius together," he said.

Evorix got to his feet. "Wake up Gius, the Rebellium is dead and so are the people who wanted to fight in it," he said.

"Allecta would tell you to help us," Gius replied.

Before Gius could get his hands up to protect himself, Evorix had him on the ground. Two punches broke Gius' nose before he knew he had been hit. He felt Evorix's large hands around his throat as if he were a chicken going to the pot.

Gius' face turned blue and with his last ounce of energy, he brought his arms up and slammed them down across the inside of Evorix's elbows. As Evorix's grip loosened, Gius gasped and smashed the top of his head into Evorix's nose, breaking his in turn.

Evorix reared back and grabbed his nose as Gius grabbed a branch lying nearby and swung it into his side. Evorix fell over with a loud groan, then rolled away. Gasping in pain, he sat up and coughed as he pushed his nose back into place.

Evorix fixed his cold stare on Gius. "If you talk about my wife again, I'll kill you. Then I'll kill everything you love—.

"Everything I love?" Gius yelled over him. "Is dead, you selfish prick. Can you think of anything else, or only your dead wife?" With tears in his eyes, Gius stared at him frostily, then spoke. "They raped and murdered my turtledove, Clovia. Fucking bastards left her hanging from a tree we planted in front of our villa. My children were burned alive as they held me in chains to watch. Octavius ordered your wife and my family's death because we believed in the Rebellium. The Rebellium lost many of its friends of all ages to kill Tiberius. Your father and brother paid the ultimate price because they believed. I know you can continue the struggle for them." He grabbed Evorix by the arm. "Help me rid Delos of Octavius and the Wolfryan aristocracy," he said, his eyes pleading.

"I don't give a shit about your wife or your kids. My motive to kill Octavius will be for coin and coin alone. That's what I'm loyal to. Aletca... Alecta is just a memory now. If you want him dead, it's going to cost you and the Rebellium more than you may be willing to pay," Evorix said.

Gius went to respond and Evorix held his hand up. "They'll just put another tyrant in his place and you of all people should know that. Does it really look like I give a shit about the politics of Wolfrya. If I risk my neck for you, it will be my self preservation that does it, not my honor," he said.

"You're a cowardly bastard," Gius shot back.

Evorix laughed. "A coward. No, I'm an opportunist," he replied.

"You killed your brother and father," Gius said.

"Sure did. They were the real traitors, so I have no regrets."

Gius frowned, clearly disgusted with Evorix's attitude. "So, how much for you to sell your soul then?"

"It'll cost you a hundred thousand gold pieces. And not that Wolfryan shit with Ovtavius' face on it," he said.

Gius nodded. "Follow me to my camp and you'll be paid."

"And where's that?" Evorix asked.

Gius smiled. "Hidden on the border between West Drathia and the Fire Lands."

Evorix chuckled. "That makes sense. Well, I'm heading back to Pistoryum for the time being. Go get my money and a plan on how to infiltrate Iceport. When you get all that together, you will find me there," he said, getting up and mounting the mule.

"You sure about that?" Gius asked.

"You have no one else so, yeah, I'm sure."

"We could find another assassin," Gius said.

Evorix tapped the mules flank with his ankles and rode off into the woods. He shouted over his shoulder, "No, Gius you can't. If you did, you wouldn't have come for me."

"Expect me within a fortnight," Gius shouted at his back.

If Evorix heard him, he didn't show it.

Gius mounted his horse shaking his head with a slight smile and cantered off in the other direction. A few minutes later, Evorix came trotting back as fast as the mule would ride.

Gius laughed, then shouted, "Change of heart?"

Trotting awkwardly past him, bouncing in the saddle, Evorix said, "Yea, something like that!"

Gius smiled and glanced over his shoulder. The horsemen that changed Evorix's mind came bursting through the undergrowth whipping their steeds.

Gius spat and shouted, "Damn luck I have... gettup!"

He slammed his ankles into his horses flanks and followed Evorix into the woods on the other side of the clearing. Gius' horse followed the donkey down the path running along the waters edge. They rode as fast as they could, glancing back occasionally to see how fast the horsemen were gaining on them. And after a few moments of riding, they knew they couldn't outrun the bounty hunters.

Evorix looked over at Gius and cut his eyes at another path further in the underbrush. Gius nodded and cut hard left at the fork in the road. Two of the men followed Gius as Evorix spun around in the saddle and faced the other two men who had overtaken his mule on the hidden path.

This is gonna hurt, Evorix thought.

He held his arms out and pushed his body forward off the back of the mule. He clothes lined the men off their mounts and then tumbled onto the muddy rock filled road.

Landing on his back, he shouted in pain as his tailbone struck the hardened earth. His attackers laid on their backs, dazed and gasping. Evorix sat up and saw his sword lying next to him. He snatched it as one of the men tackled him and pinned him to the ground.

"You bastard. I'm gonna carve my money out of you if it's the last thing I do," the man said, holding a knife to Evorix's throat.

Evorix swallowed hard and then lifted up with the bottom of his feet. He kicked the man over his shoulders as the other attacker came up from behind him. The man pulled Evorix to his feet, punched him in the face and then wrapped his arms around him in a bear hug.

Annoyed by the man's lack of professionalism, Evorix stomped on the man's foot and broke his toes. As the man reached for his foot, Evorix grabbed him by the neck, pulled it over his shoulder and dropped down to the road. The force of the blow broke the man's neck and he crumbled to the ground, his teeth scattering across the dirt path.

Evorix looked around and watched the other man run for his mount in a panic. He tripped, crawled and stumbled toward his black war horse. The horse spooked and bolted into the water, leaving the man stranded.

Winded from his sprint, the man put his hands on his knees and took deep breaths. After a few deep breaths, the merc kneeled and held his hands up. Evorix paused, let the man catch his breath and then smiled.

Savagely, he cut the man's arms off at the elbows. The man screeched for a few moments, then Evorix swung the blade down and severed his head. Blood splashed across Evorix's face and arms as the attackers head rolled to the waters edge.

Shit, Gius, he thought. He ran for the hill and thought, *Why do I care?*

Evorix's conscious answered for him, the nagging greed always got the better of him. He sighed, shook his head and sprinted up the hill, tripping a few times as he made it to higher ground. He crested the ridge and saw Gius placing the dead men's arms over their chests. Humming to himself, he placed his gold coins over their eyes for their trip with the boatman to the next life.

"You know something, Gius. If I didn't know you any better, I would say you're trying to kill me," Evorix said walking up to him.

Gius grunted and sniffed loudly, "Damn sinuses."

He wiped his nose with his tunic sleeve. "A hundred thousand coins for your help?" he asked.

"Yea, that's the price." He shoved his finger in Gius' chest. "But when we get to your little shitty hole in the earth, you better have my money or I'll kill every one of you for the headache you've caused me," Evorix said.

Gius shrugged and walked away.

Evorix walked back down the hill and over to the pond to wash away the blood that was smeared on his hands and face. A shadow loomed over him while he washed his face in the ice-cold water. He glanced up and a horse nudged him with his muzzle. Evorix fell back on his ass and laughed for a minute. He struggled to his feet and looked at the horse. Its coat was a brilliant jet black with white spots circling its eyes. He checked the under carriage and winked at the horse.

"I'll name you Whispers on account of these woods, not cause of that," he said, glancing down as the horse nudged his hand.

For the first time in a long time, Evorix felt something other than hatred. He didn't have a soul in the world he liked, but the horse made one. He looked it over thoroughly.

"Nothing that won't heal, eh Whispers?" he said quietly, looking at the scrapes from the briar patches.

He mounted him and went to round up the rest of the animals and bodies. He found the mule and the other horses wandering down by the pond.

Picking up their reins, he brought them over to his saddle and tied them off. He mounted Whispers and rode back to where Gius was. Whispers trotted up and snorted at Gius, chomping at the bit. Gius put his arm out, palm facing it and raised his index and middle finger. The horse neighed and pawed at the ground.

"Easy Gius, you're worth less than the horse. I'll eat you before I eat him," he said, pushing Gius aside with the horse's flank.

Gius stared at the horse and then pushed it aside as he mounted his own.

Evorix urged Whispers forward toward the road and waved to Gius. "Keep up."

The pair rode south along the only road that ran through Batopia. The overgrown paths slowed them to a crawl and at one point they had to dismount to lead the horses through the obstacles in the forest.

I could get used to this, Evorix thought as he watched the red, green and gold leaves fall onto their shoulders as they passed through.

"Careful Evorix, we are passing through the Datta's territory now," Gius said, watching every branch blowing in the wind.

A gutted bloody body hung from a tree limb over the middle of the road, his entrails burned. The body had been there for some time and Evorix could only guess why the man was there in the first place.

As if answering his thoughts, Gius whispered, "Some things are better left unanswered."

"These guys are serious," Evorix said, staring into the underbrush.

As he spoke, two men dressed only in loincloths stepped onto the road with blowguns at their sides. Evorix and Gius reigned in their horses and stopped a few feet away from them. One of the men shouted at them in a foreign language, raising his hands in a grandiose fashion. Gius raised one hand and with the other, he pulled a torn flag from his saddle bag.

The man softened his tone and walked up to Gius' horse, palm out. Gius reached into his saddle bag and pulled out a burlap sack tied off at the end. He said something in their native language and handed them the bag. The men slipped back into the shrubbery and disappeared as quickly as they appeared.

"What did you say to them?" Evorix asked.

"I told them you were my prisoner and an enemy of the Rebellium." He closed his saddle bag. "Ain't far from the truth," Gius said, galloping out of the woods.

Evorix stopped at the edge of the forest. He stared straight ahead, not looking at Gius. The rain started down with quick bouts of thunder.

"The God's are not pleased," Gius said, pulling his cloak tighter.

"There are no God's, Gius. Just windchimes. Now, I need supplies and armor because my chest piece is still in your damned room. And who knows what we're going to run into on the road," Evorix said.

"We can make it to my camp," Gius said, pulling his horses' reins.

Evorix snorted and pulled the horses bridle back toward himself. "Gius, we got no chance with what we have and you know that. We got lucky with those mercs," he replied.

Gius sighed and clenched his fists. "You're right. Where to?" Gius asked.

"We ride for West Drathia. The black market there is as good a place as any for quality armor," Evorix said not waiting for him to respond.

"Ah shit, I hate Drathia," Gius said.

Gius followed behind him as the forest thinned out little by little and then turned into rolling meadows. The Kingdom of West Drathia was known to house exiled murderers who escaped the hangman's noose in Iceport and Sorra. With no real laws, it was the villagers job to kill the rule breakers. It was a hard place and an unusually cold place.

All the rivers were frozen and the livestock was small and scarce.

West Drathian's didn't take kindly to strangers entering their lands. They posted pickets every mile or so down the only road into the major city, Vitadruma. The city was the black market capital on the eastern seaboard of Delos. Iceport was beautiful, the Fire Lands were deadly and Vitadruma was the place where anything could be had for a price.

It was the only major city in West Drathia. The villages and hamlets scattered throughout the barren wasteland were mostly deserted, the inhabitants were willing to give up their meager huts in order to put food on the table by working in Iceport.

A batch of eggs in Iceport was at most a silver coin, the same batch of eggs in West Drathia was a gold coin at the very least.

West Drathia was at least habitable, but the other half of the kingdom known as East Drathia, or the Fire Lands was a volcanic wasteland with deep craters and volcanoes that could easily blanket the western half if they exploded.

The Ba inhabited the volcano lands of East Drathia and killed all outsiders if they dared venture in.

The once proud tribes were forced to live in exile. Nearly wiped out by Tiberius in their entirety, a few select tribes survived. After the extermination, there were less than a thousand scattered throughout East Drathia.

The Ba dealt in flesh as a currency system. The more opulent the slave, the more money they were worth. Common everyday people in the villages were easy prey for the slavers, but didn't provide the most money. The rich aristocracy in Iceport was worth one hundred malnourished peasants.

Evorix leaned over to Gius. "Hope you brought a plate to put over your back. It's a beautiful place where the meadows run forever, but the rivers used to run red with blood and now they're frozen in time."

"I've been in this shitty kingdom before," Gius said with a hint of sarcasm.

A rat, the size of a small dog scurried across the road in front of them. "Disgusting place. I usually send other men in here to do our business."

"It's a cesspool of garbage alright." Evorix said with a laugh. "They're my kind of people though. Just remember you could find a knife in your back by nightfall. Hell it might even be me," Evorix said, concentrating on the shrubbery around him.

Small red eyes peered at them through the darkness as they continued on. They followed the road for several days as it wound its way deeper into the West Drathian wilderness. They saw the occasional village, but dared not stop in an attempt to mitigate any hostile encounters. Trash and excrement lined the road as they continued on. The rains pounded them as they approached Vitadruma. They crossed over a hill and saw several iron spires looming above the city as they rode closer.

They approached a wooden palisade with several large sections missing, the rain cascading over their shoulders.

"Why not just put a white picket fence up?" Gius muttered more to himself than Evorix.

Evorix nodded for him to go in between the gaps.

"Why me?" Gius asked.

"'Cause you're paying to kill Octavius, not to get a spear in the back. Now chop, chop."

With a sigh, Gius pulled his cloak in tighter, dismounted and stepped between the loose stakes. A spear flashed at the nape of his neck from behind the wall as he stepped through.

"A white picket fence won't keep the wolves away from our doors, animal or human, m'lord. What the rich be wantin' with us then, eh? Hands up, slow and steady," said the picket, pushing his spear closer to Gius' jugular.

Gius raised his hands and put them on top of his head. Evorix pushed Whispers in closer to them and swiftly pulled a thin blade from his boot. He put it to the guards throat with a simple flick of the wrist.

"Watch your knife, m'lord," the guard said, glancing into the tree line.

Guards in Vitadruma could be bought for a few coins by a shady merchant to protect the city from marauders. A mercenary crossbowmen with an excellent eye could put a quill through the center of a man's back in the blink of an eye. Evorix looked around for any traps and not sensing anything, he turned his attention back to the guard.

"Don't make idle threats. But now that I have your attention, we need a place to sleep and the best place around here to sell some horses and buy supplies. Where can we go?" Evorix asked.

"The knife ya lardship," said the guard, flicking his eyes at it.

"Right... now, where was we?" he asked, lowering his blade.

He slid it back into his boot and urged Whispers forward to separate Gius and the guard.

The rain showers became heavier and the wind picked up as they waited for the man to respond. Evorix held his hand up and cupped his ear, waiting for the guard to pipe up.

"The Madchester." The guard turned to face Evorix. "I can show you."

"How much," Evorix grumbled, staring at the forest again.

"A whore, it's lonely out 'ere."

Evorix kicked him in the face and said, "Not worth that to take us down the street. Fuck off, we'll find it ourselves."

They rode off, leaving the guard rubbing his chin. The horses hooves could be heard clopping down the muddy road as they trotted down the enclosed alleyway.

"Hey, you alright over there?" Gius asked, poking Evorix in the side.

Evorix didn't respond or twitch a muscle. His eyes kept scanning the upper floors of the row housing for surprises until they reached the tavern.

The Madchester was more a weapons house than a tavern. Blood pooled on the front stoop as a feral dog chewed on someone's discarded hand. Gius dismounted, slid his blade from its sheath and advanced to put the dog out of its misery. Evorix grabbed Gius from behind and placed his knife over his throat, drawing blood.

"Touch the dog and die. Did nothing to you. Best watch your sword hand Gius, or I'll chop it off. You should know what I think of dogs, because you *know* what I think of you."

Gius knew how much he cared about dogs, he'd seen him kill a few fellow legionnaires trying to kill a war dog.

Evorix barked like a dog, rubbed its head as it came over and then picked up the hand. He threw it down the opposite alleyway and watched the dog disappear. The one thing he refused do was kill an animal. He pushed past Gius and walked through the cheap double wooden saloon style doors. It felt like every eye turned toward him. Gius followed him in after tying their horses and pack animals to the post outside. He looked at the sea of unwashed faces and raised an eyebrow.

"So, you want to ask, or shall I?" Gius asked.

Evorix rolled his eyes and then walked over to the bar. A prostitute walked up to him and put her hand on his shoulder. She moved it to his crotch. "Fancy a 'gud time, soldier?"

Spinning, he slapped her across the face with the back of his hand. She stumbled back and fell over a table some of the men were gambling at. The patrons stopped drinking and watched.

"Nah, you helped enough," he said, looking down with a smile. He made eye contact with the other patrons "Now, which of you runs the black market?" he inquired, looking for his man.

"I do," said a quiet voice from under a black wide brimmed hat with a white plume sticking out of the side. Evorix squinted at the person and chuckled.

"You don't sound like a man. Show me you're no eunuch," Evorix said, walking in front of him. He grabbed the soldier by the crotch and felt around for a moment.

Something ain't right here...

His brain registered what his hand already knew. He recoiled, but it didn't stop the aggressive onslaught that dropped him to his knees. He felt several swords press against his back and then multiple blows from a knuckle duster mashed his nose to his face. Blood spurted across his assailants arm as he continued to inflict pain.

Gius charged forward, freeing his sword but two men tackled him to the floor. Evorix looked up woozy and battered. A slight smile crossed his features showing the blood in between his teeth.

"I know a whore named Bel that hits harder than you," he said.

Four men picked Evorix up and pulled his arms behind his back. The guards pulled the pair through the tavern and threw them into the back wall, head first.

"Who do you work for?" the voice asked as they sat up.

"Nobody. We're just trying to sell our stuff," Evorix said.

"Tell me who sent you. Was it Fredrick the Gray?" the voice repeated.

"Never heard of him," Evorix said.

Evorix felt a rope tighten around his neck. In a matter of moments, he was hanging from a cross beam in the ceiling. His neck muscles strained as they hung him five feet off the ground. Spitting and sputtering, he swung from the rope.

"Who do you work for?" asked the voice for a third time.

"No one," Evorix said between gasps.

"I don't believe you."

"We're from the Batopia," Gius shouted into the darkness as he watched Evorix swaying.

Evorix dropped to the ground gasping and coughing. Gius took the noose from his neck and threw it at the voice and then helped Evorix to his feet. They could hear someone walking around in the darkness behind them, the footsteps making a unique clicking sound on the floor.

"I'm the owner you're looking for," the voice said, stepping out of the shadows. "My name is Lady Corcundia of Vitadruma. I had to make sure you weren't spies of Fredrick the Gray."

"Who the hell is that?" Evorix asked, rubbing his chafed neck.

"He's the man who lives in the castle at the waters edge." She stopped speaking for a moment and poured herself a drink and then continued. "The one that my husband Duke Gadex of Vitradruma once owned, but they killed him while I was away on business. I came back and those loyal to him brought me underground and we've been here ever since. And you are?" she asked, looking at them as she stepped further into the light.

She brought her curved cherrywood pipe to her pink lips and took a drag. Her red hair looked like someone had pulled it from a fire, but it was clear she lived in the underground as dirty as it was. With a shudder, Evorix noticed her head lice.

Ugh, he thought.

The wide brimmed hat she had pulled over eyes raised a little bit and Evorix saw the faded burn marks on her face, close to her eyes. She caught him looking and pulled her hat lower.

"Names Evorix," he said and then pointed at Gius. "That's Gius and like we said, we're just looking to sell our pack horses and spare weapons. I need to buy some quality armor from you and then we'll be on our way."

Corcundia didn't speak for a moment. She motioned to one of her men to head to the bar.

"Follow me. I will sort you out with what your selling," she said, pointing at the bar.

"And the armor I can buy, right?" Evorix asked as he walked toward the bar.

She nodded as a man lifted up a trap door in the floor boards. The man handed Corcundia a torch and stepped aside. They descended into the darkness, the stairs creaking on their way down.

Chapter 7

A sinius ran across the wooden floor boards of his villa as the battle outside intensified. He heard Peltrasius roar as he covered the door. Asinius' spare armor had been neatly packed in a bag with food and other supplies that he was going to need for his journey. The only problem was that he didn't know where he was going.

He fastened his leather pack to his sword blade and crawled out of the window. He looked across the field to the swampland and shook his head with a sigh. He limped across the field, trying to stay in the high grass. He heard the howls of the emperor's dogs behind him as the sweat dripped from his brow. Not waiting to see if the large dogs were going to catch him, he kept stumbling to the swampland.

He breathed as calmly as he could, but he knew what the dogs could do if they surrounded him. He thought about the number of times he had sicked them on enemies fleeing after a battle.

His tried to lift his sandals, but they had filled with squishy brown mud. The harder he tried, the more they sunk into the muck. He switched tactics and flung the sandals over his shoulder and then started hobbling in the middle of the swampy causeway surrounded by poisonous snakes.

He ran further into the snake, rat and alligator infested land. The green and blue algae sat on top of the brackish water and floated around him lazily, hiding whatever nasties lurked beneath. He made it to a small group of tree stumps on an island to rest for a moment. The green willow tree branches from the trees nearby hung above him, hiding the swamp land from the sun blazing above. With a sigh, he wiped his face and mouth with his forearm.

An arrow thudded into a trunk by his head as he put his sandals back on. Cursing himself for a fool, he ran to a larger tree half the size of a man and hid behind it the best he could. He pulled his sword from his pack and then threw it onto the opposite shoreline, barely clearing the water.

He would run no further, it was time to die a prefect. Wincing, he looked down and saw the welts on his legs from the reeds he had run through. Holding his vine branch in one hand, sword in the other, he stepped out from behind the tree and braced himself against it.

He could hear the howls and barks getting closer. The dogs darted over the hill following his scent and then dove into the water. One of them glanced up, sniffed the air, howled and lunged forward. The algae splashed up in chunks as it bound toward him.

The six attack dogs were massive, built to kill. Wolfryan dogs were a hybrid of a wolf, hyena and the domestic dog. They were trained to kill anything their handlers commanded them too. And a good dog trainer was usually missing a couple of digits on each hand.

They were easy to identify with their silver coat with black and yellow spots. Their fur was coarse like cactus' needles and a black stripe ran down their spine. For his own pleasure, Octavius insisted their nails be sharpened with whetstones.

Twenty of the emperor's horsemen rode into the marsh behind the dogs. The first dog came within ten feet of where he stood, saliva dripping from its incisors. He crouched low to the ground, his sword pressed against the inside of his foot. He winced as his bones popped from the stress of kneeling after his run.

The dog leapt and impaled itself on his long blade. It slid down the length of it and then onto him. He closed his eyes as the dog pushed him to the ground. He managed to roll the dead dog off of him in time for another dog to jump on top of him. It pinned him and lunged at his neck. He held the dog by the throat as he reached for his sword nearby, his fingers stretching as far as they could.

He felt something cold brush against his body as he struggled with the dog. He heard the dog yelp as it was flung through the air and off of him. A wave of alligators moved quickly by him and into the water. Not losing a moment of precious time, he shot to his feet and splashed through the water to the opposite bank. He scaled a tree as the alligators bellowed in their hunt for the dogs.

The alligators were upon the riders and the dog handlers in only a few moments. They stood no chance against the ancient killing machines. The alligators tore legs from horse and rider alike, swallowing them in huge bites.

The guards formed a semi-circle and moved backward to the shore line. They screamed as they were dragged under, fragments of their blue stoles floating to the top of the swampy water. The horses that remained bolted from the swamp and trampled the riders that stood in their way.

The guardsmen fell one by one until only a few men remained when they reached the shoreline. As the legionnaires backed up, they could hear several blood chilling bellows behind them. Other alligators smelled the blood in the water and had come to investigate.

Asinius put his hands over his ears to muffle the screams of agony. It seemed to go on for an eternity, but finished in a blink of an eye. When the screams stopped, he looked around and saw the alligators had slipped back under.

They were gone as soon as they had appeared, taking whatever meat they had to the bottom of the marsh. One charcoal colored alligator remained, resting its nostrils and eyes just above the water line. It snorted as it stared at the one meal that had temporarily escaped. It slowly lowered itself under the water and then swam away.

The next morning Asinius woke up hanging awkwardly on a tree branch. He had been a prefect for many years and had seen many people die, but he had never seen a group of alligators destroy humans like that before. Bloody, intense and disturbing. He glanced around and saw his pack undisturbed below him. As he looked for any more alligators, he felt something slimy rub against his leg. He glanced down and saw a yellow and black boa constrictor.

He kicked himself free and fell out of the tree backwards and landed on his side. Dazed, he sat up and held his ribs. He saw there was no immediate danger and his breathing returned to normal. He limped over to his pack and went back to his little island. He scanned the area as he chewed on a piece of bread. He watched the corpses of both man and beast floating around him and knew it would only be a matter of time before the alligators, or something worse came back to eat what was left behind.

He carefully pulled pieces of men onto the island that he could reach. He found a pair of sandals on one body and a useable chest piece on another. He scooped up a dome shaped helmet floating by and threw it on.

He grabbed as many weapons as he could carry, shouldered his pack and then ran across the swamp to the other side. The swamp lands ran as far as the eye could see, a blue haze dancing above the water. He slowly made his way through the algae, stabbing the bottom of the riverbed to make sure nothing attacked him. He saw the long twisting road ahead of him and breathed a sigh of relief.

Several days passed on his lonely journey to nowhere. His lips were dry and cracked from the lack of clean water, the corners of his mouth collecting white spit. In the distance, he spotted an area that looked to have a small river.

A quiet farm house was surrounded by a tall white picket fence. The house sat on the edge of the pond attached to a water wheel. With his last bit of energy, Asinius grabbed the fence and pulled himself into the yard. A young man with curly black hair ran to his side and yelled for his grandfather. The old man ran to them and looked down at Asinius.

"This is an important man, Tersius. A very important man. His nails are perfect and he has all his teeth," the man said, rapping his knuckles against Asinius' gold inlaid breastplate.

The old man noticed a gold coin fall out of Asinius' pouch. He reached down and bit into it. "Go fetch your father."

Asinius opened one eye and raised his sword to the man's neck. "I've killed men for much less. Don't be a thief, sets a bad example for your grandson," he said.

"And how would you know what's good, or ain't good for the boy?" the old man asked.

"You're right, I don't. But I do know my sword arm can sever your balls right now."

The man looked down, swallowed hard and nodded. Asinius tapped the man's balls with the knife he had slid from his belt. He emphasized the words after each knife stroke.

"Do. I. make. myself. clear? Set. A. Good. Example. Now fetch me some water!" he demanded.

The old man did as he was told and ran back faster than he left. He held a cup to Asinius' lips and helped him sit up. Asinius drank deeply and then spit the water up. He dry-heaved, snatched the cup from the man's hands and took smaller sips.

Sighing, he tilted his head back and muttered, "That's the good stuff."

Tersius' father, Primus reached them and leveled his spear at Asinius' throat.

"Help you with something, prefect?" he asked, inching the blade closer to Asinius' adam's apple.

Asinius opened his eyes, cocked his head to one side and said, "I don't recognize your face behind that beard. Who are you?"

"My name is Primus of West Drathia. A man on a list you wrote for those of us loyal to the Rebellium. Come to join the cause, or be killed by it?" Primis asked, not taking his eyes off of him.

Asinius chuckled and shook his head in disbelief. He went from being hunted by his own people to landing at his enemies feet. There was no way out now. He held his hands out in front of him.

Asinius spit on Primus' sandals. "So help the God's, I will kill you for what you're planning to do," Asinius hissed.

Primus snickered and then bound Asinius' hands. "You and what army, prefect?" he asked.

Primus picked him up by the throat and shoved him in the direction of the barn.

"Primus, I should have hung you when I had the chance. I guess letting you go doesn't get me any points, does it?" Asinius asked, knowing the answer.

"Nope. We may been friends long ago, Asinius, but now I have over a thousand reasons to kill you. One for every member you had executed after the Rebellium!" Primus shouted, smashing Asinius over the head with the pommel of his sword.

Chapter 8

Evorix, Gius and Lady Corcundia descended down the stairs and into the crudely excavated basement. She put her torch into a holder on the wall and took her black cloak and wide brimmed hat off. Stepping up to the table, she pulled her red hair over the burns on her face. Several items on the table caught her eye as she walked around the room smoking her pipe.

"I see you mostly have broken shit," she said, picking up a broken dagger with two fingers. She looked at it in disgust, shook her head and then dropped it on the floor.

Gius smiled. "Lady Corcundia, we don't need much——."

"Oh we need as much as you have. He owes me a hundred thousand gold coins. He can start paying me the other ninety nine thousand five hundred pieces later," Evorix said.

She laughed and picked up a shattered sword. "The weapons are worthless, not fit for a child to wield," she said.

"Maybe, but you can melt the metal down and remake a few," Gius piped up, hoping not to come out of pocket.

"Didn't ask you old man, so shut it," she said.

"Ok, fine. How much to buy good quality armor?" Gius asked, trying to refrain from moving his hand to his sword pommel.

"A hundred coins," she replied, putting her hat back on.

Evorix guffawed. "What's in that pipe, belladonna?"

"Bellweed. I don't smoke belladonna. But that's not the point. I make the prices and they are non negotiable," she said, opening a chest on the far wall.

Gius groaned at Evorix's apparent lack of negotiating skills. They needed her much more than she needed them. The thought crossed his mind that all she had to do was kill them. No one would bother looking for them either and after carefully scanning the faces of her men, he wanted to make sure no one was thinking of surprising them. Gius butted back into the conversation, cutting Evorix off.

"Won't ask anything for the weapons then, take them. How about you take the donkey and spare horse in trade?" Gius asked.

"Ok, but I still want forty gold pieces. How does that strike your fancy?" she asked, hoisting a crude leather jerkin from the chest.

Evorix laughed as he looked at the deteriorating jerkin. "You're kidding right? That ain't quality, that's——."

"Shit," Gius said, finishing his sentence.

"You haven't got the coins for good quality," she said, dropping the jerkin back into the chest.

"Like hell I don't," Evorix said.

He liked the woman's style, she was ballsy. He looked into her eyes for a moment and saw a flicker of pain, the same pain he carried. Losing a spouse would only be seen by those afflicted by the same loss, a look of solemness, a tortured haunting of the eyes. But it wasn't a unique pain by any stretch of the imagination in Delos. It was a cold and dreary place even in the sunlight.

A kindred soul, he thought, looking in her direction.

Gius nudged Evorix as he spat on the ground at her feet. "I want real armor, not some left over piece of shit from a bygone age," Evorix paused and slid his hand to the hilt of his sword. "Actually, I have a better idea. What if I just take what I want and kill you and your men?" he asked.

Corcundia smirked. "We outnumber you four to one. Can you and the old man kill eight others before being killed?" she asked, pulling her sword from its sheath, her men following suite.

Gius touched Evorix's arm and whispered, "This is not the time for pride. Pay her, get the shitty armor and then we ride for the Rebellium," he said.

Evorix snatched the jerkin out of her hands, sniffed it and wrinkled his nose.

"By all that's holy in Delos this thing looks like it's a hundred years old." He sniffed it again. "And it smells like old Wolfryan blood."

Corcundia smiled and winked. "That's the owner in the corner the rats are chewing on."

Evorix glanced over his shoulder with a disgusted look. With an exaggerated sigh, he withdrew his pouch and counted out the coins. He begrudgingly handed them to her and donned the creaking armor.

This smells like shit and feels worse.

As Evorix opened his mouth to say goodbye and good riddance, he froze. They heard a loud pounding knock from upstairs and ran back up the steps behind Corcundia in time to see one of her men walking to the barred door.

In a boisterous feminine voice, he asked, "Who is it?"

"By order of Fredrick the Gray, open this door. We are here to serve an arrest warrant to Lady Corcundia. She has sold her last batch of illegal weapons. Now, surrender!" Fredrick's herald shouted.

In response, Lady Corcundia's men pulled their weapons and flipped the tables near them over for cover. She pulled her hat low over her eyes and tied her hair in a ponytail.

"Any of you bastards want to surrender?" she shouted.

"No!"

"I do. It ain't our fight. We're going out the back," Evorix said, keeping his sword sheathed as he straightened the tight fitting jerkin.

"What, you runnin'? Always heard you were vicious in a fight," she said with a smile, loading her handheld crossbows.

"You know us?" Gius asked.

She nodded and aimed for the front door.

"You're Gius Lupinius and he's Evorix Vispanius." She pointed to the bounty posters. "Steep price on your heads. Good thing for you I hate the emperor more than the Rebellium."

"Stay here Gius and you'll never find me again. You're money ain't worth dying for some shitty hole in the wall," Evorix said, looking for an exit.

As they argued, Evorix held up one hand and silenced Gius. He heard a loud whining sound by the door and cocked his head to the side. It was a moment to late when he knew realized what was happening.

He had heard the same sound once before. The proper name for the equipment that was whining was known as a Fire Horn. They were metallic instruments loaded with a substance called Hellrot that burned as hot as the sun, melting skin from bone. The instrument was lit at the bottom by a torch and once lit, the machinery made a high squealing noise and then liquid fire spewed from the opening. If it malfunctioned, the flame would vaporize everyone in a ten yard radius.

Evorix watched a boy stroll up to the door and put his ear and hand to it. A thought flew through Evorix's mind.

Shit, it's gonna blow.

Evorix bellowed, his voice booming off the walls. "Someone, get the bo——." He found himself running toward the door for no reason, arm outstretched.

I don't care about them, do I? Why am I running to the door?

The explosion shook the building and set it ablaze. The boy and a few men standing next to him screeched and melted into fiery puddles. The explosion from the blast launched Evorix across the room and onto a table, smashing it to pieces.

The heat coursing through the air made it almost impossible to breathe. Thick acrid black smoke that smelled like sulfur hung high in the air around them.The explosion was so loud that several of Corcundia's men nearest the door never heard their attackers barrel in behind them.

The deafened men stumbled into one another, their burnt and seared lungs holding their screams of pain as the attackers swords and axes cut them down. Gius and Corcundia coughed violently and wiped their eyes as they tried to form a defense line with the men still standing around them.

"I can't see shit," shouted one of her men, standing near Evorix.

"Then squint," Corcundia shouted.

A tall man wearing a grey cloak stepped through the hole where the door used to be and licked his lips. To look at Fredrick the Gray you wouldn't think he was anything special.

The gate guard Evorix assaulted had run to the castle after Evorix broke his jaw and told him the whole story. Fredrick was delighted by his luck when he was told of the assault. He could kill two birds with one stone, literally.

Looking around the room and sucking on his toothless gums, he said, "Clean this shit up. No survivors!"

Evorix held his head in his blistered hands as the screams around him got louder. A gloved hand pulled him off the ground and pushed him against the bar. Corcundia thrust a sword and shield into his hands.

"Fight, or die," she shouted.

Gius limped over to them with her remaining men. Corcundia shouted above the noise, "Form ranks!"

She looked at Evorix and shouted, "One hundred gold coins to fight with us!"

"Five hundred," he replied, shoving his sword into an attackers stomach.

Dodging a sword thrust, Corcundia elbowed a man in the face, shattering his teeth with a bone chilling crunch. She ducked his overhand swing and drove a thin blade into the man's chin. He stumbled back as blood seeped from his mouth. She yanked the blade free and kicked him to the floor.

"Deal, now help!" she said.

Another attacker charged Evorix. He spat in the man's face and swung his sword, severing the man's balls. Moving quickly, he cut down another three men with little effort. He saw Fredrick the Grey standing in the middle of the floor unprotected. He kicked a spear laying on the ground up to his waist and hurled it at him.

The spear flew through the air and as it was about to skewer Fredrick, he grabbed one of his men and used him as a shield. Fredrick threw the body to the side and retreated to where his men were forming a shield wall.

Damn, Evorix thought.

Corcundia's remaining men charged into the attacker's shield wall and broke it open. Evorix pulled a man closer to him by the neck, snapped it and held him as a shield. Several bolts from a crossbow hit his human shield in the face and torso as he advanced toward Fredrick. Evorix launched the dead man into a group of attackers as they charged him. He battled three men and dodged their blows as they pushed him back to the bar.

A man with a maul snuck behind Evorix and struck him across the back. The blow knocked him to the ground and sent one of his daggers clattering across the floor.

Goddammit, I'm getting slow.

He groaned as the man held the maul over his head and swung down. The blow stopped midway in its arc. The attacker fell back to the floor, the maul sliding across the floor behind him. His attacker looked surprised and yanked the quill from his stomach. He got to one knee and another bolt hit him in the face, showering Evorix with dark blood.

Evorix glanced over his shoulder and shook his head. Corcundia nodded as she stuffed liquor bottles into the bag on her hip.

She shouted, "Saving your life just cut the price in half!"

He could hear Gius laughing on his left at his misfortune. Angered, Evorix grabbed his sword and joined Corcundia's forces as they retreated. She directed a few of her men to build a barrier and fight a rear-guard action. Backing up little by little, their numbers dwindled.

Corcundia ran for the stairs, but an attacker yanked her by the hair and pulled her to the ground. She held him off the best she could as he stabbed at her throat. One of her men slit the attackers throat from behind, turned around to engage Fredricks men but was run through. Fredrick lunged at her unprotected chest with a spear.

Evorix threw a table leg at Fredrick and hit him in the temple. As he crumpled to the floor, the rest of Fredrick's men closed in. Evorix picked Corcundia up and pushed her to the back of the bar.

"Lady Corcundia, this way!" shouted one of her men, holding off another attacker.

She descended into the basement with a handful of her most experienced men hot on her heels. Evorix reached the trap door and someone pushed him down the steps behind her. As he fell, the beam in the ceiling above him broke free. The door slammed shut and the beam crushed the man who closed off their escape.

With a thud and a loud groan, Evorix hit the last step and sprawled out. Panting, he looked around.

Damn that hurt. Is this all that made it? he thought.

He counted ten men, most of them badly wounded. Screams could be heard above them as the last of her men put up a futile resistance. Corcundia ignored their screams and pushed a piece of the wall in under a torch. She wiped her temple and drew blood from her brow.

"I hate that man. I'll kill him if it's the last thing I ever do," she muttered as she pushed the door open.

Evorix walked up behind her. "Where's my money?" he asked.

"No time for that, Evorix. We have to go," Gius said.

Evorix glared at Gius and held his finger up with a shushing sound.

Corcundia cut her eyes at Evorix. "Why didn't you kill Fredrick?" she demanded.

"You didn't pay me for that," he replied.

She glanced over her shoulder and saw two of her men kneel down at the foot of the stairs, spears at the ready.

"For Kooris!" they shouted.

Kooris was the god of blood. One that demanded human sacrifices for protection. Few if any people in Delos worshipped the banned god and the penalty for the belief was to be covered with honey and left tied to ant hill. Octavius' favorite method of torture.

The wall swung open and the group quickly ventured into the passageway. Evorix was the last to go after he found a few pots of oil by the door. He pulled the torch from the holder and placed it over the pots.

"Good luck men," he said over his shoulder as he closed the door.

Corcundia led the group through the passageway as the cobwebs brushed against her face. Rats and mice scattered as she swung her torch by her feet. Her torch swung by Gius' ankles and he saw hundreds of skeletal bones. He looked at Corcundia aghast.

"What the—-?"

"Don't play innocent with me, Gius. This is for Kooris. She does not protect those who don't sacrifice in her honor," she said, shouldering past him.

One of her men collapsed in the tunnel as they began to move again.

"And that's another one!" she shouted as her men followed her obediently down the tunnel.

Evorix knelt down next to the body. He hummed as he turned the dead man over onto his back. Evorix smiled as he closed the man's eyelids down. Pulling the man's pouch from his belt, he emptied it into his. He waved Corcundia's men on until he was the last one in the tunnel. He didn't hear the explosion he was looking for, so he cupped his hand around his ear and slowed his breathing.

It should have gone off by now.

A hand grabbed his shoulder from behind, startling him. Gius pulled him back and said, "Put that money back you worthless thief. You're someone else now. Not the man I remember."

Evorix grabbed him by the throat and slammed him into the wall. "Watch yourself asshole. You came looking for me, remember?" Pointing down at the body, he said, "Guys dead, he ain't going to need it."

Evorix released his grip and then tossed the empty pouch to Gius with a snort. "I work for gold, same as you."

"What did you just say to me, thief?" Gius asked, advancing with his sword drawn.

"Watch your sword, or you never draw one again," Evorix said, picking up the dead man's sword. "What I meant was, you're a thief for the Rebellium and I am for money. Different gold, same bullshit. You kill for it like I do. We're both slaves and always will be," Evorix said.

Gius clenched his teeth and grumbled something under his breath.

Evorix laughed boisterously, then spit on the body. "What do ya know, he's still dead. Beside, I closed his eyes, didn't I? He never saw a thing. I do have some class."

The argument ended and a light could be seen down the tunnel. They heard footsteps approaching, accompanied by small shadows. Gius pushed Evorix down the tunnel and shouted, "Go!"

An explosion broke the silence and sent a ball of fire hurtling down the shaft. The force from the oil bombs Evorix built shifted the wooden beams in the tunnel. Screeches of terror and fear were heard for a moment, then nothing but darkness.

Gius ran as fast as his gimp would let him as the dirt and debris fell from the sides of the tunnel. He caught up with Evorix as the tunnel collapsed with a loud creak. They leapt the last few feet and rolled into the daylight.

Laughing could be heard above them as they brushed the debris from their scalps and clothes. Corcundia and her men held their horses reins. Evorix stood up and walked over to stroke Whispers mane, then touched his forehead to his muzzle.

To hell with the Rebellium. Got this horse, that's all I need.

Evorix looked at Corcundia and said, "Where the hell are we?"

"Under an overhang, south of the city," she said.

Gius brushed himself off again. "Where will you go now, Lady Corcundia?" he asked.

"Not sure." She took a deep breath. "I think I'll gather more men and go back to kill Fredrick the Gray."

"We could use your help to kill Emperor Octavius," Gius said, mounting his horse.

Corcundia looked at the faces of her men and then back to Gius and asked, "What's the pay?"

"We'll pay your one hundred thousand coins for your help," Gius said.

Corcundia nodded. "Deal."

The small group rode along the road single file, occasionally glancing over his shoulder.

Evorix saw riders on the horizon. "Seems someone's coming our way." He looked around the group and counted eight including himself.

Thirty riders wearing red tunics over light chain mail rode over the hill and spread out across the road. They galloped down the slope, weaving in and out of the trees in their path.

Evorix motioned for his group to lead their horses into the trees lining the roadway and hide. The riders stopped where Evorix's group was hidden and spoke for a moment. They watched the soldiers dismount, all except a man mounted on a chestnut colored mare. Evorix leaned against a tree and bit into an apple.

"They're coming to fast. We need to form a battle line," one of the men shouted.

The other riders formed a line, their spear tips gleaming in the sunlight.

"Hold the line!" one of the men shouted to his comrades.

Evorix watched a second group of riders come over the hill, riding hard. The second group urged their horses into the spear wall and as the two groups collided, the riders exploded through the defensive line. Screams and curses from the wounded and dying cracked the crisp cold silent air.

The man on the chestnut mare was knocked unconscious as he faced two attackers. One of the attackers raised their sword over the man's head to finish him. One of the fallen man's companions dove over his body and absorbed the blow. The shiny sword stuck in the sacrificial man's rib cage, preventing his attacker from attacking further.

Evorix heard a voice shout, "Cheap Wolfryan steel!"

The man put his boot on the body and yanked at his sword hilt. After a moment, he gave up and pulled a backup blade to finish the job. Evorix could hear himself suck in his breath.

That worthless bast——.

Fredrick the Gray's burnt cloak fluttered in the wind. Evorix bent over and attempted to pull a knife from his boot. As he rose to his feet, he felt two elbows lay across his back and push him back down.

"Do.not.move," Corcundia said, accentuating her words.

Evorix could hear two crossbow bolts release and fly downrange. One bolt hit Fredrick in the shoulder and one missed.

"Damn the God's. Guess it's going to be the old fashioned way," Corcundia said, lifting a branch in front of her out of the way with her blade.

She stepped out onto the road and rolled her sleeves up.

"You bitch, I'll kill you for that," Fredrick spat.

Corcundia smiled and settled into a defensive stance, her legs shoulder width apart. The men that remained with her charged out of the tree line to aid the riders in red. Fredrick roared and charged her, pushing a man in his path out of the way.

She sidestepped as Fredrick flailed wildly. She paused, stared Evorix in the eye, winked and then buried her blade to the hilt in Fredrick's neck as she dodged another of his overhand swings. He let out an animalistic screech and desperately reached for the hilt as he made loud choking sounds.

Whispering in his ear, she said, "You rotten bastard. That's for my husband."

She kicked him to the ground as the mysterious men in red that were fighting with them cleaned up the remainder of Fredrick's troops. Evorix's allies ran to their leader and carried him into the tree line. Gius pulled his blade from his opponents back and wiped the sweat from his brow.

Without being asked by Evorix, he said, "In case you're wondering, the man in red they're waking up is the King of Tramonia, fella by the name of Aksutamoon."

"I've heard of him. What's he doing in Drathia?" Evorix asked.

"Knowing his reputation, I would say making sure his shipment of wine doesn't go missing," Gius said.

The Tramonian soldiers dragged a body passed them while they talked.

"And him?" Evorix asked, his eyes following the body.

"The de—-. I mean the wounded man is Katsootamun."

Evorix stared at the man's ashen face, his grey tongue hanging out. "Gius, that guy is dead as a rat in a trap."

Gius sighed. "He is the heir...well was the heir to the Tramonian crown."

Evorix laughed. "So much for gentry. Should have learned how to use a sword, not his body to protect someone."

Gius bit his lip.

"What are you thinking about? How to pay me?" Evorix asked.

"If we could somehow get them to join the Rebellium, we may just have a chance against Octavius," Gius said.

"A king join your silly *cause*, fat chance. I'm only coming because the money is good." He pointed at the unconscious king. "He don't need money. He's rich enough to finance his own wars. But I'm sure if you pucker up, his lardship will love you for it," Evorix said, moving his tongue inside his cheek as he worked his hand by his mouth. With a sinister laugh, he clapped Gius on the back, turned around and disappeared into the shadows.

Chapter 9

The freezing green water cascaded across Asinius' face. Sputtering, he screamed as he looked at his shoulder joints separating from his arms as they hung above his head. He spit out the slimy water that had slid into his mouth and gagged.

He had been hanging with his arms tied above his head for hours. His fingertips had turned white and he had the feeling of pins being stuck into his arms and shoulders. The pain worsened by the second and it felt like every ligament and muscle he had were ripping from their sockets.

Primus towered over him, the empty water pail in his hand. With no remorse, he kicked Asinius in the ribs over and over. With a smug and sinister look, he whispered, "Who loves ya, prefect?" He sent another score of kicks into Asinius' rib cage. "Say it!"

Asinius growled and lowered his head. "You do."

"Damn right," Primus said, continuing the barrage of fists and stomps to his body.

Asinius screamed for mercy.

Primus giggled and said, "You showed no mercy to the Rebellium. You killed women and children. Innocents... and now you will pay the price," he shouted, wagging his finger near Asinius' mouth.

Asinius waited patiently and then bit down with all the force he had. Howling in pain as blood dripped from his missing fingertip, Primus held his hand in his opposite palm and began to kick Asinius in the ribs.

"You son of a whore!" Primus shouted.

Pushing the heel of his shit stained boot onto Asinius' rotator cuff, he pushed down until he heard a pop. Asinius spit out the finger and screamed in pain.

"You bit my finger off, you——

"Piss on you. It's easy to lay blame on your old leader, isn't it? You were all fools to rise against him. Everyone one of you should have been executed," Asinius shouted over him, blood dripping from his lower lip.

Boiling with rage, Primus hissed through clenched teeth, "My uncles and many others died to give us freedom. You sold us out because of misplaced *loyalty*. So where is your emperor now, you worthless rat?"

"Take these bindings off and call me a rat. The problem with you Primus is you believe that shit about the Rebellium and what it supposedly represented. Not what it really was. Lies, it was all lies. It was a group of people who wanted nothing more than anarchy. There will always be an emperor, *that* is the only truth."

Using one finger at a time, Asinius held them up. "There are three truths in life, Primus. You're ignorant, so I'll explain them. One, taxes are always due. Two, *loyalty* is just another word for services rendered. And lastly, death comes for us all. And I'll be there for yours."

"You haven't changed a bit. You're still an arrogant patronizing asshole," Primus said, pulling a blade sheathed against his forearm.

Primus placed the blade against Asinius' throat and with an ice cold menacing stare, he grabbed him and began to choke him. Asinius gasped and fought to free his hands as he began to asphyxiate. Tersius ran into the room and pulled on Primus' shoulder.

"Riders!"

Primus held his grip for a few more seconds and then withdrew. Smiling, he head-butted Asinius and knocked him unconscious. Primus ran to the barn window and saw his father meet the men at the gate.

"Shit, Wolfryan's. They must be here to claim him. Tersius, get the horses ready and tie him to a saddle. He must be brought to the Rebellium council to stand trial," Primus said.

"What about you?"

Checking his swords, Primus replied, "I'll hold them off as long as I can. You know where you're going. Find Uncle Gius and tell him what happened." Pointing at Asinius, he said, "Under no circumstance do you let him go free. Give him to the first Rebellium soldier you see. Never return to this house. Tell me you understand?"

Tersius teared up and sniffed. Primus grabbed him by the chin and punched him across the face.

"Toughen up boy. We all die and I've lived long enough. Those are real legionnaires out there. Not the ones from your nightmares. They'll flay the skin from your body and drink from your skull, or worse. Your grandfather is buying me time. Get the man on the horse and ride, son. And—."

"Then you'll follow right," Tersius asked, grasping his shoulder.

Primus chuckled. No, do.not.look.back," Primus emphasized, squeezing his shoulder.

Tersius nodded, his lower lip quivering. Primus unsheathed one of his swords and thrust it into the boys shaking hands and said, "This is the sword carried by every man in our family back to the beginning. Keep it sharp and it will keep you alive."

The guards shouted at Tersius' grandfather outside interrupting Primus. Tersius winced as Primus turned his face back to his.

Softly, he said, "Tersius, go now and let me die the way all men should."

A tear fell from Tersius' eye and he quietly asked, "And how is that?"

With a grin, Primus said, "Free, boy. Always free."

Tersius looked at him, blinking back tears and then hugged him around the neck. Primus patted him on the back and pointed to the horse and said, "Remember how we face death. Go."

Curses of pain could be heard out front as the battle began. Primus stood and cracked his back and neck. With a smile at the corner of his mouth, he waved to Tersius as he galloped off. He watched him ride off over the hill and then turned toward the door. Primus watched his father cut down two of the men and then a guard speared him through the spine. He looked down, touched the spear tip and then fell to the ground. Primus kneeled and began to make small incisions on his hand whispering:

For the cowards, the faithless and the detestable,
For the murders, the immoral and the innocent,
For the liars, cheats and thieves,
The dying and the dead...

Forgive the people like me.

Finishing his prayer, he silently pushed the barn doors open and mounted his horse. He crouched low in the saddle as the Wolfryan's came to the door.

"Long live the Rebellium!" he roared, slamming his ankles into the horses flanks.

His horse lurched forward and was cut down, throwing him from the saddle. He rolled to his feet and drove his sword through two men until a spear pierced the back of his thigh.

"Where is Asinius? We know you helped him escape," shouted the legionnaire holding the spear.

"I should have given him to you, but the honor of his execution falls to The Rebellium." He spat at their feet, pulled his knife from his arm sheath and threw into a man's throat standing in front of him.

The man gasped and clutched his throat and then fell to his knees. Primus laughed maniacally until spears entered both of his shoulders from behind and pinned him to the red and brown dirt. He grunted in pain as they pulled their swords.

"Free——." He whispered, but his words were cut short as his throat was cut.

• • • •

AKSUTAMOON, THE KING of Tramonia woke up a few hours later by a roaring fire. Overweight and pale, he looked more like a swollen red apple than a king. His men had washed the blood from his face, revealing his battered face. The king had an upset stomach and his large ears wouldn't stop ringing. He groaned and lifted his head, yawning to pop his ears.

"Katsootamun," he shouted.

No one spoke.

He shouted louder as he cleared his throat and spit, "Katsootamun!"

Lady Corcundia came to his side as he struggled to get up. "Are you in pain, King Aksutamoon?"

He looked up and smiled, "Lady Corcundia of Vitadruma, what on Delos are you doing here?"

"Until last night still selling black market goods. But Fredrick burned my inn down. I heard you were captured and being transported back to Iceport for crimes against the Empire. Any truth to that?" she asked, one of her eyebrows lifting.

He nodded and sat up. "Ain't my empire. I sell my wines to whoever the hell I feel like selling them to. Octavius doesn't own us. I'm a Tramonian and you know we bow to no man. And yes, I was captured. We were ambushed by Fredricks' men as we rode for Batopia. He confiscated our shipment saying it could only be sold in Wolfrya."

He continued, "That raggedy bastard imprisoned us a few months ago. He sent a courier to get a ransom, but my cousin told them he wouldn't pay. My cousin, Tatootamoon is a greedy bastard and wrote me off for dead. They were bringing us to the town square for execution when our escort sprinted toward your inn. We escaped and they caught us here. It was too easy to escape, I wonder why that is?"

Gius piped up behind him, "That's because of me and him, your eminence," he said, pointing over to where Evorix was sitting cleaning his nails. "If you want revenge I can guarantee that I can make it happen."

"How's that?" Aksutamoon asked.

Nodding in Evorix's direction, Gius said, "Let him do it. I know you have no love loss for the empire. And the Rebellium could use your help when we take Iceport from Octavius' greedy blood-soaked hands. What do you think?" Gius asked, sitting next to him by the fire to warm his hands.

"What can your man do my army can't do?"

Leaning toward the fire, Gius whispered, "An army during a siege is destroyable." He held up his index finger and winked, "But one man, highness. One man is always expendable."

Aksutamoon smiled and glanced over Gius' shoulder. He saw something on the side of the road on a pyre of stones surrounded by chopped up wood. He held his hand over his brow and said, "Who's that?"

No one answered him.

"I said, who the hell is that over there?"

Evorix walked up to him and said, "Your dead brother, Taksoota or some damn thing. I found his sword unused, so I'm keeping it. And this chainmail," he said, feeling the notches cut into the sword with his index finger.

"But you can have his worthless boots and his tattered stinky clothes back. His feet were to small anyway," he said, dropping the boots in the dust.

Aksutamoon shook uncontrollably, his face turning a deep red.

"One question though. Your brother, was he the village idiot? I mean, with all due respect, why carry a notched sword, known for breaking blades and then use your body for a shield?" he asked.

Evorix turned around and shrugged his shoulders. "Hell with it, he's better off dead. More coin for me... I mean us," Evorix said, picking Katsootamun's coin purse off the ground.

Gius put his fingers to his temples and groaned. He rubbed them slowly and muttered, "Damnit Evorix."

Gius watched as Aksutamoon jumped to his feet. Gius rushed to him and held him under the arms. He attempted to hold him back until the others could assist in restraining him.

Evorix laughed and bit into an apple, "What...what did I say?"

Aksutamoon shouted, "I'll murder you. If it's the last thing I do, I'll murder you."

Evorix raised his hand and spread two fingers out in front of him and blew a raspberry. A large bluish vein popped out from the center of Aksutamoon's forehead. He pulled several men with him until they brought him down in a cloud of dust at Evorix feet.

Evorix dropped the apple core on Aksutamoon's forehead with a sigh and said, "Ah forget it. I got emperor's to kill and money to make. Got no time for fake barbarian kings that drink piss wine."

The color drained from Aksutamoon's face as Evorix walked away whistling. Aksutamoon looked around, ran his hand through his hair and pulled a blade hidden near the nape of his neck. His men lined up four abreast and waited for the order to give chase. He opened his mouth, but his throat closed on him.

A voice boomed in his head, "*Leave him be. Burn your brother's corpse if you want to see the sun tomorrow. Killing Evorix will bring you no peace.*"

Aksutamoon fell to his knees choking.

Gius ran to his side and shouted, "Help, he's choking."

His men sprinted to his side and he waved them off. They looked at him suspiciously, but obeyed. From behind a tree, Lady Corcundia lowered her clenched fist and shook her wrist out. She groaned and slumped against the tree exhausted. Beads of sweat dripped from her brow and her blue eye with a yellow pupil twitched as a tear of blood fell from the corner of it.

Aksutamoon took a deep breath, trying to clear his throat. He coughed harshly as his men rushed to pull him to the fire and pour water down his throat. Corcundia watched Evorix walk away and smiled.

"Your allies will protect you long before you know we are there," Corcundia muttered.

As she walked out from the tree line, Gius stared at her. She nodded in his direction and walked up to Aksutamoon.

"I step away to piss and you look like death. What the hell happened?"

He rubbed his throat awkwardly and said, "Allergies. Mind your business."

She smirked and rolled her eyes.

Aksutamoon growled at her and stood up. Spitting into the fire, he pushed her aside and walked over to his brother's funeral pyre. Without ceremony he threw a torch onto his body. As the embers from the fire spewed heavenward, black smoke rose from the pyre. The fire raged on the pyre for a few moments and then Aksutamoon lifted his head. He slammed a bastard sword into the rough clay and then put his brothers helmet on it.

Gius walked up to Corcundia. "Missed a spot, m'lady." Corcundia's blue eye turned a deeper shade as she clenched her fist. "Easy witch, only I know," Gius said.

"Know what?" she asked, raising an eyebrow.

Gius stopped walking and motioned for her to follow him. "You're a Blood wizard, aren't you?"

Corcundia bristled. "And if I am?" she asked.

Gius spread his hands. "Oh, no problems here. You could really help us with our rebellion," he smiled. "Is it true, you lose a year of your life when you use your ability?" he asked.

She walked back to the tree line. "It's worth the price to play the part of a Goddess,"

A few hours later as everyone slept, Gius and Aksutamoon talked by the dying fire. "I'm sorry about what happened with Evorix your emine—-"

"Shut up," Aksutamoon said, staring at Evorix's back while he slept.

With a quick glance, Aksutamoon waved one of his men over. "Kill him Trakuta and then carry the body away. Chop him up and leave him for the vultures."

He looked over at Gius and said "Your assassins life ends today."

"E—-" Gius shouted.

He fell into the dirt from the solid blow that hit him from behind. Trakuta pulled his blade and rotated the hilt backward in his palm as he crept through the camp. He was slim like a reed with green tattoos on his face that had faded as he aged.

His red goatee was starting to grey, but his eyes were still as sharp as a tack. He tugged his ratty hood back and tossed it at his feet. As he came near Evorix's fire, he could hear him snoring. Trakuta sat on his heels in the shadows for what seemed like an eternity, then he made his move.

His knife hit Evorix's back and made the sound of a lead pipe hitting a brick oven. Evorix rolled into Trakuta's shins and knocked him off balance. He snatched Trakuta's testicles and gave a swift tug.

Trakuta was a powerful assassin, but no match for his vise grip. He howled, waking the camp as Evorix got to his knees and yanked his sack upwards again. Trakuta shrieked in pain as Evorix released his balls and then grabbed his penis.

"You're a good assassin. I can't kill a professional so I'll let you live," Evorix whispered, then headbutted him across the bridge of his nose, breaking it.

Evorix let him go, kicked him behind the knee and knocked him down. He slammed the cast iron plate across Trakuta's back that he had hidden in the folds of his cloak. Aksutamoon stalked toward him with the rest of his men. Evorix stood to face them, his sword resting lightly over his shoulder. As Aksutamoon closed in on him, a multi colored arrow flew from behind Evorix and thudded between the two men.

Evorix tilted his head to look at the arrow that was twice the length of a normal one. More arrows thudded next to it and Aksutamoon's men came to a halt. With an arrow nocked, a figure came out of the woods followed by others. The man with the raised longbow said nothing as he walked up. He was a full head taller than Evorix and built similarly.

"Do I know you?" Evorix asked, peering into the blackened hood.

One cold blue eye stared back at him. The man shouldered his bow, then punched Evorix in the stomach doubling him over. An uppercut snapped Evorix's head back and knocked him unconscious. The figure rotated a gloved finger in the air and then dragged Evorix by one foot into the woods.

Chapter 10

A sinius woke up bent over his saddle at the waist. His knuckles dragged against the ground and his feet dangled on the opposite side.

"Gods damnit," he muttered, turning his head in several directions, looking for his riding companion.

"Oi, anyone there?" Asinius asked.

All he could hear were the hoof beats of his horse and another horse he couldn't see.

"I said, can anyone hear me?"

"I hear you," Tersius said.

The voice sounded familiar. He knew it wasn't the Wolfryan guards following him. If it was, he would already be in a shallow grave. He looked around trying to get his bearings, but the dizziness from the blood rushing to his brain overwhelmed him. Asinius' pony came to a stop and he heard Tersius dismount.

"I will give you whatever you desire if you free me from these bonds. I'll make you a very rich——"

Asinius' legs went over his head as Tersius threw his feet over the saddle. Tersius looked down at him and said, "No promises. My family is dead because you showed up at our doorstep." He kicked Asinius in the ribs. "Make ready, we are here," he said, pulling him to his feet.

Tersius pushed him down on a nearby rock. Asinius peered at the dust clouds behind them as riders descended down the ridge. The unmistakable dark blue and white livery of Rebellium soldiers could be seen clearly as they rode toward them, no looking glass was needed.

The flag fluttering behind them was black with a broken bloody red and gold crown. Asinius closed his eyes and muttered a prayer as the men surrounded them. Their spears leveled with Tersius and Asinius' chests.

One of the men shouted down at them, "Not smart to come to these lands, who are you, boy?"

"I am Tersius son of Primus of West Drathia."

"Tersius?" the man asked, squinting.

"Aye, and I bring a traitor to the council."

The men on horseback looked at Asinius sitting on the rock. Using the flat of his spear blade one of the men lifted his chin.

"Surprise," Asinius said with a wicked smile.

A few of the men grumbled under their breath, grabbed the hilt of their sword handles and spit on him. Tersius threw them the rope he had tied around Asinius' wrists and walked in the direction the men had ridden from. The group leader yanked the rope and pulled him closer to his men. Asinius limped over to the group and stared at them defiantly. One of the men pointed at Asinius.

"Look at that Calpernicus, he's got brass balls."

"Does he now?" Calpernicus said, hitting Asinius in the balls with the shaft of his spear.

Asinius fell to his knees gasping in pain. Calpernicus' hazel eyes burned with hatred that had long simmered below the surface, just waiting to come out.

"Doesn't seem like it to me," Calpernicus said, dismounting near Asinius.

He walked up to him and pushed his forehead into his, forcing Asinius to turn away. "Oh, how I'm going to enjoy this traitor. You killed all our families in retribution for Tiberius. Now, I have no home, no wife, no life." Calpernicus shrugged and looked at his men's faces. "Well no life worth living anyway. My wife Valenia was everything."

Calpernicus' left hand clenched open and closed. "I promise you Asinius, before today is done and the sun lowers behind us, I will carve you up like a chicken dinner."

Calpernicus pulled his knife and pinched Asinius' cheeks together. The knife slashed across Asinius' flesh from his ears to the corner of his mouth on both sides.

Asinius growled at him and spit out a torrent of blood. His growl should have been a cry for help, but Asinius wouldn't give them the satisfaction.

Calpernicus gave him a cold distant smile and said, "My boys... ah my beautiful boys." He blinked away a tear, "They knew what loyalty was, even when you cut them to pieces. They never muttered a word. Do you remember how old they were?"

"Can't say I even remember ordering their executions. Then again boys should never follow the path of a traitor," Asinius mumbled, his cheeks splitting with each word.

With his forearms shaking, Calpernicus whispered, "You arrogant prick, do you have any last words before we cut you to pieces and feed you to the dogs?"

Trying to keep his face from splitting, Asinius mumbled, "To hell with your families, I did them a favor not letting them see what a terrible desolate and evil place Delos has become."

Each of the men with Calpernicus sucked in their breath and dismounted. They circled him, sharpening their blades to begin their grim duty as grandfathers, fathers and brothers.

Many men in the Rebellium had to watch from a distance as their relatives were hung, drawn and quartered, or beheaded for refusing to give them up. The spouses of the fighters suffered the most as they were slowly burned at the stake. Octavius thought he would receive their surrender and end the bloodshed. However, it had the opposite effect and the war continued until there were too few fighters left in the Rebellium and they melted into the shadows.

"By the Notella of the Drathian code of honor, I claim the traitor Asinius as my slave," shouted Tersius from behind them.

"Go to camp and find a wench boy. Leave us to our dark business. It ends today," Calpernicus shouted over his shoulder.

"I said he's mine, by law."

Calpernicus put his hand on the man closest to Asinius and stopped him from cutting him.

"Do you know what you're doing, boy?" Calpernicus asked, barely able to control his emotions.

Tersius grabbed the rope from Calpernicus' hand and said, "My father's dying command was to deliver him to the council to decide his fate. So that is where he will be taken."

The men stared at Tersius with frosty expressions but backed away. Invoking the right of Notella allowed for a slave or a prisoner of war not to be harmed. If the owner did not want to own the slave anymore, they would revoke their rights and give the individual a sword and shield in which to defend himself prior to setting them free.

Calpernicus crossed his arms over his chest and nodded. Tersius bowed at the waist and roughly put a burlap sack over Asinius's head. Asinius followed him blindly and fell a few times as they walked toward the camp. As they arrived at the walled gate, they were stopped by a sentry.

Tersius explained the situation. The guard led them into the councils tent. Walking into the tent, Tersius saw a long wooden table with ten chairs on one side of it. Four of the chairs had someone in them and three of the chairs were leaning against the table, indicating that no one occupied them any longer. The last three were pushed in waiting for their owners to return.

As Tersius entered, a man who had seen close to eighty summers was helped to his feet. He leaned on the top of his walking stick and squinted from behind his thick round wire framed spectacles. After a few more moments of squinting, the old man looked a few feet to Tersius' left and said, "Primus?"

Sliding across the floor, Tersius stood in front of where he gazed and said, "No Lord Valentinian, it is his youngest son," said a man standing beside Valentinian.

"Tersius. You should have said...," Valentinian paused and sniffed the air four times and closed his eyes. "You bring trouble and death to my camp boy. You know better."

"I know, Lord Valentinian, but please hear me out."

"Alright boy, where is your father and grandfather? Their seats wait for their return from the farm."

Tersius lowered his head fighting back the warm tears that were rolling down his cheeks. A long silence followed as he finally blinked them away.

Valentinian nodded and quietly said, "Rest Primus' and Vartis' chairs against the table. Cry not boy. We will get revenge. Who do you bring to my tent?"

Tersius pulled the sack off Asinius head. The members behind the table let out a hiss as they mumbled his name. Their old nemesis stood bleeding in front of them, but otherwise unrepentant. Valentinian sniffed the air, growled and then waved for Tersius to push him forward. As Asinius neared the table, Valentinian swiftly struck him over the head with his cane and knocked him to the floor.

Bleeding in more than one spot, Asinius slowly regained his feet. Valentinian limped around the front of the table and swung his cane horizontally across Asinius' chest and broke several ribs. He hit him twice more, once on each shoulder.

He looked over at Tersius with a smile, "Gods, that felt great. He may be your prisoner boy. But if you want to replace your family at this table, you must execute this man in a fortnight."

"As you wish, m'lord. My father said he should be judged by the council. Where is Uncle Gius?"

"On an important mission. Stand the prisoner in the center of the room and light the fire," Valentinian said to the guard closet to him.

Valentinian raised his arms and said, "I, Lord Valentinian, leader of the Free Armies of the Rebellium, hereby request the remaining members of the council to vote life or death for the prefect, Asinius Pelagius. He is charged with murder, torture, betrayal and conduct unbecoming of a Delosian officer. How does the council vote?"

"Conduct unbecoming? The hell with you, Valentinian. I was an officer and a gentleman," Asinius mumbled, holding his cheeks.

The remaining members discussed his sentence quietly and then wrote down their decisions. Valentinian took the parchment and read the verdict.

"Asinius Pelagius, it brings me great pleasure to tell you that you've been found guilty on all counts by the council and shall be punished according to the Old Laws. Do you have anything to say in your defense?" Valentinian asked.

Barely able to open his mouth, Asinius spat a stream of blood at Valentinian's sandaled feet, "Shit."

Tersius cut his eyes at Asinius while Valentinian laughed. "By the power given me by the Rebellium Council, I hereby sentence you to death. Your execution will take place in a fortnight from this evening." Pointing to a guard, Valentinian said, "Take him away."

Asinius held his head high and looked at Tersius and winked. He stopped next to Tersius, swallowed a mouthful of blood and whispered, "Careful where you walk boy. There be monsters in this camp."

"Move along, " Tersius said, pushing Asinius toward the flap in the tent.

"Tersius, I am sorry about your father and grandfather, I really am. They were valuable leaders of the Rebellium. Both of them will be missed, but their command of the Free Armies will hurt us more," Valentinian said.

"Thank you, Lord Valentinian. I will follow the councils orders and execute Asinius in a fortnight and then go back to the farm," he said, turning around to leave.

"I'm afraid I can't allow that," Valentinian said.

"And why the hell not?" Tersius asked, turning back around.

"Because we're the only family you have left. Your father gave explicit instructions should anything happen to him that we were to care for you. We were told to burn the farmhouse and keep you until you came of age. So you can either join us or—-," he said with a shrug, looking around. "Or join us. You really have no choice."

Tersius stared at the faces of the council. He pulled his sword from over his shoulder and slammed it into the ground.

"I will leave when I want. You have no authority over me, m'lord. When Asinius has been executed, I will leave. If someone at this council chooses to challenge me, we will fight to the death," Tersius said, pulling his sword free from the dirt.

He turned his back to the council and walked out of the tent.

Chapter 11

Corcundia leaned against the tree and looked at the group of men sitting cross legged around the fire ten feet away. She never heard them approach from behind and it bothered her. Not one twig snapped under their weight during their approach. She thought for a moment and stared at them trying to find out what kingdom they hailed from. A quick glance allowed her to see the souls of their shoes were covered with green leaves.

Aksutamoon and his men were bound like animals and hidden further away in the shadows. Sniffing the air, Corcundia thought she smelled a wet dog. One of the men stood up and walked over to them.

A single blue eye stared at her from under a black head wrap. She waited for the stranger to speak first so she could gain an advantage in knowing where they came from. With a slight purr the stranger kneeled in front of her and said, "Where do you come from?"

"Could you say that again?"

With a sigh, the voice purred again, "Where do you come from. North or South?"

"Lady Corcundia of Vitadruma is my name. I am from West Drathia, several days ride from here. We are headed for the Rebellium headquarters."

Unwinding his head wrap, the stranger revealed the head of a lion. Corcundia gasped and pulled back. She crossed her fingers in front of her face. "Shit, you are real."

The being sat down and licked his paws. He rubbed his ears and said, "Pardon my look. I didn't mean to scare you."

"How do you speak...?" she asked.

Holding up his furry paw he said, "Our slaves."

"You're slavers?"

The lion humanoid bowed his head never taking his pale blue eye from her and said, "Guilty." He smiled revealing his razor-sharp incisors.

Closing his fist over his heart, the lion man said, "My name's K'aro, of the mighty D'atu. We were on our way back from a hunting—-"

"You mean a slave run," she said, slicing his sentence off.

He snarled, but regained his composure. "Yes, a slave run. We live by selling flesh. You wouldn't understand human. And yes our main source of coin is from selling humans. I think there is more money in precious metals and stones in the Fire Lands, but our leader Dro'ka decides where we go," K'aro growled.

"So you follow him like he's your master. Is he your master, dog?"

Barring his incisors, K'aro growled again and then touched his muzzle to her nose. "See to your companions. We leave in a few hours." He stood up and then turned around. "I almost forgot." He pulled an apple from his pocket. "Make sure you get your strength up, you'll need it," he said, re-wrapping the cloth around his head.

The sun rose the next morning but it was hidden by gray clouds. Corcundia, Gius and Evorix walked a few paces in front of her remaining men. Aksutamoon and his men were loaded into caged wagons further back.

One of Corcundia's men collapsed next to her and she dropped to her knees to help him. She heard a roar above her. Looking up, she saw a boot swing in her direction, but it was deflected at the last moment. She rolled aside and heard a barking voice.

"Leave her Dro'ka, she is only trying to help her companion."

"You dare touch me, K'aro?"

Softly purring, K'aro said, "I claim this human as my personal slave. If I must, I will fight you for her."

Dro'ka looked at K'aro for a moment baring his teeth, "Good," he roared.

The two warriors began circling one another as the other Ba in the group roared around them and slammed their swords into the earth.

The sword ring they were forming was a traditional way for two warriors in the Ba culture to end their differences. Blood had to be taken if a challenge was issued, and if the insulted party won, they could kill the offender or make them a slave for the remainder of their days.

Dro'ka and K'aro pulled their back up daggers and crossed them in front of their faces. The beginning ritual of the sword ring was a poetic dance between two combatants. The two warriors would circle one another and exchange salutes. Their fellow warriors would hum a melodic tune as the warriors wove their knives intricately around their bodies.

The next phase saw both warriors kneeling in the center of the ring. They shoved their daggers into the ground up to the hilt in front of them. One combatant stuck his left paw out, the other stuck his right out. A rope was tied around each warriors wrist and after a count to five, the pair stood and commenced the attack.

K'aro knew he could not beat Dro'ka. He simply stayed in a kneeling position when the contest began.

"Off your knees coward," Dro'ka roared.

K'aro began to hum the same melody as his shield brothers, glancing around the ring with his one eye. Dro'ka yanked him to the center.

Holding a knife to his throat Dro'ka shouted, "Fight or die."

"Give me death," K'aro said, lifting his chin.

Shaking his head, Dro'ka roared and walked away, "Damn you K'aro, you're my only healer. You are now my prisoner and will answer to me. Take him and put him in with the other slaves."

As he was led away, K'aro made eye contact with Lady Corcundia. He lifted his head and smiled, his incisors glinting in the sun.

Dro'ka led through fear and intimidation and killed any and all who opposed him. Standing nearly nine feet in height, he had silver fur with black spots running along his arms and a crescent moon branded on each of his forearms.

He looked old, exactly how old Corcundia could only guess. As the group traveled, the tall tips of volcanoes could be seen in the distance as they crossed further into the Fire Lands.

Evorix glanced at Corcundia and nodded his head toward the volcanoes. "The ancestral home of the Ba. We won't live long now."

"Can we escape?" she asked.

"Nah, they know every trail. We would be dead before we made it a hundred feet," Evorix said.

A whip cracked near Evorix's head and they stopped talking. The group trudged through the thick ash, the air around them heavy with heat. The further they walked, the more they sweat and the dryer their mouths became. Evorix was the first to see a cluster of tents in a large circle over the next ridge and a smaller encampment could be seen near the mouth of the river a few hundred yards upstream. As the entourage came over the last dune, they saw a bridge that crossed a river of lava.

Several warriors dressed in golden armor guarded the bridge to the main encampment. They stood nine feet in height, similar to Dro'ka. Their fur was jet black, their eyes bright yellow. They crossed their weapons at the entrance as the group approached, blocking the bridge.

Dro'ka dismounted and placed his clenched fist over his heart, "I am Dro'ka, leader of the Runners."

The guards didn't move or speak to him. Growling under his breath at their insolence, he roared, "I am Dro'ka, leader of the Runners. I command you to move aside!"

The guards chuckled and stared at him. The power he once held was gone among the Protectors. K'aro approached from behind and nodded. The guards nodded back at him and stood at parade rest. With a roar, the guards slammed the butts of their spears into the ground and spun to the side.

Dro'ka bared his insiors at K'aro and continued into the encampment. The humans were led to a caged area surrounded by wooden spikes spread out every six inches.

Dro'ka shoved Evorix, Aksutamoon and their men in, but pulled Corcundia's rope as she followed the others, knocking her to the ground.

She kneeled and tried to get up before Dro'ka stomped her into the dirt. Evorix pulled with all his strength and tried to break the bars of the cage. His muscles rippled and sweat dripped from his brow.

"You furry bastard, try that on me!" he shouted.

Dro'ka glared at him and then dragged Corcundia's body away leaving a trail in the dry dirt. Evorix stood seething at the door of the enclosure.

"Well, she's dead," Gius said, with a sigh of resignation. "Damn shame, we needed her too."

Allies were hard to come by in Delos, especially for him. Running from the Wolfryan Empire through the last year had caused Gius more heartache than he wanted. His family was dead and not a single soul outside of the Rebellium camp knew he existed. He knew Octavius would hunt every member of the Rebellium down until they were all swinging from the end of rope, so he tried to stay as low key as possible.

"You don't give a shit about anyone Evorix. Why the theatrics?" Gius asked.

"You're right, I don't. I only care about that horse over there," he said, staring across the camp at the stable where their confiscated horses were being kept. "But Corcundia owes me money for services rendered. Unless you want to pay that too?" Evorix asked, cutting his eyes at Gius.

If it was one thing Evorix liked about his captors, it was their care of animals. He made mental notes about the strengths and weaknesses of the camp as he looked around.

Escape wasn't a feasible option as he counted the Ba at different locations around the camp. Slavery didn't look promising either as he saw human heads rotting on spikes spaced evenly around the campsite.

"There is no escape, only death," said a gravelly voice under a hood near them on the outside of the cage.

Evorix turned around at the sound and shook his head. "Watch who you sneak up on, cur," he muttered.

A slight chuckle escaped from under the hood. The hunchback figure moved closer to the gate, his knuckles dragging in the sand.

Evorix wrinkled his nose and leaned backward. Gagging, he drew his head back as far as he could. "You smell like death," Evorix grumbled.

"Not yet, but I will get there eventually," said the voice.

Evorix and Gius took a step forward and looked closer at the figure.

"Boo!" the man said with a cackle as he pulled back his hood.

Evorix tripped over Gius as they backed up startled by the man's features. The man's forehead was the length of two hands stacked on one another. He had a hole for one ear, the other looked like cauliflower.

"What are you?" Evorix gasped, crossing his fingers in front of his face to ward off evil spirits.

"That's funny. I'm a human, like you. Discarded by my parents in the woods north of here as a baby. The Ba found me on a hunting expedition and brought me to the Fire Lands. The named me Nigol," he said, showing them two daggers and the key to their cage. "And I'll give you these if you take me with you."

"Whaddya want in return?" Evorix asked.

"Find me a woman to settle down with. I want a family before I die," Nigol said.

"Why not find a whore?" Evorix asked, pinching his nose and trying not to stare at him.

Nigol's eyes softened and he looked down. "Because, what you see on the outside can give life to something that is beautiful inside and out," he whispered.

"Great, a cripple with a heart of gold. I've heard of a whore with a heart of gold, but this is too much," Evorix said, grasping the hilt of one of the daggers in Nigol's hands .

"Do I have your word?" Nigol asked, holding up the key for them to see.

"Aye, you have our word. When we have our other companion, we will depart. Now why don't you make yourself useful and tell us some things about this camp and our host," Evorix said, taking a knee in the dirt.

Nigol smiled, his missing front teeth poking through.

"The group that brought you in are known as Runners. Slave hunters known to go to the worst parts of Delos and bring back the best humans to trade in. The only member of their group who's not terrible is K'aro. He's their healer and if he could escape with us, he would be useful."

Evorix nodded and then pointed at the Ba wearing different types of armor. Nigol continued, "The ones wearing golden armor are known as Protectors. They are camp guards and live a life of solitude. No wife, no cubs. Death in battle is their only goal. It is the only group a warrior can be disowned from."

Nigol smiled before he continued. "The one walking over there is Dro'ka. He has the mark of the disowned," he whispered.

Evorix' ears perked up when he mentioned Dro'ka. Nigol continued, "Most of the disowned become part of the Outkast Clan, a group of outlaws sent to live by Lava Lake as punishment. They wait patiently for redemption, a redemption that may never come. Dro'ka was banished from the Protectors as well, but he's a great slave hunter, so the elders took him back."

Evorix pointed at a warrior as he walked by.

Nigol continued his story. "The ones in blue armor are Seekers. They keep the history of the Ba in their books and drawings. The everyday warriors you see wear plain green armor. They make up most of the prides warriors and do the bulk of the fighting during war. Their lioness' and cubs are never close to any humans. They believe we carry diseases they can become afflicted with. Lastly, you have the human slaves. Men, women and children plucked from Delos to do whatever the Ba require. We obviously matter little," he said, finishing his run down as he looked at a head impaled on a spike.

"Dro'ka. Tell me of him," Evorix said.

"What's there to say. He loves causing others pain. One day when he least expects it, someone is going to jam a knife in his spine."

"Who...you?" Evorix asked with a chuckle.

"No sir. I am no great warrior, but he did the unthinkable when he killed my master. He murdered his own brother and father and took control of their pride, the D'atu. In their society there is no greater evil than killing their own kin."

Glad I ain't one of these things.

Evorix spat on the ground at his feet and thought of his own brother and fathers blood on his hands still haunting his nightmares.

Dad and Palix would still be alive had they not joined that assassination attempt.

"Which reminds me. The plan we talked about prior to our mishaps," Gius said, interrupting them.

Evorix cut his eyes in Gius' direction. *We are about to get eaten and he still wants to save Delos.*

Eyebrow raised, Evorix asked him, "What did you have in mind?"

"Let's get to my camp, it's not far," Gius said.

Evorix nodded and then turned his head to Nigol and said, "I need you to steal that black horse over there and have fresh horses for the others. Find out where they are keeping our companion, Corcundia. Then find all our weapons and armor and bring them to us."

"And I'm coming with you?"

"Get me what I asked for, and yes we'll take you," Evorix hissed.

"It will be done," Nigol said, disappearing into the night.

Chapter 12

M ercy m'lord, mercy!" screamed the man being tortured by Octavius.

The cat o' nine tails ripped flesh from the man's back as Octavius swung it again. He grinned as he continued to whip the man until he passed out. The other four men hadn't fared any better in the dungeon. They were all nailed by both their hands and feet across two wooden planks.

The dungeon was poorly illuminated with rats and other vermin chasing their heels. A few torches lined the walls as stagnant water fell from the ceiling and onto the bodies. Drops of water could be heard as they landed in the puddles of blood and water mixed together on the floor. Primus' and his father's dead bodies lay beside Marus.

"Marus, did I not tell these men to return with Asinius?" Octavius asked.

The hair on Marus' neck stood on edge. He took a step back and nodded silently.

"Then why do I have two dead bodies? Not that I'm unhappy with the results. Primus and his bothersome father were on my list anyway, so killing them was perfect. I still can't believe they hid so close." He paused in thought. "However, your men—-."

"Imperator, those were not my men, they——."

Octavius moved faster than Marus would have thought. He slammed a dagger against Marus' throat. "They.are.your.men…, because I say they are. I'm emperor and that means they can be anything I want them to be."

Marus lowered his eyes and looked away.

"Tell me prefect, why do I not have Asinius or Evorix?"

Marus stared straight ahead. "They elude us Imperator. We are trying to locate them as we speak."

Octavius turned and walked over to the table were his torture tools were and grabbed another cat o' nine. He spun and slammed the whip over Marus' head, stunning him. His second blow came down before Marus could recover.

Marus threw his arms up to block the blows and then stepped back ever so slightly. As he retreated, he tripped and fell to the floor. Octavius whipped him across the back until thick red blood soaked the back of his tunic.

"You." Octavius pointed to one of his personal guards. "Kick him until you hear something break or he dies."

The man bowed and kicked Marus until he heard a sickening crunch. Marus groaned as he felt two of his ribs break. Octavius squatted on his haunches and yanked Marus' bloody head up.

"I am Octavius Victorus, the one true ruler of Delos. Remember who runs Wolfrya and the worthless people in it. I want to hear one thing from you right now," he whispered, slamming Marus' face in a bloody puddle.

"As you say..." Marus gasped as his head came out of the water. "So shall it be."

"Don't forget who owns you, Marus," Ovtavius said, oblivious to the fact that Marus' blood was seeping onto his fresh toga.

A little freckled cherub-like giddy boy ran down the steps behind them and yelled, "Uncle Octavius, uncle Octavius!"

"Ah Zactus," Octavius responded with open arms and an energetic smile. He snatched his nephew into a bear hug. "What are you doing down here?"

Zactus laughed. "You were supposed to take me on a grand adventure today, silly."

Laughing, Octavius said, "Was I...oh yes now I remember, shall we go," he asked, rubbing the boys thick black hair.

Octavius stopped at Marus' head and without looking down, he hissed, "Either Asinius and Evorix are found in a fortnight or you take their place on the chopping block. It matters little to me, any head will do. I love my nephew and I don't want him to see you tortured. He he saved your life today Marus, you should thank him."

Marus looked at the boy. "Thank you, Prince Zactus."

"Good dog, now where we, Zactus?" Octavius asked.

Cackling loudly, Zactus yelled, "An adventure."

"Ah yes, an adventure," Octavius said, walking Zactus to the door, his guards following him out.

The next morning, Marus rolled onto his side as he lay on the freezing dungeon floor. He looked at his men in their tortured positions and then crawled over to them.

Four of the men had died overnight, impaled on the boards. The room smelled of shit from the men's bowels evacuating. Their bodies were cold, frozen like stone. Marus pulled himself up, checked their pulses at the base of their necks and made sure they had expired. Only one man barely hung to life.

Marus stared at him. "You're still alive?"

"I'm still alive," the man said, making a feeble attempt at raising his head.

"You should be dead from that cat o' nine beating."

"Lucky for you, I'm tough to kill," the older legionnaire said.

"Where is Asinius?" Marus demanded, his breath hot against the man's cheek.

"I thought you told us to go out there and kill whoever harbored him. We tracked him to the farm and he escaped. You told me not to kill him, Marus. For old times sake. Don't you remember?" the old man said.

"Things have changed. It's all about self preservation now and it starts with my preservation. He won't get a pass now, but thank you for your hard work cousin. I'll take it from here," Marus said, thrusting his dagger into his cousins throat.

"Why..." mouthed his cousin, the blood draining from his face.

Marus smirked with a shrug as he wiped his blade clean and said, "Why? Why the hell not."

Marus limped over to the other men and cut their throats to ensure they were dead. He moved to the dungeon door and went back to his quarters.

His slave, Laticius was boiling water for his bath as he entered. Seeing Marus, he moved to his side and helped him into bed.

"M'lord, are you ok?"

Marus nodded and pointed to the wine carafe on a nearby table filled with Tramonian Tears. Laticius bowed and brought him a cup filled to the brim.

Marus smacked his lips together. "That's the good stuff." He took a deep breath. "Ready my pack and gear, we leave in the morning."

• • • •

ASINIUS' FINGERS WRAPPED around the slate colored bars of his cell, the wounds on his cheeks bothering him to no end. He counted seven days since the first sun set, a constant reminder of impending execution. The only thing left in his cell was a bucket to shit in and some straw to lay on.

A drunken surgeon had come to see him on the first night and cauterized his cheeks with a thin poker. The skin on his face had itched uncontrollably afterward, causing him to pat it so he wouldn't rip the wounds open again. The gray hair follicles growing in on his beard seemed to pulsate painfully as the days wore on. His captors fed him porridge and cups of water, barely enough to keep him alive.

Calpernicus, the man who had cut his cheeks walked by and stopped in front of the cell with his men. Holding a mug of ale in his hand, he hiccuped and stared at Asinius for a moment.

"I'm glad you like horse oats," Calpernicus said.

"Horse oats?" Asinius asked with his mouth full.

Calpernicus laughed. "You're eating the mill left over from our horses. You think we would feed our most hated prisoner any of *our* precious food?"

Asinius spit the porridge out of his mouth and mumbled, "You better hope they kill me, cause if they don't,

I'll repay you for what you have done to me," Asinius said, refusing to break his gaze.

One of Calpernicus' men walked up and jabbed Asinius in the side with the shaft of his spear. Asinius fell to his knees wheezing and coughing. Roaring with laughter, Calpernicus spit on him while he was bent over.

"You're no better than a slave, Asinius. You never were a great leader, we——."

"Calpernicus, that's enough!" Tersius shouted, coming out of the shadows. "You know he belongs to me, I won't say it again"

Calpernicus turned his head and said, "Watch your mouth boy or I'll eat your liver."

Tersius rubbed his clammy hands across his pant legs and advanced. Six against one were not good odds, but there was no way to back down. Standing in front of the men, he put his hand on his sword hilt and waited, shifting his weight from one leg to the other.

Calpernicus' lip sneered upward and he said, "You got your father's heart, boy." He looked over his shoulder at Asinius and said, "Lucky for you the kid showed up when he did. Real lucky. But don't fret, your luck will run out."

Without another word, Calpernicus and his men walked away. Tersius approached within a few feet of the cage and produced some lettuce he had found. Asinius tried to look disinterested in the food, but his growling stomach gave it away.

Tersius handed it to him and then sat down in front of the cell. "Asinius, you're going to tell me how you knew my father and why he was ready to kill you when you last met."

A piece of lettuce stuck out of Asinius' mouth as he nibbled it like a rabbit. With a deep groan, he pressed his back against the bars. He pursed his lips together and forcefully exhaled with a wince. Not sure how to begin, he stared into the clouds as the rays of sun tried to burst through.

"Alright, I'll tell you. But you have to make sure I get more food. I will not die on an empty stomach."

"Deal," Tersius said.

"So, you want to know what happened before you were born, eh?" Asinius asked.

"I want to know something in particular."

Asinius raised an eyebrow.

"My father said Wolfryan's ordered my mother killed. Is that true?" Tersius asked, staring through him.

Asinius' cherub like demeanor changed. "That's irrelevant. Octavius wanted everything and everyone who was part of the Rebellium killed. If they knew, or he thought they knew, they died. He ensured they suffered terribly, knowing their mates watched from a distance. Spiked heads lined the road all the way to the crossroads in central Delos."

"And I care? I'll ask you again. Who stuck their sword in my mothers stomach?"

Asinius cast his eyes down to the dirt and shook his head. "The soldier——."

"Executioner. A soldier doesn't kill innocents, old man." Tersius shouted over him.

Asinius raised his eyes and said, " Wake up boy, there are no innocents. Only the quick or the dead. And as for who killed your mother, it doesn't matter. She's dead, move on."

"You know, don't you?" Tersius asked, acrimoniously.

A thin smile crossed Asinius' lips. "Oh aye." he said, walking to the other side of the cage.

Tersius ran to the other side with him and said, "Tell me who it was slave and I will try to spare your life."

"There will come a day when you know, but it won't be from me. You want to spare my life, that's your call," Asinius said.

Tersius bristled. "Fine. But this conversation isn't over. I can make sure you get a key, but you have to give me some information about Iceport first."

"What do you want to know?" Asinius asked, licking his lips.

"How many troops does the emperor have?"

"There are three Legions totaling three thousand men, but only two are in fighting shape, the other is for show."

"How many guard the emperor at night?"

Asinius raised an eyebrow and sighed. "Boy, you ask questions that you have no business knowing. You should let Valentinian come and ask me." Smelling the air around him, Asinius said, "You reek of lies. I know your father taught you not to lie. So don't."

Feigning surprise, Tersius shrugged and said, "Valentinian doesn't know I'm here. So tell me and I'll bring you more food than you have eaten in weeks."

"Don't attempt to bribe me, it's beneath you. Octavius wants me dead, obviously, and it's why I'm here with you. If I wasn't on his kill list do you think I would be locked in this cage?" he asked, shaking the bars vigorously.

"Quiet down old man before the guard comes back."

Just as Tersius said it, a guard walked by them staring at Asinius who rested his forearms against the bars. Asinius lifted his head, flipped the guard the bird and then tried to spit on him. The guard dodged his spit and quickly smashed the end of his spear over Asinius' knuckles.

"You son of——."

"Say something about me mother and I'll kill you," the guard said menacingly before returning to his patrol.

Asinius watched the man walk away, his eyes boring holes in his back. "You were saying bo——?" He looked around.

No one was there.

Chapter 13

Fire pits blazed around the Ba camp as the sun set. The purple sunsets over the Fire Lands were always a good omen, but they only happened a few times a year and tonight marked the new year. Evorix sat with his back against the bars staring at Aksutamoon across the cage.

All you need to do is fall asleep and I'm going to slice your throat, Evorix thought.

Aksutamoon had no intention of dying with his eyes closed, throat exposed. Trakuta stared at Evorix, touched his broken nose and winced. It had been a long time since someone had gotten the drop on him and he was waiting patiently for revenge.

"When he turns his back to you, kill him," Aksutamoon said, staring straight ahead.

Trakuta nodded and walked over to Evorix.

"Mind if I sit?" he asked.

"I don't own the dirt," Evorix mumbled.

As Trakuta sat down, Evorix asked him, "How's the beak?"

"Broken, thanks for that. I—-."

"I know you're going to try to kill me. You, and the fat ape over there whisper like whores in a confessional booth," Evorix said.

"I don't know what you're talking about. I just came to get a better lay of the land for our escape," Trakuta said with a shrug.

Evorix laughed. "Glad you're an assassin and not a politician in Wolfrya. You lie like a boy trying to fuck a tavern wench. Now, either you can help us escape and we can travel together out of here, or..." Evorix paused and pulled the blade Nigol had given him from his cloak. "You'll get enough time for a prayer."

Trakuta smiled, showing his unusually pearly white teeth. His tattoos glowed in the moonlight, his eyes an unnatural light blue.

"What do you suggest?" Trakuta asked.

Evorix shrugged. What's with the tattoos by the way?"

Trakuta chuckled. "A line for every man I've killed. They were put on by a shaman in my tribe and glow in the moonlight.

Evorix glanced over his shoulder. "Nice story. To answer your earlier question, I was looking around and I found our best escape route lies through the ravine. But with lava and ash on both sides it's going to make it tough to outrun those big bastards. For a true escape, we will need some of the men to fight a rearguard action." Thinking for a moment, Evorix continued, "We have your thirty and a few of Lady Corcundia's. All told around forty men. We have to find Corcundia, rescue her and then try to reach the ravine before these things know what hit them."

Trakuta bared his open palms and said, "We have no weapons. If we try, we can only hold them for a few seconds."

"That's why I need your help. I'll get our weapons and armor. You get me four fools who will die because you asked them too," Evorix said, watching Nigol cross from one tent to another.

"I'm only a spoke on the wheel," Trakuta replied.

"Then convince your *king* to order their deaths. Doesn't matter to me."

"I'll see what I can do," Trakuta said, heading to the other side of the cage.

Evorix turned back around and watched Nigol make several trips back to the cage. He tracked down all their weapons and armor during the festivities and hauled them back to the enclosure.

Aksutamoon approached from the other side of the cage and said, "Trakuta has talked to me. What's the plan?"

"I'll save your miserable hides, but it's going to cost you fifty thousand gold coins," Evorix said, straightening his smelly jerkin.

Not moving an inch, Aksutamoon glared at him. " How can I trust you won't turn on me?"

"You don't. Now do we have an accord?" Evorix asked.

"Fifty thousand, alright fifty thousand it is. But if you betray me, I'll take my time cutting pieces off of you, starting with your feet."

Evorix smiled and looked at Nigol. "Where is Lady Corcundia?" he asked.

"She's in the tent with the other slave women."

"Other slave women? Are there other slaves?" Gius asked, butting into the conversation.

"Hey Gius, stop trying to save the world for a day and let us ride outta here without a wagon train of flesh these creatures sell to feed their young. Be glad it ain't you. Think man, we don't have the manpower to fight them. They will catch us, cook us and then eat us," Evorix said.

"Absolutely under no circumstance will I leave these people behind," Gius said.

Exasperated, Evorix said, "Why is everything so black and white with you, Gius. Come over to the gray side for a bit, it won't kill you. I might, but it won't. It will be a refreshing way to see it from a different angle."

Gius shot him a cold stare and didn't respond.

I knew I hit a nerve.

"Maybe it will kill you if I'm lucky enough. All I know is that I don't care about these people," Evorix said.

"I could care less if you agree with me, Evorix. We save these people, then we go to my camp. Do you want to get paid?" Gius asked, crossing his arms over his chest.

Throwing his hands up, Evorix said, "God dammit."

Nigol walked up and looked over his shoulder, trying to quiet everyone down. A guard came out of a tent nearby and looked over at the cages.

"Please be quiet, the guard——."

"If you slaves talk anymore, I'll kill one of you for every word you mutter." the guard growled in broken Delosian, then ducked back into his tent.

Re-emerging from the shadows, Nigol continued, "As I was saying, please don't fight. Slaves are sacrificed on nights like this for the perfect sunsets. They don't need a reason to please their gods, they enjoy killing us."

Aksutamoon looked over at him and said, "Leave slave, this doesn't involve you."

Nigol's head dropped as he began to shuffle back into the shadows.

Evorix's fist clenched by his side. "Talk to him like that again and I'll cut your royal head off ya lardship. King, or no king, I'll kill you all the same. Unlike you, he has a way to get us out of here. He holds more value than you do, so shut your rich lips, or I'll glue them shut," he said, ensuring Aksutamoon saw the blade in his palm.

Nigol looked at Evorix, as did Gius, both shocked he would stick up for him. Nigol was hardly seen, but always listening and knew every path in the Fire Lands.

Evorix glanced up at him as he peered at them from outside the cage.

"Alright Nigol, which tent is Corcundia in and how many are guarding her?" he asked.

"I don't know how many guard her, but she's in the center of the camp where Dro'ka sleeps with the Runners," he said.

"Forget the others, we get her and leave. Any man who wants to stay and help them can, but those who want to live will follow me. So let's decide who's going to go, and who's going to stay," Evorix said.

Corcundia's men quickly joined Evorix while Gius stood by himself. Aksutamoon and his men stood with their backs against the bars. Evorix scanned their half hidden features in the darkness. "Aksutamoon, are you with me, or Gius?"

"Neither. I would rather kill both of you." He walked over to where Gius stood with his arms crossed and said, "However, I ask you not to sacrifice your life for no reason, Gius. Please come to Tramonia as my guest and I will help you take Iceport. And then we can help you save these people in the Fire Lands."

Gius smiled at Evorix about his new found fortune and stepped forward to answer Aksutamoon. "I will follow you——."

Aksutamoon's punch hit Gius' chin and Evorix could hear the sound several feet away.

"That should shut up the voice of insanity. Can't save everybody," Aksutamoon whispered.

Evorix chuckled and shook his head. He glanced back at Nigol. "That solves one problem, Nigol. How many men can we safely get over to Corcundia's tent?"

"You, me and three others. There are two guards by the closest fire, another two nearby and Dra'ko's floating around here somewhere," Nigol said, glancing over his shoulder in fear.

"Let's get a plan together and get out of here," Evorix said, binding Gius by his hands and feet.

• • • •

ASINIUS COVERED HIMSELF as the rain fell into his cell. It was nice to have an open cell during the days with nice weather, but when it rained or the wind blew hard, it was murderous. He had weaved almost all the hay in the cell for his bedding and the leftovers were used to make a thatch that hung above him.

Delosian rain was warm to the touch, like the mist of a waterfall which was more of a hindrance than anything else. Asinius pissed in the corner as the thunder roared through the night sky. The longer he was held captive, the more he got used to the noise.

A pair of boots silently walked up to the cage behind him and waited for another clap of thunder.

"Get up earlier than that boy," Asinius said, buttoning his pants.

"How did you know?" Tersius asked, moving out of the shadow.

"I heard you before you opened my cell door, try again tomorrow. Now, are you here to talk again?" Asinius asked.

"Yes, I want to know more."

"Keep digging boy and you may not be able to climb out," Asinius scolded him.

"Don't treat me like a child, I'm seventeen summers," Tersius said.

Asinius laughed. "Oh, are you now? My apologies, I guess you're all grown up."

"I must be because they gave me the order to execute you."

Asinius paused as he weaved the remaining hay into a hole in the thatched roof. "Is that a fact? They're sending a boy to do a man's job now. Lord Valentinian must be getting desperate. Some of the chairs in his tent were leaning forward. Do you know why they are like that?"

"Yeah, you killed the owners," Tersius muttered.

"Is that what you think? Oh, I'm a bastard alright, but not an executioner. It is true I tracked and captured the Rebellium scum when they fled throughout Delos, but I didn't chop anyone's head off myself. I ordered it done. That's a different animal all together. Now, where is my extra food you promised?" Asinius asked.

Tersius shoved the sack into Asinius' arms, then pressed him for answers. "Is that how you sleep at night? I always thought ordering and executing were the same thing. My father told me you killed everyone. You think there is a difference?" he asked.

"Boy, don't question my ethics, or morals for that matter. I've killed men for less and while I like you, I would have no problem running my blade through your guts. I made my decision and I know the costs. You know nothing of sacrifice," Asinius replied, his voice even.

"You're right, my father and grandfather knew sacrifice, while I on the other hand know the cost. I'll tell you what I do know. Ethics are the code of right or wrong, like my belief in Notella which saved your life by the way. And morals are about what a man personally believes when faced with difficult decisions. I may be young, but I ask you to remember who I was raised by."

Asinius pressed his tongue against his teeth, clucked and said, "So boy, you believe you know what life is? I'll show you what loyalty gets you."

He pulled his tunic up and showed Tersius his battle scars. "The line across my stomach is from an axe in my first battle, nearly killed me. The stab wounds," he said, pointing over his heart. "Happens when a woman is scorned. And now this," he said, touching his cheeks.

Tersius stared at his scars for a moment, and noticed the deep purple color from his hip bone just below his waist. Asinius caught his stare.

"And this one almost cost me my life. A fight I neither wanted, nor cared about," Asinius said, pulling his breeches down revealing a long jagged scar that ran down his leg on the front and back.

"What—-."

"This is the cost of fighting for an insane emperor. I stepped in front of a blow meant for him and nearly lost my leg. And what happened to me in the end, Tiberius' dirty bastard son tried to kill me."

"My father was right, none of you get it," Tersius said.

"Get what?" Asinius asked, pulling his tunic back down.

"The Wolfryan emperors want sheep, mindless sheep he used to say. And now you're in a cage, and it fits you," Tersius said, bleating like a sheep as he shook the bars.

Asinius pushed his face into the bars and shouted, "You ever make that sound again and I will kill you. I would rather die than betray Wolfrya. My honor will not be questioned, especially not by a snot nosed little brat."

Tersius paused, rested his head against the bars and whispered, "You said you knew who killed my mother."

"Ach, yes, but——."

Tersius raised his eyes and said, "Speak, or I'll kill you before I parade you to the chopping block."

Asinius lifted his neck and said, "You're a cherry if you do."

Tersius planted his feet and kept his fingers on the hilt of his knife, but didn't move.

"Bah, you're gutless boy, gutless," Asinius said, turning his back to him.

Tersius fumbled with the key and yanked the door to his cell open and said, "Gutless?"

Asinius turned, disarmed him and then kicked the inside of his thigh, crumpling him to the ground.

"Your anger betrays your footsteps. I am not your enemy, boy. But I will leave you with this."

Asinius drew his fist back, brought it down on his chin and knocked him unconscious. He laid him down and rummaged through his waistband. He took his coin purse and knife and then sprinted for the door. As he reached the door, it slammed shut on his fingers.

"Fuck," he shouted, holding his bent fingers, blowing on them with pursed lips.

Asinius looked up and saw Calpernicus wearing a light smile on his face. "Not so fast, you muderin' bastard. I'll see your head removed from your shoulders before I die. Now bring the boy over here."

Asinius grabbed Tersius' hands and drug him to the door.

"Now back up, slave," Calpernicus demanded.

Asinius held his hands up and walked to the back of the cage. Calpernicus looked at the men with him and waved them in.

"Hands where I can see them old man, hands where I can see them."

Tersius woke the following morning with a loud groan, holding his jaw. "What the——."

"Easy boy, Asinius knocked you out. My men stopped him from cutting your throat when he attacked you," Calpernicus said, handing him a drinking horn.

Hesitating, Tesius took a long swig, spit it up and coughed violently. Calpernicus laughed and pushed the horn to his lips again.

"A man drinks, kills and dies for the Rebellium. Are you one of us?" Calpernicus asked, his right eyebrow raised.

"Don't know," Tersius said, trying to repress his gag reflex on his next swig.

He wiped the back of his hand across his lips trying to remove the sting.

"Either you are, or you aren't. It would be a damn shame for someone from such an illustrious family as yours not to follow in his father's footsteps."

"And what footsteps are those?" Tersius asked.

"Free from the yoke of the empire," Calpernicus said.

Tersius shrugged. "I don't understand."

"Do you believe all of us should bow to the crown?"

Staring at his feet, Tersius shook his head and tried to change the subject. "How do you know, Asinius?"

Smiling, Calpernicus pulled a plug of tobacco from his pocket and offered him some. Tersius declined.

Calpernicus rubbed his palms around his mouth with a sigh. "I know that piece of shit from my days as an infantry commander in the Delosian army. I rebelled with your uncle Gius, your father and your grandfather. And now, we are all that remain of the original rebels." Calpernicus pointed at his men. "They were all friends of your father's at one time or another and all of them, without exception saw their families slaughtered. Your father at least managed to capture Asinius and that will allow us our revenge. Might even make something positive out of a shitty situation." "You won't kill Asinius, Calpernicus. He is my slave, so he's mine to kill. I'll kill anyone that goes near him," Tersius said.

Calpernicus growled. "Look boy, I've spent most of my life serving people like him in Wolfrya. I've been waiting for the day I could cut his guts out and roast 'em over a fire. I wanted him alive so he could watch his own death." He paused for a moment and chuckled, "It's by luck you even knew to claim the old code of Notella and it doesn't really have a place in modern society. But Valentinian believes in it and as long as he runs our outfit, we have no other choice but to allow it. But if you turn your back for one second, I'll kill that son of a whore."

Tersius bristled, but let the comment rest. He switched topics. "So, what was your reason for rebelling?" Tersius asked, passing the wine back to him.

Calpernicus smirked. "I joined because I believe every Wolfryan citizen loyal to the crown should be tortured, then burned. If they are not peasantish in nature, they shouldn't be in power."

"Peasantish?"

"Yea, hard workers like my men." Pausing, he glanced at Tersius, "And dare I say, you."

"You don't even know me," Tersius said.

"I knew your family and that's all I need to know," he replied.

"And my family joined why?" Tersius asked.

"Everyone has their own reason. They never told me."

Tersius exhaled. "That figures."

Calpernicus spit a stream of tobacco juice between his lips. He muttered, "We all have choices, don't we."

Tersius made eye contact with Calpernicus. "What's so special about the cause?" Tersius inquired.

"Everything. If we could manage to wipe out the blue bloods—-."

Tersius interrupted him. "Blue bloods?"

Calpernicus smiled. "The aristocracy doesn't belong in power because they abuse it," he said.

"You really hate them that much?" Tersius asked.

Calpernicus nodded with a chuckle. "Damn all highborn Wolfryan's."

"Killing the aristocracy would do nothing more than put their riches in your pocket," Tersius said.

Calpernicus winked, "True."

"Greed is the root of all evil you know," Tersius said.

Calpernicus inched closer to him and said, "No boy, greed ain't the root of all evil. Coin is a disruptor, but pride and ego are the real enemy. Pride tells me I can, and ego tells me I must."

"I still don't understand why everyone rebelled. I want to know," Tersius said.

Calpernicus chuckled and then smirked.

"So, what is the Rebellium planning on doing?" Tersius asked.

"Fighting as always." He pushed himself to his feet. "But we're not doing anything until your uncle comes back.

Without his help, I would never question Valentinian's command," he replied.

"How does Valentinian fit into all this?" Tersius asked.

"Valentinian? He was Octavius' tutor early in life. He said that Octavius was pure of heart until his father's death." Calpernicus tapped his chin with his index finger and made eye contact with Tersius. "I think every man changes once his father dies. So, after Tiberius declared war on the world, Valentinian turned on him and formed the council. The council has the final say on all matters," Calpernicus said.

"Who joins the council?" Tersius asked.

"Men and women who were part of the Wolfryan senatore class. But they gave up their titles and joined Valentinian."

"Are you on the council?" Tersius asked.

Calpernicus chuckled. "Hell no, I'm not of noble birth. Some things will never change, no matter how many die for this cause. Valentinian is our *emperor* now," Calpernicus said, rolling his eyes as he walked away.

Chapter 15

E vorix gazed through the bars and watched the two guards closest to their cage as they slept. Once the festivities subsided and the alcohol had taken effect, Evorix made his move.

The key to their salvation slid out of his tunic and he inserted it into the lock. Giving the lock a quick twist, the gate swung open with a loud groan. Evorix froze and scanned the camp, his fingers wrapped around the cold metal bars. A warrior urinated out the front of his tent, glanced in their direction and then went back inside.

"That was close," Trakuta muttered, creeping up beside Evorix.

"You can say that again," Evorix said, trying to control the heartbeat pounding in his ears.

"Well, it's now or never. Lead the way," Trakuta whispered.

Evorix, Trakuta, Nigol and two of Corcundia's men snuck to the first fire and pressed themselves firmly against the ash covered boulders.

Nigol peered over the boulder and motioned for the others to follow him. "Those are the first two guards," he said, pointing at the nearest fire. "The next fire has two more warriors." He pointed at a red tent. "Once you get past them, the tent you're looking for is right there," Nigol said.

"Alright everyone ready?" Evorix asked.

He scanned their faces as they nodded, the soot mingling with the sweat pouring down their faces.

Evorix locked eyes with Trakuta who asked, "Where do you need me?"

"I need you to take Corcundia's men and kill the guards around the fires, and then follow me into the tent, get her and then ride through the ravine."

Trakuta nodded and flashed him a quick smile. "See you at the rallying point," he said, creeping into the darkness, his silhouette nearly invisible.

"Where do I need to be?" Nigol asked.

Evorix took a moment and scanned the horse pens. He looked at their horses mixed in with a larger breed of animals the Ba warriors rode known as alpurlics.

He could make out quite a few of the alpurlics in the darkness, but only a few of their horses. He couldn't see behind the alpurlics, their massive white manes were to high.

Focusing again at his task at hand, Evorix said, "Go back to the cage and make sure my men have what they need," he whispered, checking his throwing knives. "Find every horse you can. If we lack horses, we die. Can you do it?"

Nigol bowed. "Of course, m'lord."

"Go," Evorix said.

He watched Nigol disappear and then turned his attention to the guards. He smiled as he watched Trakuta's feet fall silently in the sand.

Once Trakuta's group reached the first fire, they slipped into the shadows. Evorix saw the fire illuminating the blade of his knife clenched between his teeth. Reaching the first guard, Trakuta slid under the tree trunk that his targets were using for a pillow.

Evorix watched Trakuta take a deep breath and hold it. The time between the warriors snores grew longer as he slid his blade under one guards large head. In the time it took to blink, Trakuta slammed the blade into the warriors brain stem. The warriors eyes opened wide and droplets of blood fell out of his nostrils and onto the sand.

Trakuta smiled to himself, then turned his head and rolled to the next guard. The warrior was snoring so loud, he woke himself up. The guard sat up, sniffed a few times, then laid back down.

Trakuta waited for the opportunity to strike, his thin blade catching the moonlight. Keeping focused, he slid his blade across the warriors jugular. A third guard stepped up to the fire and urinated. Evorix gagged as he watched urine drip off Trakuta's face.

That's the worst. Ba piss, that musty smell won't come out of his clothes, Evorix thought.

The guard paused, looked around and noticed the blood on the ash. He sniffed the air and then turned his head to alienate the smell coursing through his nostrils. Reaching for a horn strapped to his side, the warrior groaned and fell to his knees. His body pitched forward and landed face first into the fire. Burnt fur wafted through Trakuta's nostrils as he pulled the warrior out of the fire.

Evorix sprinted by Trakuta, pulling both daggers from his belt. He snuck up on the next two guards, their snores covering his movements. Timing their breathing, Evorix placed both daggers across the guards throats simultaneously. He exhaled and slit them at the same time.

Nodding his head at Takuta, he crouched down and sprinted toward the tent housing Corcundia.

Under his breath, Trakuta muttered. "Show off."

Corcundia's men waited by the flaps of the tent as Trakuta and Evorix joined them.

"Here's the plan." He pointed at Corcundia's men. "You two keep a lookout for any other warriors. If you see one, caw like a crow, then disappear into the shadows."

Evorix flipped a knife in his palm and handed it to Trakuta. "Wait a few seconds after I enter the tent and then come in after me. If it ain't with us, it dies. Understand?" Evorix asked.

Trakuta nodded, the faint hint of a smile at the corner of his mouth. "No problem."

Evorix laid down on his stomach preparing to crawl the ten yards to the tent. The steel from the knife between his teeth tasted gritty as he bit down on it. He crawled hand over fist to the entrance of the tent. It was deathly quiet, nothing moved as he crept further in.

No warriors... that's unusual.

He saw Lady Corcundia laying face down on a wide wooden bench, her feet and wrists bound and her mouth gagged. Blood trickled from her scalp as Evorix stared at her, looking for signs of life. His heart sunk. She didn't appear to be breathing.

He crawled to where she was and saw the Ba warrior who had protected her against Dro'ka bound to a rack with leather straps covering his limbs. Rising to his knees, Evorix looked over his shoulder and saw Trakuta slide in on his stomach behind him.

Evorix stood up and crept over to Corcundia, cut her bindings and brushed the hair from the side of her face. Both of her eyes were blackened and her hair was matted with blood. One of her eyes flickered open and a weak smile crossed her lips.

"If it ain't my hired muscle," she whispered.

"You owe me money and I plan to collect, but first let's get you out of here," he said, surveying her wounds.

"I need to help him," she said, lifting her head in the direction of the torture rack.

"Like hell we do, he's de—-."

"I'm still alive human. At least temporarily," K'aro grunted, thanking Trakuta as he helped him up.

"What the hell are you doing, Trakuta?"

"What? He helped her. I'm just returning the favor. What's right is right," Trakuta said, looking around for anything that wasn't nailed down.

Staring into K'aro's one eye, Evorix muttered, "One move in the wrong direction or I think you aren't playing with straight dice beast, I'll kill ya and then wear you as a blanket."

K'aro chuckled. "If you feel like dying for no reason other than your foolish pride human, I suggest you step closer."

Evorix stood silently weighing his options.

Mirthlessly, K'aro said, "It is as I thought it would be. Shall we move past your childish threats and escape from here?" he asked as Trakuta helped him don his armor.

"Get them out of here Trakuta and ride for the rallying point. You two stay with me." Evorix said, pointing at Corcundia's men.

Trakuta carried Corcundia over his shoulder and half pulled K'aro out behind him. A few moments later, a horn outside the tent shattered the cold crisp air awakening the whole camp.

Running to the entrance, Evorix watched Trakuta, Corcundia and K'aro mount the horses Nigol brought them. He waited for Nigol to lead them into the darkness. The group disappeared as the camp swarmed to life. Roars echoed around them as the warriors got their bearings. Evorix and Corcundia's men stood in the shadows, their breath easy to see in the air.

A group of young warriors rode past them on their alpurlics, the beast so dangerously close, they could have given away their hiding places. Evorix's back stiffened and he held his breath until they rode by.

"Looks like they made it out of here," whispered one of Corcundia's men.

"Yea, now it's your turn," Evorix said.

Nigol left Whispers and two other horses' bridles tied by the entrance of Dro'ka's tent for them. Corcundia's men wasted no time and ran to untie their horses.

"You must provide backup for us," Evorix said from behind them.

The men spun around. "No we don't! We ride with you to protect Lady Corcundia," shouted one of her men.

"You *are* helping her," Evorix said.

Like a bolt of lightning, Evorix slashed both of the men's Achilles tendons. Their screams of anguish drew the warriors in their direction. Evorix tied the other two horses to his saddle and then mounted Whispers. As he galloped off into the darkness, Corcundia's mens screams were suddenly cut short.

"Cold as ice, m'lord," Nigol said, reigning his horse in when Evorix finally caught up with them.

Evorix smiled. "Oh well, the only life that counts is mine."

"How long do we have?" Trakuta asked.

"Not sure, but we best be going," Evorix said.

"We have a few moments, m'lord. I took something they need and left them a surprise," Nigol said, holding something up in the dark.

"What ya got there?" Evorix asked.

Nigol threw him the locking pin to the horse pen, swung his horse around with a nod and joined the rest of the men riding away. Evorix smiled at the item in his hand.

Cheeky son of a bitch. He is worth somet——.

A huge explosion scattered the alpurlics and Evorix's thoughts. The blast killed a few of the warriors trying to round up the alpurlics for the warriors to ride out. A light chuckle could be heard behind him as he watched the chaotic scene from the shadows. Evorix glared at Aksutamoon.

"What?" Evorix demanded.

"Now we're in for it. You killed their mounts. They will cut us into little bits and put us in the food they serve to the slaves," Aksutamoon said.

"Hell with them," Evorix said, turning his back to the king.

"Now where do we go?" Evorix asked himself, scanning the night sky for the True star. The sound of hooves approached from behind. Evorix pulled his sword and swung Whispers around.

"Help you with something?" Evorix asked, eyeing K'aro who had ridden up behind him.

"Perhaps. If you want to survive, follow me," K'aro said more as an order than a request.

"Ha, that'll be the day. You're lucky to be breathing through your nostrils or whatever those are and not a hole in your windpipe. I will not follow a beast," Evorix said.

"He almost died protecting me Evorix and he became a slave in the process. At least he has honor. You on the other hand are low life scum and owe me two men," Corcundia said, joining the conversation, her face flushed.

"Those men volunteered to stay behind, Corcundia," Evorix exclaimed.

"I watched from a looking glass, you bastard," she said coldly, handing the looking glass back to K'aro.

Evorix growled at K'aro. "I did what needed——."

Flexing her palm a few times rapidly, Corcundia concentrated on Evorix's face. He began to choke and spit, then looked around nervously. His swollen tongue pushed his lips apart as he scratched at his constricted larynx. His sight became hazy as he stared at her wondering what else he could do. Gasping repeatedly, he fell from Whispers back and rolled around on the ground.

"I would never kill any of my men again," she said, staring down at him, tightening her grip. "Do I make myself clear?"

K'aro put his paw on her shoulder and said, "Enough m'lady. There is no honor in killing thieves."

A blood red tear fell from the corner of her eye as she loosened her grip. She whistled at her remaining men and rode off behind K'aro. Air flooded into Evorix's oxygen starved lungs as he gasped.

What in the hell was that.

Trakuta and Aksutamoon extended their arms, guffawing at him.

"So, shall I make dinner plans with her, or should you?" Trakuta asked with a chuckle.

Evorix cleared his throat and spit. "I'll kill that women before our trip is out, mark my words," he said.

Evorix heard Gius groan as he woke up. He thought about leaving him behind after he was unconscious, but he still needed to get paid. It would be useless trying to get his money from the Rebellium council without Gius being there.

Nigol had ridden with Gius draped across his legs for quite awhile without complaint. And after they stopped for a moment, Gius fell off the saddle and plummeted into the sand. He rolled over and sat up taking in his surroundings.

He squinted at everyone in front of him and shouted, "Someone take these bindings off of me, now!"

Evorix motioned for Nigol to untie him. Gius scrambled to his feet and stormed up to Evorix.

"I demand a sword and shield to settle this in combat," Gius shrieked.

Evorix chuckled. "No time, we've been attempting an escape while you've been napping."

Gius stammered for a few minutes. His face flushed red, hands shaking. "I'm going to kill you. I don't care if we need you to kill the emperor or not."

"We'll fight later, Gius. Now we need to escape, but I'll kill you when we get to the Rebellium's campsite if you wish," Evorix said dismissively over his shoulder as he mounted Whispers.

"Nigol, give him a horse of his own and follow me," Evorix said as he rode off.

Their company followed K'aro as he led them deeper into the Fire Lands. Lava Lake appeared on the horizon in front of them, its heat cascading over them. An ash storm, similar to a sand storm swirled around them as they galloped across the valley until their horses began to slow.

"If we don't rest soon, these horses will die," Trakuta said, peering into the ash behind them.

A horse near Evorix reared up on its hind quarters with a screech and fell over.

"Cover," Evorix shouted.

The rider shouted in pain from underneath the dead horse, half his body pinned to the ash. Trakuta rushed to the soldiers aid and tried to pull the dead carcass of him. As he bent down an arrow buzzed by his head and cut the man's screams short.

The rest of their group dismounted as another horse slammed head first into the gray ash, throwing its rider. A long thin arrow protruded from the horse's thick mane.

"Where did that come from?" shouted a voice as the group formed, backs to one another.

Shadows loomed above then, their large bows strung. K'aro stepped out from the group and ran up a path to the top of the ravine.

"If I catch you coward, I'll gut you!" Evorix bellowed, pulling his sword.

As soon as the shadows appeared, they disappeared. Evorix shouted for his group to form two rows. "Front rank, kneel. Second rank, pull drawstrings."

"Wait for the command," Trakuta shouted stepping in front of Aksutamoon.

K'aro re-emerged from the pathway with his fist closed above his head. Corcundia tried to leave the group, but Evorix grabbed her by her shoulder.

"Oi, you still owe me money," he said.

Corcundia looked at his hand and then raised her other hand. "Do we have a problem?"

Shit... He withdrew his hand. "Nope, no problem."

K'aro led a small group from the path and met with Corcundia and her men in the middle of the ravine. Evorix watched the exchange and wrapped his sweaty fingers around the hilt of his sword. He watched K'aro's movements closely and looked at Trakuta.

"I'm going to see what's going on, something doesn't feel right. Keep an arrow aimed at my back, Trakuta. If there's trouble, I'll fall back with her. Order the men to kill whatever may be chasing me," Evorix said.

"Don't be a hero," Trakuta muttered, nocking an arrow.

Smiling wide, Evorix said, "Never happen."

Evorix walked with a sense of purpose to the exchange. As he approached the people in front of him an arrow slammed in front of his next step.

Looking down at the arrow, Evorix dropped to a knee and pulled it from the ash. He slid the arrow under his nose and smelled it.

Ah, pine resin, no other smell like it.

He stood up. "I'm Evorix Vispanius. I'm with Lady Corcundia, don't shoot."

He raised his hands above his head and walked the last few feet to Corcundia. He gave K'aro a cold stare, the hatred burning from his eye sockets. K'aro shook his mane and then continued to speak to the cloaked figure next to him in deep guttural growls.

Puzzled, Evorix watched them talk and his eyes drifted over to Corcundia. Nigol ambled up behind him and said, "Careful with the words you use here, m'lord. These be the monsters every Ba warrior fears. They don't like slaves at all."

"I'm no man's slave, Nigol. And that's enough out of you," Evorix hissed, pushing him back.

K'aro moved his hand in Evorix's direction and made a few gestures. The figures K'aro was speaking with gave a low growling laugh.

Evorix looked at Nigol who translated, "K'aro of the Runners told them——."

"What?" Evorix demanded.

Nigol lowered his head.

Evorix cut his eyes at Nigol. "Last chance before it gets messy in here," Evorix said, sliding his palm to his sword hilt.

Pushing his arm down, Nigol said, "Wait m'lord, wait. He said you would make a good wife."

Evorix never lost a step as he ran into K'aro full on. The unexpected blow broke several of K'aro ribs. Roaring, K'aro chomped down on Evorix's arm as they rolled around in the ash. Evorix shouted in pain as the teeth broke through his skin. He cursed at K'aro and landed two solid blows on the side of his furry ear. K'aro roared again and applied more pressure to Evorix's arm. Someone grabbed Evorix by the back of the neck and launched him a few feet away into the ash.

He got to his feet and pulled his sword free. "You crazy cat thing, I'm no ones wife! No one's, you hear me! When I get my hands around that furry neck, I'm going to squeeze it till your head pops off!"

He charged forward again, sword raised. A kick from the side knocked the air from his chest. He landed on his back with a loud groan.

Shit.

He could hear the sounds of men rushing by him, but he could only gasp as he attempted to catch his breath. Two ranks formed in front of him led by King Aksutamoon.

"Rank one, advance on the double. Second rank, hold here!" Trakuta shouted.

Waving her hands in front of her face, Corcundia held both groups at bay.

"King Aksutamoon, back down, now! They're allies" she said.

"Unlikely love. I don't much like the dark skinned man in the ash, but I like that lion thing even less," he said, pulling his bastard sword from the scabbard strapped across his back.

He stepped over Evorix in a defensive position. Trakuta crossed his blades in front of his chest as he stepped in front of Aksutamoon.

"Wait!" K'aro roared, holding his side with one paw, the other outstretched. "These are the Outkast. They are the sworn enemies of the Runners and the other Ba prides."

The lion men behind K'aro untied their red scarves, revealing their scarred faces. Some were missing incisors or clumps of fur. A large eye was branded onto their right wrists, identifying them as having lost their honor. They were warriors convicted of heinous crimes against their fellow warriors with crimes ranging from adultery with a shield brothers wife to fratricide and patricide.

Trakuta helped Evorix to his feet. He coughed, cleared his throat and then nodded his thanks. He turned his attention back to the warriors and arched his back.

"So, which of these things says I'll make a good wife?"

"Wife, no one said wife human. I said warrior, warrior," K'aro roared, putting pressure on his side.

Nigol cleared his throat nervously and looked at the ash. Evorix chuckled as he walked up to him. He raised his chin and looked into his eyes. "Explain," he hissed.

Nigol chuckled nervously and said, "Um, those two words are very——."

Evorix headbutted Nigol and sent him crashing into the ash. Trakuta walked up and grabbed Nigol by the feet and dragged him away.

Evorix watched them for a moment, then turned to K'aro. "My apologies. I thought my translator spoke your language."

"He does, but our words differs from pride to pride. The slave Nigol speaks D'atu, not R'atu." K'aro pointed at the warrior next to him. "This is Vitkalla of the mighty R'atu. He only has half his tongue, so he's hard to understand," K'aro said, watching Nigol's head bounce up and down as it passed over mounds of ash.

"They were laughing at me being a great warrior, why?" Evorix asked.

"You're a slave, nothing more. They have never seen a human take up arms," K'aro said.

"I'll show you a slave," Evorix said, taking a step forward.

"Watch yourself human," Vitkalla said in perfect Delosian, raising a hand with a missing index finger.

White tips passed through Vitkalla's slicked back greying mane. Evorix noticed flesh missing throughout his body, lumps of pink scar tissue taking their place. An arrow thudded between them from the ridgeline.

"These are my lands." Vitkalla said, pointing to the ridgeline. "Not yours."

Evorix spit at his padded feet, sheathed his sword and raised his hands. "So be it."

A loud roar echoed into the ravine as one of the Outkast above them fell off the ridge and into the ash. His brain matter splattered across Evorix's worn boots as he landed.

A deep horn blew as the Outkast prepared themselves for battle. Roaring, K'aro pulled his sword, then pointed to where he wanted Corcundia's men.

"Archers to the back, spearmen to the front, calvary bring up the rear," K'aro said.

"I ain't fighting for you," Evorix said, stepping back.

"Then die," K'aro said, leading Corcundia and her men over to Vitkalla.

God damnit, I don't want this.

As he looked around for an escape, Trakuta jogged past him with Aksutamoon and his men. "Aren't you leaving with me?" Evorix asked.

Turning his head, Trakuta looked back and smiled, "No, no, those bastards over that ridge got plenty of treasure on them. I'm going to get mine and eat until I'm suckled like a sow."

Evorix looked at his boots and wrapped his hand around the hilt of his sword.

I'm going to regret this, I just know it. I'm nobody's hero, he thought as he charged after Trakuta.

Chapter 16

Perspiration dripped from Tersius's brow as he scanned the encampment. The smell of shit after a night of drinking made him throw up into the cool blue water. Knees skinned from a fall earlier, he lifted his head with a groan, hoping no one had seen him. As he straightened himself, he wiped his tunic sleeve across his sunburnt lips.

"I'm never drinking again," he muttered, holding his head in his hands.

Casting a shadow over him, surrounded by guards, Valentinian said, "When you're done acting like a child, Tersius, I would like to see you in my tent."

Sluggishly, Tersius stumbled behind him, head lowered. Valentinian was always the stalwart leader of the Rebellium, but the years hadn't been kind to him. With his eyesight nearly gone and walking with a limp, he knew it was only a matter of time before he would not rise one day soon.

The closer they got to Valentinian's tent, the more Tersius' mind raced. Looking around, he felt the hairs on the back of his neck stand on end. It only lasted a moment, then left. They crossed into the tent and Valentinian held his hands by a candle wick that had burned down to the brass holder.

Tersius looked around the inside of the tent. A globe of Delos sat in a stand in a corner of the tent with tomes of books surrounding it. The tent was plain in every respect, except for the hundreds of books lining its leather walls. A straw bed and a basin of cold water were his only luxuries.

Calpernicus stood with a few of his men by a table in the opposite corner, pouring over a battle map.

"It can't be done, believe me when I tell you. If we attempt an assault with our numbers, the cause is lost," Calpernicus said to one of the burly men on his left.

Valentinian walked over to the table, crossed his arms over his chest and took a deep breath. "Are you a Drathi*can* or a Drathi*cant*, Calpernicus?" Valentinian asked.

After hearing the question, Calpernicus' face reddened. He placed both palms on the table and leaned forward. "I am a true Drathian, m'lord. And I have the scars to prove it."

"Then prove it."

Calpernicus smoldered as he watched Valentinian walk away. He turned back to the map, grinding his teeth and said, "If it can be done, who can do it?"

One of his men paused and shrugged, "What...assassinate the emperor?"

Calpernicus growled. "Yes." He sighed and rubbed his red eyes, casually tracing the lines of Wolfrya on the map. His finger slid over the trees and mountains leading up to the city of Iceport. "It's going to get bloody and many of ours will die, needlessly."

"Don't pout, Calpernicus." Valentinian said as he spun his globe. He looked at Tersius and said, "What news of Asinius?"

"He tells me nothing."

Walking with his hands clasped behind his back, Valentinian spoke out loud, "It doesn't matter, we will kill the emperor all the same. How many we lose will be substantially higher than I first anticipated. But I think we may need his help and I will do anything to kill the emperor, no matter how many men I lose."

"M'lord, we have precious few remaining, how can you ask them to sacrifice more?" Calpernicus asked, stomping up to Valentinian from the table.

Valentinian looked up from his book, over the rim of his eye glasses, then tapped his chin with a smirk and said, "Because I command them to die for the cause and that includes all of you as well."

"My life is worth more than dying in a headlong assault, m'lord. Octavius will die, but not with my men's lives needlessly thrown away to make it happen," Calpernicus spat.

"I still command the power here. Know your place, Calpernicus. If I command it, it will be done. In fact, I want your men to lead the charge when we mobilize the army."

The smudge from Valentinian's finger on the map smeared the area around Iceport, emphasizing his point. "Asinius will take us to the throne room after we breach the gate." Slamming his hand onto the map, Valentinian finished. "And I will kill Octavius, well I won't, your men will. Are any of you stupid enough to challenge my authority?" He glanced at Calpernicus. "What about you, Calpernicus?"

Calpernicus lowered his head and muttered, "No m'lord, but why rush? We have lived this long by being cautious."

Valentinian chuckled, rolled his eyes and looked over at Tersius and mouthed, "Cowards."

A slave with an olive complexion, black hair and leathery skin approached Valentinian and filled his cup. Valentinian's hand slid over the rim of the goblet and he slammed the contents. He licked his lips. "I need something stronger. Tersius, bring me my favorite drink." He pointed to the table.

"What's your plan m'lord?" Tersius asked, handing him the lead goblet.

With his goblet full of Tears of Tramonia, Valentinian took a sip, adjusted his spectacles and said, "When we bring Asinius aboard, he will help us smuggle an assassin I sent your uncle Gius to find." Valentinian burped lightly, then tapped his chest. He stared at the goblet. "This whiskey has gone south. Shouldn't waste it though," he said, pouring more into his glass.

The sound of Valentinian clearing his throat was raspy, allergic sounding. He smacked his lips together, looked at the goblet, then dropped it.

"No use wasting good whiskey. My, I feel.... I feel peculiar. As I was say——-," Valentinian said, swallowing hard as he sank to his knees.

Dropping to catch him, Calpernicus held him as the first convulsions coursed through his body. A bloody froth exploded from his mouth, covering Tersius. He sat up and vomited dark pools of blood. "It's not supposed———."

Calpernicus held Valentinian as the guards rushed in with a physician. He pointed at Tersius and yelled, "He killed our lord, capture him."

Valentinian frantically opened a book by his hand and ripped out a page. He thrust it into Tersius' pocket, gasping for breath. His chest heaved and his head snapped side to side like a teeter-totter. So much to say, so little time,

Valentinian opened his mouth, tried to say something, but nothing came out.

His chest stilled and the blood gurgling in his throat subsided. Calpirnicus lowered him onto the ground and looked at Tersius with watery eyes.

Reaching his feet, Calpernicus squared his jaw and said, "Tersius of Drathia, you are charged with killing Lord Valentinian, ruler of the Rebellium. Guards, take him to a holding cell until his trial in the morning."

The physician looked at the blood flowing from Valentinian's nostrils and right eye. He knelt down and stuck his finger inside Valentinians mouth and pulled it back out. Lifting the blood to the tip of his tongue, he tasted it, then vigorously spit on the ground. "Ach, poison."

Calpernicus' men chased down the slaves who served Valentinian in the last week and brought them back to the tent. Calpernicus lined them up and assigned guards to interrogate them. He noticed a thin man with black hair easing his way out of the tent as the guards selected the other slaves.

"Stop him!" Calpernicus shouted.

Tersius shook off his guards and turned to stop the man. The assassin's blade bit into Tersius' neck, snapping off at the hilt in the process as he sprinted by. A guard overreacted and thrust his long spear into the assassins stomach, disemboweling him.

In a fit of rage Calpernicus drew his sword. "You idiot." he shouted, swinging his sword at the man's neck, cutting it wide open. The dead guardsman's long spear clattered to the floor. Calpernicus' men and Valentinians guards squared off in the cramped quarters, weapons at the ready.

"Now there's more than one way out of this and bloodshed can be avoided," Calpernicus shouted.

A guard tentatively stepped forward and stabbed at Calpernicus in response, barely missing him. Calpernicus shouted to his men outside the tent. They rushed in and took Valentinian's guards from behind, quickly putting them to the sword.

• • • •

MARUS PEERED THROUGH his grubby telescopic lens, blinked, then refocused as he tried to make out the violent scene transpiring below them. Everything had gone as planned and he never stepped foot in the camp.

Valentinian appeared to have been killed and with him the Rebellium. A shadow snuck up to his outcropping and grunted with strained effort.

"I'm gettin' too old for this shit," Marus' companion said.

Marus nodded, ignored the man and then looked back down his spyglass. Squinting downrange without a spyglass, the figure excitedly raised his hand and said, "This is the perfect time to attack, m'lord."

Marus yanked the man's arm down with a glare and returned to what he was doing. If anything, Zillas his companion was more of a liability than an asset. He drank too much wine which made him impetuous and a drunk man was a bad omen who cost soldiers their lives when they talked out of turn.

But he was Octavius' cousin and afforded the luxury of being a pain in the ass. During the suppression of the Rebellium, he was a great warrior and leader, but the Tears of Tramonia had transformed him. Zillas now ran errands for the commanders and went out with the scouting parties. Usually, the scouts brought him back over their shoulders.

As Marus scanned the cells, he saw an individual leaning against the bars in a white Wolfryan tunic and tan breeches. "It can't be...." Marus mumbled.

"What do you see?" Zillas asked.

"My unicorn," he replied.

"Your unicorn? What the hell does that mean?" Zillas asked.

Marus cawed like a crow and one of his men crawled to him. The new man lay flat on his stomach waiting for a command from Marus. Marus handed the new man the spyglass, then rolled out of his way. The commander scanned the landscape and murmured, "Can't be that easy, can it?"

"What do you think, Precipitous?" Marus asked.

Snickering, Precipitous said, "That's him alright. I know that arrogant stance anywhere. I can't believe he got caught by the rebels. Serves him right though." He glanced over at Marus with a shrug. "So, why do we need to intervene?"

Marus growled. "Because I want his head. But no one moves from this bluff until I give the order. Once I get Asinius, kill everyone else in the camp, but not before."

"Don't let your hate get you killed or miss an opportunity the emperor insists on being done, m'lord," Precipitous said.

"When I want your recommendations, I'll give them to you, Precipitous," Marus replied.

Precipitous paused, looked over at him and then shook his head. "You, and what army, prefect? Have you already forgotten what happened in the dungeon with the emperor?"

Precipitous had followed Marus through the Rebellium Wars and in the process lost his right wrist, courtesy of a Ba warrior. He also carried a single jagged scar that ran across his leathery face at an angle.

"Remember Marus, I've saved your ass more times than you can count on your fingers and toes. You want to talk to Zillas like that, do it. He's a drunken bastard, but watch how you speak to me," Precipitous said, handing Marus the spyglass.

Precipitous waited for Marus' response and stared into his troubled eyes. Marus' lip twitched at his comment. He rolled away and then walked back to the campfire.

"I don't think that was what he expected from you," Zillas said.

"I don't care. He's quick to see red and stupid enough to do something irrational. Now I won't start trouble, but should Marus need me to finish it, I will," Precipitous said.

"Does that mean kicking him when he's down?"

Precipitous cut his eyes at him. "My emperor commands, I follow."

"I bet and if I didn't know you any better, I would say you were plotting on him," Zillas whispered.

Staring intently at the men rushing to the tent, Precipitous spoke out the side of his mouth. "And that's why you'll always be a runner and an errand boy."

The pair waited in silence, wiping the sweat from their faces. Precipitous waited patiently as he watched the valley floor. The tent they had seen Valentinian enter and exit from had blood smeared across the opening. Someone drug a limp bloody body out of the tent and tossed it into Asinius' cell.

He didn't recognize the man's face, nor did he care. He knew a surprise attack would destroy them, but if he didn't follow Marus' order, he would be executed along with any rebel survivors.

Precipitous and Zillas snuck back to their camp and sat by Marus who was slowly chewing on a piece of raw meat. He ground it between his teeth and stared at them as they approached. He took a sip from his wine skin, then handed it across the smouldering fire to Precipitous as he sat down.

Hesitating for a moment, Precipitous reached for it. Marus dropped it into a pile of horse shit beside them.

"Prick," Precipitous mumbled.

"That and worse, much worse," Marus said with a smirk.

The other members of their small raiding party came and sat down beside them after they returned. Marus grabbed a stick at his feet he had sharpened and picked his teeth.

Sucking his bleeding gums, Marus said, "So, what's the plan, Precipitous? Since you think you're the mighty general."

Precipitous shrugged and grabbed a rock from the ground. "How should I know, it's your command."

Marus glanced across the fire at the scouts he sent out.

"What did you men see?" he asked, turning his attention away from Precipitous.

"The only way in is a frontal assault, unless you send someone in to unlock the gate from the inside. It would take several towers that we will need to build to breach that wall," the leader responded.

Maris nodded. "I think——."

Precipitous cut him off. "The emperor commands Asinius' head. We need to go tonight, Marus, damn the cost."

Marus slapped Precipitous across the face for cutting him off. "Do.not.interrupt.me.again," he said with emphasis, staring into his eyes.

Precipitous pulled a blade from his forearm and swung it at Marus' neck. A sword swung out of the shadows of the bonfire and struck his wooden hand, knocking it off. It was followed by a fist and a vicious knee to the temple. The stars danced around Precipitous' head for a moment and then he fell to the ground. Zillas stood by Marus and nodded at him.

Marus waved his hand dismissively, ignoring the fact Zillas had saved his life. "Take him away."

Marus waited while Precipitous was dragged away and then continued, "As I was saying before I was rudely interrupted. We will pull back and get the rest of our army and once we have re-assembled both legions, we will return. I need a volunteer to surrender to their patrols and then reach my man on the inside who can unlock the gate for us. Any volunteers?" he asked.

"You have a man on the inside? Why do we need someone to speak to him?" asked one of the scouts.

"Because, I want the gate opened quickly. I want our calvary through the gate first, followed by our legionnaires. Once we're in, put everyone to the sword. So, who's my volunteer?" Marus asked.

Marus knew none of his men would go, it was to risky. If the person were discovered, they would be tortured and killed. He looked around and saw his chance to get rid of Zillas.

"Zillas, you will surrender," Marus said, after taking another sip of wine.

"Wait, wait a hot damn minute. I didn't volunteer," Zillas said with a hiccup.

"No, you didn't but when your cousin finds out you did, he will probably promote you to prefect. You up for it?" Marus asked.

"You really think he would do that?" Zillas asked, both eyebrows raised.

"Ofcourse I do. I wouldn't have said it if I didn't think so. Get captured, then speak to my ally and make sure he unlocks the gate."

"Who's your contact?" Zillas asked.

"He will reveal himself to you," Marus said.

Zillas nodded with a smile, grabbed a wine skin and stumbled off alone into the darkness. His curses could be heard as he walked into something past the tree line.

Marus felt along his neckline and drew blood from the wound Precipitous had given him. "Rat bastard," he murmured.

One of Marus' men walked up and began sewing the wound using dirty fingers. "Clean your hands," Marus said, pushing him away.

The man paused and washed his hands with wine. He glanced up at Marus, "Do you really believe what you just said, prefect Marus?"

"Ofcourse I don't, but Zillas doesn't know that and if he dies, Octavius will burn Delos to the ground in retribution. After all his son is Octavius' spawn."

The healers jaw dropped.

"Come man, you didn't know?" Marus asked. He took a swig of wine. "I mean he did impregnate his cousin's wife and the fool actually believes Zactus is from his loins. Learn this fact about Octavius. He's a real bastard, but the real problem for Delos is hope. The Rebellium scum still believe in hope and hope is dangerous."

The point of Marus' knife scraped across one of the rocks in the fire pit. He looked into the sky, his breath catching the cool night air. "Ach, he's a worthless drunk anyway and either he's to stupid or to ignorant to know his wife had a child with another man. He would serve Wolfrya better by getting himself killed during his capture."

"I see your point, prefect."

Marus looked around the campfire and noticed he was the only one left. "Leave me," Marus said to his healer.

"As you wish, m'lord."

Marus stood up, brushed himself off and then walked toward his tent for a few hours of sleep.

Chapter 17

An arrow twice the length of a human one snapped by Evorix's face and thudded into the back of the man behind him.

Damn that was close.

He looked around and saw Dro'ka throw his bow to the ground, bare his incisors and then mount his silver and blue alpurlic.

"Hold the line," Trakuta shouted, pulling his drawstring back and firing two arrows high into the sky. He shoved the men around him to their knees and stood behind them continuously firing.

"Easy boys, easy," he shouted, encouraging them.

One of his arrows struck one of the warriors next to Dro'ka, tumbling him from the saddle as they rode hard across the ravine floor.

"Nice shot," Evorix said.

"I was aiming for that guy," Trakuta said, pointing at Dro'ka as he strung his bow and fired another arrow.

"I hate getting old. My eyes aren't what they used to be," Trakuta mumbled. He turned his head toward his archers. "On my command."

He watched Dro'ka's warriors close the gap. "Loose!" He glanced at Evorix after giving his command, "So, you with me, or are you running?"

"I'm here, aren't I?" Evorix replied, picking up two spears at his feet. He slammed one of the spears into the ground and shouted, "First line, brace shields. Second row, spears at the ready."

Trakuta smiled as he watched Evorix readying the men.

"See you in the afterlife," Trakuta shouted to Evorix.

A volley of arrows landed among the defenders, killing several men caught in the open. The D'atu roared as they galloped faster across the ash. Some of the Tramonian's turned to flee, pushing past the Outkast as Dro'ka blew on his horn.

Aksutamoon rode in front of them as they retreated. He held his hands up and stood up in his stirrups. "Tramonians... Tramonians, hear me! Return and die with your fellows. Are you true Tramonians, or cowards?" he bellowed above the din of battle.

Most of the men stopped, only a few continued by him. The men stared at Aksutamoon mounted on his chestnut mare, the Tramonian flag fluttering by his side. There was nothing special about the plain red flag with a brown barrel of wine on it, but his men would die for it.

"Come with me! Who will come with me?" He slammed his visor down, the sun reflecting off of it. He yanked the reins on his mount, standing it up on its hind legs. A few of his men gave half hearted cheers and returned to the line.

Evorix saw Gius and Nigol walking toward the line. A soldier carrying spears and arrows knocked Gius down as he rushed to re-join his comrades. Evorix picked Gius up by the nape of his neck, untied his rope bindings and shoved a sword into his hands.

"Fight or die Gius. Your choice."

"If we survive this Evorix, watch what you eat and drink."

"You haven't got the balls," Evorix said.

"A weapon please, m'lord," Nigol said.

"Can you fight?"

Nigol shook his head no. Evorix smiled and turned to Nigol and tossed him a spear. Nigol ambled to the front line, his hunchback lowered as far as it could behind one of the Tramonian's shields. Evorix glanced at Gius with contempt.

• • • •

THE D'ATU RODE EIGHT across as they thundered through the valley. Row after row of Dro'ka's warriors bore down on them, even as they fell from the barrage of arrows.

K'aro looked around and calmly said in Delosian, "Spears at the ready, archers nock." He heard the click of the arrows as they were pulled against their bow strings. "Loose!"

Their arrows flew downrange and slammed into both warrior and beast. Howls of pain could be heard from the warriors mixed with screeches from the alpurlics.

Aksutamoon's men cheered and then watched in horror as the D'atu ride over their dead and wounded. Groans could be heard up and down the line as they watched them continue on. A warrior missing an ear stood near Evorix and roared an order.

"Brace!"

The R'atu, led by Vitkalla sprinted in front of the Tramonian lines in a wedge formation, their red scarves fluttering behind them. Vitkalla looked over his warriors faces, then back at Evorix.

"Human, they say you can fight. I doubt it, but on the chance you are a warrior, prove me wrong."

K'aro walked up to Evorix, picked a target, fired and knocked an attacking warrior out of his saddle. Evorix smirked and looked at both Vitkalla and K'aro. He spit at their feet and pulled his bowstring to his chin. Never breaking Vitkalla's gaze, he smiled arrogantly and fired his arrow.

Dro'ka caught the arrow as it descended, snapped it and threw it to the ground. Evorix wasn't sure, but he thought he heard him laughing as he rode over the last bit of ash.

Dro'ka snatched a javelin from the side of his saddle and threw it along with the other riders. Instinctively, Gius pushed Evorix to the ground as Dro'ka's javelin slammed into a shield behind them. Evorix looked up and spit out a mouthful of ash.

Gius smiled. "It must hurt that I'll always be smarter than you," Gius said.

He stepped over Evorix and engaged the D'atu.

K'aro looked down and yanked Evorix to his feet. "Let's go!"

By all that's holy, that's the last time anyone knocks me to the ground.

A Tramonian commander shouted. "Loose!"

As more arrows flew from their lines, K'aro and Evorix ran toward the Outkast who stood in two rows. The left row held their spears at an angle, their ten foot oiled spearheads forming similar to rows of teeth. The tips gleamed in the orange volcanic light, a mix of obsidian and iron.

Looking straight ahead, Evorix muttered under his breath, "I owe you, beast."

He gave him a curt nod. "Start by calling me, K'aro."

Evorix took a swig from a bottle he had hidden and sighed, "So this is the end, eh K'aro."

Trakuta shouted beside them, "Give them everything you got. Loose!"

K'aro shook his mane at Evorix and smiled. "Nothing is ever as it seems."

He raised his arm, a bright red sash flowing from his elbow. Fire arrows flew down from the ridgeline above, wiping out a group of D'atu riders at the back of the attacking column.

Dro'ka's warriors were unable to reign their mounts in and crashed into the raised spears of the Outkast. The bodies of both warriors and alpurlics hung limp, impaled on the long shafts. Shouts and screams reverberated through the ravine as the two groups collided.

The agonizing shouts, curses, roars, neighing horses and roaring alpurlics made men clamp their teeth, some shattering their roots. Piles of intestines, blood and shit were plentiful as the scene of carnage unfolded.

The bodies of both friend and foe mixed together, the dead tripping the living as they continued their scramble for survival. A small group of humans formed a phalanx and surrounded Aksutamoon.

The phalanx surged forward around him, impaling the D'atu warriors as they crashed through the first spear line.

Evorix watched Gius lead a few injured men to plug the gap in the center and then watched him disappear into the ash falling around them. As the Tramonian's pushed the D'atu back, a large vase flew over the phalanx.

K'aro sniffed, his ears perking up. "Fire pot!" he roared.

He bounded onto one of the Outkast who held his paws cupped near his knees. The warrior bent over at the waist and lifted K'aro into the sky.

K'aro leapt, but a javelin tore into his helpers neck, knocking him to the ground. The javelin caught the back of K'aro's leg and he plummeted to the ground near the other dead warrior. Rising to his feet, two arrows thumped into his armor. He dropped his spear and collapsed into the blood stained ash.

A dismounted D'atu warrior roared. "Push!"

A few of the men in the phalanx retreated and left Aksutamoon vulnerable to attack. Aksutamoon didn't seem to notice as he ran his sword through the warrior in front of him. He buried it up to the hilt and then lost control of the weapon as the warrior fell under his horses hooves. He glanced around his saddle bag and pulled one of his spares.

Another D'atu warrior yanked on Aksutamoon's leg from below and held him still as another warrior galloped toward him and leapt. Evorix's arrow slammed into the leaping warriors eye and sent him crashing to the ground. Aksutamoon hacked the other warriors arm off, then lifted his sword and saluted Evorix.

Fire pots exploded over the phalanx, melting most of Aksutamoon's men's heads. A cloud of black smoke and screams were all that remained of the Tramonian's.

The screeches of agony around Evorix echoed in his ears. As the number of humans in the fight dwindled, Aksutamoon ordered a retreat and was finally cut down from behind. Trakuta fell to the ash beside him as a D'atu warrior with one arm leaned over him with his sword raised.

Evorix searched madly for Corcundia and saw her across the battlefield. Sprinting through the mass of bodies, he slowed as the blood soaked the ground around him. A young boy beat Evorix to Corcundia's side.

A Da'tu warrior nearby swung his sword at her as she wiped her soot stained face. The young Tramonian boy stepped in front of the sword strike meant for her, then fell to the ash, his head split open.

As he reached Corcundia, he lowered his shoulder and drove his sword into the warriors back. Another warrior approached them and raised his spear over his head. A knife flew through the air and embedded into his attackers throat. The warrior stumbled forward and fell on Evorix, crushing him to the ground. A horn pierced the air around them.

Can my life get any worse? Evorix thought.

Roars from the victorious D'atu could be heard drowning out the sounds of the humans screaming. Before his eyes closed, Evorix thought he saw red scarves coming down behind them, then a large paw thumped his skull.

Chapter 18

A sinius watched from the other side of the cage as a guard opened the door and threw a body in. After they left, he approached and prodded the person with his foot. The person lay still and every few seconds a shudder would run through it.

Asinius nudged him and a gasp escaped the person's lips. Confused for a moment, he knelt down and rolled the body over. Asinius saw a knife blade embedded in the man's clavicle.

"Can't be," he muttered, wiping the bloody matted hair from the man's forehead.

Tersius lay still and ashen, barely alive. Asinius cautiously leaned over his chest and tried to feel a heartbeat. He felt Tersius' heart flutter a few times, then it went silent. Asinius crossed his hands over Tersius' rib cage and pushed down repeatedly breaking several of his ribs. Gently, he blew air into Tersius' mouth and after a few moments, Tersius' heart beat and his eyes opened slightly.

Like a weed from the ground, he sat up, winced and then gasped. The blade from the assassin had missed its mark. Somehow it hit him instead of its intended recipient. A cough sent paralyzing bursts of pain through his body. Instinctually, he reached for the blade but Asinius slapped his hand aside.

"Pull that blade out and you're dead," Asinius said.

The seasoned veteran ripped the top of Tersius' tunic off and put it around the blade. Whimsical sounds emanated from Asinius' closed lips as he felt along Tersius' clavicle. With a few grunts of satisfaction, Asinius blew into his ear.

Tersius jerked his head away and as he did, Asinius caught the blade, yanked it free and then smothered him. Tersius' cries of anguish and pain sounded like the death chant from a Ba warrior.

"Quiet boy, quiet. You're alright I promise," Asinius whispered in his ear.

The hot blood rolled down Tersius' shoulder and onto his chest. Asinius covered his mouth as he screamed and screeched in utter agony until he finally passed. He picked the cleanest straw from the remaining pieces near them and pressed them to the free flowing wound. He wrapped the cleanest piece of his tunic around the wound and tried to stem the flow of blood. The binding looked like it would burst, but it would hold, for the moment.

Asinius had not been honest with Tersius from the start and kept as many secrets as he could from him. The boy didn't need to know he trained as a surgeon prior to Tiberius coming to power, or that the dead emperor wanted to marry his wife and adopt his son for the throne. It was also unnecessary to inform him that he joined Tiberius to kill him because he killed both his wife and child. To save his own life, he swore loyalty. And he knew that if he hadn't, he would have been executed too.

The memory of his family had been buried deep down inside himself for many years, but Tersius reminded him of what his own son would have been like. However, in Asinius' mind one memory would never surface and he had no trouble keeping it that way. Just the thought of it rearing its ugly head was enough for him to change his thoughts.

Delicately, Asinius pushed the hair away from Tersius' eyes and looked down at his fevered face with a sigh. He could never tell him why Primus always referred to him as a traitor. Tersius would never understand the choices one has to make to stay alive in a Wolfryan viper pit and he hoped he never would. He looked around the cell for anything that may help keep Tersius alive. He had seen many battle wounds, some more egregious than others during his campaigns. Tersius' clavicle would never be the same, even if he managed to survive.

Asinius' eyes rested on a small group of flowers and moss growing under a rock in the shadows at the back of the cage. His eyes lit up when he saw that the moss would bind the wound, if there was a salve on it.

Laying on his stomach at the back of the cage, Asinius stretched his arm out as far as he could, fingernails scraping the dirt. He picked the marigold flowers and then slowly peeled the pale green moss from the rock face. He thought for a moment and then pulled the tops of the marigold from the stems and chewed them. He squeezed the moisture from the moss across Tersius' cracked lips and laid it out to dry. He mashed the chewed marigold petals on top of the moss as the sun began to set.

Several hours passed before Tersius finally opened his eyes. He motioned Asinius closer and whispered in his ear, smiled and then passed out again. Asinius stared at the boy for a moment, then reached into his pocket as instructed and unfolded the bloody parchment. Upon closer inspection, he could see some scribbling, but some of the words had been blacked out by dark blood stains.The writing was hard to see, even when he squinted and held it close to his eyes.

"Can't see shit," he muttered.

He moved his head so the moonlight could assist him in reading. The torn paper read:

'I have been watching my fellow members of the Re———- for the last several weeks and I constantly feel someone staring at me from the shad—-. I believe my p—- has be— discovered by those unfaithful to **OUR** *c——. As much a-it pains me to think this, we need Asin—-'s help.*

I think if he were to help Ev—— ,we could kill Octavius. It will fall to Primus' son to follow Evorix, kill him after his job is done and get Asinius out of the castle. Evorix, Tersius and Asinius shall be the light that leads the way. I will record the outcome of our meeting tonight. I question—-.'

Asinius turned the paper over but the rest had been ripped off the sheet. He dug in Tersius' pockets, finding only pocket lint. Tersius' chest rose and fell rhythmically. The sweat dripped from his forehead as he tossed and turned in the moonlight. The moss had dried and Asinius knew if he didn't get better supplies, the boy would die.

Lost in his thoughts, he heard Tersius say, "Evening, old man."

"Watch your tongue boy, or I'll put the knife back in."

Swallowing hard, Tersius ground his teeth. "You don't have any whiskey, do you?"

"Nope, you took it, remember? Now pay close attention to what I am going to tell you. If you listen, you'll live, and if you don't, you'll die. Do I make myself clear?" Asinius asked.

Tersius nodded.

"I'm going to pull this makeshift bandage off, apply this moss, then we need to get out of here," Asinius said.

"I'm game, but how do we get out?" Tersius asked.

"All in due time, all in due time," Asinius replied.

"They're going to kill us in the morning, aren't they?" Tersius asked.

Asinius ignored the question, rose to his feet and waved a guard over. He whispered between the bars. "Bel, you and I have had a few conversations and if I don't help this boy, he will die. He's done nothing wrong and you know that. Why keeps us here to die?"

"They murdered my brother in that tent tonight, but I will die if you escape. You know that," Bel said, stealing looks around him.

"Are you wanting to live life like a scared whipped dog, or will you die to regain your brothers honor and kill the men responsible for his death?"

"I'm only seventeen summers, I can't help—-."

Blood splashed across the bars in front of Asinius' face. Bel's eyes widened as he squirmed on the ground.

"He definitely can't help you now and as for tomorrow, you will die just the same," Calpernicus said.

"You're a coward Calpernicus and if you come in this cage, I'll show how real men fight. I'm not a boy you can kill from behind."

With his hands clasped behind his back, Calpernicus licked his lips, anger clouding his voice. "Valentinian's dead and with him his plan to use you to storm the castle. And tomorrow you will be dead too. So save your strength,

Asinius. You'll need it when I walk you to the executioner's block," he said.

Calpernicus turned on his heels and whistled a sweet melody as he walked back into the pitch black night as Bel's blood pooled under Asinius' boot. Asinius lifted his boots in disgust and flicked away as much blood as he could. He glanced into the shadows, saw no one was paying him any attention and then dropped to his knees.

A glint of light from Bel's body drew his attention to the ground. A silver necklace hung loosely from his neck. He snatched it and shoved it in his pocket. Searching further, he felt a sharp pain through his index finger. Blood fell from his fingertip as he pulled a knife from under Bel's tunic. Asinius pawed at his coin purse and managed to rip it from his belt, "Damnit Bel, not a key or a lockpick," Asinius grumbled.

As Bel's life blood drained away, he knew he and Tersius were finished. A rumbling in his stomach made him wonder if he was nervous, hungry, or both. A fir was raging twenty feet away, barely casting any heat in their direction. Tersius groaned and gasped for breath between coughs that raked his body.

"Water," Tersius whispered.

Asinius shook his head and stood over him. "I'm sorry boy, fresh out."

"Kill, kill me...please," he pleaded between coughs.

Tersius sweat and groaned as he rocked side to side, holding his arms. Reaching down, Asinius peeled the straw away from Tersius' wound and inspected it. Yellow pus oozed out, the smell of rotten cheese accompanying it.

"I'm dying, aren't I?" Tersius asked with a groan, his eyes no more than mere slits.

"That is a distinct possibility. I do not have the tools to save you."

Tersius forced air from his lungs and nodded. "That's not good. What can I do?"

"Pray to the Gods. It's in their hands, now," Asinius said.

• • • •

SEVERAL HOURS LATER, three Rebellium riders galloped over the ridge, one rider carried something over his worn leather saddle. The riders pulled in their reigns and stopped outside the wooden palisade of the encampment.

"Open the gate!" the guard in the tower shouted.

The rider gingerly threw the large burlap sack off his saddle as they entered. A low cry emanated from it as it struck the hard earth.

Calpernicus walked out of his tent wearing a white and black bear skin draped around his shoulders. He looked around and then kicked the bag.

"What is this?" he asked the man who had thrown the bag to the ground.

"Octavius' men are close by, m'lord. This is one of their spies," one of the other riders replied.

Calpernicus knelt down and untied the bag. Zillas' head burst from the open hole. He gasped and wiggled the rest of his body out of the encasement.

Calpernicus looked at him, then mounted his horse. "Guard, take him to the cells. Scrub him clean, he's covered in bugs." He wrinkled his nose and then finished his sentence, "And horse shit."

The guard yanked Zillas up by his braided hair. Zillas was always a mess, his rich black hair was graying at the temples and several of his fingers were missing from to many unfortunate run-ins with Wolfryan attack dogs.

"Hey Zillas,"Calpernicus said, pulling his horse next to him.

Zillas looked up in time to feel Calpernicus' boot connect with his chin. The ground swirled around him for a moment and then he collapsed at the horses feet. The guards surrounding Calpernicus laughed and gave him a few kicks for good measure.

"Welcome to the jungle," Calpernicus said before riding away.

The guards dragged Zillas to the back of the camp. Reaching the cage Asinius was in, they threw him in. The hard ground in the cage jarred Zillas awake on impact. His eyelids fluttered, then closed.

Tersius' eyes opened for a moment and he groaned. He tried to wipe his forehead, but his limp wrist just slapped against it. Asinius hurried to his side and wiped his brow. "Easy boy, I know it hurts."

Zillas coughed and groaned as he drug himself to the bars of the cage and then pulled himself to his knees. He pulled the cork from the glass flask in his pocket and tilted his head back.

Asinius kicked him mid swallow and sent the flask to the ground and shattered it. Zillas looked up with a hiccup and reached behind his back. He hiccuped again, smiled and said, "I always carry a backup."

Asinius sighed. "You're a worthless drunk Zillas and to think you were one of my best pupils."

"You know why I drink, so leave me to my buzz before they kill me," Tersius grumbled.

Asinius thumped his back up bottle. "This is what kept you from advancement, not me," he said.

"Same old man with the same old story. You betrayed every one of us to survive and climb the ranks. At one point you were one of the best physicians in Delos. Now look at you." He hiccuped and swayed. "A trapped rat, just like me. Which is worse Asinius, a coward or a betrayer?"

Asinius scoffed. "You'd never understand the sacrifices I've made for the empire," he said, walking back to Tersius.

"What? You mean about your wife, son and Tiberius?" Asinius turned his head and stared through him. "Hell everyone knew, Asinius. There are no secrets in the palace," Zillas said with a curt chuckle.

"I would stop talking if you value your life, Zillas."

"Prefect, I worry more about making it to the privy for a shit, than what you'll do. You scare no one, especially not me. Yes, I was your pupil once, but now like you, I do what I must to survive." Staring at him with haunted eyes, Zillas downed the rest of his flask, sighed and then looked at it with a smile. "Pity, I'm all out."

He glanced at Asinius, his eyes unable to mask his pain. "Almost forgot. Marus saw you from the ridgeline last night. I was *voluntold* to get captured and open the doors when they attack."

"And I care? Anyway, how's Zactus?" Asinius asked with a chuckle.

Smiling maliciously, Zillas murmured, "Screw you, prefect. You really believe I'm so incompetent that I don't know my wife had an affair with Octavius and that the boy isn't mine? You're going to have to try harder to hurt my feelings."

"I didn't think you knew," Asinius said, raising an eyebrow.

"I know more than people think I do. I'm not as drunk as I appear. Fact is, I can't ever seem to get drunk enough," Zillas said.

"So, why tell me? You know I could care less about your problems," Asinius said.

Zillas chuckled. "Because I'm going to help you get your revenge,"

Asinius shrugged. "My revenge? What revenge?"

"I'm going to help you kill the emperor."

Asinius stared at Zillas coldly. "You speak of treason," he said.

"Hate to tell you this, prefect." Zillas glanced in the direction of Wolfrya with a smile, and then faced Asinius. "But we're marked men. That's not treason, that's the life we now live. We can never go back to our old ways. That's why we have to kill the emperor, because no one else will."

Asinius smirked, then nodded. He put his forearms against the cold iron bars with a long sigh. "Would have been a good idea, but it's too late now, they'll hang you tomorrow."

"You mean us," Zillas said.

"I mean *you*. They will go light on you, Zillas, but me... Calpernicus will take his time with me."

"What if we break out?" Zillas asked.

"I've looked for a way every waking moment. All I found is this and it doesn't help us very much," Asinius said.

Hesitating, he went into his pocket and handed Zillas, Valentinian's note. "I don't know why I'm showing you this, but it looks like we're going to need each other. This is where we are with everything in the camp."

After reading for a few minutes, Zillas looked up and gave him a coy smile. "So, Valentinian is going to use Evorix and you to take out the emperor." He giggled. "That's not a very good plan. The guards will kill you on site."

"Tell me something I don't know. Let's not waste any more time. What is Marus' plan?" Asinius asked.

"They are pulling back to gather the army south of here. And then they're going to ride through the open gates and slaughter what's left of the Rebellium," Zillas said, staring south.

Asinius spat between the bars. "Perfect plan. Marus always was a good tactician. You were supposed to open the gates? How do you plan that now?" he asked.

"He has a traitor in this camp," Zillas whispered, tipping his empty flask to his lips.

"Who?" Asinius demanded.

Zillas shrugged. "I was supposed to get captured and then the person would get me out just before the attack," he said.

"That's suicidal," Asinius said.

Zillas smiled knowingly.

"I've known you far too long not to know what your thinking. So, what's your plan?" Zillas asked, eyes gleaming.

● ● ● ●

THE PAIN IN EVORIX'S head was excruciating. He felt the back of it and drew blood from a gash behind his right ear.

A warrior knelt beside him and said, "You'll live. Get up slave."

The smell of wet fur wafted into his nostrils again. He rolled over onto his back and sat up slowly. The bodies surrounding him were stacked like a dam in a river of blood. The limbs of both human and Ba warriors were intermingled throughout the battlefield. After getting to his feet, Evorix put his hands on his knees and coughed.

That was a terrible idea. Should have ran. I doubt anyone's alive.

A shadow appeared above him and spoke, "Don't expect me to say thank you, you still owe me two men."

Growling in anger, Evorix said, "Now wait a minute. I saved your life and this is the thanks I get?"

"You protected an investment, not me personally."

After he thought for a moment, he went to speak but heard a neighing behind him and turned. Whispers lay mortally wounded near several D'atu corpses. Evorix pushed through the men around him and took a knee in front of his beloved horse.

"Easy boy, easy now," Evorix said, stroking his mane.

Whispers had only been with him for a short time, but he had loved again, no matter how brief. He clenched his teeth and laid his head on Whispers neck fighting back his tears. It was only a matter of time and he was beginning to suffer.

I'm sorry it happened like this boy. I wish we could have plowed fields and rode through pastures, but it never happens that way from me. Everything I touch dies or disappears. Why should this be any different?

Corcundia walked up behind him and cleared her throat. "You want us to help?"

His sword pierced Whispers heart as she asked, silencing his pain. A single salty tear fell onto his dirt stained cheek, the first since the death of his wife.

"No. My horse, my problem," he said in a hushed tone.

He slowly lowered Whispers head into the ash and slid his fingers over his eyelids.

Death...all this death. I hate the Ba, nothing more than talking animals.

Whispers death quieted those around him. Men and warrior lay wounded side by side moaning, the dead frozen in one last desperate act of defiance.

"What the hell happened?" Evorix asked, spitting blood onto the ground and wiggling one of his teeth.

Corcundia spoke. "I'm sorry about——."

Staring straight ahead, Evorix said, "Save it."

She nodded. "To answer your question, the rest of the Outkast came to our defense. They captured Dro'ka and a few of his remaining warriors."

"How did they know we needed help?" Evorix asked.

She shrugged.

Evorix asked, "And our losses?"

"The rest of my men and almost all of Aksutamoon's are dead. Not very many wounded, these are some big tough bastards."

"And our group?"

Her head lowered as she chewed her lower lip, then looked up. "I haven't found Trakuta, K'aro, or Aksutamoon, but I found Gius." Evorix peered over her shoulder at the spear sticking out of Gius' chest.

Fuck.

"Is he dead?"

"Will be shortly. He asked to see you."

Evorix walked up to Gius and stood over him. "Looks like you're done this time," Evorix said.

Blood trickled out of the corner of Gius' mouth. "So it would seem."

"Who's going to pay me now?" Evorix asked.

"Valentinian... sent me to find you, so he will be the one to pay you," he said as coughs shook his body.

"If I don't leave for Batopia," Evorix replied.

Gius' smile revealed his blood stained teeth. "You'll stay. Not for the cause, but because we are paying you to kill the emperor and you want to kill him more than I do. Don't you want to stop running?"

Evorix blinked a few times, trying to shed the eyelash that was bothering him. "Would be nice."

Gius' eyes flicked back and forth, "I can't see. I... I can't see." His voice took an anxious tone, "Evorix, are you there?"

Evorix knelt down and grabbed his hand. "Ain't left you yet." A look of ease and comfort crossed Gius' face. He wanted to use the right words, but all that crossed his lips was a low guttural groan. "I'm s——."

More blood cascaded from his mouth as he squeezed Evorix' hand.

"Go easy, old friend," Evorix said.

Gius' eyes glazed over and a bloody froth escaped his lips. His chest rose a last time, then stilled. His dull open eyes stared into the grey volcanic sky. Evorix got to his feet and watched the dead being dragged into separate piles. The humans were missing most of their limbs, their bodies covered in extensive bite marks. The smell of shit overwhelmed the senses.

Those untested in battle vomited where they stood. Flies buzzed around the dead horses and alpurlics scattered around the battlefield. Vitkalla limped up to them with a bandage around his forehead. Evorix noticed he was missing more patches of black hair along his arms and legs. His mount lay behind him, multiple spears in its flank.

"Good fight," he grunted, leaning against his broken spear shaft.

A warrior dressed in a studded bronze and black leather cuirass came to Vitkalla's side and snapped to attention. He placed his hand over his heart, then removed his helm. His mane was ebony with a white stripe, his body merle.

The white apurlic hair on top of his helm flowed in the breeze as the two warriors spoke in their native language. Nigol walked up to Evorix, knelt by Gius and folded his arms across his chest. He placed two gold Wolfryan coins over Gius' eyes and smiled.

Evorix listened to the conversation across from him and waited for Vitkalla to finish. He waved Nigol over and told him what he wanted to say. Nigol's head bobbed up and down as he did his best to understand their dialect and what they were saying.

"He is introducing the warrior in black as his son, Tro'ka, heir to their pride. His warriors were the ones who saved us," Nigol said.

Evorix shrugged and walked away. Corcundia followed behind him, keeping pace. "Why did you not thank them?"

"Because they rode to save the other beasts, not us. We're slaves, remember?"

The two reached the center of the battlefield where the fighting had been the worst. Aksutamoon and Trakuta sat on a dead D'atu warrior passing a bottle of Tramonian wine between them. Only a handful of Aksutamoon's men were left. They sat around him nursing their wounds. Heads were missing bodies, bodies were missing arms and legs and men's torso's were strewn about in a macabre scene. Trakuta smiled wide, opening a wide gash across his brow.

"You alright?" Evorix asked.

"I'll live. More than I can say for our men," Trakuta replied.

"Gius is dead," Evorix said.

Trakuta spit on the ground and lifted his wine flask. "Good luck to the Gods. He was a testy one."

Aksutamoon stood up and extended his arm. "You fight well. Thanks you for watching my back."

"I didn't. You fell anyway. I should have been faster," Evorix said.

Aksutamoon patted his arm and tilted his head back roaring with laughter, the giblets on his neck shaking. "You did better than my men." He glanced at the corpses and winked. "Much better."

A warrior climbed over a pile of bodies holding his side. Corcundia noticed K'aro immediately and ran to him. She hugged him around the neck, burying her head in his mane.

"How are you still alive?" she asked.

"The Gods," he chortled.

One of the Outkast healers wandered over and helped him lay down. One arrow was stuck in his side, the other deep in his shoulder. The healer and K'aro growled at each other. Bracing himself, he roared as the healer pulled both arrows out. He inspected their tips and then threw them into the ash before moving on to help the others.

"How bad?" Corcundia asked.

"Not bad, my armor is made well," K'aro said.

He smiled at her, then spotted Dro'ka across the field. Sprinting as fast as he could, K'aro reached him with only a few bounds. He grabbed him by the neck and squeezed, trying to crush his larynx. Vitkalla grabbed K'aro by the mane and threw him to the ground. "You're a slave, you can't kill him."

K'aro balled his fist and sprung at Vitkalla. Calmly, Vitkalla side stepped him and wrapped K'aro around the neck with the inside of his elbow. The headlock took K'aro's breath away and knocked him unconscious. Vitkalla dropped him, pulled Dro'ka to his feet and then dragged him away snarling. Mounted on a blue alpurlic, Tro'ka galloped up and looked down at Evorix.

"You're free to go," he growled.

"Oh, how kind of you. We were leaving anyway," Evorix said.

"Don't press your luck, slave," he purred, his eyes turning to slits and his ears flattening against his skull.

"Call me a slave again and you won't be quite so elegant when I finish with you," Evorix said.

Corcundia elbowed him and bowed stiffly. "Thank you for rescuing us. We are in your debt," she said.

Muttering under his breath, Evorix said, "The hell I am."

Tro'ka tilted his head. "What was that, slave?"

"Nothing honored host, we will be leaving," Corcundia said with a disarming smile.

"You can take K'aro with you. He's no use to us," Tro'ka said.

K'aro held his head as he came too and looked at Tro'ka with a sneer.

"I am freeing you from your duties. Travel well K'aro, last of the D'atu," Tro'ka said.

"You're mistaken, I'm not the last of my pride."

Howls of agony could be heard from where the Outkast had dragged Dro'ka and the rest of the Runners. A body impaled on a long spear through the rectum, exited through the warriors mouth.

Arms flailing wildly, Evorix watched a spray of blood project from the body and soon after the remaining Runners were in the same position.

With a chuckle, Tro'ka watched K'aro's face, "You are now."

Dro'ka was the last to be impaled. His eyes were swollen shut and his broken arms flopped around at different angles by his side. The R'atu dragged him back to the center of the battlefield. Vitikalla viciously kicked him behind the knees, sending him to the ash. The other warriors circled around roaring in joy. A warrior placed a spear smeared in animal feces at Tro'ka's feet.

Tro'ka picked it up, wrinkled his muzzle and then glanced at K'aro. "Now you better be going shield brother, we have a dirty business to attend to," he growled.

Dro'ka saw the blade and growled at Tro'ka. "Give me a sword and let me die with honor."

Tro'ka slapped one of his warriors on the shoulder with a loud roar. "Honor, you're talking to an Outkast, we have no honor."

Evorix didn't watch the exchange as he got some horses and helped everyone mount. A warrior shouldered him aside in excitement and joined the group circling Dro'ka. Corcundia watched Dro'ka howl in agony as they impaled him. After a moment she shook her head, looked down at her bloody hands and massaged her knuckles.

"All this death," she whispered to herself.

Evorix glanced at her without a word and then turned his horse around and rode off. Sitting in her saddle, she watched the Ra'tu begin to make small cuts on Dro'ka' body causing him to wiggle as he continued to howl.

K'aro cantered up and asked, "Lady Corcundia, shall we ride?"

A drop of blood welled at the corner of her eye. She closed her fist, twisted it quickly and snapped Dro'ka's neck twenty feet away. His head rolled forward on his chest, then stopped as the blood dripped from his incisors. The R'atu were silent as they turned their attention to her in disbelief.

"Enough. Revenge is not the answer, forgiveness is," she shouted.

Tro'ka and Vitkalla approached her cautiously from the crowd. "You are a Last Blood?" Tro'ka asked.

She smeared the bloody tear away with the palm of her hand. "I was once, yes. Now, I am all that's left."

"The wizards of your group helped us reach the safety of the Fire Lands," Vitkalla purred more to himself than her.

"Yes and we were exterminated by Wolfrya for it."

Vitkalla nodded. "This I know." He stepped closer to her, his shadow flowing over her. "I thank you for helping my pridesmen escape. We number less than a thousand now, but if your people hadn't helped we would be far less," he purred in perfect Delosian.

Corcundia nodded and cut her eyes at K'aro who watched with mild amusement as Vitkalla stared at his paws for a few moments.

"Brother's of the Outkast, hear me!" Vitkalla turned around and roared, raising his spear into the air. "We have to repay a blood debt, one that the old warriors like myself remember. All of you remember the shield brothers who died holding the human's back. What the young warriors don't know is the Last Bloods stayed with those shield brothers, so our cubs could escape."

A few warriors who had survived that costly retreat were standing in the front rank. They nodded at Vitkalla and kneeled.

Vitkalla continued. "The young warriors here must pay it back." He pointed at Corcundia. "That's a Last Blood, the only one of her kind. Many of you don't know but a pact was signed by the elders in every tribe. We promised that we would protect any and all Last Bloods should we ever see them again." Vitkalla paused. "Who will follow me?"

Corcundia whispered to K'aro, "What is he saying?"

K'aro shrugged and dismounted. He pulled his blade and slammed it into the ash. Taking a knee in front of her horse, he said, "I, K'aro, last of the D'atu will follow you into death."

The other warriors roared and raised their spears and shields high above their heads. In unison they shouted, "We of the Ba will ride with you."

Individually, hundreds of Ba warriors made a mark on their forearms and drove their bloody sword tips into the ash. Riding up beside her, Evorix chuckled.

"Whenever you're ready your Highness of Fur. We have to get to Rebellium Headquarters."

She shot him a grim look, unimpressed with his cynical comments. She raised her sword, swung it over her head and pulled the reins of her horse. "On me!"

Chapter 19

"Lord Marus, if we don't attack now, we will lose our advantage," one of his infantry line commanders said.

Marus turned his back to him and looked at the weathered map he was holding. A group of men had ridden back to Iceport and gathered one of the legions, the other two were left in the castle for Octavius' protection.

"Cowardly bastard wont give me all the legion's that I need," Marus muttered.

"Your orders, sir?" asked one of the men at the battle table.

"How many men are battle ready?" Marus asked, not bothering to look up.

"The legion is still marching in. At the moment we have a little over five hundred men. The other half stopped at the crossroads and made camp," his line commander said.

"Shit. They will take at least three more days to straggle in and when they do, they won't be worth shit," another commander added.

Marus looked at the faces around the table, then swiped the battle pieces off the table. "Set it up again and tell me how it's possible with the numbers we have."

"M'lord, perhaps if we had someone on the inside, we could send a band of men to hold the gate," one of his more seasoned officers said.

One of the archery commanders moved a wooden sword and shield representing Legion I closer to the Rebellium camp.

Marus smiled. "We already have a man in there." He stared at the map as a man walked in with a few others and bowed. Marus looked over his shoulder and waved them over.

"What's the news in the camp?" Marus asked.

"It has been done as you planned it, m'lord."

"There will always be a place for you in my war council, Calpernicus," Marus chuckled.

"Thank you, m'lord. I poisoned Valentinian as you asked and the assassin you sent was killed trying to escape, so there are no witnesses. What are your next orders?" Calpernicus asked.

Marus' eyebrow raised. "Did you use his Tears of Tramonia?"

Calpernicus nodded.

"Good. Are you willing to go back in to the camp for more work?" Marus asked.

"You show me my money and I will return to kill anyone you ask."

"Follow me to the treasure chest over by the fire." Calpernicus followed closely behind him and kneeled in front of the chest and ran his hands through the gold with child like pleasure. He picked the coins up and then dropped them through his fingers. The clinking noises gave him a hard on.

"How many soldiers are in the camp?" Marus asked.

"We have roughly six hundred infantry, two hundred archers and a few hundred calvary," Calpernicus replied.

"Any other news?" Marus asked.

"Asinius will be executed tomorrow."

Marus tapped his finger on the table top, tracing the area around them. "I can't let that happen. He must be executed in Iceport, Octavius' orders."

"As you wish, m'lord," Calpernicus replied.

"The legion will wait three nights before we attack. Delay his trial until we appear. Expect us on the fourth morning before the sun rises."

"M'lord," said Calpernicus, bowing low.

Marus followed Calpernicus out and the pair walked into the cold night air. Calpernicus pulled his hood closer to his cheeks. "Always hated the cold," he said.

"Ain't so bad. It beats a wet spring. When we crush the Rebellium and the emperor, what do you want?" Marus asked.

"Crush the emperor?" Calpernicus asked in an octave higher than normal.

"We both have goals and aspirations, Calpernicus. Mine are to rule the world," Marus said.

Calpernicus smiled. "Well in that case, I will be your prefect, your eminence."

Chuckling under his breath, Marus said, "You can read minds?"

"No m'lord, soldiers."

The pair walked around the camp watching the legionnaires clean their weapons and grumble about their porridge. The night sky was clear and the stars above them appeared like drops of silver. Marus stopped in front of a bonfire and warmed his hands. "If you betray me Calpernicus, I'll kill you. You know that right?"

The fire warmed Calpernicus' hands as he stood next to him. "I'm loyal to position and money, Lord Marus. So promote me and pay me." He shrugged and continued. "And I will be loyal to you."

"Like your loyalty to Valentinian?" Marus asked.

Calpernicus ground his teeth at the comment. "I'm no common brigand, prefect, so watch your arrogant tone. I am a simple man with a simple plan. *He* made the mistake of trusting me and died for it. Plain and simple."

With a malicious smile, Marus said, "You are a vicious bastard, aren't you?"

Calpernicus laughed before he responded. "Oh if you only knew Marus, if you only knew," he said, pulling his hood tighter and disappearing into the woods with his fellow conspirators in tow.

Precipitous lay prone in the briar bush he was hiding in during the conversation. He had stayed in the shadows after Marus humiliated him in front of his men, something he could never forgive.

Marus stared intently at the hedgerow for several minutes before walking away. After another few moments passed, Precipitous slowly climbed out of shrubbery and folded his notes.

"Now the fun begins," he said to himself, rubbing dirt across his flesh to blend in to his surroundings.

• • • •

EVORIX'S BAND AND THEIR R'atu entourage arrived outside the Rebellium ringfort thc following morning. A group of Rebellium riders met them halfway from the gate and slowed their horses as they approached.

"You will ride no further until we know who you are and what you want," a man with a pointed goatee said.

"I am Evorix Vispanius, former prefect of Tiberius Victorus. I carry the body of Gius Flavius for the council to see and convey his dying wishes. Now move aside, *commander*."

The riders whispered amongst themselves for a moment and turned their shoulders away from him. "You may follow us, but your slavers aren't welcome," the leader said, pulling his sword from his scabbard.

Corcundia pulled her sword from her right hip and urged her mount forward."Tell me my warriors are not welcome again and I.will.kill.you."

K'aro and Vitkalla followed her and nudged the Rebellium horses with their alpurlics. "Stand down Lady Corcundia. We are here to gather our forces and ride for Tramonia," Aksutamoon said, riding to the front with Trakuta.

Using his mount to create a barrier between the two groups, Evorix held his hand up and pointed to the cart. The leader acknowledged him and pointed to his men to lower their weapons. Evorix smiled, dismounted and then pulled back the tarp covering Gius.

"Here is one of your council elders. Let us pass with our men and bury him with honor," Evorix said, clearing his throat.

"We will give you the road, Lord Evorix. You may follow us, but we must say again——."

Corcundia threw a right hook and knocked the man with the silver goatee out of his saddle. Her warriors roared with laughter and pounded their breastplates in approval.

"Don't get up on my account, I'll show myself in," she said, cantering by the unconscious body.

The peasants inside the ringfort watched partly in terror, partly in awe as the Ba rode two abreast past them. After gawking, most fled inside their homes and shut their doors, hoping to ward off the mythical beasts.

"Why are they frightened," one of the warriors asked K'aro.

"Because of the Runners," K'aro replied before galloping after Corcundia.

Evorix rode to Valentinian's tent and saw the blood splattered across the opening. Calpernicus stepped out covered in white wolf pelts.

"Greetings my fellow travelers and welcome to the Rebellium," he said with a closed fist over his heart.

"We bring Gius Flavius home," Evorix replied, attempting to hide his contempt for Calpernicus.

"Where, where is my old friend?" Calpernicus asked, looking over Evorix's shoulder.

Evorix pulled the tarp back from Gius' bruised and blood splattered face. Calpernicus slowly approached the cart and clenched the railing.

"Who killed him?" he asked.

"A D'atu warrior. We were captured and during our escape from captivity, he was killed. I wish to speak to Lord Valentinian and ask his council on some personal matters.

Calpernicus stared at the Ba warriors in front of him. "You bring slavers with you into my encampment?"

"Call them what you wish. Gius died fighting side by side with them," Evorix countered. "Now, where is Lord Valentinian?"

In a monotone voice, Calpernicus replied, "Lord Valentinian is dead. I am the temporary regent until——well it looks like I'm the true leader with Gius dead," he said, covering him up and motioning for two soldiers to take his body to be cleansed. "I didn't figure you would show up," Calpernicus said.

"Shit, Valentinian is dead?" Evorix muttered.

"Yes."

"Then who's paying me and the Ba?" he asked, glancing at the warriors over his shoulder.

"I will talk to the other elders and arrange payment. Unlike you, rebel commanders honor their debts." He paused and adjusted one of his wolf pelts. "Personally, I was against finding you. You have no honor after killing your father and brother," Calpernicus said, trying to egg him on.

Evorix approached him and closed his fist to strike. "Remember Calpernicus, I would gladly kill you for free."

Calpernicus chuckled. "We will see about that. Come with me and we will talk about the situation with Octavius," Calpernicus said, walking into the tent.

As they approached the war table, Calpernicus asked, "Fancy a drink?"

At the mention of a stiff drink, Evorix's thirst got the better of him. "You know I'd love to have a drink. What have you got?" Evorix asked, licking his dry lips.

"Tears of Tramonia seems the popular choice these days. It was Valentinian's favorite." He stooped down. "Now where is it? It's the damnedest thing when you are looking for something and can never find it."

"Happens to me all the time." Evorix said, looking down at the ash.

He followed the orange trail to the door flap and saw the blood smear across it. He noticed small pieces of flesh mixed in with the ash as he scanned the room.

"Looks like you had a pretty bad fight in here," he said, kneeling down.

"An assassin tried to kill me, but he didn't do well," Calpernicus replied, pointing to the man's head on a spike near the Delsoian globe.

"When did that happen?"

"A couple weeks ago. Why?"

Lightly touching the blood on the flap behind him, Evorix asked, "You sure it was a couple of weeks ago?"

"Ofcourse, ofcourse, ah here we go, I found the bottle. Here let me fill your glass," Calpernicus said, approaching him.

"Speaking of Valentinian, what did he die of?" Evorix asked, taking the full glass from his hand.

"Sudden thing, heart attack. He was over eighty summer you know." Staring through him, Calpernicus didn't try to conceal his hate and contempt. "I wish it had been you," he muttered.

"What was that?" Evorix asked.

"Nothing," Calpernicus said, spinning the globe.

Evorix glanced up from the map with a solemn look on his face. "Don't misunderstand me, I came back because Gius thought I could get to Octavius. I doubt I can, but we will soon find out."

"Yes, we will. I will pay you in full when the job is done," Calpernicus said.

A quick thought jumped into Evorix's mind. *I would love to crush your arrogant throat with my boot. Did you just say you would pay after the job?*

"Pay half up front and I will get ready," Evorix replied.

"Fine," Calpernicus said, raising his glass to his lips.

Evorix lifted his glass in Calpernicus' direction. "Here's to the memory of Gius Flavius and a short life."

Fucking hell, I'm thirsty.

The cup called to his lips. He raised it, but at the last moment something caught his eye at the back of the tent. He saw a body with a white linen cloth covering it. He placed his drink down and walked over to it.

"So rests Valentinian, leader of the Rebellium," Evorix said, staring through the shroud.

A few feet away seated at the table drinking from a mead horn, Calpernicus raised it and said, "He will be buried side by side with Gius. Long may he live."

Blood stains marred the cloth. With a slight movement, Evorix peeled the sheet back and saw the black specs under Valentinians nose and at the corner of his eyes.

This is no heart attack, he was killed by something. He shouldn't smell this bad. Is that the smell of nightshade?

Evorix inhaled deeply and it nearly took his breath away. He turned to ask Calpernicus why there were black specs under Valentinian's nose and just before he turned around, a knife came from behind him. He heard a shriek as Calpernicus' arm was severed at the elbow.

A cloaked figure quickly put a tourniquet on Calpernicus arm as the blood spurted in every direction. Calpernicus' guards and Corcundia's warriors rushed into the tent.

One the Calpernicus' guards tackled Evorix from behind and slammed him into the table. They knocked Valentinian's corpse into the ash as they tussled. Calpernicus' guards formed a circle, backs to one another protecting Calpernicus as he screamed, but the Ba immediately overpowered them.

The screams from the guards slaughter brought more men into the tent. Evorix gasped as the guard attacking him choked him and pummeled his broken ribs. As they fought, the guard reached for a dagger hanging from his belt. Blood sprayed from the guards throat, covering Evorix, temporarily blinding him. The sweet taste of blood touched Evorix's lips as he dry heaved.

Shit, I'm blind.

K'aro grunted and lifted him off the ground. With a swipe of his paw, he cleaned Evorix's face off. He pushed him down into a chair and grabbed one of the last guards, bit into his neck and tore a chunk out, killing him.

Calpernicus whimpered on the floor, his blood draining out into the already orange ash. The new figure swooped down and tightened the tourniquet to stop the flow of blood. Evorix turned to the man, placed his sword at the nape of his neck and pressed down. "I should kill you, but you saved my life. Talk."

The man paused and then pulled his hood back. Evorix smiled wide and embraced his old friend. "Precipitous, what in the hell are you doing here?"

"Saving your life. What does it look like?"

"I thought Octavius executed you. Where have you been hiding?" Evorix asked.

"Working as one of Marus' personal bodyguards. Wasn't too many jobs left for a one handed legionnaire after Tiberius died. Marus gave me work."

Evorix's hand touched Precipitous' shoulder. "I owe you and I'm sorry I didn't take you with me."

Shrugging, Precipitous winked and said, "Glad I could help. There's something you should know though."

Blood dripped from Evorix' sword as he cleaned it with a rag. "What's that?"

"Asinius was captured and is being held in the cages on the outskirts of the fort. Marus will be attacking within a few days time and this piece of shit killed Valentinian with poison. He is Marus' top spy in your camp."

"Is that a fact?" Evorix asked, running his thumb over his blade.

In the blink of an eye, he took his sword, bent down and cut Calpernicus' ear off and threw it over his shoulder.

"I'll take all the time in the world to make sure you suffer. K'aro, keep him alive."

K'aro shook his mane no, looked at Corcundia who nodded, then begrudgingly carried Calpernicus over his shoulder and worked to keep him alive. The other leaders of the Rebellium were sent for and brought to the tent.

Evorix bent down after everyone arrived, snatched the ear off the sand and held it up to his lips as he spoke. "I'm only going to ask this once. Did anyone know or help Calpernicus with the enemy bearing down on this camp? If you tell me now, your death will be quick, but if I find out later, I will have you impaled and marched to the top of a volcano and thrown in. But that will be after I take all your parts," he said, wiggling Calpernicus' ear.

A frail woman stepped forward, head bowed. In a squeaky voice she said, "I have betrayed my oath and helped Calpernicus murder Valentinian."

Before anyone could move, Evorix expelled his hidden dagger from his wrist and slammed it under her larynx at the top of her chest. She made a choking sound, gasped, her eyes wide with terror.

She collapsed and Evorix stepped forward. "Any other honorable souls, or will I find out later?"

The last man in line bolted for the door, knocking Corcundia over. Vitkalla pounced on the man, slashed his throat and threw him back to the center of the room.

"Never touch a Last Blood!" he roared.

The one man left quivered and fell to his knees. Out of nowhere, a bright red apple rolled by Evorix's hand as he leaned against the table. Precipitous smiled at him and ducked out of the tent. Evorix picked it up and bit into it. The juices rolled down his chin and onto the ground.

"What's your name? I don't recognize your face," Evorix said.

The man sobbed uncontrollably as he held the dead woman. Evorix kicked her with his boot. "Why cry over this traitor?"

"This was my sister, Lord Evorix. I had no idea she was aiding the enemy. Please let me take her body and bury it."

"You know what we do with traitors. I don't recognize you. Where are you——?"

Aksutamoon barged in and said, "Kristdrum and his sister Pierrette where once nobles of my father's court in Tramonia. They assassinated him, my mother and brothers when Tiberius was killed, then they disappeared. Is this where all the trash from the realm ends up?"

Looking up with a deep sigh, Kristdrum held his sister close to his chest, salty tears streaming down his cheeks. He heard Aksutamoon's sword slide from its sheath, and then closed his eyes to await the death blow. Aksutamoon's sword crossed another sword above Kristdrum's head sending sparks down his neck.

"No innocents," Corcundia said, slapping the flat of Aksutamoon's blade to the ash.

The skin around Aksutamoon's nose turned beet red, the capillaries flaring blue. "You'll regret this choice. He's a killer and if you turn your back for even the slightest moment, he will gut you and leave you face down in a ditch." He stormed out of the tent followed by Trakuta.

Corcundia took a knee in front of Kristdrum and lifted his quivering chin. "I will protect you, stand and join me."

Kristdrum stood up and bowed low. "Thank you, m'lady."

The Ba warriors walked out of the tent without acknowledging him. "Don't worry human, they will trust you once you prove yourself in battle," Vitkalla said, pulling his helmet over his mane. "That is if you live that long." He said as he followed the others out.

Evorix sent runners to assemble the army within the fort and then walked to Asinius' cage. He approached through the shadows, his hands shaking. He watched Asinius tending Tersius, the rage roaring through his veins. Approaching the cage, Evorix cleared his throat as he stepped out of the shadows.

Asinius chuckled, glanced up and then went back to fighting Tersius' infection. "Asinius, do you not remember what I look like?" Evorix asked.

"Sure I do. However, the boy is dying and I'm no longer a perfect, so I could give two shits where on Delos you are," Asinius said.

With a tortured darkness in his voice, Evorix said, "You killed my wife and now I am here to repay your cowardly move." Pointing to the door, Evorix shouted, "Someone open this door, now!"

A guard ran over and blocked it. Evorix raised an eyebrow not sure why the guard was protecting Asinius.

"No one enters unless Lord Calpernicus says," the guard stammered, keeping his hand on the hilt of his sword.

"Calpernicus, is minus an arm and an ear, move boy!"

"N—."

Evorix's sword ripped into the guards stomach and exited through his back. "Don't worry, I'll let myself in." He lifted the guards chin. "I admire what you did, really I do."

He pushed him off of his blade and onto the ground. He took the key ring from his belt and opened the door. "Now where were we, Asinius?"

Asinius didn't bother to look up and said, "You were about to take my head. Fine with me, but let me finish tending to Primus' boy, Tersius."

"Who?"

"Tersius, son of Primus of West Drathia, nephew to Gius Flavius."

Evorix moved closer. "Shit." His look softened. "I'm going to regret not taking your head and mounting it on a pike, but follow me. I have someone who will help you save him." He squeezed Asinius shoulder, nearly breaking his clavicle. "But our problems are far from over."

Chapter 20

Octavius stood on the senate floor and stared at the faces of the Wolfryan aristocracy. He felt the bile in his throat rise as he looked around in disgust.

A man from the crowd shouted, "Imperator, what you ask of us is lunacy."

"Lunacy? Lunacy to me is why you're still alive Senatore Brilla."

"I can not be touched. Not without the consent of the senate," Senatore Brilla said smugly.

Octavius snapped his fingers as several crossbow bolts flew from the elevated balcony above them and slammed into Brilla from the front and back simultaneously.

"And now you can," Octavius replied.

The senatore's body rolled down the black marble steps. His white toga opened slightly as he hit the floor, blood oozing from his wounds.

"Now that I have everyone's attention. We will be going to war as soon as I can muster the legions. My prefect isn't dealing with my problems fast enough. I have received word about the location of the Rebellium camp," Octavius said, once again scanning the faces.

The senators grumbled amongst themselves, ensuring the emperor didn't hear them. If we attack the Rebellium camp, we will be open to attack from the Kingdom of Draco to the south, Tramonia to the west and the northern tribes in Batopia," shouted one of the younger senatore's.

Octavius ran his fingers across his throat. One of his guards fired a bolt and hit the young senatore between the eyes. His brain matter splattered on the senatores behind him as he slumped onto the bench he had been sitting on.

"That's one less vote to contend with. Now, who is going to disband this law so the legions may march into Iceport and ready the conscripts?"

The senatore's stared at their brown leather sandals while Octavius strutted like a peacock in front of them, looking for allies.

Only one senatore held his gaze.

"So, let this be a lesson to the rest of you. You can be killed whenever I deem it. I run Delos, you just visit to lick my sandals. Is there not one man here who sees my dream?" Octavius asked.

"I do your highness," said the middle aged senatore who was missing both hands.

The senatore who had spoken had lost his hands during the Rebellium campaign and had been medically discharged from the infantry. The physicians experimentally attached hooks to the end of each of his wrists to help him cope with the loss. The other senatores hissed their disapproval as he walked down from the top tier.

"Senatore Quillen, I heard word you returned to your home in the countryside. Why come back?"

"I'm not much of a farmer Imperator, I'm your senatore."

Octavius smiled. "Good. I need a new prefect."

"What of Marus, your highness?" he asked.

A droplet of blood fell from Octavius' nostrils as he screamed, "I have demoted him. Do you understand me?

When I see him again, I will have him executed," he screeched.

"As you wish," Quillen said, bowing low.

"Follow me, senatore Quillen," Octavius said, his voice returning to normal.

As they neared the door to the senate floor, Octavius turned around. "Now, I am fed up with this group of cowards. I don't need your approval."

He raised his arm up and the guards leaned over the balcony with their crossbows strung. Shouts of confusion could be heard as the senatore's tried to run as the command was given.

"Fire!"

As the doors closed, Octavius waved to the senatore's as they attempted to flee. "The meek will never inherit Delos, I am an immortal god," he shouted, holding Quillen by the back of neck, forcing him to watch.

Screams echoed from the senate floor as bolts penetrated flesh. The men tripped and pushed each other in a desperate attempt to escape. A lone figure ran for the door and slipped through as it closed. He tripped as he took the marble steps two at a time.

The senatore rose to his knees and held his hands up. "Please Imperator, I beg for my life. I have a wife and children. I have been loyal to you."

Octavius stood over the senatore and asked Quillen, "Do you have a wife and child?"

"No, I married the senate, Imperator."

He smiled at Quillen's answer. "That's the answer I'm looking for. Go in peace senatore and marry the senate."

The pair strolled further down the road. The senator smiled and sighed and then brushed himself off. A bolt slammed into his shoulder knocking him forward, two more hit him in the lower back. He sank to his knees, arms outstretched. "Imp——." A last bolt hit him in the center of the back, cutting him short.

The pair turned around and Octavius said, "I love giving men hope, but he should have married the senate."

Quillen stared at the man's body, palms clammy, and then continued down the cobblestone path. He tried to look busy, rubbing the dirt off of his toga with his hooks.

"Your first order of business as prefect is to round up all of the senator's families and execute them."

"What of the women and children?"

"Perhaps you misunderstood me, prefect. I mean kill everyone. Women, children, pets. They must all die so no one will come for revenge. Never leave a girl or boy to turn into a threat after the bones of their ancestors have been ground to dust."

"I understand, Imperator. It shall begin tonight," Quillen whispered.

"Never question me again, Quillen, or you will be next." He patted Quillen's cheek. "I have killed for less, much less."

Octavius moved on with his entourage of guards that had caught up to them and left Quillen standing in the roadway. Once he was back at the palace, Octavius walked to his room. His bed lay in the center of the room with stained glass windows on either side.

Blood ran from his nostrils as he closed the door behind him. He put a rag up to his nose and tried to stop the bleeding. Once it subsided, he took his wine glass and filled it to the rim. He searched frantically for his belladonna leaves, then felt a sense of ease and comfort after he found them.

The hallucinations began an hour later, causing him to grin wildly and foam at the mouth. A slave was brought to his room and Octavius took a long wooden paddle off the wall.

He bent the man over, lifted his toga and whispered, "I rule the world!"

He swung the paddle against his rear end until he began to bleed. The man begged for the torture to stop, crying out in agony. Octavius lifted his head by the hair and slowly slid a knife across his throat. Laughing, the emperor sat on the bed, drank more wine and ate more belladonna leaves until he passed out.

• • • •

THE FOLLOWING MORNING, Quillen walked over the bodies in the road stifling his gag reflex. It had been a horrific night for the senatore class. He saw the men, women and children hanging from lengths of rope, the others lay where they had been standing when the legionnaires ransacked the neighborhood.

Wisps of smoke rose from the burned out huts that housed the senatores families. A boy no older than twelve tried to pull on his pant leg and plead for help with his eyes. As Quillen bent down to help, the boy sighed, laid his head down and died.

"This is what I wanted to see, prefect. You take care of what I want without question. I like it." Octavius lifted a man's head near them with one of his sandals, clicked his tongue and sneered. "Dead."

"It's as you wish, Imperator," Quillen said, bowing low to keep his clammy hands hidden from view.

A wide grin crossed Octavius' lips. He stepped on the bodies to keep from stepping in the torrent of blood flowing through the streets. Quillen watched him and tried not to look at the bodies as he passed them. The guards sent to kill the families walked past him and saluted. He returned the gesture and wiped the water from the corner of his eyes.

"Quillen, are you ready for your next task?" Octavius asked.

"I am."

"Then ride with me to find Legion II north of here." Octavius leaned closer to Quillen's ear. "Help me wipe out Legion I."

Quillen's eyes grew large as saucers. "Imperator, they——."

"Are dead men," he screeched, his voice breaking an octave.

He struck Quillen, then kept striking him as his guards stood by and watched. No one intervened when Octavius was beating someone or they would be next. Quillen sank to his knees and took the beating. He knew if he touched the emperor even in self defense, he would be killed.

"Now, do you understand me?" Octavius screeched.

"Yes Imperator, I do," Quillen replied, staring at the ground.

"Good, now ready the men and meet me at the palace."

An hour later, Quillen and the Imperial guardsmen waited in the palace courtyard. The emperor walked down the palace steps wearing a gold breast plate and a silver helmet with red horse hair that was a little too tight for his head.

A few chuckles could be heard from the men as they watched the overweight peacock mount his horse. The emperor farted as he mounted the horse.

"Let's get a move on, prefect. Unless you need another beating."

Quillen rode behind him and didn't speak the first day until they made camp. Octavius walked up to him and said, "I'm sorry I lost my temper earlier. It happens sometimes."

"That's alright your highness," he replied, tepidly, making eye contact.

Octavius struck him over the head and shouted, "I'm not sorry, you ignorant ape. I should never apologize to the likes of you. You do as I say."

Quillen put his hand over his bloody scalp and said, "Yes."

Octavius sneered. "Yes what?"

"Yes, Imperator."

"Pathetic," Octavius muttered, mounting his horse.

The emperor disappeared into the night followed by his men. Cursing under his breath, Quillen galloped behind them trying to ignore the pain from his bloodied skull. They finally stopped where Legion II was camped at the crossroads. Octavius cantered into camp as the men got to their feet and bowed their heads.

The lead infantry commander strode from his tent and said, "Imperator, I didn't know you were coming. I'm afraid I'm not prepared, but you may take my quarters."

"They will do," he replied.

Octavius whispered to one of his guards and pointed at the infantry commander. The legionnaire walked up to the commander and stuck a knife into his neck. The commander stared at him, his mouth flapping like a fish caught in a net.

"Now, who wants to take his place?" Octavius asked.

"I will," Quillen said, stepping in front of the other commanders.

"Quillen, haven't you had enough trouble for one day?"

"Allow me to redeem myself, Imperator," Quillen said.

"Not likely, but I will honor your request. I will more than likely kill you tomorrow," Octavius replied with a flick of his wrist.

Quillen bowed low. "As you wish, Imperator."

"Get this army in order. We leave at daybreak," Octavius said, putting a belladonna leaf in his gum line as he walked into the tent to lay down.

Quillen looked around at the men and shouted, "Infantry commanders on me."

The commanders walked up to the bonfire he stood in front of warming his hooks. An old habit that he didn't mind keeping. "Legion I will decimate Legion II tomorrow as the emperor commands."

The men grumbled under their breath and one was even bold enough to ask, "And what of the senate. He must have their approval?"

"They do not exist anymore commander, nor do their families. Octavius runs Iceport by himself now and if you want to live, you will follow his command and attack Marus' legion. Any questions?" Quillen asked.

The men stared at their feet, noticing every pebble in the dirt. "Dismissed."

Quillen took a knee and scraped some dirt onto his other hook and let it fall to the ground. He whispered, "Like sand in the wind."

Chapter 21

Tersius rested peacefully on a bed in the medical tent, his wound scabbing over. K'aro had been able to save him with a salve only used on Ba warriors. Evorix glanced in K'aro's direction and nodded his head in thanks.

Calpernicus lay by a fire outside whimpering, praying for a miracle that would never come. He was tied to a tent pole that had been hammered into the ground. K'aro had expertly cauterized his wounds, nearly killing him in the process. Evorix smiled and took a knee next to Calpernicus and held his chin up.

"Calpernicus," Evorix whispered.

Calpernicus ignored him as he wept, staring into the fire. Evorix slapped him viciously across the face and shouted, "Calpernicus, listen to me, you're dying. Do the right thing and help us win this battle."

Calpernicus' smile dripped with blood. "Fuck you! I chose a side a long time ago."

"And what side is that?" Evorix asked, raising an eyebrow.

After a desperate laugh, Calpernicus hissed, "Mine."

Evorix bristled, tightening his grip on Calpernicus' chin. "This is either going to happen the easy way, the hard way, or my way. It's your choice."

Calpernicus spit blood in Evorix's face and chuckled. "Do your best."

Evorix pulled a hammer from behind his back and brought it down on Calpernicus' toes. Eyes bulging in pain, he shrieked as white bubbly spit flew from the corner of his mouth.

"Ready to talk?" Evorix shouted.

"Fuc——." His sentence was cut short from the blows of the hammer hitting his shin bones. The pain felt like a horse kicked him as he tried to roll around holding his shattered shin bones. "Oh you mot————."

Evorix brought the hammer down on his ribs, breaking several per blow. Blood dripped from both sides of Calpernicus' mouth. Some of the Ba warriors watched and growled amongst themselves, nodding their manes in approval. They watched the bloody hammer rise above Evorix's head and slam down on Calpernicus' fingers a few more times, turning his other hand to a bloody pulp.

"Now, tell me what I want to know," Evorix shouted again.

Blood leaked from Calpernicus' lips as he let out a tittering laugh. "Fine, I'll tell you. Just make it stop."

Evorix threw the hammer over his shoulder. "Fine, talk."

"Marus will attack three nights from tonight, on the fourth morning. I was supposed to keep the gate open with my men."

Looking over his shoulder, Evorix made eye contact with Trakuta and said, "Take some warriors and kill his men."

Trakuta turned to go. "Trakuta," Evorix said.

Trakuta turned around. "Do it slowly."

Trakuta nodded and left the tent. Evorix turned back to Calpernicus and slammed his knife through his pulpy hand, pinning it to the sand. His tortured screams caused the men standing around them to cover their mouths and more than one man gagged.

"How many men does he have?" Evorix shouted.

"Two." Blood dripped from Calpernicus' bottom lip. "Agh fuck, one thousand in camp and the other thousand are still marching up from Iceport."

"What's Marus' plan?" Corcundia stepped up, joining the conversation.

Gasping in pain, Calpernicus spit up pools of blood. "He will attack once they receive the signal from me that all is clear."

"What's the signal?" she pressed.

"I can't——."

"Like hell you can't. Perhaps a little motivation." Evorix said, pulling a scalding hot poker from the fire. He laid it across Calpernicus' eyes and burned them out.

"Now, tell me and I will end your suffering."

Rolling in the ash made the pain worse. Finally in a moment of clarity, Calpernicus screeched, "Two fire arrows at the same time. Kill me. For the mercy of the Gods, kill me."

Evorix pulled a blade from the back of his boot, flipped it in his hand and then slammed it into Calpernicus' brain stem. He caught his head and lowered him gently into the ash with a sigh.

Gods, I despise torture. But it's the only way for me to find out the good information.

"Sound the assembly horn. I need to speak with the army," Evorix said, wiping the blood from his hands.

One of the men with him nodded and blew the assembly chords from his bugle. Trakuta returned and threw Calpernicus' tortured men at Evorix's feet. Trakuta had left one man alive for the information needed. Evorix looked at the man with disgust.

"Find out what we need to know and assemble the army," he said to Trakuta.

An hour later, the army assembled and Evorix stood erect on top of a supply wagon and addressed the crowd.

"I am Evorix Vispanius of Wolfrya, many of you know me and for those who do not I am a disgraced prefect. I came here on a job that paid me to kill Octavius, not to protect you, but here we are. You people are here because you believe in a cause. Personally, I care more about two goats trying to fuck a doorknob in Iceport, than I do about your Rebellium."

Boos and curses resounded from the crowd.

Evorix gave a curt laugh, then continued, "And what's worse, you idiots believe we aren't dead. I pity you ignorant fools. But we have a common problem coming down the road to wipe this place out because of a traitor in our midst." The crowd booed again. "But we have found him. Behold the ones who sold you out for coin."

The Ba warriors hoisted Calpernicus and the others into the air, their bodies dangling like marionette puppets to the poles holding their weight.

"Here's what we do with traitors. Those who aren't with us, are against us. I will open the doors for an hour for those who want to leave. If you stay, gear up."

Evorix got down and walked to the armory. Upon entering, he found a cold forge. "Someone get this thing going, now." He glanced at some of the men with him and said, "They will have ladders, ready the repelling poles. We will dig a ditch and drive stakes into the ground to help stop their calvary."

"Where do you want us?" K'aro asked.

"In reserve. This is not your fight," Evorix said.

He purred with laughter and said, "We fight and we die, Evorix. It is what we do and it's the only way we live." K'aro roared as the others with him pumped their fists. "We will help forge weapons and armor. How much time do we have?"

"Two, best case scenario three days," Precipitous said, walking up to the forge.

How do I make a rock solid defense in two days. I can't run anymore. I'll take Marus with me though.

"Evorix, what are your orders?" Precipitous asked.

Evorix's scalp glistened as he ran his fingers over it. The men looked on in anticipation, waiting for orders.

How did I ever get myself into this?

After a few moments someone said, "Evorix, what do——."

His mind snapped back from his daydream. "Precipitous, you and the Ba are in charge of the armory. Get the smiths going and make as many traps, projectiles, swords and shields that you can." He looked at Trakuta. "You have the stakes and ditch digging operations. When we get into battle, you will lead the archers."

Asinius approached the group and said, "And what of me?"

Evorix picked up an ingot of steel, inspected it and ignored Asinius. "Ain't your fight either. Back to your cage, slave."

A guard walked over to Asinius to tie his hands behind his back. As the guard tied his hands, Asinius said, "Gius is dead, hell all the leadership of the Rebellium is. You need me, so give me a sword."

"No chance," Evorix said.

Digging his heels in the ground, Asinius pushed the guard off and crossed his arms. "Let's clear the air shall we, prefect Vispanius. I did what I was ordered to do, no more, no less. You want to blame someone, blame Octavius."

Evorix glared at him. "Don't be an asshole, Asinius. Does Tersius know you killed his mother?" he asked, looking up from the map he was studying.

Asinius gave him a frozen stare and replied, "He wouldn't understand."

Evorix chortled, then shrugged. "What, that you fucked his mother and he could possibly be yours? And that it was easier to pawn him off on Primus' stupid ass. You really are a piece of work, Asinius. I don't believe he would like you as much if he knew. What do you think?"

Asinius stammered. "I did as my emperor comm——."

Evorix moved with lighting speed from the table and stared him in the eye with his finger inches from his nose. "Screw your loyalty. You should get what's fair, but life isn't fair. I'll kill Octavius and you too. It's only a matter of time, only a matter of time."

Asinius pushed him back and said, "I don't care about your threats. I may only have one eye, but I can still see enough to kill you. Now where do you need me?"

Evorix stared around the room for support and found none.

I should kill this son of a whore right now.

Evorix's hand crept slowly to the hilt of his sword. Corcundia walked up behind him and pushed his hand away.

"We need all the swords we can get and this is a sword if I'm not mistaken."

"No, it's not. He's a walking death dealer and he will slit our throats while we sleep," Evorix said.

Corcundia moved in front of him. "You owe me two men and now I have them. I'll take Asinius and Kristdrum as replacements."

Shit, she's right.

"Whatever you need to do, m'lady. But when you get your throat cut, I'll make sure I bury you in a shallow grave," Evorix said.

"Why shallow?" K'aro asked.

"For the dogs to find her," Evorix said, walking out of the armory.

• • • •

TWO NIGHTS HAD PASSED before Marus led the men of Legion I into the valley. Evorix looked through his spyglass at the individual faces marching in. The army came to a stop half a mile from the fort. A lone horseman rode in front of the assembled men with his pennet snapping in the wind. Evorix's commanders stood on the rampart with him.

Alright you dirty bastard. Now, we'll see who the better man is, Evorix thought.

"They have a lot of men," Corcundia said, wiping the sweat from her eyebrows.

Asinius, who was standing next to her instinctively touched the hilt of his sword. "The best in Delos. They've never lost a battle."

"That's right and we are going to use it to our advantage," Evorix said.

"We are outnumbered two to one. How do you propose we win?" Aksutamoon asked.

Tapping the stone wall in front of him, Evorix said, "They don't know the Ba are here. Let's give the signal for them to attack and then see where we are when the dust settles."

"Figured you would run like a coward," Corcundia said.

Evorix's spyglass glinted in the sun as he scanned the legion ranks again. "Nah, can't run anymore. Got to fight."

Corcundia laughed. "You're a coward, why not run?"

He glared at her. "I wasn't always and I can choose when and if I run. If you value your neck attached to your body." He stared through her. "I would shut it."

Trakuta looked around at the legion as it assembled. "Let's get this fight started. My daggers are itching for a body."

K'aro, Vitkalla and Tro'ka waited for Evorix at the bottom of the rampart. The Ba stood a head above the average soldier. Their shields rested side by side in a phalanx, the butt of their ten foot spears in the ash.

Vitkalla walked away with Corcundia as K'aro and Tro'ka sat on a wagon wheel nearest them and spoke to Evorix. Tro'ka handed Evorix a flask of wine. Evorix declined.

"Human, we will lead this fight. Open the gate and let them in," Tro'ka growled.

"No, I said it before. It ain't your fight."

"And we told you how we live our life. Now, a handful of our best warriors will guard Corcundia, the others will march out into the valley after we slaughter the men at the gate."

"There are a thousand legionnaires out there, many who I trained. They are good, real good. You have at best four hundred warriors. It's nearly three to one," Evorix said.

Tro'ka purred softly. "Good odds for any warrior. We are the Outkast for a reason. Do you know why?"

Evorix shook his head. "Because we have killed our own people and it carries a sentence of death." He showed him the brand of the open eye on his arm. "Human, behold warriors who are already dead, their bodies just don't know it yet."

"You're mad. You know that right?" Evorix asked.

Growling their approval, they nodded.

Trakuta ran up to Evorix. "Are you ready?"

"Yes, bring all commanders here," Evorix said.

A few moments later the commanders kneeled in front of him. "This is our plan," Evorix said, grabbing a stick to draw the fort in the sand.

"The Ba will be at our center and when the gate opens let Marus' calvary ride through and engage. Archers will line the wall, here, here, and here," he said, pointing to the front and sides of the fort.

"And what about the infantry and our calvary?" Precipitous asked, looking down at the crude drawing.

"We will open the back gate and our horsemen will ride out and flank them. Should we be overwhelmed, fall back to the inner wall. Now, who will lead the cavalry charge?"

"I will," Zillas said, stepping forward with a hiccup, sipping on a wine bottle.

"Zillas, you're dead drunk. Go and sit down somewhere," Evorix said, tightening his own armor.

The tip of Zillas' blade nicked Evorix's chin. Trakuta and Precipitous' moved their blades to his throat before he could blink.

"Not a smart move, drunk," Trakuta said, pushing the blade harder against Zillas neck.

"Easy Trakuta." Evorix touched his bloody chin. "You owe allegiance to Octavius, Zills. Why the change?"

Moving Trakuta's knife from his throat, Zillas replied, "I was told to get captured. Asinius knows my story and so does Precipitous. I asked to lead the charge because I have the most knowledge of where they are—-" He hiccuped. "The weakest. I may look drunk, but I ain't as drunk as I look," he said, swaying.

"The calvary will be outnumbered four to one. You can't commit. It must be a shock hit, then retreat. Understand? Evorix asked.

"Agreed, now can I ride one of those?" he asked with another hiccup.

"You really are a drunk idiot," Precipitous muttered.

"If this human is crazy enough to charge their flank, we will give him an alpurlic," Tro'ka said.

"I'll take that one," Zillas said, pointing at K'aro.

He sneezed and fell over. Evorix roared with laughter after K'aro understood what Zillas said. K'aro growled and looked down at him with disgust as he was drug away.

"And who will lead my infantry?" Evorix asked.

"I will," Tersius said, pulling his chainmail over his head.

"You are in no shape to fight," Asinius said, pushing to the front.

"You're not my father, Asinius. Butt out." Evorix guffawed and looked over at Precipitous who tried to hide the smile that crossed his lips. "What's so funny?" Tersius asked.

"Not a thing Tersius, not a thing. Do you think you're strong enough to lead them?" Evorix asked.

"Ofcourse I am. Why would I say it if I weren't."

Evorix smiled. "I bet you are." He handed some papers to Asinius. "Asinius leads, you follow."

Tersius opened his mouth to protest, but Evorix stared at him and shook his head. Muttering curses under his breath, Tersius stormed out of the tent followed by Asinius.

"Now back to business. I will be on the rampart with Precipitous and Trakuta." He glanced over at Aksutamoon. "I will need you and a handful of men firing the repeating crossbows on the ramparts. Load your quills and aim for the flanks."

"Why the flanks?" Aksutamoon asked.

"It will bunch Marus' men closer together and when the calvary hits them, hopefully, they'll break and run."

Aksutamoon's face reddened. He pointed at Evorix, then outside and shouted, "You're an idiot. Those are the members of Legion I and they will not break and run. They took out half my army on a field like this one years ago. Breaking and running just isn't their thing."

Tro'ka stepped forward. He eyed Aksutamoon as if he were an ant on a hill and said, "They may have, but you never had us. Let us begin."

"And what are you going to do?" Aksutamoon asked.

Tro'ka pulled his helmet over his mane. "We'll win."

The Rebellium army slowly came into formation as the stars moved in overhead. The flames from the torches around the fort fluttered in the cool breeze as it cascaded over the walls.

The army lay in wait for the signal, a look of anticipation crossing most of their features. Evorix walked over to Trakuta and asked, "Ready?"

"Heaven holds a place for the dearly departed," Trakuta replied with a wink.

Pulling back his bow string, Trakuta fired both arrows at the same time to give Marus the signal. They thudded into the ash a hundred yards away from the wall. A few moments later hoof beats could be heard echoing across through the darkness, hiding whatever was riding to meet them.

Trakuta looked at Evorix and said, "See you in Hell."

I'm glad all these nuts are on my side. I pity my old friends in Legion I.

Evorix waved to Trakuta and walked to the center of the rampart with Precipitous and yelled down into the fort, "Open the gate!"

The gate groaned open, making it appear empty in the darkness.

Precipitous glanced at Evorix and smiled. "Got a surprise for you."

He glanced at a Rebellium soldier and nodded. Lighting an arrow, the soldier waited until he heard the hard breathing from the horse's. Evorix heard Precipitous mutter, "Boom."

The area twenty yards in front of the fort illuminated, blinding anyone looking directly at it. The wall of flame drove across the ash for several hundred yards, swallowing both man and horses. Their screams chilled Evorix's blood as he watched the scene of terror. Skin melted from fat and tissue down to the bone. Evorix ground his teeth as he watched.

Precipitous laughed and then walked over to his section of the front wall. Over his shoulder, he cackled, "Packs a punch, don't it?"

The second wave of horses rode over the flames, the pitch sticking to their hooves. Evorix shouted, "Nock!"

Precipitous shouted a command a few feet away. "Loose!"

Riders were thrown off wounded horses, trampled or flung from the saddle by the arrows. As the waves of calvary continued forward, deep growls and roars were heard from inside the fort. In a wedge formation the Outkast surged through the open gate, their spears shimmering in the moonlight. They stabbed everything in sight as they weaved through the legionnaires.

Tro'ka shouted, "Who are we!"

"Outkast!"

"What do we do?" Vitkalla roared, ramming his spear through two legionnaires.

The warriors advanced a few steps and made a shield wall. "Kill.Die.Repeat."

Aksutamoon raised his arm "Ready!" He dropped his arm and shouted, "Loose!"

The large quills from the mounted crossbows flew at a fast cyclic rate and impaled the men and pinched the edges of the legion together. Fire pots raked the stone walls from below and killed some of the Rebellium soldiers. Their bodies tumbled onto the Ba warriors below them in the courtyard. The Rebellium soldiers began to retreat in a panic as the legionnaires surged forward with ladders, oblivious to the carnage at their feet.

"Hold the line, damnit. I said hold the line," Evorix shouted, pushing his men back to the wall.

A legionnaire leapt over the wall and swung his sword at Aksutamoon who tripped over his own feet. The legionnaire's sword flew back over the wall, a thin misericorde blade stuck out from the man's forehead. Evorix pulled the blade out, grabbed the man by the throat and then threw him off the rampart. Evorix reached his hand down and pulled Aksutamoon to his feet.

"And that makes two, *King* Aksutamoon."

"Shut it."

The stone earthworks around them exploded, covering them as more clay jars were thrown over the wall.

"What the hell are they throwing at us?" Trakuta shouted at Evorix as he dabbed blood from his temple.

Evorix shrugged. "Wolfryan Pots."

"What the hell is a Wolfryan Pot?"

Yelling above the din of battle, Evorix said, "They explode with some kind of black powder. The thrower lights a wick, it burns down and then." He swung his hands and made the sound of an explosion.

A legionnaire scampered over the wall, knocked Evorix down and raised his sword over his head. Tersius grabbed the legionnaire from behind, slit his throat and kicked him back over the wall. Another legionnaire came over the wall and stabbed at Tersius. He parried the blow and slammed his sword through his attacker's eye socket.

Legionnaires swarmed over the wall a few at a time, then in larger numbers killing all in their path. More Rebellium soldiers ran up the rampart, attempting to push them back.

"Line up, and hold.this.line!" Precipitous shouted as Evorix ran to the Ba in the courtyard.

Evorix tried to block out the sounds of the children screaming in pain and fright as the women of the Rebellium fought and died side by side with their men.

Bounding down the steps, Evorix knocked a small boy over as he clutched his mother's corpse to his breast. Evorix stared at them for a moment, his own mother's face staring back at him.

"Boy, you need to run to the rallying point and hide. I'll make sure your mother gets evacuated." The boy hesitated, kissed his mother's forehead and then ran. Evorix saw the women gasping and finished the job.

Looking at her body, he felt a tug at his heart. He grabbed the woman's dirt and blood caked arms and crossed them over her chest. Searching for the Ba warriors, he watched them re-form into a wedge and push the legionnaires out of the gate. Horses, alpurlics, soldiers, warriors and legionnaires lay dead around him, their limbs contorted and crushed.

Corcundia stayed in the center of the group as it surged forward and rolled back. An arrow flew by Evorix's head, hit her and knocked her to the ground. Vitkalla threw his helmet off, ran to her and picked her up. He roared and his men parted as he sprinted to the rallying point. A small band of warriors formed a line and step by step followed his retreat.

I hope she isn't dead.

Evorix ran to Zillas and the calvary waiting by the back gate. Their leather armor creaked as they sat in their saddles.

"Zillas, ride into their flank. Show no mercy."

Zillas saluted and urged his alpurlic toward the door. Evorix saw him sway in the saddle and sighed.

My victory depends on a drunk.

A soldier opened the gate and the calvary began to ride out. Evorix turned around, grabbed Zillas' bridle at the last moment and said, "And Zillas, a bottle of Tramonian wine awaits your return. Come right back."

"You know how to get my loyalty. As you wish, m'lord. Gettup," he said, urging his alpurlic forward.

A pale soldier limped up to Evorix bleeding from numerous wounds. "Asinius sent me to tell you the left flank is caving in, m'lord. What are your orders?"

"Fall back to the rallying point. The Ba will hold them back. Sound regroup," Evorix shouted to the bugler as he looked for his commanders.

Asinius' messenger stumbled toward the crumbling wall. As he crossed the corpse laden courtyard, a flaming arrow hit him in the neck, killing him and the message.

Evorix swore under his breath and looked at the bugler as he sounded retreat. He rubbed the perspiration from his neck as he watched the left flank disintegrate, his men slaughtered. The remaining rebel soldiers routed, their numbers dwindling as the few trained men left formed a shield wall and fought a retreating action.

The soldiers stepped back calmly, one step at a time. The blue livery of the rebellium mixed in with the white tunics the Wolfryan's wore. They fell one by one during the retreat, trying to hold back the overwhelming force of legionnaires swarming around them. Wolfryan pots broke across the shield wall causing more chaos.

Evorix rallied as many veterans as he could and shouted, "Turtle formation on me. Head for those buildings."

His veterans were cold, calculating and calm. They moved into position, shields interlocking. The rear guard action bottle necked the legionaries between the two burning buildings. He looked at one of his grizzled veterans and said, "Hold them as long as you can. I must organize the last defense. Can you hold?"

The old man standing with a young boy smiled, knowing what the order would take to complete. "We will hold the line, m'lord. Get a move on," he said and then shouted, "Turtle formation, push forward, push them back boys, push them back!"

The soldiers groaned in effort and began to push the defenders back.

The archers on the second ring wall covered the last of the defenders as they retreated. The soldiers were barely able to close the gate behind them as more legionnaires sprinted past the formation and stood in front of the gate.

"Bring it down," Evorix shouted, his hands cupped around his mouth.

The last trick Evorix had up his sleeve were the most potent liquids known on Delos. The molten black, red and silver liquid flowed down the connecting pipes and spewed from the gargoyles mouths mounted on the wall. The boiling pitch, harvested lava and boiling mercury melted everyone within ten feet.

Precipitous ran up to Evorix, his false hand missing. "The calvary, by the gods, they did it."

"Where's your hand?"

"Some bastard ripped it off when I kicked him over the rampart."

Evorix slid his hand over his mouth, stifling a laugh.

Sad, a man can't even keep his fake hand.

Cheers from behind the wall started low, then grew louder. "Zillas, Zillas, Zillas!"

Zillas' black alpurlic with a white mane reared up on its hind legs, then ripped into the disorganized line. The calvary chewed a gap through the legionnaires seven horses across and then swung around the fort and reentered. The remaining men from the legion retreated as the calvary crushed their flank. Evorix scanned the horizon.

Maybe we can win this.

"Never in Wolfrya's history has a legion retreated. Especially not Legion I!" Precipitous exclaimed.

It's surreal, how could they break and run. Unless...

Fireballs soared silently over them and crashed into the castle wall, sending bodies through the air.

Shit, I knew it.

"Take cover," Evorix shouted as another fireball exploded around them, setting more men on fire.

"The wall can't take many more hits. We have to retreat to where they can't hit us," Trakuta said, supporting Aksutamoon.

"King Aksutamoon, are you ok?" Precipitous asked, helping support him.

Aksutamoon nodded.

"Retreat to the last ring and hold the line. I will take a few volunteers out there and disable the catapults."

"It's suicide, you can't do that," Precipitous said.

"Who's going to stop me from going, you?"

Precipitous bit his lip. The remaining commanders avoided making eye contact with him. "Now, who's coming with me?" Evorix asked.

"I'll go," Kristdrum said, stepping forward.

"Survivors guilt getting to you?" Evorix asked, rubbing the grey ash across his face.

"No, redemption for my family's name," he replied.

"I see. Just make sure you know whose side you're on. Any other volunteers?"

"I'm in," Tersius said.

"I forbid it," Asinius replied, stepping forward.

"I can take care of myself," Tersius said, stripping down nude with the others and covering himself in ash.

"We will return shortly. In the meantime retreat and organize our final defences. We will burn those catapults, then flee back here. Cover us with the archers and crossbows if we have any left."

A few more young soldiers volunteered to help and then the group disappeared into the air. They waited in the ash for most of the night after the legion retreated. The fireballs had stopped an hour before, having run out of ammunition.

Evorix's group slid across the valley floor and crawled hand over fist to the legion's perimeter. The guards dozed, oblivious to the fact that someone would assault their camp.

"Split into three teams of two. Tersius, you're with me. There will be a pile of clay pots somewhere near here. Find them, light one and destroy your catapults before they collect more ammunition," Evorix hissed, his voice shattering the silent air around them.

"Then what?" one of the soldiers asked.

Evorix got into a squatting position. "Run like hell."

The groups split up in search of the pots and discovered them close to the center of the camp. Kristdrum motioned for the men with him to destroy their catapults. He saluted Evorix and waited for the explosion.

"What is he doing?" Tersius asked, watching Kristdrum crawl forward toward the sleeping guards .

"Being a damn fool, move boy." Evorix said as he shoved him back toward the fort. He lit his clay pot and then followed behind him. The explosions killed several of the volunteers who couldn't get far enough away from the blast.

Kristdrum stood up and rotated his sword in his palm, a look of serenity on his face. A moment later, the sane face had a warlike expression. He cursed at the legionaries, pounded his bare chest and stood his ground as the legionnaires barreled toward him.

His voice boomed above the heat from the burning catapults and dead bodies.

"I am Kristdrum of the Rebellion. Killer of the Tramonian royal family. Who will challenge me?"

The legionnaires charged him. He slew three before a sword nicked the artery on his sword arm. He picked up a spear and ran it through two more men. He pushed on the spear handle until they crashed into the bonfire.

A sword blow from behind chopped his head off and it rolled away. Kristdum's body dropped, then fell into the fire, his dead eyes looking up at his killer. Marus picked his head up by the hair and then threw it in the fire.

"Bring me their heads!"

Marus and his horsemen galloped behind Evorix and Tersius as they sprinted for the fort. The arrows from the legionnaires bows came within inches of their heels.

"Run boy. I'll draw them off," Evorix shouted.

Evorix ran parallel to the fort and continued sprinting until he could hear the horses behind him. The tip of a spear hung inches from the middle of his back as a rider bore down on him. He could feel the steel tip probing him. His breath grew haggard, his lungs screamed for air.

The spear jammed into his back and sent him tumbling into the ash. He rolled and came to his knees as another blow from behind knocked him to the ground. Marus dismounted and walked up to him and stomped on his back and neck.

As Marus continued stomping on him, the screech of an alpurlic broke his focus and frightened the horses. The horses bolted, throwing their unsuspecting riders from their saddles. The crazed alpurlic ripped huge chunks of flesh from the bones of both horse and legionnaire.

With an explosive warcry, Zillas leapt from his mount and engaged the men surrounding Evorix. His old comrades didn't expect such a vicious attack from a man who was always more or less drunk. Zillas' sword entered a legionnaire's body and withdrew as fast as it entered. He spun as another legionnaire tried to impale him.

With a flick of his wrist, Zillas threw a long blade from his belt and caught the man in the throat. Marus looked around him and realized he was the last man left. He vaulted onto his horse as it lashed out at the alpurlic. He yanked the reigns and rode back to his camp.

Zillas found Evorix laying in the ash covered in blood. He scooped him up and threw him on the alpurlics back as more of Marus' riders approached. Zillas' black alpurlic sprang forward and outran the horses on its way back to the fort. The legionnaires closed the gap and raised their short bows. A wave of arrows from the forts walls flew over Zillas' head and hit his pursuers.

A voice from above bellowed. "Open the gate!"

Zillas rode through the burned out rings of the fort, his mount leaping over the mounds of bodies lying in its path. The warriors and soldiers stood together on the rampart above him watching. Nearly half the Rebellium force had been killed and most of the others were wounded. Vitkalla walked up to Zillas and took Evorix from the alpulic's back.

"Is he dead?" Tro'ka asked.

"Not sure, someone get K'aro. The rest of us have to keep fighting," Asinius said, checking Tersius for wounds.

War drums could be heard in the distance as the men in the fort watched more men march over the hill toward Marus' camp. Asinius wiped the sweat from his eyes and peered through his spyglass at the newest pennett coming over the horizon.

"Now we're in trouble," he muttered.

A soldier ran up to Precipitous and handed him his fake hand. Precipitous smiled. "Thank you boy, what's your name?"

"Sillas. I was Lord Valentinian's slave, m'lord."

Precipitous looked at his hand and saw three of the fingers had been broken off. He reattached it with a frown and said, "You now serve me. Ready the war table and send word to all remaining commanders to rally on me."

As the boy sprinted off, Asinius looked over at Precipitous and said, "The emperor has arrived. There will be no retreat now. We must get as many people out of here as we can."

"Any ideas?" Precipitous asked, sheathing his sword.

"Octavius marched with the army. He will finish what he started. Some of us are going to have to stay behind. Any others who can escape must."

During the conversation, the remaining commanders rallied around them. Precipitous noticed several faces missing. "Where is everyone?"

"Corcundia, Evorix and Aksutamoon are with the wounded in the tent. Word has reached me that Nigol is dead, killed in the retreat. Vitkalla and Tro'ka are on their way," Trakuta said.

"Asinius and I have been talking about what we will need to do to escape this situation. If they rally the remnants of Legion I then we stand no chance."

"So what did you come up with?" Trakuta asked.

Precipitous paused knowing his next statement would seal some of their fates. "I am asking for volunteers to stay behind and delay the emperor's army."

The awkward silence seemed to last an eternity. The soldiers and warriors that were left gave each other grim glances. An old man, badly wounded made his way to the front with a young boy.

"We'll stay behind," he said, placing his sword on his shoulder.

"As I live and breath, Litus. I thought I spotted you forming the turtle earlier. You know what's going to happen in a little while?" Asinius asked.

Litus smiled, showing his missing teeth. "I do. Take care, prefect. Glad you joined us." He groaned as he felt his scorched side. "Long live the Rebellium."

Without another word, the pair walked back to the rampart, the boy supporting his father. A few greying warriors looked at Vitkalla and roared and then followed the two soldiers back to the front line. Little by little the severely wounded soldiers and warriors helped each other back to the wall.

Precipitous looked at Asinius and smiled. "I'll tell Octavius you send your regards."

Asinius grabbed Precipitous' upper arm. "Precipitous, if you or I stay and they capture us, the emperor will torture us for days," Asinius hissed so the men wouldn't hear him.

"I know and that's why I'm sending you out with the rest of the men. Follow Trakuta to Tramonia, get Aksutamoon's army and then slaughter the emperor," Precipitous said.

Trakuta mumbled under his breath as the decision was made. "I wish Aksutamoon were here to help with this plan."

Pale and clammy, Aksutamoon approached with the help of two orderlies. "I'll stay behind," he said, standing by them.

"Aksutamoon, you're the King of Tramonia. We need you to lead the remaining men to Sorra and lay siege to Iceport," Precipitous said, objecting.

Aksutamoon sat down with a sigh and showed him the wound to his side. The sword cut was deep, it had a dark red froth escaping it. He had been hit by a Wolfryian pot also that seared his side and neck with third degree burns.

"I'm dying, Precipitous. Trakuta and you will take the army west to Tramonia."

"Hell no, I'm staying with you," Trakuta shouted.

Smiling weakly, Aksutamoon said, "I know you're loyal, Trakuta. That's why I want you to escape with those well enough to travel and take Iceport." He spit up more blood in his hand before he continued. "Bring me my sword," he bellowed as an old warrior helped him to his feet.

Trakuta nodded, snapped to attention and tried to swallow the lump in his throat. "On me you lucky bastards," he shouted to the men standing next to him.

He smiled again, then looked at Precipitous and Asinius. "You both need to help Trakuta plan for the final assault on Iceport." He grabbed his side, sweat dripping from his brow. "I'll hold them off as long as I can."

"As you wish your highness," Asinius said, saluting.

Aksutamoon lifted his bastard sword and then slung it over his back with a grunt. He took one last look at the companions who had become his friends, then turned around and limped to the stone wall with the rest of the men staying behind.

"And there goes the last King of Tramonia," Precipitous whispered to Asinius.

Asinius and Precipitous gathered the remaining men and ran to the tent where the wounded were housed. They looked for Evorix and found K'aro wrapping a bandage across his back. Corcundia lay still, her skin waxy. Precipitous walked over to K'aro.

"Will they live?" he asked.

"Lady Corcundia may, time will tell. Evorix..."

"Is he dead?" Asinius asked, a hint of hope filtering through with his question.

"Nearly. Somehow he is hanging on. He's a tough human," K'aro said, wiping his paws.

Precipitous nudged Asinius' arm. "Probably waiting to kill you, prefect."

"Then let us pray he wakes," Asinius hissed.

K'aro continued. "If we get the proper medical supplies, I may be able to save him. The spear blow into his back was deep, but the blow to the head is what nearly killed him. I'm surprised his neck isn't broken."

K'aro walked over to Corcundia brushed her bloody hair from her forehead. "The arrow hit her in the side of the throat. I was able to apply our salve and plug the wound. You should take a look at this, I found it to be disturbing."

Pulling back her tunic, he showed them the black stitches on the wound that ran from her ear to her collar bone. He picked up the arrow head he had removed from her neck and handed it to Asinius.

"Look familiar?" he asked, his cold blue eye burning with hatred.

Asinius stared at the barbed arrow, then took a closer look and cursed under his breath. "These arrows are outlawed," Asinius said, handing it to Precipitous.

"They have been outlawed in Wolfrya since the reign of Tiberius. Who would have these?" Precipitous asked.

"If I have one guess," Asinius said, flipping it in his palm.

Precipitous growled. "I never saw Marus use them. When we finally do catch up with him, I'm going to take my tim."

"We have to go," Trakuta said, donning his armor as he waved the men to the back of the fort.

"Put the wounded on stretchers and load them into the wagon," Asinius said.

"Those to critical to move must be left," Trakuta said, looking at the men as he nudged them out.

The wounded who were unable to travel watched them leave, and those few who could grabbed the weapons that were lying around. Shuffling into a broken spear wall, they took up a defensive position.

Asinius led his group to the back of the fort and helped everyone mount their horses and alpurlics. Aksutamoon watched them disappear into the cloud of ash swirling at the back of the fort.

He faced the attacking army, spit a bloody wad of phlegm at his feet and yelled, "Steady on the wall boys, steady!"

Chapter 22

Octavius smacked the back of his neck, killing the mosquito that was drawing blood. "I hate the woods. More wine!"

A slave ran to his horse and lifted the flask up to him. He lifted it to his lips and spilled the wine across the front of his breastplate.

Quillen rode up from the baggage train. "Imperator, we must leave the baggage train and the slaves in order to reach Legion I before they break camp."

"I travel with slaves and my clothes, there is no other way."

"Imperator—-."

He waved his hand and rode off. "Kill the slaves, bring my clothes."

Quillen gave the order, his voice shaking. He rode behind the emperor as the screams from the slaves faded into the distance. The group had traveled slower than Quillen anticipated. They came to a stop in a glade as the night closed around them. After watering the horses, Quillen walked over to the fire and sat by Octavius, his eyes cast downward.

"Prefect, must you question every decision I make?" Octavius asked.

"I am only trying to help you, Imperator."

"As many have done before you. However, you're not a coward, so I'll listen to you. I absolutely despise cowards. Asinius and now Marus have betrayed me." He put another belladonna leaf in between his teeth, ground it with a sigh and then spit the juice into the fire.

"We are a days ride from Legion I. I will ready the horses so we can attack them by mid afternoon," Quillen said, rising to his feet.

Octavius' eyes that were normally glazed over, brightened. "Stay a moment, prefect. Do you know why I am the way I am?" Octavious asked, a slight bit of drool starting to form at the corner of his mouth.

Quillen stared at the emperor for a moment and realized he wasn't toying with him. He shook his head as Octavius dabbed at his nose with a sigh.

"You knew my father, but you didn't really *know* my father. He was a hard man, worse than people remember, much worse. Before you joined the senate, he killed my mother and her lover in a fit of rage when I was a young boy. And with no one restraining him, he believed a strong hand was the way to raise a strong boy." His eyes softened and he stared into the darkness. "You see when you take a beating every day, you begin to feel like there is no hope. Not that it mattered, I was always going to feel that way, but his acceptance meant everything. I knew I would be loathed when I took the throne."

Quillen cleared his throat ready to object. Octavius held up his hand and said, "There is no need to try and cover anyone's tracks. I know what I am and why I'm hated. And it is much deserved, but I rule the way I rule because no one respects a weak emperor. My father wasn't weak and so I must not be. You see prefect, when you kill, you have to keep killing or they won't respect you. If you plan on staying as my prefect you had better learn that."

He spit into the fire again, stuck another leaf in his mouth and continued, "The moments of clarity I have are few." He held his palm open showing him his belladonna leaves. "I'm addicted to these and they kill my judgement. I wish I could wake up tomorrow and be someone different," he said, his eyes suddenly glazing over. A long string of drool fell from the corner of his mouth.

"Imperator?"

Octavius' eyes grew cold and withdrawn. "We will kill everyone who has betrayed us. Every——"

His head hit his chest and he was lost in a swirling darkness. Quillen picked him up and carried him to his tent. He returned to the fire and sent word to bring the commanders.

His commanders assembled ten minutes later, some only in their underwear. "Wipe the sleep from your eyes, danmit. We leave at first light. The only one who lives when we attack is Marus. I want every other legionnaire killed. Any questions?"

A young commander stepped forward and asked, "Are you suggesting we kill our brothers, fathers and uncles?"

"You will kill whoever our supreme emperor dictates."

Quillen clasped his hooks behind his back and walked closer to the fire. He stared at the flame in silence, his throat itching for a drink. After pausing for a moment, he opened his hooks and slashed them across the young commanders throat who had questioned him and then stomped him into the ground.

"Once you kill, you have to keep killing. Assemble the horses, we leave at dawn," Quillen said, his voice like steel.

Daylight broke over the cloudy horizon as the horses pranced on the roadway in the drizzle. The emperor slept in and the army waited an hour while his retainers readied him. He walked out of the tent, up a wooden stairway and then onto his horse. Without a word, he cantered out followed by the army.

The infantry marched double time attempting to keep up. As they marched, they saw a war raging on the horizon. Octavius saw the siege equipment burning at the edge of the woods, the smoke wafting through his nostrils. The attack had broken off and Legion I sat around campfires awaiting orders.

"You see Quillen that coward Marus has retreated against a weaker enemy. We must purge *all* the rebels from Delos one last time."

"Understood Imperator. But last night you thought of a plan around the campfire. It was to ride into their camp, help them defeat the Rebellium and then kill them. I believe you said something like two, oh what was it."

"Two birds, one stone?" Octavius asked a little more than confused.

"Yes, that was it Imperator. I should have known you would remember."

"Yes, that was a good idea wasn't it. I'm glad I thought of that. Do what I suggested then," he said with a wave of his hand.

He rode out with his personal guards leaving Quillen with the army. One of the commanders came to Quillen's side, helmet in hand. "You're not really going to attack the other legion are you, senatore?"

Refusing to answer the question, Quillen clicked his hooks together and said, "I wouldn't question my plans, commander Fillas. Do your job and I'll do mine. Understood?"

Fillas bowed low. "Then what is the next plan, Senatore Quillen?" Fillas asked.

Quillen stared at the battle maps lost in thought.

"Prefect Quillen," Fillas asked, glancing out the corner of his eye.

Quillen snapped back to reality. "We will ride into camp, reinforce the legion and then kill the remaining defenders. Have some of our legionnaires construct a battering ram. It ends today."

"And what of the men who surrender?" Fillas asked, before Quillen walked away.

Quillen lowered his head and shook it."Kill them, Fillas, kill them all. Traitors to the crown must die."

• • • •

OCTAVIUS WATCHED FROM the tree line as the battering ram rolled from the defense line and stopped just out of arrow range from the fort.

Marus saw the emperor's flag, galloped up to him and saluted. "Imperator, I didn't know you were coming."

"There are many things you don't know, Marus. Evidently, you don't know you're a coward, but I do. A worthless coward." He nudged his mount next to Marus', and snatched him by the chin. "And you will die a coward."

"Imperator, what have I done to anger you?" Marus asked.

"You can't kill them you worthless shit," he screeched as he pointed at the smoldering fort. "They mock you from their walls. Their flag is still flying overhead. Look!"

The torn and shredded flag of the Rebellium went up the pole as he pointed, incensing him even more.

"But Imperator, they are behind———."

The wooden cudgel Octavius had hidden on the side of his saddle struck Marus across the jaw. He tumbled out of his saddle with a small grunt and as he hit the ground several of his teeth fell out.

Dazed by the blow, Marus lay still for a moment trying to collect his thoughts. Octavius stared down at him, his eyes full of hate. "You're fired, Marus."

He nodded to Quillen after he was satisfied Marus wouldn't move and then rode off with his men. Quillen dismounted and held his hook out. Marus got up, spit more teeth out and nodded his thanks.

"I want you to hear it from me, Marus. You have been replaced by me as prefect and I think you know what that means." Quillen said, trying his best to hold his gaze.

Spitting out a stream of blood, Marus said, "It means I don't have a friend in the world."

A guard with Quillen shouldered him aside and kicked Marus to his knees. He pulled his sword from its scabbard and raised it over his head.

The guard staggered back and dropped into the ash, his throat slashed open. Quillen mounted his horse and sighed, the guards blood dripping from one of his hooks.

"Marus, it's a damn shame you killed that guard. And it's too bad I couldn't fight you off. Now run and hide and never show your face in Iceport again. We are even now. You saved my life in the war and I just saved yours. If I find you again, I'll kill you," Quillen said, urging his mount forward.

He caught up with Octavius a few moments later."Imperator, Marus has escaped."

Octavius sat on his saddle stunned. He reached for his club, but found it missing. Enraged, he reached for Quillen's throat, nearly falling out of his saddle in the process.

"I will kill you for this screw up, Quillen."

"As you wish, Imperator."

"Meet me in my tent in an hours time for your punishment," he screeched before riding off.

Quillen rode into camp and had his tent assembled. One of the commanders from Legion II walked into his tent behind him after it was assembled. "Damn shame Marus escaped."

Quillen spun around. "What are you doing in my tent?"

The man stood by the tent flap and peeked outside. "Relax Senatore Quillen, I mean you no harm."

Lifting an eyebrow, Quillen said, "What do you want?"

The commander rubbed his brow. "I wanted to thank you in private for allowing Lord Marus to escape. He was a good leader who inspired loyalty amongst his troops. He will be missed."

Quillen nodded. "I owed him my life anyway. I was just repaying the debt."

The man shrugged and smiled. "The Rebellium Wars were hell," the man said.

Quillen stared at the man. "You were there?"

"Damn right I was." The man stuck his hand out. He slightly shook Quillen's hook with two fingers. "Name's Calatinius, commander of the Nightshades."

"Never heard of you," he replied, watching Calatinius walk around.

"No, I don't think you ever would. We are the legions ranger battalion, unknown to the senate. Hunting, spying and sabotage are what we do best. No one really knows we even exist, except the boy king and Marus." Calatinius smiled. "You want a way into that fort to stop the body count from rising right?"

Quillen nodded.

"I can help you, but it's going to cost you."

"Name your price," Quillen said.

"Name me head commander of Legion II and help me kill the emperor."

Feigning surprise, Quillen slowly looked up from unpacking his bag and said, "What was that?"

"You heard me. You become emperor and I lead your armies." Calatinius replied.

"Are you suggesting we kill the emperor ourselves?"

"You know it's what you want. And if you don't, you'll be dead by nightfall. I can do it, no one would suspect me. It's what the empire needs. We don't need another crazy dictator like Tiberius. Do you want another large scale Rebellium War?" he asked.

"You speak of treason like a whore speaks to a soldier about what she costs. I should have you arrested right now," Quillen hissed.

"If you wanted to do that, you would have already. Can I count on you when I make my move?" Calatinius asked.

Quillen paused and bit his lip. "If we get caught, we die."

Washing his hands in the water basin, Calatinius muttered, "We're screwed already, senatore. It's only a matter of time before the emperor turns on us during one of his imaginary drug induced slights."

"I suppose you're right, Calatinius. But how would we kill him and keep most of the men alive?" Quillen asked.

"First off, we need more men to help us. My brother Calpernicus is behind those walls. He would give us the Rebellium troops if it meant killing the emperor," Calatinius said, looking through the tent flap cautiously.

"And how do you propose we get in?"

Calatinius went into his pocket and pulled out a worn key and showed it to him. In the darkness it was hard to make out, but he thought he saw a skeleton key.

"And what's that going to do?" Quillen asked.

Snickering, Calatinius said, "He gave me this many years ago if I promised not to ever attack. Now we are here and I need to make sure we get to my brother before the emperor does. I get him out, you get more men. Deal?"

"You drive a hard bargain, Calatinius, but I'm in. Now leave my tent before someone hears us," Quillen said.

"One last thing m'lord. If you write to Valentinian about our plan, he should be more than willing to help us along with my brother," he said, walking out of the tent.

As Calatinius walked away, Quillen stepped outside. The smell of rotting animal corpses and bloated bodies baking in the heat caused him to cover his nose and mouth with a rag dampened in salt water from the baggage train. He stepped back into his tent and a slave brought him food and wine. The slave washed his face, neck and feet, then helped him out of his armor and hung it on a mannequin.

Quillen turned to his slave. "I need you to write a letter for me."

The slave fetched some papyrus and a quill and prepared to write. Quillen dictated what he wanted written to Lord Valentinian and after the letter was drafted, he said, "Thank you, you're dismissed."

The slave bowed and left. Quillen looked at the dried blood on his hooks and lowered his head to pray. He laid back on his bed for a moment and fell asleep.

He woke to the sound of legionnaires barging into his tent an hour later. He watched them throw his dead slave at the foot of his bed before he tried to rise. A blow to the temple from behind knocked him unconscious. Calatinius walked in with the emperor, grabbed the letter and smiled. "I told you he was a traitor, Imperator."

"You're as dishonorable as your brother, Calatinius. When he helps us eliminate the Rebellium, I will make you both lead commanders."

"And what of the traitor?" Calatinius asked, drinking from a wine bottle nearby.

"Put him in chains and throw him in with the other prisoners." He looked Calatinius in the eye. "You're a vicious bastard, Calatinius. You betrayed a man I liked. Only the most ruthless are loyal to me and it's a damn shame he wasn't. I was actually going to forgive him for his blunder earlier today. I want you to burn him at the stake when you finish torturing him," Octavius hissed, taking one last look at his former prefect.

"As you command, so shall it be so," Calatinius said with a deep bow.

Octavius left the tent. Calatinus smiled as the for a moment and then pulled Quillen's helmet on. He admired the handiwork and then picked up a piece of bread. As he brought the bread to his mouth, a knife entered the back of his neck and exited out of his throat.

Marus crept from the shadows as Calatinius collapsed and said, "Should have been looking behind you."

He bent down, scooped Quillen up into his arms and snuck out the back of the tent. There was only one place they could find refuge as he watched the bulk of the legionnaires marching past him.

He looked into the sky and muttered, "Better to die standing, than swinging at the end of a rope."

His keen eyes had seen a small contingent of warriors and soldiers riding out of the back gate near the volcanoes edge. He threw Quillen over his saddle and then the pair disappeared into the mist heading for the Batopian frontier.

• • • •

AN HOUR AFTER QUILLEN and Marus made their escape, Octavius' men scaled the walls and killed the remaining defenders. Octavius walked through the burnt gate of the fort and looked around at the charred bodies of women, children, warriors and soldiers that were all mixed in with his legionnaires. The smell from the carnage was overwhelming.

He gagged and dry heaved as he walked a little further and saw a few soldiers in red tunics from the Tramonian army. Aksutamoon lay against a stone wall surrounded by his men and several old warriors. His fingertips spasmed as he reached for his sword hilt.

Octavius stepped on his hand and, "King Aksutamoon, what in the hell are you doing here?"

Aksutamoon winced. "Son of a whore." He looked up and smiled. "Trying to kill you."

Blood trickled from the corner of his mouth and his beard had burned away, leaving his face with large white calluses.

Octavius stared down his nose and said, "You're going to regret that."

"Nah, I'm already dead. You can't do anything to me," Aksutamoon said after a light chuckle.

"On the contrary. I will keep you alive and torture you for information, then I'll roast you on a stake."

Aksutamoon stared at him for a moment and then said, "The plan dies with me."

His hand reached his knife and slit his own throat. He gasped for several moments, eyes searching madly for a solution, then his head came to rest on his chest. His eyelids didn't close, a look of shock burned into his corneas.

"So much for you," Octavius muttered, picking the remnants of a leaf from his teeth.

He watched as his men dragged all the bodies into the center of the fort. Lined up, they were stacked neatly in six foot piles. Hundreds of bodies lay in front of Octavius in different positions. Shaking his head in disbelief, he reached for more of his belladonna leaves. He looked around and saw that he was alone.

Muttering to himself with a giggle, he said, "I guess I'm the prefect and emperor." He waved one of his guards over and said, "Assemble my generals, destroy the remnants of Legion I, and burn this shithole to the ground."

Later that evening back at their camp, Octavius watched the Last Keep burn to the ground. He had left Aksutamoon's body impaled on the road as a warning to other rebels.

After making camp, the generals walked into Octavius' tent weary and filthy from the gore of battle. After they assembled around his war table, Octavius spoke.

"We have killed all those responsible for my father's death. What are my losses?" He stuck another belladonna leaf in the side of his cheek.

"Legion I has been destroyed. A total loss—."

"There is no loss, do you hear me. No loss." He pointed to the man who spoke. "Bring me his head."

Before the man could pull his sword to defend himself, a blade entered his back and severed his spine. It took Octavius' guard a few swings, but he finally separated the man's head from his body. The guard picked up the head, put it on the table and handed Octavius a spear.

"Now, you men should know what I expect." Octavius walked to where the head was. "We will withdraw to Iceport and celebrate this great victory." He grabbed the head by the hair and slammed it down on the spear.

The other generals shifted their weight as Octavius walked around the room shoving the severed head in their faces.

"We have defeated the Rebellium. And we will celebrate," Octavius said.

One of the commanders cleared his throat. "We haven't killed them all, a small group escaped."

Octavius glanced at the commander. "What was that?"

"I was informed the Rebellium scum disappeared into the ash," the man said, taking a step back.

Octavius growled. "I want the survivors brought before me and executed. I want...no I need the Nightshades to track them. Where is Calitinius?"

A moment of silence followed his question. "Where is the commander of the Nightshades?" he asked, pressing his generals.

A guard walked in dragging Calatinius by the feet and dropped him in the center of the room. Octavius glanced down at him and saw his throat.

"Where was he?" Octavius asked.

"Quillen's tent, Imperator," the guard said.

He blinked and glanced up. "And Quillen?"

"Gone," the guard said, stepping back and sliding his hand to his sword. Octavius nodded his head for a moment, then looked at a legionnaire.

"You're a Nightshade, right?" Octavius asked.

"I am, Imperator," the man replied, his voice cracking, eyes wide.

Octavius took the spear, licked his lips and struck the man with the severed head he was holding, spilling blood across his armor and face. The other generals dabbed at their sweating necks with their blue stolls and cast their eyes to the ground.

"Kill him," Octavius said.

A guard standing behind the beaten man pulled his hair back, cut his throat and then kicked the body onto the war table.

"Failure and desertion are not an option. Nor will they ever be," Octavius shouted, watching the body slump to the floor. The men around the table tried to avoid eye contact with him. "Kill all the Nightshades," Octavius screamed.

The guards slaughtered the small group that were in the tent, then rushed into the camp and killed the remainder of them. Octavius walked around the camp mingling with his legionaries as the bodies of the Nightshades where dragged into the center of the encampment and set ablaze.

He stuck another belladonna leaf in his mouth and looked at one of his guards. "Never fail me," he muttered and then staggered into his tent.

The next morning the commanders shouted at the men to assemble. Octavius stepped onto a platform and addressed them. "We will be returning to Iceport to regroup and rest for a few months. Then we ride to wipe out the Tramonians to the west. Kill all of the stragglers we have who fall behind, or I'll kill you myself."

Chapter 23

After riding for a fortnight, Evorix's ragged band rode into the Tramonian frontier. Withered naked tree branches drooped down over the path they rode on, hindering their progress. Trakuta scouted ahead and found a small brook deep in the woods. As they reached it, the men unpacked and set up camp.

Asinius walked up to Trakuta and said, "Where the hell are we?"

"Foghorn Forest. The castle lies a mile from here," Trakuta replied.

Asinius waved the men over and everyone kneeled by the edge of the brook. Precipitous spoke first. "We're going to need a plan."

Trakuta cracked his knuckles and looked around. "Tro'ka, can you find other warriors to help us take Sorra?"

"I can ride to the other tribes," Tro'ka replied with a slight nod.

"We're going to need you, K'aro and Vitkalla to scrounge up as many warriors as you can and meet us outside the castle walls. As long as this flag flies, so does the Rebellium." Trakuta said as he pulled a torn and bloody black flag out of his bag. "This represents all that remains of the men and women who believed Tiberius' lineage line should be wiped from Delos. I for one never thought I would fight for this cause, but these are dark and twisted times. I hope to one day understand why this war ever took place."

Tro'ka growled in agreement. "Well said human. I have been killing humans since I was a young cub and here I sit, one of the last of the R'atu. I will follow your suggestion and find warriors to help take Sorra, but I wouldn't get my hopes up. Many will say this isn't their fight."

"I understand. But some did pledge to protect all the Last Bloods, did they not?" Trakuta asked, playing on Tro'ka's emotions.

Tro'ka glanced at Vitkalla and then nodded.

"See to it, please," Trakuta said.

Tro'ka, Vitkalla and K'aro gathered their remaining warriors, said their goodbyes and then rode for the northern Fire Lands, a place most Outkast wouldn't dare tread. There was no guarantee that if they rode into the north, they would come back.

All of the prides lived separately, scattered around different patches of volcanic ash. A few prides aligned during times of war with each other, but that hadn't happened for a hundred years. Not since the days of A'tu the Unifier.

Almost all of the Outkast were members of the different tribes with nowhere to go but down the social ladder. It was a dangerous plan and success didn't seem likely, still they knew they had to go.

Later in the evening, Trakuta ducked into Evorix's tent and found him propped up against his bed, head back, drinking Tramonian wine.

"You look comfortable," Trakuta said.

Evorix raised his middle finger.

"Straight to the pleasantries I see. Amazing thing you did with those catapults. It saved a lot of lives," Trakuta said with a smile.

Easy for you to say, you're not a cripple. Evorix glanced down at his right hand. The spear blow severed his ulnar nerve, turning his hand into a claw. It would never again hold a weapon or a mead horn.

"It's just my luck. I should have let the kid take the blow," Evorix said, attempting to flex his fingers.

"The boy will be a great warrior one day. Saving him may help our cause years from now. You on the other hand are cynical and the devil himself doesn't want you, but I came here to ask for your help one last time," Trakuta said.

Evorix put the flask to his lips and drank for a minute and then sighed. "What do you want, Trakuta?"

"I need you to train Tersius."

Evorix laughed so hard that the wine spilled on his tunic.

"I am sending him to assassinate Octavius. Would have asked you to go, but..." He shot a quick glance at Evorix's hand.

Evorix tucked it under his arm, then spit some of his wine at Trakuta' feet. "He's a child and Asinius will kill you if you send him."

"You're right. He is a child, but he has the drive because Octavius had his father killed." He paused and took a seat next to him. "I left my king in defense of this bloody flag." He tossed the flag in Evorix's lap. "I want revenge and you're the only one who can prepare him," Trakuta said.

"What about you?" Evorix muttered.

"I'm here for a higher purpose, now," he said, standing up.

Evorix stared at him with a blank expression. "I'll think about training him, but his blood is on your hands if he dies."

Trakuta smiled at him. "Understood. Now, there's something I've been meaning to ask you. Why are you so bitter at life, Evorix?"

After a long pause, Evorix shrugged and said, "You wouldn't understand."

"Try me."

Evorix paused and looked at his feet. "My life as the prefect to Emperor Tiberius was a good life, a real good life. Full of wealth, education and looting." He sighed. "Oh, how I loved the looting. My wife and I lived in a villa on the sea outside of Iceport, near the town of Tygrim. I was gone on campaigns quite often to subdue the Ba and as the years went by, so did Tiberius' paranoia that someone would kill him."

He took another swig of wine. "My father and brother ambushed the emperor and I reacted too late. I lost my honor, my position and my self respect. Gius and I were arrested by Asinius and as a special treat, Octavius killed my pregnant wife Alecta. And then he killed Gius' family as he watched. Gius swore revenge and hired me to kill Octavius once and for all."

"Why are you still here then? Gius is dead and with him the Rebellium," Trakuta said, towering over him.

"Funny you should ask. I never wanted to be here, but I'm here nonetheless." He chuckled. "I gave my word and to me and that's worth more than money. It's about respect. And you're right, Gius died before he could pay me. Now it looks like I'll never get paid. So, I'm just surviving," Evorix mumbled under his breath. "There is a phrase my father once said," 'Angelus mortis venturus est.'

Trakuta laughed and stretched his back. "And what's that supposed to mean?"

"The angel of death is coming."

"Well when you see this angel, tell him I need some killer angels," Trakuta said as he left the tent.

• • • •

A FEW NIGHTS LATER, Evorix sat by the brook staring at his reflection. The last few months had not been kind to him. Dirt was jammed under his fingertips and bags hung under his eyes.

Now I'm stuck. I hope like hell the end comes quickly and painlessly. I wish I was already dead. He looked at the knife hidden under his sleeve. He pricked his index finger with the razor shape tip.

It would only take a moment, wouldn't it.

He sighed and took another drag from his wine skin. Like a school boy, he giggled and ran his finger over the blade.

"Nobody would care anyway," he muttered out loud.

"I would," Tersius said, walking over to him out of the shadows. "Die in battle with honor, not by your own hand, old man."

"Mind your business *boy* and fetch me more wine."

"Train me. Then do what you want, I could care less," Tersius said.

Evorix stood up, then bent over and vomited. He wiped his mouth and looked at Tersius. "You're like a gnat at a bonfire, annoying."

"Train me and I'll leave you be," Tersius said.

Evorix got to his feet and swung his right fist in Tersius' direction. Tersius grabbed it, turned on his heel and threw him over his shoulder.

Evorix lay on his back for a few moments coughing. Tersius walked over to him and nudged him with his toe. "You alright old timer?"

Evorix grabbed his heel and pulled up. Tersius fell back and hit his head on a rock. Seeing stars, he held his hand to his temple and tried to get back on his feet. Evorix scrambled to his feet first, pulled his knife and tackled Tersius from behind.

Tersius pushed up and rammed his head into Evorix's chin. Evorix instinctively put his fingers to his chin and dropped the knife. With a quick barrel roll forward, Tersius grabbed the knife and put it to Evorix's throat.

"Yield."

Evorix sat with his knees in the dirt for a moment.

The kid's quick. Probably should train him.

He tapped Tersius' forearm. "I yield."

Tersius withdrew the knife and handed it back to him. "I want to know everything you can teach me."

Evorix winced as he touched his chin and said, "Ok boy, but if you don't keep up, I'll kill you."

Tersius nodded with a smile and turned around to head back to their camp.

"And I'm going with you to assassinate Octavius."

Tersius turned on his heel. "Fine. Just don't get in my way, fall behind and I'll kill you."

"Looks like you're all grown up, boy," Evorix said.

Tersius smiled and walked away.

A few nights passed before all the commanders met in Trakuta's tent. "We need to attack and hurry this up," Precipitous said.

"Brilliant. Let's kill the soldiers we need to take Iceport, not to mention our own and then show up with less men than we have right now," Evorix said, shaking his head.

"What's your idea then?" Zillas asked after he took a swig of wine.

"Keep drinking that wine and you won't be any help to us," Tersius said.

Evorix smirked. "We attack under the cover of darkness while they sleep."

Trakuta chuckled. "Great plan." He walked over to the tent flap and opened it. "Would you like to go through the gate or scale the walls of the mightiest city in the world?"

"Smart ass," Evorix muttered.

Corcundia walked into the tent and lit her cherrywood pipe. She winced when she touched the scar forming on her neck.

"M'lady, you need to rest," Tersius said.

"I've had enough rest. Where are my warriors?" she asked.

"They've ridden north," Trakuta said.

"On whose orders?"

"Mine," Trakuta replied.

"What for?" she asked.

"We needed more troops," Trakuta spat back.

"You need my warriors to help take Sorra?" she asked.

"Yes."

"Well that won't happen on my watch, so while we wait on my warriors to return from the task you asked of them without my approval. But let's get a group together and sneak in."

"I'm in," Zillas said, swaying side to side.

"Great, the drunk's in. Who else besides me and Zillas?" she asked.

Precipitous touched his fake hand and smiled. "The God's hate a coward," he muttered. "I'll go."

Asinius stared down the flat of his blade, humming. "I'm in."

Tersius raised his sword with a wide smile. "Looking forward to it."

Trakuta sharpened his knives at the table. "Guess you'll be needing a tour guide."

All eyes turned to Evorix who had stepped back from the group. "You're all insane," he mumbled, stepping further into the shadows.

"Maybe, but we need your help," Trakuta said.

Evorix shrugged. "I won't be of any help," he said.

"I'll give you your weight in gold when we take the castle," Trakuta said.

Evorix glanced at his hand and then made eye contact with Corcundia. She waited on him to excuse himself and ride back to Batopia. He exhaled, his head hung low. "I only have one hand. It would only be a hindrance, not a help."

"Maybe, but we still need you, even if it's to absorb a sword blow meant for someone else," Trakuta said.

Evorix stuck his middle finger up at him and blew a raspberry. "And I might get lucky enough to wedge a knife into yours."

Trakuta laughed and said, "I guess that means he's in. I'll scout ahead and make sure our entrance will be open." He moved to the tent flap and stared at the bright full moon. "Be ready in an hour."

Later that evening, Trakuta slipped back into the foliage where everyone was hiding. The willow branches swung lazily in front of them, blocking the view of the guards a few hundred yards away.

"You scared the shit out of me. What did you find?" Evorix asked, moving aside.

"Follow me and I'll show you," Trakuta said, slipping back onto the road.

They transversed through the foliage until they reached the river bank. Trakuta motioned for them to melt into the shadows and then scouted ahead. He returned some time later to where they were hiding.

Taking a sip of water with a sigh, he said, "I hate to say it, but we need to go through—-."

"If you say the sewer, I'll kill you," Precipitous said, pulling his knife.

"It's the only way in unless you want to storm the gate and face the army with just us," Trakuta said, motioning to the thick front gate. "But I don't think we'll win."

Precipitous crawled over to a log and laid against it. Evorix crawled over next to him, careful not to slide through the sludge.

"You alright, brother?" Evorix asked.

Precipitous smiled. "Never been better. But I'll be damned if I'm going into a shit infested sewer."

Evorix chuckled and crawled back over to Trakuta. "Is he alright?" Trakuta asked.

"Oh yea, just peachy," Evorix snorted.

The group waited until three in the morning to ensure everyone was asleep. They waded through the cool crisp water to the rusted sewer grating Trakuta scouted. A toxic smell radiated from the dark tunnel making them pinch their noses shut.

"Fuck me it stinks. What is it?" Evorix hissed.

"Shit and more shit," Trakuta said, trying to pick the rusted lock.

Some time later, Trakuta managed to pry the lock open, breaking two dagger blades in the process. The tunnel was grimier than they anticipated. They stared into the dark tunnel until Precipitous spoke up. "Where's the light?"

All their faces turned in his direction. "There is none you fool. We keep going until we hit something," Evorix said.

"Or until something eats us," Precipitous replied.

Trakuta opened the grate."Welcome to Sorra."

"To hell with you, Trakuta," Precipitous said, passing by him.

"Stop your bitching," Evorix said, pushing Precipitous into the tunnel first. They hunched low and duck walked down the tunnel, staying nose to ass the whole way down.

Everyone vomited as they crawled through the parasitic shit infested slush.

"There ain't even rats down here. How stupid are we?" Precipitous asked after he vomited for a second time. He fell forward into the rancid water and cursed loudly answering his own question. "Pretty stupid I'd say."

A sliver of light shined through a hole in front of them. They continued crawling for several hundred more feet until they felt the wall. Trakuta pressed his palms against it and after what felt like an eternity a piece swung open.

The group pushed each other into the opening, all of them becoming entangled as they rolled into the room. A mess of hands and feet spread out in every direction. Their hushed curses echoed around the room as they fought to retract their own limbs. They landed behind rows and rows of Tramonian wine barrels.

Trakuta touched the barrels and smiled. "I had more than a few wenches in here in my day."

"Ugh, men," Corcundia said, pushing Evorix's arm off her shoulder.

"Thanks for the trip down memory lane with your wenches, but let's kill this guy and wash ourselves clean," Evorix said.

"I smell like an overfull privy," Tersius said, wrinkling his nose.

"What's our next move, Trakuta?" Precipitous asked, rubbing the filth out of his hair.

"Before we go any further I want to mention a few things. Tatootamoon will most likely be asleep in his chambers, next to the throne room."

"Should be easy then," Zillas said, wiping his dagger blade across his smelly shirt to smear the shit on the blade.

Trakuta laughed. "Before you go wild in your killing spree. Tatootamoon will be guarded by an elite unit of men who have sworn to die with him. They drink a hallucinogenic cocktail called Sitas to keep fear from their minds and pain from their bodies."

"Great, drug fueled bodyguards. How worse can it get?" Corcundia asked, picking a piece of sewage from her hair.

"Now you tell us?" Asinius asked, kicking sewage from his boot.

"I forgot earlier," Trakuta said.

Asinius grunted and wiped the hilt of his sword clean. "And I'll forget too when I run my blade through your chest."

Evorix pinched his fingers shut in front of Asinius face to quiet him and then looked at Trakuta. "You lead, we'll follow."

"Right, we're going to go down a hallway to a room holding the armor, change into it and then attack the throne room. There should be a few guards in there and at least five in his chamber. Everyone good?" Trakuta asked.

He moved over to the door and pressed his hand to the knob and opened it. There were no guards in the hallway as they snuck out of the room. The group slipped down the hallway and snuck into a room at the opposite end. The room was full of discarded armor, clothing and weapons. They stripped down and put on the Tramonian guardsman uniforms. As they changed Corcundia caught Evorix staring.

"This ain't a peep show, look the other way," she hissed.

Trakuta looked over at Precipitous as Evorix smiled at her before looking away. "You're in Tramonian armor, how does it feel?"

"If I die do.not.bury.me.in.this," Precipitous barked.

"You don't like our armor?" Trakuta asked.

"I'm a Wolfryan, not a winemaker," he snapped back.

Everyone chuckled as he tugged on one of the leather straps. Finally, Trakuta came over and tightened it for him. They checked their weapons and proceeded to the door with Zillas bringing up the rear. He filled his wine skin and took a pull.

"Let's go, drunk," Evorix hissed.

Zillas smiled wide. "Not without my energy potion."

Trakuta turned around before they exited. "Evorix, Corcundia and Tersius are with me. Asinius, Precipitous and Zillas, you take the guards in the throne room." He put his hand on the door knob. "After I open this door, we will go down the hallway and up a stone stairwell. Should we become separated, the throne room is on the left, Tatootamoon's chambers on the right."

Evorix paused. "I just want to thank everyone for coming with me. I'll see you all in the throne room."

"Bah, move your ass," Precipitous said, pushing him out of the way.

They crept behind Trakuta to the stairwell. The few men patrolling the castle never bothered to go into the lowest levels where they were hiding. Climbing the stairway, they snuck to the throne room unmolested. A handful of guards stood talking by the throne, another five by the kings chambers.

Trakuta made hand signals to the group and Precipitous nodded. The throne room team crept along the darkened wall and waited. The guards stood in the middle of the room laughing amongst themselves.

Trakuta's team went to the opposite wall outside of the kings chambers and waited. Evorix knelt in anticipation as the throne room team snuck behind a marble column to wait.

Trakuta made eye contact with Precipitous and nodded toward the guards. The throne room group sprung from the shadows, taking several guards by surprise. As the groups slammed together, Asinius noticed the men had a possessed look in their eyes.

Asinius shouted, "No prisoners!"

Zillas yelled back, "No mercy!"

The throne room team fought as well as they could, but the more noise they made, the more men rushed up from below.

"Form a line here and hold your ground!" Precipitous shouted.

Evorix heard the screams of the wounded and the last gasps of the dying as their swords and spears clattered onto the stone. Tatootamoon sprung from his bed as his guards engaged Evorix's group. Tersius was knocked to the ground as he entered the chamber, a guard poised over him to deliver the killing blow.

The guard stumbled forward, a crossbow quill buried in his neck. Corcundia reached down and picked Tersius up. He nodded his thanks and pressed his attack. Evorix could see Precipitous fighting several guards, numerous wounds on his arms and legs.

Precipitous gasped as an axe was buried in the center of his back. He spun around, grabbed a bodyguard by the throat and tumbled over the balcony with him.

Evorix parried a sword blow from his left. He spun his sword handle in his palm and decapitated the guard attacking him. Trakuta stepped by Evorix and deflected another sword blow aimed at his knees. The mass of guards in the bed chamber pushed Evorix's team back into the throne room.

Evorix turned from where he was fighting and shouted at Trakuta. "Go get him!"

Trakuta slipped by the guards as Evorix and Corcundia took his place. He sprinted into the back of the room and saw Tatootamoon slip behind a false door. He followed Tatootamoon down the corridor and ran into the last guard protecting him.

The guard snarled, foam dripping from his upper lip. Trakuta pulled a hand held repeating crossbow from behind his back and fired both quills. The guard stumbled, but regained his footing. Trakuta rushed forward, knocked the guard over and left a knife in his stomach just under his breastplate.

Tatootamoon reached a stairwell and tripped over his toga. He fell headlong down the stairs, grunting as each stone step slapped him in the face. Trakuta watched him from the top of the stairs and then sprinted down after him.

He leapt off the last five steps and slammed Tatootamoon into a long table. Tatootamoon got to his feet and snatched a spear from the wall.

"Nice try, Trakuta. I knew you would come!" Tatootamoon shouted.

Blood splattered across Trakuta as the king fell onto him, his neck sliced to the bone from a hatchet. Tersius stood over them, smiled and then fell over with a groan.

Evorix and Corcundia ran down the stairs a moment later and stood over Tersius. Asinius ran down the steps and as he turned to lock the door a quill caught him in the chest, knocking him to the ground. Evorix ran to the door, locked it and pulled Asinius back to the rest of the group.

"It was a good fight wasn't it, prefect," Evorix said, pulling him to his feet.

Asinius winced and then smiled. He spit blood onto the floor in response.

"Where is Trakuta?" Corcundia shouted.

"Who cares. We're going to die whether we like it or not. Prepare last defenses!" Evorix said.

The group flipped over the long table in the center of the room and stood behind it. The door shook, the dust catching the early morning light.

"Never thought I'd die fighting beside you," Asinius said, holding his hand over the quill, trying to stop the flow of blood. "But I'm glad I did. Now go on and get Tersius and Corcundia out of here."

"You can't hold them off," Evorix hissed.

"I can hold them long enough for you to escape. Kill Octavius and free Delos from the darkness. Tell Tersius I said goodbye." He winced and took a deep breath, then coughed violently. "Tell him... Tell him I'm sorry,"

He yanked the quill from his upper chest and coughed violently again. He snapped the quill with a growl and tossed it at his feet.

Corcundia threw Tersius over her shoulder and ran with Evorix for the exit. The door in the back of the room burst open as they reached it. Trakuta ran in with several soldiers.

"Run!" Trakuta shouted, surging forward.

Asinius, Trakuta and their reinforcements charged into the the remaining bodyguards as they broke the door down. As the groups met, loud shrieks of pain carried down the stairs. Blood, guts and lifeless bodies fell to the stone floor, then an eerie silence hung in the room.

Chapter 24

Evorix walked back up the stairs after Trakuta yelled down into the courtyard that everything was clear. The banquet hall where they made their last stand was littered with bodies, mostly the king's guard. He found Asinius first as Trakuta's soldiers pulled three bodies off of him. His body contorted in a final position of defiance, a look of determination across his brow. The sword strike that killed him opened his neck where it met his shoulder.

Evorix walked up another set of stairs and into the kings chambers where body parts littered the floor. The blood on the stone was so thick it was hard for him to keep traction. He saw Zillas laying up against the king's bed, his wine bottle broken by his side. Evorix looked down at him and couldn't tell what wound had killed him.

Several quills had broken through his breastplate and one was buried in his throat. Evorix pulled out the sword lodged in his stomach out and then laid him out on the stone and crossed his arms over his chest. He picked up what was left of his wine bottle and laid it between his bloody hands. A Tramonian soldier waited patiently to take the body to the graveyard.

I guess I owe ya one. I'll see you in Hell, Zillas.

He stood up and nodded to the young man who was ready to carry him out. He walked into the throne room where more bodyguards lay strewn about the floor. Evorix kicked their limbs out of his way as he walked over to the balcony.

He peered over and saw what was left of Precipitous. His head was smashed open on the stone, the axe lodged in his back. Precipitous' hand rested on the bodyguards throat crushed underneath him. Evorix shook his head as he watched a soldier pull him out by his feet. The guard picked him up and carried him toward the graveyard. Precipitous' fake hand lay destroyed by his side, the fingers pointing toward Iceport.

"Boy, take that armor off him and burn him on a funeral pyre," Evorix said.

The young man nodded and walked out into the courtyard. Corcundia walked up behind him and put her hand on his shoulder.

"I'm sorry about your friends."

Evorix glanced over at her and grunted. "They weren't my friends, just pawns. How's Tersius?"

"Bad, the wound is deep," she replied.

"Where is he?"

"In Trakuta's quarters. The best surgeon here is attending him," she replied, running her fingers through her matted hair.

She caught Evorix staring at her. "Help you with something?" she asked, tying her hair into a ponytail.

"No, just admiring the view," he replied with a smile.

She chuckled and took a deep breath. Exhaling with a loud sigh she smiled back at him. "Evorix, if you were the last man on earth I wouldn't fuck you, not even to keep civilization alive." She patted him on the shoulder as she walked by him. "And I do mean that."

Evorix watched her walk away, mesmerized by her hips. Trakuta walked up from behind him, sharpening his knife. "Out of your league. Stick to easy tavern wenches, nothing else."

"Fuc——."

Before Evorix could finish his sentence, a blade rested on his collarbone. "Careful how you speak to our king, *mercenary*," said one of the men with Trakuta.

Evorix pushed the tip of the blade away with his index finger with a roll of his eyes. "King?"

"It seems I'm the only one left," Trakuta said.

"Even if you're a *king,* you'll never get Corcundia. You jealous of her wanting me," Evorix said.

"Jealous? Ha, that's a good one. No, I don't care who you screw. I just need you focused to kill Octavius. Like I said, find a tavern wench to relieve your stress," he said with a chuckle.

"Whatever. So, when are they crowning you *king*?" Evorix asked.

"Tonight," Trakuta said.

"That's quick. Have you seen Tersius yet?" Evorix asked.

"No, but they say he won't last the night."

"He's been close before. He may just pull through. Either way, I think we need to rest until the spring rains thaw the snow, or we risk losing the siege in Iceport. The winter is brutal on the coast and it will give us a chance to drill the men," Evorix said, running a blade under his bloody fingernails.

Trakuta nodded. "Alright." He turned to one of his men. "Assemble the army in the square. Tonight we bury our dead and crown me king."

The army assembled a few hours later in the vast courtyard shoulder to shoulder. Trakuta and his entourage walked down the lines of assembled soldiers and inspected them.

They reached the stone steps of the castle and walked up to the landing. Trakuta sat on the throne and one of his heralds slammed a scepter onto the stone and made a loud thumping noise. The men below them snapped to attention almost in unison.

"Today is a new day. A day of rejoicing for all of Tramonia. The new king will be crowned. You will witness this glory," shouted the herald.

The men roared their approval, banging their swords against their shields. An old man weathered by age walked up in front of Trakuta and in a surprisingly loud voice said, "Today marks the new day, my king." He placed the gold and silver crown on his head. "May you rule as long as the God's see fit. All hail King Trakuta, the first of his name!"

Keeping with tradition, the men in the courtyard took a knee. "All hail King Trakuta, first of his name."

Trakuta rose from the throne, took the scepter and slammed it at his feet. He swung it over his head with both hands and shouted, "God's save Tramonia!"

The men cheered for a few minutes until Trakuta held up his hand. "King Aksutamoon would be thrilled to see you in arms today, free from the yoke that bound you while we were away. The Wolfryan emperor, Octavius killed him in battle not long ago. The king bought us the time we needed to escape, but his dying wish was for us to destroy Iceport. I say we pay him back and teach him why you never kill Tramonian's."

His men drowned him out with their cheers. He continued, "We will train through the winter and when the spring comes we will attack and dispose of Emperor Octavius. Are you with me?" he asked.

"Long live the King," they chanted.

Evorix looked around and took a sip of wine as he scanned their young faces. He leaned over to Corcundia. "Where are their veterans?"

"Dead," she said, staring straight ahead.

Evorix cut his eyes at her. "Well then, we're dead as well. Do you fancy a toss in the hay?" he asked.

She scoffed and stared ahead at the men. "In your dreams." A slight smirk crossed her lips. "I'm going to check on Tersius."

"I would treat you real good," Evorix said after her.

Thinking of her smirk, he slipped away from the celebration behind her and walked into Tersius' tent. Blood covered the operating table and drenched the floor. The doctor stood over Tersius wiping the blood from his chest. He handed the rag to an assistant and put his ear to his chest. The faint heartbeat stopped and then fluttered again. Evorix walked over to him.

"How is he?"

The doctor glanced up at him and then back at Tersius. "Bad. The boy has received terrible wounds. He's lucky to be holding on. So now we wait and see," the healer said, preparing more stitches.

"Do your best," Corcundia said.

The healer nodded and went back to work.

Corcundia and Evorix walked out of the tent. Corcundia glanced over at Evorix staring at her.

"You really got it for me don't you?" she asked.

Shocked by her question, he said, "Ofcourse, if you were me, you would too."

"I won't screw you, but I will let you buy me a drink," she said.

"Oh, I'll buy you a drink alright and give you a nightcap," Evorix muttered.

She turned around and caught him staring again. "What was that?" she asked.

He smiled at her. "Oh, nothing, nothing at all."

• • • •

QUILLEN AND MARUS RODE into the Batopian wilderness, their horses slowly cantered along the dirt trail. Approaching a fork in the road, the pair made eye contact and Marus instinctively reached for his sword.

As his hand tapped the corded hilt, several men on horseback dressed in black leather armor surrounded their horses. The warhorses they were on snorted and nudged Marus and Quillen horses.

"Halt," said a man as he rode into their path.

The men with him raised their crossbows and guided their horses with their knees.

Marus spoke first. "I am Marus of Wolfrya, former prefect to Emperor Octavius."

At the mention of Octavius' name, the mercenaries fingers slid over the triggers of their crossbows.

Quillen raised his hooks. "We're not working for the emperor anymore. We have defected to your side and want an audience with Warlord Three Toes."

The man in the middle of the road took off his black hollow cow head mask with red horns and spit at them from his elevated position. "Wolfyrians are not welcome in the Warlord Three Toes presence. We have orders to execute anyone who crosses his borders." The man raised his arm.

"Wait, wait. I have coin," Quillen said.

He pulled a large purse from within his cloak and handed it to the man nearest him. The soldier handed the bag to the leader who pocketed the money and then looked at Marus' sword. He pointed at it.

"It'll cost you his sword too."

"Fat chance," Marus said, sliding his fingers around the worn hilt.

A quill slammed into the ground at his horses hooves, making the horse prance. "I would give him the blade, or." The man closest to him put a little pressure on the trigger. "I'll put this through your eye and take it for the boss anyway."

Quillen looked at Marus. "Give him the blade, Marus, or they'll kill us."

Marus waited for a few moments, gauging the situation. Reluctantly, he handed over his sword. As he passed the crossbowman, he said, "I'll be getting that back, just so you know."

The other man laughed, turned his horse around and then galloped off. The leader waved for them to follow him down the left fork in the road. The escort rode for several miles until they came to a town tucked in between two mountains.

Cascade Lake was nothing more than a village with several brothels and bars. A few miles further up the road was the coastal village of Pistoryum. Most of the mercenaries that lived at Cascade Lake slept in tents that they set up next to the main roadways.

The way it worked among the mercenaries in Batopia was simple. The mercs who lived there could fight for the Warlord, or seek money elsewhere as long as they gave him his share.

Quillen and Marus were brought into the village. The escort stopped at a small fountain with bubbles floating to the top. Marus' thirst took over, and he went to touch it, but a man snatched his hand away.

"You don't want to stick your hand in there, it's a trap." Marus made eye contact with him. "It's filled with oil. One spark and it goes sky high," the man said.

"You two come with me," the leader said after he dismounted.

Marus and Quillen were escorted to a burned out castle long since forgotten in the wilds. Vines grew up the sides and disappeared over the broken ramparts. Walking into the main hall, they saw a figure sitting on a throne to large for his frame. A few gold trinkets lay against the wall among broken wood and pottery.

Warlord Three Toes was brutish, nasty in every way, from his bulging eyes to his rusted boots. His young grizzled face had dozens of scars running across it and his hair was shaved to the scalp. By his side was a double sided axe with blood still caked on it from some animal, or human, whichever had been his latest victim.

"My lord, these two vagabonds have come to see you," said the man who led them into the room.

Three Toes stared at them, Quillen's hooks drawing his attention. "Why do you come to my great hall?"

Marus scoffed. "Great hall?" This looks more like a pigs paradise, than a hall."

Quillen stepped in front of him and bowed low, his hooks extended, diverting Three Toes attention.

"Nice hooks. Can you take them off?" Three Toes asked.

"M'lord?" Quillen asked.

"Your hooks, can—-?"

"No m'lord. My hands were cut off in a battle long ago and these took their place. I am Senatore Quillen of Wolfrya and this is Marus, my loyal servant."

Marus glared at him.

Three Toes smiled. "I see, so again, why have you come to my court?" His hand slid to his battle axe. "I hate Wolfryan's."

"I know that m'lord. We have come to offer you a chance to help us take down the Wolfryan empire," Quillen said.

Three Toes roared with laughter and held his chest until he recovered. "You are suggesting we storm Iceport?"

"Yes m'lord. If you help us take Iceport, we will ensure you are crowned king and establish a new lineage line there," Quillen said.

Three Toes chuckled. "New lineage line?" He looked around the room. "Does it look like I have children. Look around you old man, there is nothing here except my mounds of treasure," he replied.

Quillen looked around. "Yes m'lord, your wealth... is vast." He tried to find an object worth something. He picked up a broken gold cross from nearby and walked toward the throne.

One of Three Toes bodyguards intercepted him and pushed him back with the butt of his spear. "Step back or get a spear through your guts." The guard said before he looked at Three Toes.

Quillen approached and knelt before the throne. "M'lord, Iceport has more gold than anywhere in Delos. It's streets are paved with it. If you help us destroy Octavius, you can loot the palace and with it the city," Quillen said.

Three Toes stared at the broken cross and a smirk crossed his lips. "There will be more gold than I can imagine?" he asked.

"I give you my word as a senatore of Wolfrya."

"Words are cheap, senatore. What plan do you have to take Iceport?" he asked.

"I can sneak into the city and open the gate. Your men can ride inside and pillage as much as they want. All we ask is you kill Octavius," Quillen said.

Three Toes stretched and stood up. "I don't have enough men to take the castle. There are thousands of legionnaires there. I will not lead my men into a slaughter," he replied.

"What if we poison their water supply?" Marus asked, walking up to Quillen.

"Kill the women and children too?" Three Toes asked. "We're not devils, we're mercenaries. We don't kill women or children."

Marus didn't budge. "Are they *your* women and children?" he asked.

"Well, no——,"

"M'lord, I don't mean to interrupt, but if you want those lands some people must die. There is not enough grain to feed the populace and Octavius has no intention of helping them. It would be more humane to kill the women and children with poison rather than let them starve to death," Marus said, standing behind Quillen.

Three Toes scanned the sparsely finished room. "You have a point."

Compared to Wolfrya, he was a pauper and what was worse, he knew it. He tapped his chin with his index finger as delusions of grandeur danced through his mind.

"I'll agree to your plan." He turned to the man who brought them in. "Assemble our men. Tell them whatever lies behind Iceport's walls is there for the taking. Give our guests a tent and food. We will meet again in the morning."

The guard bowed at the waist and wiggled Marus' sword in his direction to mock him.

As morning came, the sound of drunken men snoring woke Quillen and Marus. They sat up and watched the sun rise over the horizon.

Marus spat. "Never thought this would happen."

"What would happen?" Quillen asked.

"That I would be assaulting Iceport and killing the emperor. What has my life become?" Marus mumbled.

"I'm not sure. I didn't see myself turning into a traitor either. But Octavius wants us dead, so this is the only way."

Marus chuckled. "I wish there was some way for us to regain his favor."

"Only way to do that is to bring Evorix Vispanius to him, alive," Quillen said.

A glint of hope came to Marus' eyes. "What if we convince Three Toes to kill Evorix if we can track him down?"

Quillen was quiet for a moment in his own thoughts. "That may just work, but where would we find him?"

"My guess is he is going to find an army and march on Iceport, same as us. Let's beat him there and set up an ambush. If we destroy his army, we will get back into the emperor's good graces."

Quillen scratched his chin with his hook. "And if they outnumbered us?"

Marus gazed straight ahead and spit. "Then we fight to the last man."

Chapter 25

"Tro'ka of the R'atu, what you are proposing will be the end of our society," the warrior seated at the opposite end of the table said, his fur white as the driven snow. The other warriors surrounding him growled in agreement.

"I understand how you feel, Hu'taka, leader of the Free Prides, but if we help the humans, we can be rid of the Wolfryan Empire. The very same line of humans that hunted us and drove us into the Fire Lands," Vitkalla said.

"You're an Outkast and have no say at this table, Vitkalla. You, or Tro'ka for that matter." Hu'taka scanned the room looking for someone. "You, K'aro of the D'atu, what say you?"

K'aro sat in the shadows by himself eating an apple. "I have no say, Lord Hu'taka. I'm the last of a pride and therefore have no vote," he replied.

"I know your pridesman are gone, but you still hold a vote. What are your thoughts?" he asked again.

"I rode with Lord Tro'ka and Lord Vitkalla to request your aid. I believe in what this human Evorix proposes. I have sworn allegiance to Lady Corcundia, a wizard of the Last Bloods. So I have no choice but to return," K'aro said, his blue eye catching the firelight.

At the mention of the Last Bloods, the warriors around the table stopped eating and drinking. They looked at one another and then back at K'aro. "What was that?" Hu'taka asked, leaning forward in his chair.

"We follow a human woman named Lady Corcundia. She is the last of her kind and if we follow anyone it will be her, m'lord. Not some Wolfryan slaves," K'aro said.

Hu'taka tapped his paws in front of his muzzle. "That's what I thought you said. This puts us in a bit of a spot. Last Bloods must be protected if ever found in the world. We agreed to that for their help."

"That is true m'lord," K'aro said.

"Leave us," Hu'taka said, looking around the room.

"M'lord——-," said one of his men.

Hu'taka roared. "I said leave us." He waited until the others left and continued, "So K'aro, how do you propose we help the Last Blood?"

"We help her re-take Iceport. And after we finish, we can come out from the volcanoes," he replied.

"What assurances do I have that they won't finish us off?" Hu'taka asked.

K'aro slammed his blade onto the table and cut his paw, smearing the blood over his brow. "I give you my word as an oathsworn."

Hu'taka stood for a moment and collected his thoughts. He placed his paws behind his back and stared into the smoldering fire. "If what you say is true, how much of a difference would a thousand warriors make? Even if we could summon the prides, some may still seek a sword ring," he said.

"M'lord, if we can convince them to help us, we may live in peace with more land than we have had in a hundred years," K'aro said.

"And then what?" Hu'taka asked, raising an eyebrow.

K'aro smiled. "We would be the tip of the spear and the first ones to glory."

Hu'taka growled with laughter. "I see. You were always a good diplomat, K'aro. Perhaps you have something here. Call the others back into the tent, we have work to do."

The other warrior lords returned to their seats, a look of concern on many of their faces. Hu'taka clapped his paws and their human servants brought more food and drink to the table.

He stood up from his chair. "I want riders sent to each pride in the Fire Lands. Tell them I want to convene a war council to decide this matter of going to war aligned with the humans."

Some of the lords of the Free Prides growled in protest. Hu'taka slammed his paw on the table. "Does anyone here question my position?"

The lord's quieted down and looked around. Lord Na'tu of the Grey Cloaks, a slaver group within the Free Prides stood up and said, "I will send some warriors to the other tribes. Who's with me?" he asked, looking at his fellow lords.

The others stood one by one. Hu'taka waved a runner over and said, "Ready the alpurlics."

• • • •

SEVERAL DAYS PASSED and then one morning the sand swirled on the horizon as the different prides rode over a sand dune to the gate of the encampment.

"If anything, this should be entertaining," K'aro said, watching the dust floating around the alpurlics riding toward them.

A warrior nearly ten feet tall dismounted from his abnormally large alpurlic in front of the other warriors and walked up to the earthen mound protecting the encampment.

The warrior had a misanthropic personality and didn't mind letting humans know he saw them only as slaves. K'aro turned to Tro'ka.

"Thought he was dead," K'aro whispered.

Tro'ka growled as the warrior approached. "I will always despise him," he said, sliding his paw to his sword.

K'aro lifted Tro'ka's paw from the hilt of his sword and said, "No sword rings, m'lord."

Chewing on a warm human femur, the ten foot warrior glanced up at them. "Cousin, how are you?"

Tro'ka leapt from his position and rose to his feet and nodded his head. "Ba'tu."

Ba'tu roared with laughter at Tro'ka's response. "Come now cousin, let us not dwell on the past."

As Tro'ka was about to reply, Vitkalla walked up behind them, his mane slicked back with bacon grease. "Tro'ka, prepare the war table."

Without a word, Tro'ka turned around and walked back into the council's tent.

Ba'tu raised an eyebrow as he walked away. "Does my cousin wish a sword ring," he asked, his paw tapping the pommel of his sword.

"You're cousin would take that challenge without thought, however, I forbid it. Now, form your pride for entrance into our camp.

As Ba'tu walked away, the other five pride leaders rode up to the fort and dismounted. The others that arrived were the Ta'tu, A'tu, Era'tu, Pa'tu and the Ca'tu.

The Ra'tu warriors inside the fort lined up in two rows down the ash covered road and held their spears by their sides, their helmets shining brightly in the setting rays of the sun. The ceremonial herald beat his war drum as the leaders approached from their respective prides. As they neared the gate, he roared their names.

"Xa'tu of the Ca'tu," announced the herald as the warrior ambled on all fours through the gate. He roared and headed towards the war tent, his black spots loud against his yellow fur. The Ca'tu walked on all fours for the most part, but a few warriors like Xa'tu walked on all fours and on two when it was needed.

"Lord Ja'tu of the Pa'tu," shouted the herald. A fifteen foot warrior walked forward and slammed his ten foot obsidian tipped spear into the ground and roared as he looked around. Red and blue bird feathers adorned the head of his spear, marking him as the holder of power in the pride. The Pa'tu were few in number but were the tallest of all the prides, their strength unparalleled. Most warriors stood at least eleven feet, but the leader, Ja'tu was the tallest.

"Lord Gra'tu of the Era'tu," said the herald, an extra beat on his war drum. Supported by two warriors, the ancient warrior limped forward. The oldest warrior in the pride, he was nearly two hundred years old. The trio stopped several times for Gra'tu to catch his breath. This would be his final meeting as the head of their pride, his son Su'tu waited patiently with the others, keeping his paw on his knife handle.

"Lord Ma'tu of the A'tu," said the herald. The warriors were from the painted tribe founded by A'tu, first king of the united prides. Each of their faces were painted in different colors, symbolizing their hierarchy. Those who held power wore blue streaks through their manes and faces and the lowest rung of their caste system wore white throughout their manes, no better than the human slaves that traveled with the baggage train. They were mostly warriors who had lost their honor retreating in battle, or through desertion. Chains adorned their necks, a mark of their cowardice.

"Ba'tu of the Ta'tu, said the herald, spitting his name out venomously. The herald threw his war drum down in protest and walked away. The other pridesmen grew wary and mumbled obscenities as he walked by. Ignoring their stares, he sneered at anyone who kept his gaze.

"Bunch of scared lionesses," said Ba'tu with a scoff.

No matter how much food could be harvested among the prides, the Ta'tu preferred the taste of the dead, human or warrior. Wiping his paw across his mouth, Ba'tu flung a bone over his shoulder he was chewing on and burped.

Vitkalla approached him and said, "Ba'tu, I will tell you once more, know your place in my council. Your cousin is the chosen heir of the R'atu and you will respect him. You were banished for your lifestyle choices, remember?"

"How could I forget, uncle."

"You put yourself in that position," Vitkalla said heatedly, refusing to break his gaze.

Ba'tu roared. "It's none of your——."

Holding his hand up, Vitkalla said, "You ate my brothers in an attempt to usurp my crown, one of them your own father. I asked you to do what I needed and that plan was to kill my father because of his cowardice, instead you killed everyone. And my son and I were banished. If we met outside this council, I would kill you. But you're protected here under a banner of truce."

Ba'tu roared with laughter and shouldered past Vitkalla. He walked into the tent and took a seat at the center of the table. Sitting down, he looked at the food in disgust and then grabbed something from his pouch and unrolled it. He licked his lips and picked up the cold bloody paw of a warrior in front of him.

Ja'tu gave him a harsh look, then pushed his seat back with a growl and walked away. Ba'tu shrugged and used the open chair as a footstool.

"Now, what's all the fuss about?" he asked, taking a bite out of the paw.

Tro'ka shook with fury at the open disrespect he showed the council.

"If you address this council, you know the proper way to do so. If you do not, we will put it to a vote for someone to accept The Challenge and face you in the sword ring," Vitkalla said.

Ja'tu stepped up from behind and said, "I will take that challenge."

Vitkalla chuckled. "Ah, the first challenger. If you lose the fight, you lose the power as head of your demented pride. Are we going to have a problem out of you, Ba'tu?"

"No problem uncle," he purred and threw the half eaten paw over his shoulder, hitting Ja'tu.

Ja'tu lunged forward, but his warriors grabbed him and pulled him back. Ba'tu glanced over his shoulder and bared his incisors.

Vitkalla shook his mane. "Let's bring this war council to order. Thank you all for coming. We only expected your envoys, not your warriors. We are grateful though, so I will cut right to the chase. We need all the warriors in this camp to take Iceport from the humans. If we can assault their castle, we can settle the blood debt against the Wolfryan humans."

Gra'tu glanced up from a thick leather book he was reading from and made eye contact with Hu'taka. "Why should we care about a blood debt?"

Hu'taka stood up and said, "You and I stood together at the signing with the Last Bloods when they helped us escape."

"Right you are, but the Last Bloods are dead. The Wolfryan king wiped them out, just like us. We have been replenishing our ranks among these accursed volcanoes for years and now you are suggesting we lose all of our warriors taking a castle none of us care about?" Gra'tu asked.

Hu'taka pointed at K'aro who stepped out of the shadows. "Lord K'aro of the Da'tu, what say you?"

K'aro stepped up to the table. "I follow a human—."

Ba'tu pounded the table. "You follow a human?" He shook his mane. "Where's your spirit K'aro, you weak—-."

Ja'tu lunged forward and snapped Ba'tu's neck and threw him out of the chair. "My lords forgive my actions, I could no longer abide his behavior." He knelt in front of Hu'taka. "I am prepared to be an Outkast should the council deem it."

Tro'ka and Vitkalla roared their approval of Ja'tu's actions and picked Ba'tu's body up. They threw it outside and returned to their seats.

"Any in this council intend to vote for Ja'tu to be an Outkast?" Hu'taka asked.

No one's paw went up.

Gra'tu chuckled. "And that's the end of Ba'tu of the Ta'tu. Go inform his warriors they are no longer needed at the council."

Tro'ka grinned and left the tent with his warriors to ask the Ta'tu to leave, or die in a sword ring.

"You may continue, K'aro," Hu'taka said, sitting back down.

K'aro stammered as he continued to speak, then refocused himself. "Yes my lord, I was informing the council that we follow a human named Lady Corcundia, the only remaining member of the Last Bloods."

The lords that were gathered glanced down the table at K'aro and then amongst each other. "Did you say a wizard from the Last Bloods?" Gra'tu asked with a pur.

"Yes Lord Gra'tu, we have found the last one and fulfilled our end of the blood oath."

Gra'tu pondered the information for a moment, then nodded. "Then my warriors will help you fulfill our duty I signed with my father. Anyone else?"

Ja'tu growled and stared at Hu'taka. "Where do you need my warriors, Lord Hu'taka?"

Hu'taka smiled. "I knew I could count on you, Lord Ja'tu, thank you."

A large warrior in a studded leather chest plate stormed into the council tent. He slammed the shaft of his battle axe into the sand and bowed low. Two guards leveled their spears and put them on either side of the warriors shoulders.

Hu'taka glanced at him and said, "Lord Za'tu, what can we help you with?"

The warrior growled and then spoke. "I have assumed leadership of the Ta'tu, Lord Hu'taka. Many of my warriors would like to stay and fight."

Hu'taka looked at Gra'tu who finally nodded. "One condition, your pride stops eating the flesh of warriors. We don't care about the humans. Do we have an accord?" Hu'taka asked.

Za'tu nodded and raised his chin. "We will do whatever you ask, Lord Hu'taka."

"Fine. Assemble your warriors. You will lead the charge when we reach Iceport," Hu'taka said.

Za'tu smiled, one of his jagged incisors peeking through. "Thank you for the honor, Lord Hu'taka."

Tro'ka stared at Hu'taka after Za'tu left, his eyes mere slits. "Why Lord Hu'taka?"

Hu'taka glanced at the warriors faces. "The Ta'tu pride has lost its honor with Ba'tu as their leader. I will allow them to regain it."

Gra'tu nodded and waved a warrior over to help him out of the chair. "I will retire for the evening, my lords. Su'tu will take command of the pride while I rest."

"Good night Lord Gra'tu and thank you for your support," Hu'taka said.

"Xa'tu, are you with us?" Hu'taka asked after Gra'tu left.

Xa'tu stood on his hind legs and roared.

"I'll take that as a yes," Hu'taka glanced to his immediate left. "Lord Ma'tu, are you with us?"

Ma'tu sighed and shook his blue mane. "We will follow you, but how do you plan to take Iceport?" he asked.

"The plan will come together in due time," Hu'taka said, glancing over at one of his lords that stood up.

"Lord Hu'taka, I know some may think this a fool's errand." The warrior raised his cup. "But my warriors are with you."

"So, this is everyone?" Vitkalla muttered, looking around.

The lord's stood together and raised their goblets as one. Hu'taka slammed his goblet down and the others roared in response.

• • • •

THE NEXT MORNING, THE sun peeked over the horizon. A long line of warriors riding on the backs of their alpurlics stretched a mile back. The warriors rode through the black sand and across the burned out ruins of long forgotten stone forts.

As they approached Last Keep, the road was lined with crucified Rebellium soldiers and Ba pridesmen. Hu'taka held his paw up and stared at the corpses, his incisors bared.

"Who did this?" he growled.

"The Wolfryan emperor, Lord Hu'taka," Tro'ka replied.

Hu'taka rode in front of the column with his bodyguards and said, "Make camp. I want the Gray Cloaks to strip the dead and burn them. After all the bodies have all been pulled down, I want the lord's to assemble by the great fire."

The Gray Cloaks cantered down the road and stopped every few feet to cut someone down. After a day in the beating sun with the volcanoes at their backs, the warriors stacked all the corpses in piles and then built a large fire.

All the Ba lord's reassembled in Hu'taka's tent, except K'aro. He led a pack horse with a body slung over the saddle, a burlap bag by his side. He walked up to the fire and gently laid the man on the ground. The burlap sack swung from his saddle in the dusty wind.

"Who is that?" Vitkalla asked.

"King Aksutamoon," K'aro said.

"Is that his head?" Tro'ka asked, walking over.

K'aro nodded. "I need a wagon to transport the king's body to Tramonia for a proper burial."

"Fetch him a wagon Tro'ka," Vitkalla said.

A few minutes later, Tro'ka returned and lifted Aksutamoon onto the wagon and then draped a wool blanket over him.

"Find the rest of his men and load them in as well. They may not have burials like ours, but they should go home," Vitkalla said.

K'aro nodded and then placed the sack on Aksutamoon's chest with his hands covering it. After he was done loading the wagon, he returned.

A horn sounded behind Hu'taka. The prides formed as he stood on a rock outcropping. "Tonight, we bury our brethren, both human and warrior."

The warriors slammed their spears and roared. "Each life is precious and must be treated with respect. I want the emperor's head on a spike by the end of this," Hu'taka said.

The warriors spears slammed into the earth in response. Hu'taka nodded to a warrior who lit the bonfire he was standing next to. The burning hair in Hu'taka muzzle made him gag. After the oil sparked, it meandered through the wooden boxes lining the pridesmen and their human counterparts.

The wooden boxes had been built intrictly throughout the grave pit making the shape of an A, in respect to the original member of the prides, A'tu the Unifer.

"Those of you who fear no death will ride with me when the assault on Iceport begins," Hu'taka roared, his face partially covered by the white smoke in the air.

The warriors slammed their spears one last time. Without another word, Hu'taka walked off the rock outcropping and back to the other lords.

"Prepare to move out at first light," he said, strolling past his guardsmen.

Chapter 26

Evorix smiled at Corcundia laying on the bed of furs in his tent. She moaned, opened one eye and smiled.

"Told you I'd treat you good," he said.

"Indeed you did." She rose from the bed and poured two glasses of Tramonian wine. "Now what?" she asked.

A guard ran into the tent unannounced and saw them naked holding their glasses of wine.

He stammered. "Lord..."

Evorix let his penis sway side to side. "Yes."

"King Trakuta requires you and Lady Corcundia's presence," he said, trying not to stare at Corcundia.

Evorix looked at Corcundia as she got back in the bed, her lips turned in a seductive grin. She motioned for him to come closer.

He shrugged. "Tell the king I have more pressing priorities."

Several hours passed when Evorix and Corcundia finally walked into Trakuta's hall. Evorix walked up to the throne and made an exaggerated bow.

"Enough already, we have a problem," Trakuta said.

"And what's that?" Evorix asked.

"The rains are flooding the crossroads and it won't recede before we assault the castle. If we go, we have to go now."

"The army isn't ready," Evorix said flatly.

Trakuta shrugged. "This isn't their first battle."

Evorix scoffed at the comment. "You and I are old, Trakuta. Not a man in this army is our age and none of them have ever scaled a castle wall with arrows, or whatever else those legionnaires are going to be throwing down on us. If we leave now, we will be slaughtered at the gate."

"I know that, Evorix. But Octavious killed Aksutamoon. Someone has to pay," Trakuta snapped at him as he handed a map to a soldier standing nearby.

"Trakuta, think of what you are saying. Aksutamoon wouldn't want you to needlessly throw away lives and that's precisely what you're about to do," Corcundia said.

"Lady Corcundia, may I remind you that you are guests in this hall. But that can quickly change," Trakuta said, eyeing a guard slipping closer to them.

Evorix growled. "Trakuta, if you do this we all die. Is that what you want? Remember, it was my men who died so you could be king. And now you want to lose your entire army over a dead one. You're stupider than I gave you credit for, don't do this," Evorix said.

"I am the king and I make the rules. I have decided to invade Iceport before the rains block us in. Now, you are the lead general. Assemble *my* army. We leave at dawn."

Evorix shook his head and stormed out of the hall with Corcundia. "Power hungry, asshole," Evorix said as they walked out.

"Aren't they all?" she asked.

Evorix picked the dirt from under his fingernails as they walked and chuckled. "Yea, they are."

"Let's arm these soldiers the best we can. You have to speak to them before we leave. They won't follow a man just because he leads, they will follow him because he helped them believe. They deserve to know what you are asking of them," Corcundia said.

Evorix waved a guard over. "Sound the assembly horn."

An hour later every soldier in the castle stood shoulder to shoulder in the square. Evorix stood on the gallows ready to address them.

Ironic, he thought touching the hangman's rope.

At the top of his lungs, he shouted. "Men of Tramonia. My name is Evorix Vispinius, former prefect to Emperor Tiberius, commander of the Tramonian army. I wanted to let you know we will be moving out in the morning and our destination is Iceport. I'll give it to you straight. A lot of us will not be coming back. So, any man here who wants to stay behind, can. No man here will think less of you."

A few men raised their swords in the air and left the line. The army was primarily made up of conscripts during Tatootamoon's reign. Barely any of them were over the age of twenty one. Evorix took a sip of wine to quench his parched throat.

"For those of you who do leave with us prepare for a long campaign. Hopefully, whoever is with the emperor convinces him to make a run for it. If not, we're in bigger trouble than I thought we were. Division commanders and squad leaders meet at the war council tent in one hour. Dismissed."

Later that evening, all of Evorix's commanders were seated at the council table. He stood at the head of the sandbox with his pointer and drew Iceport's castle and the moat surrounding it.

"This will be the hardest battle you men have ever fought. There are at least two legions and our best guess is there are around two thousand battle hardened men eager for a fight." He pointed at the castle walls. "Our plan of attack is simple. We will assault on two fronts, the west and east walls. We will be outnumbered two to one. Once we're inside the walls, we will form in rows that are no more than five men across. We'll have to take it street by street. I know the layout and will lead a group of men into the castle as the others advance."

A scraping sound could be heard outside the tent. A guard hurried to the flap and swung it open, his sword inches from the person's throat.

"Put that sword away before I chop your hand off," Tersius said as he walked in with the help of an orderly.

His face was waxy, a look of hatred showing in his features. "Tersius, why are you not in bed?" Corcundia asked.

"Lady." He coughed and spit, his phlegm speckled with blood. "Lady Corcundia, I will storm the castle with you. Octavius' men killed my family. I will have my revenge, even if it costs me my life."

Evorix nodded and continued. "As I was saying, I want twenty volunteers to enter the castle with me. Lady Corcundia, you will lead in my absence. Unlucky for us, we'll be moving out without the aid of the Ba warriors. Once we scale the walls there are a few ground rules. Unless a woman, or child attack you there will be as few civilian casualties as possible. Our fight is with the legionnaires, not the populace. Any questions?"

A soldier in his mid twenties stood up. "And if we are taken prisoner?"

Evorix chuckled. "Legionnaires do not take prisoners. Save your last dagger for yourself. I want a team of healers to follow behind us when we open the gate. As our men fall, cover them and have runners bring them to the rear.

What I would give to have Precipitous and Zillas with me. Evorix mused.

Reading his thoughts, Corcundia smiled and slipped her hand into his. "We will see them again."

Evorix bowed his head and then glanced at the faces of his men. "Everyone understand the plan?"

Silence met him in reply.

"Good, now feed your men heartily. Tomorrow we march on Iceport."

The next morning Evorix mounted a white alpurlic, a gift from Tro'ka. The animal purred when Evorix petted its mane. He looked at the crisp Tramonian tabards marching past him and smiled.

I should be drinking in Batopia.

Evorix glanced at Trakuta in his silver plated armor.

"Are you ready your highness?" Evorix asked, not bothering to look at him when he responded.

Trakuta ignored him, raised his hand in the air and then swung it down. His horse neighed and trotted off as the war drums and bagpipes accompanying them broke the silence of the early morning air. They marched off and traveled for several days until their wagons finally bogged down in the slick mud from the constant rain.

Trakuta stayed with his staff the whole trip. He didn't talk to, or even bother to ask about the plan. Evorix stared at him talking to his men, trying to block out his anger.

Corcundia walked up beside Evorix. "He's changed," she said.

He laughed. "Yea, you're right, but I think this was his plan all along. I don't think he expected you or I to live through the castle fight."

"That coward will get his day, they always do," she replied.

"I don't understand. He became king and overnight he changed. Why?" Evorix asked.

"If there's one thing I have learned during my life; men with the wrong ambition who hold resentments will get everyone killed," she replied.

"Why have you stuck around as long as you have?" Evorix asked.

A slight smile crossed her features. She rubbed her ring finger, oblivious to the fact that the ring that was once on it had been buried with her husband. "You wouldn't understand."

"Probably not, but tell me anyway," he replied.

She looked at her boots and wiped a single tear away. "My husband, Falgor was one of the people who hated the empire and sold stolen arms to the Rebellium. Octavius ordered his cronies to kill him and then me when I got back from a trading venture in the south."

"What happened?"

"Fredrick the Gray captured him during a banner of truce. The offer from Octavius was simple. Give up our black market trading and be absolved of any crimes against the crown. From what I've been told Falgor turned his back to transfer the lead wagon and surrender ..."

"And they killed him," Evorix said, finishing her sentence.

She nodded and wiped another tear away. Evorix pulled her close and kissed her. She gazed into his eyes and smiled.

"I never thought I would be with you. I don't usually fall for brutes, but you are changing, Evorix. You may end up being a good man," she said.

A deep roar of laughter sounded from Evorix's throat as he let her go. "Not bloody likely."

• • • •

AFTER BREAKING CAMP, the army moved over the hill and down into the next valley.

A fire arrow flew out of the treeline to the east and landed on the dirt path the army was on. Nearly a thousand men rode out the woods in a wedge formation. Evorix calmly freed his sword and shouted orders to his commanders. "Form lines."

"Form ranks, gods damn you, form ranks!" one of the commanders with Evorix shouted as he stepped forward.

The soldiers hurried to their positions looking over their shoulders at the onslaught of men riding towards them.

"Pikes to the front, archers to the back," Evorix commanded.

A command was given from somewhere beside him as they formed battle lines. "Archers, nock!"

"Who the hell is that?" one of the commanders shouted, pushing a soldier into line.

"Doesn't matter, kill them all," Evorix roared back.

The arrows snapped from their bowstrings and flew downrange. The arrows thumped into the oncoming riders, knocking many of them from their saddles. Evorix scanned the men dressed in black, his eyes darting to each one.

Why the animal masks?

He cursed when he saw a familiar face.

Marus, you rotten son of a bitch.

Looking around, Evorix shouted a command to his archers, "Loose."

Another round of their arrows knocked more men from their saddles. A moment later, the horsemen crashed into the line, the blood mixing with the mud as both men and beast fell into the slop.

"First rank, push!" one of the front line commanders yelled.

The young Tramonian's listened to the command and pushed the first wave of attackers back. More screams could be heard as the second wave crashed in behind the first, killing many of the Tramonian's in the front ranks.

"Who the hell is this?" Trakuta shouted.

"Batopian mercenaries led by Marus," Evorix hissed back.

"The prefect you're always talking about?" Trakuta asked.

"The very same. Trakuta, I need you to lead the calvary and buy us the time we need to reach the high ground before we are obliterated, " Evorix replied, firing an arrow at one of the horsemen breaking through the line.

Trakuta shook his head. "I'm a king now. I can't ride into an enemy. What if I'm killed? You would have utter chaos."

Evorix glared at him and shook his head. "Fine, I'll go. You should probably retreat your eminence." Evorix looked for Corcundia. "Take my position, I'll be right back."

A boulder exploded next to them as Evorix stepped forward, scattering everyone. Evorix woke up and pulled his helmet off, his ear drums pounding. The smoke obstructed his view as he looked for everyone. He only had a split second to react as a man barreled through the smoke.

Evorix dodged the wide swing and sunk his knife into the man's throat. He kicked him off the blade and searched for Corcundia. He saw her laying on her side, blood trickling from a wound somewhere on her head. He knelt by her and picked her up. Throwing her over his shoulder, he sprinted to his alpurlic and threw her over the saddle.

He heard a warcry from behind and spun around. He caught an attacker by the throat and crushed his windpipe.

Tersius hobbled up as Evorix launched the body away from himself. Checking her wounds, Evorix shouted, "Take her to the rear. Her life is in your hands, boy."

He helped Tersius onto the alpurlics back, slapped the animal on the rump and then turned around to organize whatever troops remained.

Pandemonium had broken out, the first line all but disintegrating. The men who remained fell behind the second rank to regroup. The blood and mud had men slipping and fighting each other with their fists and knives.

Through the haze, Evorix saw a catapult fire and watched helplessly as it killed another score of young Tramonian's.

One of his commanders sprinted up to him. "Our men are retreating on all sides."

"Go to the left and reorganize them. I will do the same with the right. Have the center fight a rear guard action. Shit, look out!" Evorix shouted, hearing a boulder whistle near them.

The boulder crashed near them, killing the commander and knocking Evorix down again.

Fuck!

He snatched a horn from one of the dead heralds by his side and sounded retreat. He heard another horn in the distance, followed by another. He watched the calvary form up and charge toward the attackers.They collided and held them just long enough for the infantry to regroup.

"Form a line here," Evorix shouted, discarding his dented helmet.

He watched in horror as another boulder slammed into their lines. Evorix grabbed a horse and mounted it. "Hold the line!" he shouted to the closest sergeant.

He yanked the horses head to the right and rode hard for the catapult.

This is a really bad idea, he thought.

The enemy didn't see him flank them as he hung onto the side of the saddle. Riding hard, the horse began to foam at the mouth and a second later it gave out and collapsed. Evorix rolled to his feet and ran the rest of the way. He counted five men guarding the catapult. Sprinting through the dead bodies in his way, he pulled both of his swords from their scabbards.

The men guarding the catapult saw him, fired their crossbows and advanced with swords drawn. One of the quills struck Evorix in the shoulder and knocked him down. Before he could regain his feet, they were on him. He swatted their swords strokes away and killed a few of them in quick succession. One man swept Evorix's feet out from under him and pressed his attack.

Evorix tripped over a body behind him and fell back on the dew covered grass. One of the attackers sword blows severed his crippled right hand as he lay unprotected. Roaring in pain with blood gushing from the wound, he stood up and managed to parry the last two men's sword strokes. One of the men stepped forward and slipped, his arms flying out in front of him to catch his fall. Evorix dropped his sword, gripped the man's throat and crushed his adams apple.

The last attacker sneered at him, showing him his missing teeth. He tackled Evorix and threw him to the ground. Evorix clicked the back of his boot as they tumbled to the ground.

The mercenary stood up, leaned forward at the waist and swung his sword down. At the last moment, the man noticed a glint in the mud, but before he could react, Evorix buried the hidden knife blade deep into his stomach. The attacker spit out a mouthful of blood as Evorix withdrew the blade. His attacker put pressure on the wound and looked up at him. As he glanced up, Evorix slammed a blade into the man's right eye.

Kicking the body to the ground, Evorix fell back into the mud with a sigh. He wiped his hand across his mouth as a slight chuckle escaped his lips.

Damn shame I didn't get to kill Octavius.

A foreign note on a horn sounded, then another until the earth shook. Evorix lay back with a cough, holding the bloody stump that had been his hand.

"To the Last Blood!"

Evorix heard the roar behind him and smiled. A thousand Ba warriors rode over the hill and into the center of Three Toes army. The mercenaries weren't able to form a battle formation as the alpurlics galloped down the slope. The roars from the warriors deafened the attackers, causing some of them to flee. They rode through the mercenaries like a scythe through wheat and the mercenaries folded soon after.

A warrior rode up to Evorix and dismounted. He grabbed a silk cloth from his sash and tied it around Evorix's lower arm just above his wrist, stemming the flow of blood. Evorix glanced up.

"K'aro, should have figured you would show up."

"Where is Lady Corcundia," he growled.

"Wounded. Tersius took her to the rear," Evorix mumbled.

K'aro picked him up and put him on his alpurlic's neck. He mounted, held on to Evorix's belt line and rode after the rest of the prides.

Tro'ka and Vitkalla's personal flags were in the thick of the fighting. The Ba'tu not wanting to be outdone dismounted and fought hand to hand using their large double bladed axes, killing scores of mercenaries.

Hu'taka, flanked by the other pride commanders watched the battle with a look of amusement on their faces. He watched a head of bright red hair ride into the center of the retreating men, the Rebellium flag fluttering behind her. Hu'taka pointed at the woman.

"Who is that?" he asked.

The other pride leaders shrugged. Hu'taka urged his mount forward toward the Tramonian tents by the river.

"Let us go and find out," Hu'taka said.

The other lords followed behind him. The mercenaries were soon surrounded and captured. K'aro had managed to ride through the throng of soldiers to the medical tent to drop Evorix off.

Screams of men having their limbs amputated echoed through the valley. K'aro waved a few of the Ba healers over and gave them instructions on treating the wounded Rebellium soldiers. He pulled Evorix from the saddle, went into the tent and threw him onto an empty table. He grabbed a hot poker from a fire in the center of the tent, walked over to him and then began his gruesome work.

On the battlefield, the Ba collected their prisoners. They led them over to Corcundia and shoved them down into the mud. She dabbed at the blood running down her temple as she stared at the prisoners faces. Three Toes and his men sat bound in a circle with a few warriors keeping a close eye on them.

The battle had been fierce. A few hundred Tramonian's and a handful of warriors had been killed. A few of Three

Toes mercenaries survived the attack and of those that did, only a few had survived without major wounds.

The warriors and the Tramonian's that were well enough helped pull the bodies of both friend and foe to a pit and roll them in. The deep pit claimed several hundred bodies before they were ready to burn them. A lone warrior chanted and then threw a torch on the oil covering the pit. Tersius watched as a huge flame roared ten feet into the air in front of him.

He walked over to Corcundia. "What's the plan with these prisoners?" he asked.

Corcundia looked at the men huddled in a circle. "Can't take them with us as captives, so I have an idea."

She walked up to the group. "Who is the leader here?"

Three Toes stood up. "I am."

Corcundia pointed to two guards and they brought him over. "Why did you attack us?"

"I was told by those two over there that there was gold in Iceport. They told me I had to destroy you before we could proceed."

Corcundia stared past him. "Who told you?"

He pointed at Marus and Quillen. "Them right there."

"Guards, take those two in for questioning. If they refuse to talk during the interrogation, kill them."

The guards ripped them off the ground and marched them past Corcundia as she sniffed the air around them.

"Those two are Wolfryan's, high born if I had a guess. I can smell it on them, like stink on shit. But they'll talk soon enough." She glanced at Three Toes. "Where are you from?" she asked.

"Batopia, near the village of Pistoryum."

"Come with me, friend. We will dine and talk about your opportunities," she said, leading him to a tent.

Corcundia walked into the tent to the sound of Rebellium commanders sitting around the table studying maps, arguing whether or not holding in their current location was the best plan.

She pointed to a seat for Three Toes to sit down. "Bring our guest food and water." She sat down and lit her cherrywood pipe. "What's your name?"

"I am Warlord Three Toes of Batopia."

"What did the Wolfryan's tell you?" she asked, her eyebrow raising.

"They said Iceport has an overflowing amount of gold. And if we could ambush this Evorix, I would be handsomely rewarded."

"Ah, they have a problem with Evorix. That figures," she replied.

She got up and walked to a slave in the corner of the room and took the wine glasses from him. She put a glass in front of Three Toes, broke some bread and handed half of it to him.

"You know the emperor has been spending his gold rapidly."

Three Toes stopped eating. "That figures, nothing is ever as it seems."

"You never had enough troops to take Iceport, you know that right?" she asked, after taking a sip of wine.

"We were supposed to poison their water supply and wait them out."

"Water supply? You would kill the women and children?" she asked, running her hand through her matted hair.

"I thought the same thing, but they aren't my kin. So if some will die for our advancement, then so be it. But all we had to do was kill Octavius."

"Is that a fact." She looked around and then whispered, "I have an idea on how to save your life. What do you think about joining us?" she asked.

Three Toes smiled.

"Let's raise our glasses in a toast to the death of Octavius," she said in her regular voice.

They raised their glasses, clinking them together and then downed the wine.

Three Toes licked his lips. "Spicy."

He picked up his bread again and stopped suddenly. He pulled at his tunic and coughed. Blood trickled from his ears and his skin flushed.

"What did you do to me?" Three Toes gasped in a raspy voice.

"Oh, I forgot to tell you. I slipped a little extra in there for you. The spicy taste is snake poison." She grabbed the glass and handed it to a slave. "Bury it," she said in an emotionless voice.

She stood from the table as Three Toes foamed at the mouth, gasping for air. The commanders at the table smiled, a few nodded. He fell from the chair, blood dripping from his lip. She knelt down next to him and put her hand on his shoulder.

"The problem with this poison is it takes awhile to die. Wasn't sure how much it would take. Can you still hear me?" she asked.

Three Toes tried to speak but a torrent of blood exploded from his mouth.

"You should never try to kill someone you don't know," she said, leaning closer.

Blood curdling screams could be heard outside the tent. "The last thing you'll hear is your men being impaled, then crucified." She waved one of her commanders over. "Pick him up and bring him outside."

She walked out behind them and watched the mercenaries as they were impaled and left to die. Three Toes collapsed to his knees throwing up blood and bile. She squatted down next to him and watched his shoulders shaking from the spasms wracking his body.

"The next sight you see will be the devil."

Three Toes glanced up, his cheeks bursting with fluid and then he fell to the ground.

"Boy that took a minute," she said, walking back into the tent.

• • • •

LATER THAT EVENING, Marus and Quillen sat in a tent bound by their wrists and feet. A large warrior stood outside blocking any access from curious onlookers.

The pair hadn't fared well in the battle. Quillen suffered a concussion and Marus had a nasty gash over his left eye.

A soldier ducked into the tent behind them. "You boys know what comes next, right?" he asked.

Marus chuckled. "I fuck your mother."

The soldier pulled a cat-o-nine tails from his belt and smashed it across Marus' face. Marus tried to stand and fell into the sand, his blood soaking into the dirt around him. He winced as the welts formed on the right side of his face.

"Now we get to go to the interrogation tent and believe me this will be the last day of your miserable lives," the soldier said, his crooked teeth poking out from behind his large lips.

The guard whistled and three other soldiers came in and pushed them out of the holding tent. Marus and Quillen were paraded past the impaled corpses of the mercenaries, their blood and guts slick on the stake below them.

They walked past the infirmary and the soldiers stopped them, forcing them to look at the tent. The pile of limbs outside were a few feet tall. Marus smiled, but it was immediately replaced by a frown when he saw Evorix emerge from the tent with his arm in a sling, his wrist padded in silk.

K'aro had barely saved his life. The wound had been cauterized, but there was still a risk of infection. It would take multiple remedies and months of rest to bring him back to full strength.

Evorix made eye contact with Marus and before anyone could react, he was on top of him stomping him into the ground. K'aro came out of the tent, his apron dark with blood. He shook his mane, snatched Evorix from behind and drug him back into the tent.

The guard pulled Marus to his feet and dusted him off.

"Thank you," Marus said.

The soldier reared his head back and slammed it on the bridge of Marus' nose. Blood squirted in every direction as Marus held his hands to it. "That's my brother's arm right there, you bastard." The man pointed at the pile. "You're lucky I don't stick that hand up your ass," he said, shoving him forward.

The soldiers brought them into a nearby tent. It was dim on the inside, only the coals on a small brazier illuminated it. The soldiers kicked Marus and Quillen in the back of the knees to help them reach the ground faster. Three shadows appeared above them as Tro'ka, Vitkalla and Na'tu stepped forward.

"Leave us," Tro'ka purred.

The guards left and closed the tent flap.

Marus glared at Tro'ka, not breaking his gaze.

"Impudent human," Tro'ka roared, backhanding him onto his back.

Tro'ka reached down and untied each of them. Quillen kept his eyes closed, his whimpering drowned out by the low guttural laugh of the warriors.

"And this one wines like a cub," Na'tu said.

He bent down and pushed his muzzle against Quillen's nose. "Don't y—-."

Quillen's hooks tore his throat out before he finished his sentence. Na'tu bled out next to him. "I'll be seeing you soon, Marus," Quillen said, staring straight ahead.

Tro'ka's mouth was wide open and he bit Quillen's head off. The headless body fell to the ground spasming. Tro'ka spit out Quillen's mangled head and picked his teeth with a claw.

"Tasty," he said.

Vitkalla picked Na'tu's body up and carried him out without a word.

"That's going to cost you, human," Tro'ka said, rolling out his selection of torture goodies.

"I didn't kill him," Marus replied.

Tro'ka pulled out two thin knives and sharpened them. "It matters not. You know something human, I picked these knives because they will keep you alive long enough for you to say my name."

Marus stared at the knives and swallowed the lump in his throat.

"What's my name, human?" Tro'ka asked.

Marus watched the knives come closer "How the hell should I know." Tro'ka chuckled and with a flick of his wrist, he cut both of his eyes out.

Marus screeched in pain and doubled over.

Tro'ka grumbled with laughter. "And now the fun begins."

Marus screamed all night and then a new day began.

The next morning saw Marus impaled, his head hanging low on his naked chest. Evorix stared up at him with a smile as the blood dripped around him.

Corcundia stood next to him. "Feel better?"

Evorix shrugged. "Wish I could have killed him." He nodded at Tro'ka. "But I'll settle for his handiwork."

Tro'ka waved as he wiped the blood from his paws and walked over. "The other human killed my shield brother, Na'tu, so this one paid for it."

He looked up at Marus. "Took him about six hours to finally die. I saved his ears for last, so he could hear my laughter. He never did know my name. Pity too, I would have stopped hours ago."

"How would he know your name?" Evorix.

Tro'ka raised an eyebrow and chuckled. "He wouldn't."

Evorix stuck his only hand out. "Thank you."

Tro'ka shook his hand and smiled. "Now, what's next?"

Evorix shook his head. "Best case scenario, we wait for the rain to pass, then we march on Iceport and kill Octavius."

He waved one of his commanders over. Covered in gore, the man snapped off a salute. "What are our losses?" Evorix asked.

The commander cleared his throat. "Two hundred dead, times two wounded, and only a few commanders left."

"Dismissed," Evorix said.

The soldier snapped to attention and left as Evorix lit his pipe. "Nearly half our force," he muttered.

Tro'ka nodded. "We have roughly a thousand warriors. Is there anywhere else to get men?" Evorix clicked his tongue. "Nope."

"So, what do we do?" Corcundia asked.

Evorix tapped the silk padding on his wrist and sighed. "We wait."

• • • •

THE MONTHS PASSED, the wounded healed and the rains finally passed through. The morning before they were to leave for Iceport, Corcundia found Evorix up on an overhang, his gaze focused toward the city.

"You ready to do this," she asked.

He chuckled and looked down. His hand had been replaced by a prosthetic dagger. He turned it in several directions. "Don't know if I'll ever get used to this."

"You don't have to, you just need to fight," she replied.

"There's only two things I'm good at. One's fighting, the other——."

"Is fucking," she said with a sly smile.

He winked and stood up. "Where's Tersius?"

"Never more than a few feet away," Tersius said, walking up to them with a slight limp.

"Still limping, eh?" Evorix asked.

Tersius looked at his leg. "Of all the wounds, didn't think this one would be the worst. I'm glad to be alive though. If this limp is what I carry, then this is what I carry."

"Spoken like a true warrior," Evorix said.

"Come Evorix, the *king* has summoned us," Tersius muttered.

King Trakuta had barely spoken to the three of them since the battle. He spent most of his time watching his men drill. The battle brought the men closer together and now they were looking like a well oiled machine ready to fight.

The trio walked into the command tent and watched Trakuta knock the clay pieces that represented his different units off of the table.

"I don't want excuses, I want solutions." He went nose to nose with one of his commanders. "Now find a way in."

"Why the despair, Trakuta?" Evorix asked, trying to hide his pleasure at Trakuta's stress level.

Trakuta turned around and said, "King Trakuta."

Evorix mockingly bowed low. "Your ever faithful servant Evorix, my king."

Trakuta turned his back to him. "I'm in no mood for your patronizing." He studied his maps for a few more minutes. "Leave us," he said to the men at the table.

After his commanders filed out of the tent, Trakuta said, "Evorix, I shouldn't have to remind you that I'm the king of Tramonia now."

"Yes I know, but—-."

"But nothing. I have an obligation to the people of Tramonia, the ones who have died for it too." He looked up from the map. "They made the ultimate sacrifice because I ordered them to and half of them died for it," he said, picking up one of the clay pieces.

Evorix glanced down at the map. "Men die, Trakuta. They followed *me* because I asked them to. Those boys didn't die for you, they died for their wives, mothers, fathers and children. Their death's are on my shoulders and it really doesn't bother me." He shrugged. "Maybe it should. It is what it is, nothing's going to change what happened.

"I suppose you're right," Trakuta said.

"Back to the business at hand then," Evorix said, looking at the map. "If you want to win this battle, I would build a lot of catapults."

Trakuta smiled. "And once their built, how would you assault walls?"

Evorix looked over at Corcundia. "Any ideas?"

She stared at the map for a long moment. "We could use some of the men as decoys, but the casualties would be catastrophic. A complete loss," she said.

"Sometimes in order to succeed, you need to sacrifice," Evorix muttered, flicking some bread crumbs from his tunic.

Tersius spoke up from the opposite side of the table. "I'll lead the decoy's."

Everyone looked in his direction. "Out of the question," Evorix said.

Tersius stepped up to the table. "I said I'll lead them," he said more forcefully. "And I won't take no for an answer. Give me the men and I'll take the rampart."

Trakuta clicked his tongue. "Alright."

Tro'ka, Vitkalla, K'aro and the other Ba warrior lords walked into the tent from outside. "We will go with him. We have a few warriors to spare and it gives us a great death," Tro'ka said.

"You know this is suicide, right?" Trakuta asked.

Tro'ka shrugged. "Human, a few months ago we captured your people and sold them into slavery among our tribes. And now we fight side by side with you." He exhaled deeply. "Stranger things than death have happened so far."

"True, but this isn't your fight. You follow me, right?" Corcundia asked, butting into the conversation.

"Lady Corcundia, yes we follow you, but we must preserve our honor as well. And if we watch mere boys throw themselves into an unwinnable battle, you'll see them slaughtered. Human or warrior, we can't watch that," Vitkalla said, joining the conversation.

"Vitkalla, you and some of the other lords can go with Tersius, but K'aro is a healer and I need him with me," Trakuta said as he traced the outlines of the castle walls.

K'aro growled. "I don't follow your orders, King Trakuta. You have no authority over me."

"You follow me and it's my order," Corcundia said, glancing up from a separate map she was studying.

K'aro roared and pushed his way out of the tent. Corcundia glanced at Vitkalla. "Get him to see my reasons," she said.

Vitkalla nodded and walked out of the tent.

"Orderly, " Trakuta shouted.

A man hurried to his side. "All commander's ready their men. We must prepare for the attack," he said.

• • • •

THE NEXT EVENING THE camp came to life, the newly appointed commander's shouting orders in every direction. Men scrambled into formation and after a few minutes, the disorganization turned into organized chaos. The Tramonian's led the march through the Crossroads with the Ba warriors bringing up the rear. After marching for several days, the newly minted Rebellium flags came into the marshland just west of the city. The war council met in Trakuta's tent to prepare for the battle.

Once everyone was settled, the soldiers and warriors went to work constructing ladders and catapults for the assault.

Evorix and Corcundia took the commander's on a scouting mission into the marsh lands. Trakuta didn't understand why Evorix needed a few wagons, but he gave them to him anyway.

Evorix knew every twist and turn in the swamp and led his group through the snake and alligator infested waters.

The kingdom had changed since Tiberius' assassination. Evorix looked over at Corcundia. "When I was a boy all of this land was a green open plane." He glanced at the scorched earth, fallen trees and fresh sinkholes that now inhabited the landscape. "And now it has been destroyed. When I get a hold of Octavius I'm going to skin the flesh from his bones and roast him over a fire pit. I just hope to beat Trakuta to the prize."

"As long as he dies, why do you care who does it." she asked.

Evorix shook his head, his face a wall of stone. "He killed my wife Alecta and my unborn child in her belly. There will be consequences. Trakuta lost a friend. I lost everything and had to live in the Batopian wilderness while the boy responsible destroyed a kingdom and its people."

"I'm sorry, Evorix. He will pay for his crimes. The question is; how many lives are you willing to throw away in the process?" she asked.

"Enough to destroy the Tramonian army in its entirety. But they aren't my brothers, so I don't care how many it takes. Let's get what I came here for and then head back."

"What do we need?" Corcundia asked, following him deeper into the marsh.

"You'll see."

The group walked along the narrow trails overrun with weeds and alligator dung. One of the soldiers with them stepped into a pile of it and cursed.

Evorix chuckled and said, "Watch your step in here soldier."

The group finally found what Evorix was looking for. He stopped the column and pulled a branch down from above his head and yanked the fungus free.

"Now we're in business," he whispered to himself.

Back at camp, Trakuta watched the sun pass overhead with no word from Evorix. He wiped the sweat from his brow as he watched his men drill the rest of the day.

Vitkalla walked up behind him and smiled, well what could have been a smile. "King Trakuta."

Trakuta nodded and spit. "I wish my soldiers were as good as your warriors."

"Impossible. We live for this exact reason," Vitkalla purred.

Trakuta chuckled. "I see that."

Vitkalla nudged him and winked. "Watch this."

He raised his horn to his mouth and trumpeted a loud whining noise.

"Not very awe inspiring, " Trakuta said.

"Doesn't have to be," Vitkalla said.

The warriors formed ranks and chanted as they slammed their spear butts into the rain-soaked earth. The chants rose and fell in rhythm as their spears slammed into the earth with each step. The warriors formed a shield wall and at the end of each line a warrior roared something that Trakuta didn't understand.

"What do the words being chanted mean?" he asked.

Tro'ka, who had been standing by roared with laughter. He translated as Trakuta watched the warriors line up.

They chant, "Bring me a glorious death," he said.

The warriors finished their chant and crouched down in position.

Trakuta stared at them, his mouth agape. "Now that's quite a sight."

Tro'ka chuckled. "Wait to see what happens in front of the odds we're going against."

"How many of your warriors volunteered to scale the west wall as decoys?" Trakuta asked, his eyes transfixed on the large spears gleaming in the sun.

"All of them," Tro'ka said.

Trakuta's eyes opened wide.

"Don't worry King Trakuta, only the wounded and the old will take the rampart. That's about two hundred warriors to help pull the legionaries away," Tro'ka said.

"Need I remind you—-."

Tro'ka held his hand up. "We know the cost of glory."

Hu'taka walked over with his warriors. "Tro'ka, you will lead my army now that Na'tu is gone." He glanced at Vitkalla. "What say you Vitkalla, son of my old shield brother, Titkalla. Will you regain your honor with me?"

Vitkalla roared and pounded his breastplate.

Hu'taka roared and shook Vitkalla's shoulders. "To glory, shield brother," Hu'taka said as he looked at the other lords with them. "Who will go with Vitkalla and I? And who will lead the other warriors?"

Gra'tu smiled. "I will go with you, Lord Hu'taka, but I will need an alpurlic to get to the wall. I'll help draw their fire from above with the other elders. Su'tu and my other warriors will go with Lord Tro'ka on the other wall."

Su'tu roared and then slammed his spear into the ground. "No, I will not watch you die!"

Gra'tu touched his shoulder, a simple reminder who was in charge of the pride. "I'm still lord of my pride. You go where I tell you to go," he replied, his mouth barely moving.

Su'tu nodded as he embraced him and then stormed out of the tent. Gra'tu watched him leave and turned back around. "Cubs."

The other lords roared with laughter and continued their discussion.

"I would love to go with Lord Vitkalla," Ja'tu said with a sigh, his mane waving as he shook his head. "But I think we'll be needed on the other flank."

Xa'tu stood on his hind legs. "I will go in with my warriors once the gate is opened from the inside," he said, lowering himself to all fours.

Hu'taka glanced over at Lord Ma'tu and watched him move his paw across the battle lines.

"What say you, Lord Ma'tu of the A'tu?" Hutaka asked.

Ma'tu growled and shook his mane. "How many are in the fortress?" he asked.

"Two thousand, maybe more," Trakuta said.

Ma'tu chuckled and waved his human slave over and whispered something in his ear. The human sprinted from the tent and into the darkness.

"I promised you warriors, but this is madness. They have the fire that burns the more it touches you and after my warriors get through that, they will face thousands of well trained humans to get past and into the palace. I will not subject my warriors to a death like that. We will return to the Fire Lands and hide in the ash," he said, walking past the other lords and mounting an alpurlic outside the tent.

Hu'taka shouted after him. "You will lose your honor, Ma'tu."

Ma'tu ignored him, blew his horn and then rode off into the darkness. Tro'ka raced after him, but Hu'taka held his paw up. "Leave him. How many warriors did he have?" he asked.

Ja'tu went to the tent flap and opened it. "I see two hundred warriors, maybe more."

Trakuta swore under his breath. "That's two hundred less than we *need*."

"They will live in shame for eternity," Hu'taka said. He looked around. "And his pridesmen will starve. They are banned from future war councils. They are now dead to us," Hu'taka said, without glancing at the Trakuta.

Za'tu stood in the back, the only spot for disgraced warriors. He shouldered past the other lords and said, "Are my warriors still leading the charge?"

"Yes Lord Za'tu, prepare your warriors for their glory," Hu'taka said.

Za'tu roared, pounded his chest and then rushed from the tent.

Tro'ka stared into the dying light of the candle, his paws twitching. "Lord Tro'ka, what bothers you?" Hu'taka asked, coming over to stand by him.

Tro'ka glanced over at him. "I have no cubs to carry on my legacy," he replied.

Hu'taka grunted and put a hand on his shoulder. "After this final charge you will be sung about in many tales by the fire," he said before walking away.

Trakuta watched the exchange and then stepped outside for a breather, leaving the Ba lords to discuss their plans. He rubbed his hands around his mouth with a sigh as Evorix walked into the camp leading the covered wagons.

"What did you get?" Trakuta asked.

"Something worth more than gold," Evorix said.

"Tramonian wine?" Trakuta asked. "I have plenty of that."

Evorix chuckled. "No, Trakuta. But this will help the warriors storming the rampart."

Trakuta lifted the cover and smiled. He closed it, lowered his head and ran his hand through his hair with a sigh.

"Something wrong, Trakuta?" Evorix asked.

"One of the Ba warlords left the council. He believes his warriors will die for nothing," Trakuta replied.

"How many warriors did he take?" Evorix asked.

"Two hundred, maybe more," he replied.

"Win some, lose some," Evorix said, walking toward the tent. "Come, we must tell the others what I have."

"Does it not bother you that we will be without several hundred warriors?" Trakuta asked, following behind him.

Over his shoulder, Evorix said, "No, not at all. It's more glory for me."

Chapter 27

A scout rode into Iceport covered in mud first thing the next morning. He ran into the palace and waited for Octavius to rise.

After several hours, Octavius walked into the throne room, half his toga at his feet.

"Imperator, we have reports of troops on the horizon," the scout said.

Eyes glazed over and wearing half a frown on his face he said, "Don't bother me with such trivialities. It's probably a Batopian raiding party."

"I wish it were Imperator, but I have seen beasts nine feet tall and men carrying red banners with a barrel on them."

Octavius spit up the wine he was drinking. "Did you say nine foot beasts?"

"Yes, Imperator. They walk among the other men and they are heading this way. It looks like——."

"It can't be the Ba, can it," Octavius mumbled, cutting the scout off. His head jerked up, half a belladonna leaf hung from his lower lip. "Assemble the army. Bring me my generals," he shouted.

A few minutes later, his general's rushed into the throne room still adjusting their armor. Octavius screamed. "Where...where is my general, Marus?"

The assembled commanders stared at one another until finally a young man stepped forward. "Imperator, he has turned on you. Senatore Quillen too. Don't you remember?"

A crazed look crossed Octavius' features. He pointed to one of his guards. "Kill him."

A guardsman walked over, rapped his sword across the man's knuckles reaching for his sword, and then rammed his blade through his stomach. He kicked him to the floor and returned to his post.

Octavius sneered at the men assembled. "He didn't tell me what I wanted to hear. Who...why, why am I so tired?" He fell to his knees and then collapsed.

An older commander walked up to him and whisked his hand. The guards picked him up and carried him back to his chambers. The commander rubbed his beard for a minute.

"Assemble the others, we have a battle coming," he said.

The commander that took over the army was named Lazerus Quintus, a hard man with a leather tanned face. The scars that peppered his body were too numerous to count. He was once Asinius' pupil and when Asinius was condemned to death, Lazerus slid into the shadows until the storm blew over.

"Men to the walls, commanders on me," he shouted as he entered the courtyard with his other generals.

The legionnaires followed his orders without question. The two thousand defenders rotated through the armory to receive extra armor and weaponry. It was easy to follow Lazerus, he was one of them, a man of the people who killed to be at the top.

The commanders followed him to the war room across from the throne room. He cleared a table and pulled the scout forward. "Now, tell me what you saw."

The scout nodded and looked at the map of Delos. "The enemy is a few miles west of here." He pointed to the crossroads. "They have built catapults and are heading this way. With a fast horse, they will be here within a day, m'lord."

"Enough with this m'lord shit. It's Commander Quintus. How many men did you count?" he snapped.

The scout shrugged. "Few hundred Tramonian's, but the warriors stretched back beyond the horizon."

"The Ba have left their hiding spots, interesting." Quintus moved around the map, his footwork silent across the marble flooring. He hummed the Wolfryan anthem and traced his fingers along their route.

"What Legions are ready?"

A voice to his left said, "Last count Legions II & III are at full force."

Lazerus nodded. "And what of our Hellrot stores?"

Another voice popped up. "Fifty barrels in the keep."

Lazerus looked up. "Where the hell is the rest of it?"

A frail alchemist named Justinius spoke up. "The emperor thought it wise to trade it to the southern tribes to levy the money for the takeover of Delos."

Lazerus' mood darkened. "So, now the enemy to the south has most of our Hellrot?" he asked.

Justinius was bald with sunken eyes. The white robe he wore was stained from something he spilled on himself earlier in the day. He was the only remnants of Tiberius' reign. After the assassination, he went into hiding and came out when the emperor offered an amnesty for all non combatants.

Another commander spoke up for Justinius, interrupting Lazerus. "Commander, they aren't the enemy right now."

"You're right, but they will be once we crush this menace at the gate. And when we do turn south, they will have more Hellrot than we have," Lazerus said after contemplating his options.

"I want the legions split in half, five hundred men on each wall. Any questions?"

The commanders saluted and ran to rally the men. Shouts and curses could be heard above the clinking of arms and armor as the men scurried to their posts. Lazerus stood in the center of the chaos and watched them with a veteran eye.

"Legionnaire, pick up that sword," he shouted at the man running by.

The man obeyed and ran to catch up with the rest of his unit. Lazerus walked among the streets giving orders and checking on the populace who attempted to barricade themselves inside their homes. Hours passed and it appeared Octavius wouldn't be returning from his latest episode.

"Lazerus," Octavius shouted from above.

"Imperator?" He looked up and snapped to attention.

"To my chambers," Octavius said, his voice cold.

Lazerus and his staff walked to the throne room where Octavius was drinking wine and chewing more leaves. He didn't even try to cover his nose bleeds anymore. He was past the point of caring. All he wanted to do was stay in a drunken rage.

"More wine," he shouted as Lazerus and his entourage entered. Octavius' eyes darkened. "What did you do with my army, Lazerus?"

"Imperator?"

"Why are my legionaries on every wall?" he asked, his fingers tapping his throne.

Lazerus smiled. "We're being attacked, your eminence. We must man every point of impact to meet our foes. At this moment we are readying the Hellrot to help repel the attackers. You requested that before you took your nap," Lazerus said.

Octavius looked confused for a moment and glanced at one of his guards. "Is what he says true?"

The guard looked at Lazerus and watched his fingers twitch over his sword handle. "It is, Imperator. You instructed him to do what he said you did."

Octavius stared at his guards expression a while longer and then nodded. He drank a glass of wine and burped. "Commander Lazerus, I have changed my mind. I want Legion III pulled back to the palace courtyard. My safety is more important than the populace at this point. Without an emperor, the people will ruin the city. We must have law and order. I want every man who isn't in the legions suited with armor as the first line of defense, then Legion II and the last line of defense is my thousand personal bodyguards."

"Imperator, I must object. If we put untrained men on the walls, they will cave as soon as the Ba warriors come over the top. And the unlimited Hellrot we had was sold to the southern tribes. With only fifty barrels left, we can only man two of the four walls with it," Lazerus said.

Octavius smiled, his stained teeth made his already disheveled appearance more gruesome. "Did I ask for your council, commander?"

"No, Imperator, you didn't."

"Good, then follow my orders. I will be in my chamber with my——." He stared at a young man and licked his lips. "Slaves."

Lazerus bowed low at the waist and waited for Octavius to leave. He grumbled as he walked back to the ramparts followed by his men."If you listen to him, we all die," said one of the commanders, trying to keep pace with him.

"If we don't, we'll be hanging by our entrails. If we stay in the palace with him, we may be able to escape through the catacombs. No one knows they are there. Only three others did know and they're all dead. They killed Evorix in the Batopian wilderness, remember?"

"You sure about that?" Justinius asked.

"Yes I'm sure. Marus said he accomplished that when we rode to Last Keep. Aksutamoon put up more of a fight than I expected though. I don't even know who leads the Tramonians now, or why they are here. I have no idea what lies in front of us." He glanced at the commander standing next to him. "I want you to siphon off one in every ten legionnaires and keep them on the walls mixed in with the peasants."

"If the emperor finds out, he will impale you just like the others," Justinius said.

"He will be in a drunken stupor when he wakes up after screwing his slaves. Trust me, he'll sleep it off," Lazerus said.

Following Octavius' orders, the legionnaires went from house to house, pulling every man and boy from their homes. As the peasants shuffled through the armory, the two hundred legionnaires he selected showed up in the courtyard.

"I want fifty men defending each wall. You will be surrounded by untrained men, so keep them at the wall. Our lives depend on it," Lazerus barked at them.

The legionnaires trotted to the walls, helping the young boys and men to their positions. The Hellrot was brought to the east and west wall and poured into canisters overhanging the ramparts.

The ramparts were crowded, at least two men to each crenellation on the wall. Lazerus walked down each rampart encouraging the men and comforting those who shook with terror. He found a small boy, no older than eight standing by himself shaking. Lazerus smiled and took a knee.

"Remember boy, the worst thing you can do is fight a losing battle." He took his dagger from his belt and handed it to him. "When the warriors come over this wall take this to Wilten Road, find my son and help him escape. It's the house with a blue roof, you know where that is, right?" he asked.

The boy nodded.

"Good lad, leave when they get close and then slip into the Batopian wilderness," he said, patting him on the head.

"M'lord, what should I tell your son?" the boy asked.

Lazerus stopped and made eye contact with him. "To die like a Wolfryan when the end closes in," he said and then walked away.

The landscape in front of them was ready for battle and the Hellrot would be the great equalizer. An idea popped into his head as he stared at the landscape. He looked over the rampart.

"Justinius, get up here."

Chapter 28

E vorix stared at the moon. "It's going to be a bad day."
Corcundia nodded and looked at her warriors. "They're ready to die."

K'aro walked up to them. "As long as our cubs survive, we'll survive." He chuckled, his mane a sweaty mat. "Besides, we don't have anything in the Fire Lands. We were waiting for this day. Evorix has made that possible."

Evorix's half smile was the only answer to K'aro statement. One of Trakuta's men shouted to him from behind. "King Trakuta requests all commandes to the war tent."

Evorix sighed and lowered his head. "Here we go again."

All the commanders assembled in the tent and gathered around the makeshift table. Trakuta glanced at Evorix. "What's the plan?"

Evorix's fingers tapped the edge of the table. He felt like he could hear the sweat dripping from everyone surrounding him.

"We need to march our main force within catapult range. Our volunteer's should lay in wait in the forest and attack when the battle is well under way on the western wall. We will attack from the east and stay away from the front gate. They will be using Hellrot and they don't have any shortages. If our volunteers manage to pull half their force to the west wall, then we can go over the east rampart."

Trakuta stared at the map and rubbed his chin. "I want the Tramonian's over the wall first and then the Ba behind them—-."

Hu'taka slammed his paw on the table. "No, we've discussed this. Our warriors will lead the charge. Your men have done enough and they need a break. We will take the east and west wall. Ca'tu will lead his pride to the gate and your soldiers will go in there. If they can hold the legionnaires in the square, my warriors can reinforce them. We have seven hundred less than they do, it's good odds."

"I don't like it, but you're right. The warriors will be our best advantage," Trakuta said.

Hu'taka traced the outline of the castle with his sharp nail. "King Trakuta, have your men operate the catapults. How many do we have?"

"We managed to make five, but they're small. I have no idea how long they will last."

"How many ladders?" Evorix asked.

"Around fifty," one of the commanders said.

Evorix nodded and closed his eyes. He was silent for a few moments. "Prepare the men. Gods be with you."

He walked out of the tent with Corcundia. "I want you to stay with the archers. Once we go over the top, run them to the gate. Crossbows in front, the longbowmen in the rear. Can you handle it?" he asked.

"Of course I can."

"I'll see you on the inside," he replied, mounting his white alpurlic.

"Evorix, I—-."

Evorix cut her off. "I feel the same."

He rode toward the warriors as they assembled. He found Tro'ka roaring orders and suiting up.

"I had all of your shields covered in Ice flower oil," Evorix said.

The secret weapon they brought back from the marshes was Ice flower oil. Evorix had the warriors paint it on the their shields prior to the assault. It was a fire retardant, specifically designed to quench Hellrot. It would only be a minor help for the first rank of warriors as they scaled the ladders, but he hoped it would be enough to carry them over the top.

"They are ready for war," Tro'ka said.

"And what will you do if the first rank is wiped out?" Evorix asked.

"The second rank will charge right over them. It will be a glorious day. A day when Delos will know it was the Ba who restored order to their realm," Tro'ka said.

Evorix smiled, a genuine smile. He stuck his hand out. "It's been an adventure, Lord Tro'ka. I hope to see you on the inside."

Tro'ka bared his teeth. "If I live human, I'm cursed. When you do find my body, it will be on top of many legionaries." He grabbed Evorix's shoulders warmly. "Don't worry, we'll open the gate. Make sure Lady Corcundia and Ca'tu lead the forces in before they can retake it."

"I'll make sure of it," Evorix said.

The army assembled and marched the rest of the way to Iceport. The castle was a beehive of activity. Evorix scanned the ramparts for any faces he may know. Seeing none, he motioned for the catapults to move forward. The men soaked the boulders with pitch and brought them to the front line.

Evorix handed the commander running the catapults a torch. "Begin commander and don't let up until we've breached the gate. Try to aim for the pipes that are hanging over the rampart," he said, handing the commander a spyglass. The man scanned the wall, located the pipes and nodded.

"It will be done," he said.

"When we have breached the gate, follow Lady Corcundia in and advance on the palace," Evorix said, before he walked away.

The warriors assembled out of Iceport's catapult range. The ladder bearers were small Tramonian's who could set them up and then retreat before the majority of the Hellrot could kill them. It was a risky venture, a risk they had to take. Octavius would never come outside the gate to fight.

Hell, he may not come out of the palace when we reach the gate, he thought.

He rode back and forth in front of the first battle line with the other Ba commanders. "Over that ridge and behind those walls lay the men responsible for killing a king and exterminating your prides. We are going up against the best troops the emperor has." He pointed at Tro'ka. "But look there! Here stands Lord Tro'ka of the Ra'tu, mightiest of your warriors."

The Ba smashed their shields and spears together and roared.

"Who will follow us into death?" Evorix shouted.

The Ba roared again, a sound so deep and horrifying that Evorix watched a few men on the ramparts retreat.

And so it begins.

Trakuta stood in front of the catapults and shouted, "Fire."

The catapults groaned and fired their flaming boulders at the east wall. They soared over the rampart and into the courtyard.

"Re-adjust," shouted a Tramonian commander. The ropes were slackened and reloaded. "Fire."

The boulders flew downrange and hammered the rampart. The screams from the wounded could be heard among the first line of attackers. The first rank of Ba warriors kneeled and slammed their daggers into the ground.

Evorix looked at Tro'ka who shrugged and said, "It's a challenge for any on the wall to face us in hand to hand combat."

Evorix laughed, "Yea, that will happen."

"Reload," shouted the catapult commander.

The catapults creaked and fired again. As the boulders collided with the walls, Evorix held his hand up.

"March."

A thousand feet stomped in the dirt as they advanced toward the wall. Tramonian bagpipers carried a lively tune as Tro'ka hoisted the Rebellium flag onto the tip of his spear. Evorix glanced at him quizzically.

Tro'ka glanced over his shoulder as he marched forward and said, "If I die, it will be under the flag that freed us."

The Ba chanted as they led the way to the castle. The sound of horns and bagpipes kept pace with the chanting and roaring. Evorix reared his alpurlic onto its hind legs and then dismounted.

Tro'ka, Evorix and the other commanders walked shoulder to shoulder in front of the army and descended into the valley.

• • • •

TERSIUS WALKED WITH Gra'tu, Hu'taka and Vitkalla among the kneeling warriors in the shadow of the west wall. He stared up at the ramparts and held his breath, then exhaled. Gra'tu led his alpurlic to the treeline with his helpers and stood beside him.

"Now begins the battle to end all wars," Gra'tu said.

Tersius nodded and moved his palm to the hilt of his sword. "You will bring up the rear, human. We will be the first ones in for glory," Gra'tu said, without waiting for an objection.

The Ba assembled behind Gra'tu and adjusted their armor. They watched the defenders on the west wall stare across the square to the east as the catapults raked the ramparts. The screams from the defenders had a few men running across the adjoining ramparts to help their fellow legionnaires.

Vitkalla, Gra'tu and Hu'taka huddled together. Tersius watched them smear blood across their brows and embrace one another. He shook his head in wonder at the warriors calmness and focus. Every eye in the trees were trained on the west wall. Some warriors spoke softly to one another, others kneeled towards the wall, their long arms reaching out in front of them to grasp the soil.

The three Ba leaders walked up next to him. "Boy, you will lead our most capable warriors, the ones who will help you hold the square should you survive. You must move quickly, the battle will be raging above you," Vitkalla said, offering him a Ba hatchet the size of a human axe.

Tersius took it and shoved the weapon into his trousers with a smile. "Never thought this is how it would end."

Vitkalla looked down at him. "Nothing ever really ends Tersius, it just pauses until a new day comes over the horizon."

They watched a fire arrow fly through the sky, a mark that the east wall was under attack from Evorix's forces. Gra'tu groaned as he mounted his grey alpurlic and tried to catch his breath. Vitkalla put a horn to his lips and instead of the normal whining sound, the horn carried a powerful chord. All at once the Ba warriors made low growling noises that built up to a roar.

They formed four abreast, shields together and walked out beyond the treeline. The roaring crescendoed and then silenced. Gra'tu rode his alpurlic to the front of the army, raised his spear in the air and then dropped it with a flourish.

The warriors waiting for his order sprinted across the plane. As they reached the wall, the warriors in the front cradled their shields and launched the others up to the rampart above them.

For every few warriors that made it onto the rampart, several fell back over the wall impaled by a spear or a sword. A handful of warriors made there way in with ladders and helped the others up the ramparts.

At first, only a few made it over, but as the minutes ticked by a few more survived long enough to form a pocket around the two ladders at the top, allowing the rest of the pridesmen to climb up unhindered.

Tersius heard a screech on his left side as he sprinted to the ladder. He watched both Gra'tu and his alpurlic speared through by a large bolt fired from a mounted crossbow at the far end of the wall.

Hu'taka ran over to Vitkalla and shouted, "Lord Vitkalla, regain your honor and take five of my best warriors. Scale the wall at the far end, capture their weapon and turn it on them."

Vitkalla roared and slammed his visor down over his face. An older group of warriors followed him to the edge of the wall and snuck under the rampart with a single ladder. The warriors bounded up the ladder and overtook the crossbow crew and turned it on the legionaries.

As Vitkalla made it to the top he roared, "Fire!"

A warrior rotated the large handle and sent large crossbow quills downrange with deadly efficiency. The men on the rampart began to retreat as the warriors flooded over the rampart. Tersius climbed up the ladder that Vitkalla had gone up and watched him lead his warriors into the thick of the battle to join Lord Hu'taka and the remainder of his warriors.

The plan had worked for the most part. As the men on the east wall were pushed into the square below, several hundred legionaries ran from the west wall to reinforce them. Barely thirty warriors on the east wall remained, unbeknownst to the legionnaires running to their comrades aid.

Tersius watched a warrior near him take a spear through his abdomen. He killed the legionnaires who stabbed him and then dropped a slow burning torch onto a barrel by his side.

The warrior stood up and took a defensive stance. The last of the elder warriors led by Vitkalla and Hu'taka formed a semi circle around the burning barrel, holding the legionaries at bay.

As the legionary reinforcements ascended the stairs to repel the warriors, the hellrot exploded, killing everyone. The heat from the blast washed over Tersius several feet away and knocked him and his remaining warriors off the rampart and onto the spikes in the square below.

Chapter 29

"**G**et up those ladders, get up there," Evorix shouted from the base of a ladder.

The Ba held their shields over their heads as they took one rung at a time to the top of the rampart. Most of the first wave had been ineffective. Pieces of burnt flesh and singed hair fell on top of Evorix, making him gag.

Za'tu lay at the foot of the ladder horrifically wounded. He pulled himself to the bottom rung of Evorix's ladder and climbed up the next rung.

Collecting his breath, Za'tu roared, "To glory!"

As the warriors behind him surged forward, Za'tu scrambled up the ladder two rungs at a time, dodging the hellrot. He leapt onto the top of the wall, grabbed two of the legionnaires commanders and dove onto the stones below, one locked in each scorched arm.

Evorix heard a roar above him on the parapet that shook his eardrums. He looked up and saw Tro'ka waving the flag of the Rebellium back and forth as he kicked several legionnaires in the face. He picked one of the men up by the throat with his spare hand and slammed him onto the shaft of his spear.

Evorix climbed the ladder behind him and dodged a sword strike as he grabbed the last rung of the ladder. He grabbed the legionnaire by the tunic and threw him over the ledge and onto the warriors below. He made it through the crenellation in the rampart and killed several more legionnaires as they attacked him.

"Kill the commanders," he shouted, snapping another man's neck.

In one moment, all was clear across the courtyard and then a huge ball of Hellrot came up over the west rampart across the courtyard. Evorix watched the explosion and the bodies combust, then heard the howls of the dying warriors. He saw two distinct bodies on fire and saw them tackle several of the Wolfryan commanders and then throw themselves onto the sharpened stakes below.

Tro'ka pounded his fist against his breastplate and roared, a tribute to his father's last stand. Tro'ka and Evorix leaned against one another and fought back to back, killing anyone that dared go near them.

"Evorix, this is where I leave you and join the long ride!" Tro'ka shouted, pulling a large double sided battle axe from behind his back.

A sword slashed across his stomach as he brought the battle axe around. Tro'ka glanced at the wound and held his paw across it. He snarled and bit the attackers head off. Raising his axe high above his head, he gave the sign for his warriors to charge the main gate.

Evorix glanced over his shoulder and saw Corcundia's hair flying behind her as she led the archers to the gate with Ca'tu and his warriors.

Evorix looked for the closest legionary commander on the ramparts, the smoke so thick it watered his eyes. Seeing a young legionnaire commander, he hurled his knife end over end and hit him in the back, sending him sprawling out into the courtyard.

Evorix grabbed a warrior that was sprinting by him by the shoulder and shouted, "Hold the line. Push these bastards off this rampart and into the square. Kill the commanders first, then their men."

The pridesman roared and blew his horn. The warriors roared their response and closed ranks, shields locked together. Their chanting drowned out the screams of the dead and dying legionnaires.

Evorix sprinted behind Tro'ka and took the steps two at a time down from the rampart. He arrived in time to see Tro'ka and his men surrounded. They formed a circle at the main gate, the warriors with battle axes killing scores of legionnaires. Tro'ka stumbled to the door, blood dripping down his legs. He reached the gate and pushed up on the wooden beam that lay across it.

Evorix fought his way through to the warriors and pushed his way through the circle. He pushed his shoulder under the beam with his weight, trying to ease Tro'ka's burden. Tro'ka smiled at him and laid his mane against the door.

His muzzle contorted in pain as he was speared from behind and stuck to the gate. He roared and snatched the spear from his back. Spinning around, he hurled it at a man atop a white horse and then fell to his knees with a gasp. His paws clenched the blood soaked earth.

Evorix felt as if everything was in slow motion around him. Blood splashed onto the ground, against the stone walls and smeared across his face. Finally, the door groaned open and a crossbow quill zipped by his ear from outside the gate and slammed into the legionnaire with his sword raised over his head.

Corcundia came through the gate as the Tramonian's pushed by them, screaming like men possessed. She picked Evorix up and pushed him against the wall.

Tro'ka managed to push himself up, blood dripping from his incisors. He pulled his knives from his belt as three attackers bore down on them. Roaring, he collided with them and slashed wildly. He pushed them back as their swords cut him to pieces. He held them just long enough for the Tramonian's to push the defenders back with what remained of the gate team.

Legion III stormed out of the palace and separated into different shield walls down each street. The warriors above them were throwing the defenders down the steps, off the rampart and over the wall they had just scaled. Forming a wedge, the warriors ran across the rampart and then slammed into Legion III from the side, punching a hole through it.

Hundreds of warriors stormed into the drill square from above and pushed half of the defenders toward the closed gate of the palace.

Evorix ran down one of the streets and saw two repeating crossbows at the end of it. Wolfryan archers leaned out of the windows and showered them with arrows as the repeating crossbows battered the front line.

"Shields up," Evorix commanded, firing an arrow at the crossbow team. The archers with him fired back, killing a few of the men above them as well. Evorix waved to a few warriors and pointed to the windows. The warriors kicked the doors to the houses down and a few moments later the rest of the archers plummeted down into the square around them.

Evorix picked up a spear in one hand and skewered a man who broke through the front line. "Archers, fire at the crossbows."

The warriors lifted the archers up on their shields, drawing the crossbow fire. A few of the Tramonian's men fell back, gored by the large crossbow quills.

A contingent of warriors led by Ja'tu charged down the cobblestone street. The arrows snapped by the warriors felling several of them. Ja'tu and a few others survived the onslaught of quills as they flew downrange. They pounced onto the crossbow teams and slaughtered them. Evorix was pushed forward by one of his men and lost sight of Ja'tu and his warriors.

"Push forward and turn those crossbows around," a warrior shouted before an arrow passed through his throat.

The Tramonian's formed a phalanx and pushed the defenders back, step by step. Evorix's men surrounded the crossbows, holding their defensive line.

"Runner, I need a runner," Evorix shouted.

A runner came to his side, panting.

"Tell the king we need reinforcements and the catapults moved forward!"

The runner disappeared into the mass of Tramonian's coming down the street. The warriors and soldiers with him regrouped and prepared to charge the last gate.

Legion III fell back, a small group holding the door as the rest escaped. The doors clanged shut as the attack surged forward. Evorix shouted to one of his heralds to sound regroup. As the bugle blasted out the notes, an arrow slammed through the young boys eye as he finished the last note. He fell dead at Evorix's feet, a serene look on his face.

The remaining Tramonian and Ba commanders huddled around Evorix. His men held their shields over them as they tried to come up with a plan. When one the shield men fell, another took his place.

"We need most of our men to feign a retreat. I will take a mix of soldiers and warriors with me. I know a way in that probably won't be protected," Evorix said as an arrow ricocheted across a shield with a ping.

"Who goes?" asked one of the Tramonian's.

"Pick the best from your remaining units and then have them crossover to the next street. Find some cover and have your men meet me under the overhang of an inn. During the fake retreat, we will go in and open the gate from the other side. Corcundia is now in command," Evorix said, nodding in her direction.

The group broke apart and Evorix sprinted into the next alley. The horns sounded retreat and the chosen soldiers and warriors made a break for the alley. A few were killed as they ran for the inn. After they assembled, Evorix stood in the middle of the group and took a knee to explain the plan.

"There is an old back door into the castle courtyard. The legionnaires use it to smuggle in women and mead. But we can only go in single file. It will lead right into the courtyard. Once we're in, I want everyone to break left. Hustle to the gate and the first one to arrive will open it and let the rest of our force in," Evorix said, staring at each of their faces.

The grim nods didn't make it any easier to give an order that would condemn most of them to death. Each of them knew the score, the penalty for being the best. Evorix tightened the leather strap to his prosthetic.

"I want the Ba in first to draw the majority of their men away from the courtyard, the rest form up in a turtle formation and cover the gate. Let's move."

The group snuck along the buildings and stayed out of view of the wall. Evorix sprinted to the door and kicked it in.

Someone would have heard that, he thought.

As the men followed him in, a large boulder smacked the rampart above them. Huge chunks of stone tumbled over the side, crushing some of his group. The continous onslaught of boulders drove most of the defenders off of the wall. He smiled broadly as the last of his men formed in the tunnel.

"Attack," Evorix roared.

The group pushed forward and into the courtyard. He saw a light at the head of the tunnel and heard the Ba warriors with him roar as they burst through the opening. A blinding explosion on his right side knocked Evorix off his feet and everything went black.

• • • •

LAZERUS STOOD UP IN his stirrups shouting orders during the hasty retreat from the first set of walls outside the palace. At first, he didn't see the Ba warriors enter the courtyard, but as soon as he saw them, he ordered the powder kegs near the opening blown. It took a while for his men to fight through the throng of warriors cascading through the open doorway. One of Lazerus' badly wounded men slipped through and threw the torch he was carrying onto the kegs.

The explosion rocked the courtyard and the blast blew a five foot hole in the wall, killing most of the legionnaires stationed on top of the stone ramparts. The main gate gave way with a groan as the timbers scattered across the courtyard, killing everything in its path.

Lazerus attempted to rally his fleeing men, but the fierce roars of the Ba warriors charging through the breach didn't persuade many to hold their ground. After a few moments of fighting, Lazerus was overtaken.

He screamed in pain as a Ba warrior bit his arm off at the elbow. His view only lasted a few moments until he was torn in two by several bloodthirsty warriors. The remainder of his legionnaires retreated into the palace.

Corcundia cleared the breach and found Evorix bloodied, but alive. The bodies of his men lay burnt and broken around him. As the rest of Legion III crumbled, only a few hundred of them made it to the confines of the palace.

Evorix shouted orders to form a line. None of his commanders had survived the attack and only scared young sergeants were left to run their platoons.

He sent another runner back to Trakuta to wheel the catapults forward again and continue their barrage. The men formed a protective shield around Evorix as he thought of how they would proceed. The pristine walls of the palace crumbled as the boulders smashed into them.

Corcundia reloaded her crossbows and glanced over at Evorix. "You ready?"

Evorix chuckled. "Going to be one hell of a fight."

They watched the boulders smash into the palace walls until the catapults ran dry. Evorix regrouped his army and split them in half. Corcundia would lead the warriors to engage the rest of the legionnaires and Evorix would enter through the large hole in the palace wall and attack the throne room with the Tramonian's.

He walked up to Corcundia. "I'll see you on the inside."

She nodded, unable to say anything through her clenched throat. He smiled and pulled a coin from his pocket.

"Gius gave me this and I haven't looked at it in a while. Seems fitting." He handed it to her, his hands calloused and bloody. He whistled to his men and ran for the palace wall.

Corcundia stared at the bit of gold for a moment and then flipped it over. Stamped on the back was a picture of the Rebellium flag. She blinked back her tears and pocketed it. The horns from her warriors were blowing made her glance up. She saw Evorix standing at the wall, his sword raised in her direction and then he disappeared inside.

She straightened her back, adjusted her bloody breastplate and shouted at the top of her lungs, "For the Rebellium!"

She charged into the palace, followed by her roaring warriors. The warriors rushed past her in a frenzy, their insors barred. The legionnaires were leaderless, but they were hardened. As the two forces collided, Corcundia unloaded her crossbows and drew her sword. As she advanced a crossbow quill hit her in the kneecap, knocking her to the ground. Her warriors dove in front of her, absorbing the sword blows meant for her.

As her warriors engaged the legionnaires in the palace, more legionnaires flanked them in the outer halls. Corcundia regained her feet and swung her sword at an advancing legionnaire and decapitated him. Another man kicked her to the ground and as his sword swung down to finish her, she held her hands up. The man groaned and fell backward.

Trakuta ran past her with his entourage, pulled his blade out of the man's chest and continued on. She felt someone pull her up from the ground.

Tersius smiled at her and blocked a sword blow coming at them. He chopped the man's hand off and shoved his sword through the legionnaires gut.

"Lady Corcundia, shall we?" he asked, kicking the body off of his blade.

Corcundia looked at the boy who had become a man. As she touched his brow he winced. The burns on his face had left him horribly disfigured. She tried to stifle her gag reflex.

"Tersius..."

He turned around without responding and led the rest of the reinforcements into the fray. The hall was choked with the dead and dying. The legionnaires had fallen back to the next hall leaving a trail of dead in their wake. They made their last stand outside of Octavius' throne room.

• • • •

EVORIX HEARD THE FIGHTING down the hall near the throne room. He picked the best men with him and sent the rest to help Corcundia. The men that went with him adjusted their armor one last time. An older man with one eye smiled at him.

"To a united Delos," he said, pulling his shield from his shoulder.

Evorix could only nod as he watched the rest of Octavius' guards stand in a shield wall two rows deep in front of Octavius' chamber. A small man in a robe stepped forward. Evorix stared at him and ran his sword blade across his prosthetic.

"Justinius, you traitor. I hope you have said a prayer to the God's. Because tonight, you and I meet again in hell."

"Lord Evorix. I come on behalf of the emperor. He is willing to offer you terms for your surrender."

The Tramonian's with Evorix laughed and banged their swords against their shields. The old man with one eye winked at Evorix with the other.

"You best be getting along to kill the emperor, Lord Evorix. We'll deal with these bastards." The man looked at his friends, raised his sword and shouted, "For King Trakuta and the Tramonian Republic!"

Crossbow quills hit the first men who charged at the legionnaires. Evorix saluted them with his sword arm as they pushed past him. He left the group behind and sprinted down the hallway as a few of Octavius' guards chased after him. He ran into a side chamber where the palace slaves were hiding and as the guards rushed in, Evorix shouted, "Fight for me and win your freedom."

The unarmed slaves blinked for a few moments and registered what he had said. They threw themselves onto the guards, slaughtering those who couldn't escape. Evorix fought his way through the two groups and back into the hallway.

This was a really bad idea, he thought as he slipped into the room adjacent to the royal chambers.

He walked over to the far wall and pushed a stone in that was smaller than the rest. The old trap door hadn't been opened in years and the cobwebs were still in the door frame. It was the very same door Gius and his men used to assassinate Tiberius. He crept to the other side of the wall a few feet away and pressed his ear to the false door. He could hear Octavius screaming at his men as the sounds of battle drew closer.

Without thinking, he pushed the door open a crack and saw the guards moving things around. Try as he might, he couldn't see what they were doing. He looked up at the sky.

You still owe me money, Gius.

He stepped into the room and slid behind a marble pillar. He miscalculated the number of guards. He watched from the shadows as they slammed the solid oak doors shut.

It's now, or never.

He stepped from behind the pillar and saw the barrels of Hellrot waiting for the Tramonian army on the other side of the door. A guard strolled over to the door with a smug look on his face.

Octavius screeched. "Light it, light it."

The guard glanced over his shoulder. "Imperator, if I light this with you in the room, you'll die."

"I'm immortal you fool, light it."

Evorix pulled a small hatchet from his belt and threw it. The axe head sunk into the guards neck, and the torch clattered harmlessly to the ground.

"No need to kill my men, boy," Evorix said.

Octavius cut his eyes at him and when he finally realized who it was, he staggered back. Evorix pulled back his black hood.

"That's right. It's me, the one you've been looking for. The angel of death."

Octavius screamed, "Kill him, kill him."

The remaining guards turned in his direction. A slight smile crossed Evorix face, a look of relief and anger as the five guards approached him.

"You boys should know, I'm taking your emperor with me. Now, if you wish to cross swords with me, it will be your doom." Evorix moved gracefully around them. He pointed his sword at the lead guard. "My quarrel isn't with you. You can leave now, or die when my men break through the door."

The door behind them shook. "Go back to your wives and children. Live a long happy life. *Or...*

He crossed his sword over his prosthetic and bowed his head. Two of the younger guards backed away, dropped their swords and walked out of the room through the back door. Evorix glared at one of the remaining guards and raised his dagger.

"You first," Evorix said as he released the spring loaded dagger from his sword arm. The blade struck the man in the neck.

The other two guards advanced, swords raised. Evorix sidestepped one man and slashed his stomach open. The other man sliced Evorix across the back of his knees, cutting his tendons. He roared in pain and fell to the floor. The guard seized the moment and stabbed Evorix in the thigh and twisted his blade.

Evorix could feel the bone grinding as the guard twisted harder. He could hear Octavius clapping in the background as he gripped the guards sword blade, slicing his hand open in the process. Growling, Evorix hooked the man's knee with his free ankle and knocked him to the ground. He spit in the man's eye and then shoved his dagger through it.

He lay dazed and bleeding on the ground. He struggled to his feet and swayed for a moment. A crossbow quill hit him right above the heart and slammed him back to the ground. He squinted at Octavius and watched him drop the crossbow.

"Shit..."

The crossbow made a loud thud as it hit the marble floor. Drool fell from Octavius' lips as he walked with a slight sway over to Evorix's broken body.

"Looks like I finally killed you," Octavius sneered, glancing down at him.

Teeth drenched in blood, Evorix coughed and spit. He spit on Octavius and then said, "Guess I killed us both."

He lifted his arm and threw the torch end over end toward the barrels. At the last moment, he looked up at Octavius. "For the Rebell—-."

The explosion rocked the palace and set the throne room on fire. The legionnaires at the door were blown up with the remainder of the Tramonian's battling them. The blast was deafening, shattering windows and doors alike along the palace corridor. A stillness rolled across the palace and a single crow could be heard cawing in the distance, then it flew away.

• • • •

CORCUNDIA HELD HER head as she pushed a dead legionnaire off of her. The explosion had brought part of the ceiling down on the groups as they fought each other in the great hall. She could hear groaning around her as she stood up. Tersius limped over to her, dust covering his hair and face. He brushed her shoulders off and smiled.

"Have you seen Trakuta?" he asked.

She shook her head and blinked. Her sight came back into focus and through the smoky haze, Trakuta walked over with what remained of his army. She saw something in his hands as he crossed over the bodies. Tears welled in her eyes as she saw what he carried.

"Lady Corcundia, this is all we could find of Evorix, please accept our condolences."

He handed Tersius the sword, and the prosthetic dagger to Corcundia. Hands shaking, she clutched the dagger to her chest as a single tear fell from the corner of her eye. She nodded and handed it to a warrior standing nearby. Tersius cleared his throat and stared at the floor, dabbing his eye.

Taking a deep breath, Corcundia shouted to her warriors. "Follow me."

Trakuta and his men followed behind them and out into the courtyard. K'aro led a merle alpurlic over to Corcundia. She mounted it and swung its muzzle around.

"King Trakuta, I will ride with my warriors into the Fire Lands. Do what you want with the government of Iceport. Once my warriors get their cubs and lionesses, we will ride for Batopia and take control of the kingdom. Should you need to find me, make sure you wave a white flag high in the sky."

Without a further word, Trakuta watched her fire red hair fade into the distance. Tersius mounted his horse with the help of some of the warriors. He swung Evorix's sword over his shoulder.

"Where are you going boy?" Trakuta asked.

"With the only family I have left," he replied.

"Who's that?"

He nodded at the warriors. "Them."

He saluted and rode off behind Corcundia.

One of Trakuta's commanders stood beside him. "What now my king?"

Trakuta rubbed his eyes, smearing the soot at the corner of them. "We rebuild."

Later in the evening after riding for several hours, Corcundia's group rested in a glade not far from the Crossroads. The Ba had lost three quarters of their numbers in the assault. Lord Ja'tu, Lord Xa'tu of the Ca'tu and Lord Su'tu of the Era'tu had survived.

Only one young warrior from the Ta'tu tribe was left after the opening charge. Corcundia glanced across the fire at the bloodied warrior. "Warrior, what is your name?"

The warrior blinked and stared into the fire as he watched the embers fly skyward.

K'aro leaned over to her. "He is La'tu, son of Za'tu. He is all that remains of the Ta'tu."

"Lord La'tu," she said again.

He kept his eyes transfixed on the fire, one of his incisors missing. "My Queen?" he growled.

"Raise your head when you speak to the queen," K'aro snapped.

La'tu lifted his chin and made eye contact with her. Corcundia smiled and said, "Lord La'tu, you are now in charge of my personal guard. Pick the best warriors from the remaining force and meet me in my tent in two hours."

She stood up and walked over to where Tersius was sitting by himself at another fire. She stood over his shoulder and warmed her hands.

"Tersius, are you alright?" she asked.

He nodded and pulled an animal roasting on a stick from the fire. He took a bite and winced, his jaw disfigured from the hellrot. K'aro did his best to help him by putting his salve on it, but it would take many months to heal.

"May I sit?" she asked.

Tersius moved over on the log and handed her the stick. She sat down and took a bite and gagged.

"Ugh, what in the God's name is this?" she asked.

Tersius chuckled. "Some rodent I found in the bushes, m'lady."

She swallowed the meat and wiped the juices from her chin. "Tastes awful," she said, handing it back.

"Let's me know I'm still alive," he replied, a hint of sarcasm in his voice.

"That you are Tersius of West Drathia, that you are," she said with a smile.

"I'm sorry for your loss, my queen," he said.

Corcundia's smile quickly faded as Evorix's face and smile seared through her memory. "Thank you," she said, her voice distant.

"Where to now?" K'aro asked, walking up to sit beside them.

Corcundia stared into the fire with Tersius and said, "To a quiet and simple life in the Batopian wilderness."

• • • •
THE END

Don't miss out!

Visit the website below and you can sign up to receive emails whenever Christopher Metcalf publishes a new book. There's no charge and no obligation.

https://books2read.com/r/B-A-LWXG-XGBAB

BOOKS 2 READ

Connecting independent readers to independent writers.

Also by Christopher Metcalf

Fire Lands

About the Author

Christopher Metcalf has been writing stories for a few years and loves to lose himself in them.

When he's not writing, he's spending time with his beautiful wife and their three dogs, Chin, Juno, and Sushi.

71216737R00234

Made in the USA
Middletown, DE
29 September 2019